Terry Pratchett is o................................rs writing today. He lives behind a keyboard in Wiltshire and says he 'doesn't want to get a life, because it feels as though he's trying to lead three already'. He was appointed OBE in 1998 and his first Discworld novel for children, *The Amazing Maurice and His Educated Rodents*, was awarded the 2001 Carnegie Medal.

Hogfather is the twentieth novel in his phenomenally successful Discworld series.

Register to receive news from Discworld! Simply *email: news@discworld.co.uk*

www.**booksattransworld**.co.uk/terrypratchett

HOGFATHER

Terry Pratchett

CORGI BOOKS

HOGFATHER
A CORGI BOOK : 9780552155106
0552155101

Originally published in Great Britain by Victor Gollancz Ltd

PRINTING HISTORY
Gollancz edition published 1996
Corgi edition published 1997
Corgi edition reissued 2006

3 5 7 9 10 8 6 4 2

Set in 11/13pt Palatino by
Kestrel Data, Exeter, Devon.

Corgi Books are published by Transworld Publishers,
61–63 Uxbridge Road, London, W5 5SA,
a division of The Random House Group Ltd,
in Australia by Random House Australia (Pty) Ltd,
20 Alfred Street, Milsons Point, Sydney, NSW 2061, Australia,
in New Zealand by Random House New Zealand Ltd,
18 Poland Road, Glenfield, Auckland 10, New Zealand
and in South Africa by Random House (Pty) Ltd,
Isle of Houghton, Corner of Boundary Road & Carse O'Gowrie,
Houghton 2198, South Africa.

Printed and bound in Germany by
GGP Media GmbH, Poessneck.

Papers used by Transworld Publishers are natural, recyclable
products made from wood grown in sustainable forests.
The manufacturing processes conform to the environmental
regulations of the country of origin.

To the guerilla bookshop
manager known to friends as
'ppint' for asking me, many years
ago, the question Susan asks in
this book. I'm surprised more
people haven't asked it . . .

And to too many absent friends.

HOGFATHER

Everything starts somewhere, although many physicists disagree.

But people have always been dimly aware of the problem with the start of things. They wonder aloud how the snowplough driver gets to work, or how the makers of dictionaries look up the spelling of the words. Yet there is the constant desire to find some point in the twisting, knotting, ravelling nets of space-time on which a metaphorical finger can be put to indicate that here, *here*, is the point where it all began . . .

Something began when the Guild of Assassins enrolled Mister Teatime, who saw things differently from other people, and one of the ways that he saw things differently from other people was in seeing other people as things (later, Lord Downey of the Guild said, 'We took pity on him because he'd lost both parents at an early age. I think that, on reflection, we should have wondered a bit more about that.')

But it was much earlier even than that when most people forgot that the very oldest stories are, sooner or later, about blood. Later on they took the blood out to make the stories more acceptable to children, or at least to the people who had to read them to children rather than the children themselves (who, on the whole, are quite keen on blood provided it's being shed by the deserving*), and then wondered where the stories went.

And earlier still when something in the darkness of the deepest caves and gloomiest forests thought: what *are* they, these creatures? I will observe them . . .

And much, much earlier than that, when the Discworld was formed, drifting onwards through space atop four elephants on the shell of the giant turtle, Great A'Tuin.

Possibly, as it moves, it gets tangled like a blind man in a cobwebbed house in those highly specialized little space-time strands that try to breed in every history they encounter, stretching them and breaking them and tugging them into new shapes.

Or possibly not, of course. The philosopher Didactylos has summed up an alternative hypothesis as 'Things just happen. What the hell.'

The senior wizards of Unseen University stood and looked at the door.

---

*That is to say, those who deserve to shed blood. Or possibly not. You never quite know with some kids.

There was no doubt that whoever had shut it wanted it to stay shut. Dozens of nails secured it to the door frame. Planks had been nailed right across. And finally it had, up until this morning, been hidden by a bookcase that had been put in front of it.

'And there's the sign, Ridcully,' said the Dean. 'You *have* read it, I assume. You know? The sign which says "Do not, under any circumstances, open this door"?'

'Of course I've read it,' said Ridcully. 'Why d'yer think I want it opened?'

'Er . . . why?' said the Lecturer in Recent Runes.

'To see why they wanted it shut, of course.'*

He gestured to Modo, the University's gardener and odd-job dwarf, who was standing by with a crowbar.

'Go to it, lad.'

The gardener saluted. 'Right you are, sir.'

Against a background of splintering timber, Ridcully went on: 'It says on the plans that this was a bathroom. There's nothing frightening about a bathroom, for gods' sake. I *want* a bathroom. I'm fed up with sluicing down with you fellows. It's unhygienic. You can catch stuff. My father told me that. Where you get lots of people bathing together, the Verruca Gnome is running around with his little sack.'

---

*This exchange contains almost all you need to know about human civilization. At least, those bits of it that are now under the sea, fenced off or still smoking.

'Is that like the Tooth Fairy?' said the Dean sarcastically.

'I'm in charge here and I want a bathroom of my own,' said Ridcully firmly. 'And that's all there is to it, all right? I want a bathroom in time for Hogswatchnight, understand?'

And that's a problem with beginnings, of course. Sometimes, when you're dealing with occult realms that have quite a different attitude to time, you get the effect a little way before the cause.

From somewhere on the edge of hearing came a *glingleglingleglingle* noise, like little silver bells.

At about the same time as the Archchancellor was laying down the law, Susan Sto-Helit was sitting up in bed, reading by candlelight.

Frost patterns curled across the windows.

She enjoyed these early evenings. Once she had put the children to bed she was more or less left to herself. Mrs Gaiter was pathetically scared of giving her any instructions even though she paid Susan's wages.

Not that the wages were important, of course. What was important was that she was being her Own Person and holding down a Real Job. And being a governess *was* a real job. The only tricky bit had been the embarrassment when her employer found out that she was a duchess, because in Mrs Gaiter's book, which was a rather short book with big handwriting, the upper crust

14

wasn't supposed to work. It was supposed to loaf around. It was all Susan could do to stop her curtseying when they met.

A flicker made her turn her head.

The candle flame was streaming out horizontally, as though in a howling wind.

She looked up. The curtains billowed away from the window, which—

—flung itself open with a clatter.

But there was no wind.

At least, no wind in this world.

Images formed in her mind. A red ball . . . The sharp smell of snow . . . And then they were gone, and instead there were . . .

'Teeth?' said Susan, aloud. 'Teeth, *again*?'

She blinked. When she opened her eyes the window was, as she knew it would be, firmly shut. The curtain hung demurely. The candle flame was innocently upright. Oh, no, not again. Not after all this time. Everything had been going so well—

'Thusan?'

She looked around. Her door had been pushed open and a small figure stood there, barefoot in a nightdress.

She sighed. 'Yes, Twyla?'

'I'm afwaid of the monster in the cellar, Thusan. It's going to eat me up.'

Susan shut her book firmly and raised a warning finger.

'What have I told you about trying to sound ingratiatingly cute, Twyla?' she said.

The little girl said, 'You said I mustn't. You said that exaggerated lisping is a hanging offence and I only do it to get attention.'

'Good. Do you know what monster it is this time?'

'It's the big hairy one wif—'

Susan raised the finger. 'Uh?' she warned.

'—*with* eight arms,' Twyla corrected herself.

'What, again? Oh, all right.'

She got out of bed and put on her dressing gown, trying to stay quite calm while the child watched her. *So they were coming back.* Oh, not the monster in the cellar. That was all in a day's work. But it looked as if she was going to start remembering the future again.

She shook her head. However far you ran away, you always caught yourself up.

But *monsters* were easy, at least. She'd learned how to deal with monsters. She picked up the poker from the nursery fender and went down the back stairs, with Twyla following her.

The Gaiters were having a dinner party. Muffled voices came from the direction of the dining room.

Then, as she crept past, a door opened and yellow light spilled out and a voice said, 'Ye gawds, there's a gel in a nightshirt out here with a *poker*!'

She saw figures silhouetted in the light and made out the worried face of Mrs Gaiter.

'Susan? Er . . . what are you doing?'

Susan looked at the poker and then back at the

woman. 'Twyla said she's afraid of a monster in the cellar, Mrs Gaiter.'

'And yer going to attack it with a poker, eh?' said one of the guests. There was a strong atmosphere of brandy and cigars.

'Yes,' said Susan simply.

'Susan's our governess,' said Mrs Gaiter. 'Er . . . I told you about her.'

There was a change in the expression on the faces peering out from the dining room. It became a sort of amused respect.

'She beats up monsters with a poker?' said someone.

'Actually, that's a very clever idea,' said someone else. 'Little gel gets it into her head there's a monster in the cellar, you go in with the poker and make a few bashing noises while the child listens, and then everything's all right. Good thinkin', that girl. Ver' sensible. Ver' modern.'

'Is that what you're doing, Susan?' said Mrs Gaiter anxiously.

'Yes, Mrs Gaiter,' said Susan obediently.

'This I've got to watch, by Io! It's not every day you see monsters beaten up by a gel,' said the man behind her. There was a swish of silk and a cloud of cigar smoke as the diners poured out into the hall.

Susan sighed again and went down the cellar stairs, while Twyla sat demurely at the top, hugging her knees.

A door opened and shut.

There was a short period of silence and then a

terrifying scream. One woman fainted and a man dropped his cigar.

'You don't have to worry, everything will be all right,' said Twyla calmly. 'She always wins. Everything will be all right.'

There were thuds and clangs, and then a whirring noise, and finally a sort of bubbling.

Susan pushed open the door. The poker was bent at right angles. There was nervous applause.

'Ver' well done,' said a guest. 'Ver' persykological. Clever idea, that, bendin' the poker. And I expect you're not afraid any more, eh, little girl?'

'No,' said Twyla.

'*Ver'* persykological.'

'Susan says don't get afraid, get angry,' said Twyla.

'Er, thank you, Susan,' said Mrs Gaiter, now a trembling bouquet of nerves. 'And, er, now, Sir Geoffrey, if you'd all like to come back into the parlour – I mean, the drawing room—'

The party went back up the hall. The last thing Susan heard before the door shut was 'Dashed convincin', the way she bent the poker like that—'

She waited.

'Have they all gone, Twyla?'

'Yes, Susan.'

'Good.' Susan went back into the cellar and emerged towing something large and hairy with eight legs. She managed to haul it up the steps and down the other passage to the back yard, where she kicked it out. It would evaporate before dawn.

18

'That's what *we* do to monsters,' she said.

Twyla watched carefully.

'And now it's bed for you, my girl,' said Susan, picking her up.

'C'n I have the poker in my room for the night?'

'All right.'

'It only kills monsters, doesn't it . . . ?' the child said sleepily, as Susan carried her upstairs.

'That's right,' Susan said. 'All kinds.'

She put the girl to bed next to her brother and leaned the poker against the toy cupboard.

The poker was made of some cheap metal with a brass knob on the end. She would, Susan reflected, give quite a lot to be able to use it on the children's previous governess.

'G'night.'

'Goodnight.'

She went back to her own small bedroom and got back into bed, watching the curtains suspiciously.

It would be nice to think she'd imagined it. It would also be *stupid* to think that, too. But she'd been nearly normal for two years now, making her own way in the real world, never remembering the future at all . . .

Perhaps she *had* just dreamed things (but even dreams could be real . . .).

She tried to ignore the long thread of wax that suggested the candle had, just for a few seconds, streamed in the wind.

* * *

19

As Susan sought sleep, Lord Downey sat in his study catching up on the paperwork.

Lord Downey was an assassin. Or, rather, an Assassin. The capital letter was important. It separated those curs who went around murdering people for money from the gentlemen who were occasionally consulted by other gentlemen who wished to have removed, for a consideration, any inconvenient razorblades from the candyfloss of life.

The members of the Guild of Assassins considered themselves cultured men who enjoyed good music and food and literature. And they knew the value of human life. To a penny, in many cases.

Lord Downey's study was oak-panelled and well carpeted. The furniture was very old and quite worn, but the wear was the wear that comes only when very good furniture is carefully used over several centuries. It was *matured* furniture.

A log fire burned in the grate. In front of it a couple of dogs were sleeping in the tangled way of large hairy dogs everywhere.

Apart from the occasional doggy snore or the crackle of a shifting log, there were no other sounds but the scratching of Lord Downey's pen and the ticking of the longcase clock by the door . . . small, private noises which only served to define the silence.

At least, this was the case until someone cleared their throat.

The sound suggested very clearly that the purpose of the exercise was not to erase the presence of a troublesome bit of biscuit, but merely to indicate in the politest possible way the presence of the throat.

Downey stopped writing but did not raise his head.

Then, after what appeared to be some consideration, he said in a businesslike voice, 'The doors are locked. The windows are barred. The dogs do not appear to have woken up. The squeaky floorboards haven't. Other little arrangements which I will not specify seem to have been bypassed. That severely limits the possibilities. I really doubt that you are a ghost and gods generally do not announce themselves so politely. You could, of course, be Death, but I don't believe he bothers with such niceties and, besides, I am feeling quite well. Hmm.'

Something hovered in the air in front of his desk.

'My teeth are in fine condition so you are unlikely to be the Tooth Fairy. I've always found that a stiff brandy before bedtime quite does away with the need for the Sandman. And, since I can carry a tune quite well, I suspect I'm not likely to attract the attention of Old Man Trouble. Hmm.'

The figure drifted a little nearer.

'I suppose a gnome could get through a mousehole, but I have traps down,' Downey went on. 'Bogeymen can walk through walls but would be very loath to reveal themselves. Really, you have me at a loss. Hmm?'

And then he looked up.

A grey robe hung in the air. It appeared to be occupied, in that it had a shape, although the occupant was not visible.

The prickly feeling crept over Downey that the occupant wasn't invisible, merely not, in any physical sense, there at all.

'Good evening,' he said.

The robe said, Good evening, Lord Downey.

His brain registered the words. His ears swore they hadn't heard them.

But you did not become head of the Assassins' Guild by taking fright easily. Besides, the thing wasn't frightening. It was, thought Downey, astonishingly dull. If monotonous drabness could take on a shape, this would be the shape it would choose.

'You appear to be a spectre,' he said.

Our nature is not a matter for discussion, arrived in his head. We offer you a commission.

'You wish someone inhumed?' said Downey.

Brought to an end.

Downey considered this. It was not as unusual as it appeared. There were precedents. Anyone could buy the services of the Guild. Several zombies had, in the past, employed the Guild to settle scores with their murderers. In fact the Guild, he liked to think, practised the ultimate democracy. You didn't need intelligence, social position, beauty or charm to hire it. You just needed money which, unlike the other stuff, was available to everyone. Except for the poor, of course, but there was no helping some people.

'Brought to an end . . .' That was an odd way of putting it.

'We can—' he began.

The payment will reflect the difficulty of the task.

'Our scale of fees—'

The payment will be three million dollars.

Downey sat back. That was four times higher than any fee yet earned by any member of the Guild, and *that* had been a special family rate, including overnight guests.

'No questions asked, I assume?' he said, buying time.

No questions answered.

'But does the suggested fee represent the difficulty involved? The client is heavily guarded?'

Not guarded at all. But almost certainly impossible to delete with conventional weapons.

Downey nodded. This was not necessarily a big problem, he said to himself. The Guild had amassed quite a few unconventional weapons over the years. Delete? An unusual way of putting it . . .

'We like to know for whom we are working,' he said.

We are sure you do.

'I mean that we need to know your name. Or names. In strict client confidentiality, of course. We have to write something down in our files.'

You may think of us as . . . the Auditors.

'Really? What is it you audit?'

Everything.

'I think we need to know something about you.'

We are the people with three million dollars.

Downey took the point, although he didn't like it. Three million dollars could buy a·lot of no questions.

'Really?' he said. 'In the circumstances, since you are a new client, I think we would like payment in advance.'

As you wish. The gold is now in your vaults.

'You mean that it will shortly be in our vaults,' said Downey.

No. It has always been in your vaults. We know this because we have just put it there.

Downey watched the empty hood for a moment, and then without shifting his gaze he reached out and picked up the speaking tube.

'Mr Winvoe?' he said, after whistling into it. 'Ah. Good. Tell me, how much do we have in our vaults at the moment? Oh, approximately. To the nearest million, say.' He held the tube away from his ear for a moment, and then spoke into it again. 'Well, be a good chap and check anyway, will you?'

He hung up the tube and placed his hands flat on the desk in front of him.

'Can I offer you a drink while we wait?' he said.

Yes. We believe so.

Downey stood up with some relief and walked over to his large drinks cabinet. His hand hovered over the Guild's ancient and valuable tantalus, with its labelled decanters of Mur, Nig, Trop and Yksihw.*

'And what would you like to drink?' he said, wondering where the Auditor kept its mouth. His hand hovered for just a moment over the smallest decanter, marked Nosiop.

We do not drink.

'But you did just say I could offer you a drink . . .'

Indeed. We judge you fully capable of performing that action.

'Ah.' Downey's hand hesitated over the whisky decanter, and then he thought better of it. At that point, the speaking tube whistled.

'Yes, Mr Winvoe? Really? Indeed? I myself have frequently found loose change under sofa cushions, it's amazing how it mou . . . No, no, I wasn't being . . . Yes, I *did* have some reason to . . . No, no blame attaches to you in any . . . No, I could hardly see how it . . . Yes, go and have a rest, what a good idea. Thank you.'

---

*It's a sad and terrible thing that high-born folk really have thought that the servants would be totally fooled if spirits were put into decanters that were cunningly labelled *backwards*. And also throughout history the more politically conscious butler has taken it on trust, and with rather more justification, that his employers will not notice if the whisky is topped up with eniru.

He hung up the tube again. The cowl hadn't moved.

'We will need to know where, when and, of course, *who*,' he said, after a moment.

The cowl nodded. The location is not on any map. We would like the task to be completed within the week. This is essential. As for the who . . .

A drawing appeared on Downey's desk and in his head arrived the words: Let us call him the Fat Man.

'Is this a joke?' said Downey.

We do not joke.

No, you don't, do you, Downey thought. He drummed his fingers.

'There are many who would say this . . . person does not exist,' he said.

He must exist. How else could you so readily recognize his picture? And many are in correspondence with him.

'Well, yes, of course, in a *sense* he exists . . .'

In a sense everything exists. It is cessation of existence that concerns us here.

'Finding him would be a little difficult.'

You will find persons on any street who can tell you his approximate address.

'Yes, of course,' said Downey, wondering why anyone would call them 'persons'. It was an odd usage. 'But, as you say, I doubt that they could give a map reference. And even then, *how* could the . . . the Fat Man *be* inhumed? A glass of poisoned sherry, perhaps?'

The cowl had no face to crack a smile.

You misunderstand the nature of employment, it said in Downey's head.

He bridled at this. Assassins were never *employed*. They were engaged or retained or commissioned, but never *employed*. Only servants were employed.

'What is it that I misunderstand, exactly?' he said.

We pay. You find the ways and means.

The cowl began to fade.

'How can I contact you?' said Downey.

We will contact you. *We know where you are. We know where everyone is.*

The figure vanished. At the same moment the door was flung open to reveal the distraught figure of Mr Winvoe, the Guild Treasurer.

'Excuse me, my lord, but I really had to come up!' He flung some discs on the desk. 'Look at them!'

Downey carefully picked up a golden circle. It looked like a small coin, but—

'No denomination!' said Winvoe. 'No heads, no tails, no milling! It's just a blank disc! They're all just blank discs!'

Downey opened his mouth to say, 'Valueless?' He realized that he was half hoping that this was the case. If they, whoever *they* were, had paid in worthless metal then there wasn't even the glimmering of a contract. But he could see this wasn't the case. Assassins learned to recognize money early in their careers.

'Blank discs,' he said, 'of pure gold.'

Winvoe nodded mutely.

'That,' said Downey, 'will do nicely.'

'It *must* be magical!' said Winvoe. 'And we *never* accept magical money!'

Downey bounced the coin on the desk a couple of times. It made a satisfyingly rich thunking noise. It *wasn't* magical. Magical money would look real, because its whole purpose was to deceive. But this didn't need to ape something as human and adulterated as mere currency. This is gold, it told his fingers. Take it or leave it.

Downey sat and thought, while Winvoe stood and worried.

'We'll take it,' he said.

'But—'

'Thank you, Mr Winvoe. That is my decision,' said Downey. He stared into space for a while, and then smiled. 'Is Mister Teatime still in the building?'

Winvoe stood back. 'I thought the council had agreed to dismiss him,' he said stiffly. 'After that business with—'

'Mister Teatime does not see the world in quite the same way as other people,' said Downey, picking up the picture from his desk and looking at it thoughtfully.

'Well, indeed, I think *that* is certainly true.'

'Please send him up.'

The Guild attracted all sorts of people, Downey reflected. He found himself wondering how it had come to attract Winvoe, for one thing. It was hard to imagine him stabbing anyone in the heart in case he got blood on the victim's wallet. Whereas Mister Teatime . . .

The problem was that the Guild took young boys and gave them a splendid education and incidentally taught them how to kill, cleanly and dispassionately, for money and for the good of society, or at least that part of society that had money, and what other kind of society was there?

But very occasionally you found you'd got someone like Mister Teatime, to whom the money was merely a distraction. Mister Teatime had a truly brilliant mind, but it was brilliant like a fractured mirror, all marvellous facets and rainbows but, ultimately, also something that was broken.

Mister Teatime enjoyed himself too much. And other people, also.

Downey had privately decided that some time soon Mister Teatime was going to meet with an accident. Like many people with no actual morals, Lord Downey *did* have standards, and Teatime repelled him. Assassination was a careful game, usually played against people who knew the rules themselves or at least could afford the services of those who did. There was considerable satisfaction in a clean kill. What there wasn't supposed to be was pleasure in a messy one. That sort of thing led to talk.

On the other hand, Teatime's corkscrew of a mind was exactly the tool to deal with something like this. And if he didn't . . . well, that was hardly Downey's fault, was it?

He turned his attention to the paperwork for a while. It was amazing how the stuff mounted up. But you had to deal with it. It wasn't as though they were murderers, after all . . .

There was a knock at the door. He pushed the paperwork aside and sat back.

'Come in, Mister Teatime,' he said. It never hurt to put the other fellow slightly in awe of you.

In fact the door was opened by one of the Guild's servants, carefully balancing a tea tray.

'Ah, Carter,' said Lord Downey, recovering magnificently. 'Just put it on the table over there, will you?'

'Yes, sir,' said Carter. He turned and nodded. 'Sorry, sir, I will go and fetch another cup directly, sir.'

'What?'

'For your visitor, sir.'

'What visitor? Oh, when Mister Teati—'

He stopped. He turned.

There was a young man sitting on the hearth-rug, playing with the dogs.

'*Mister Teatime!*'

'It's pronounced Teh-ah-tim-eh, sir,' said Teatime, with just a hint of reproach. 'Everyone gets it wrong, sir.'

'How did you do *that*?'

'Pretty well, sir. I got mildly scorched on the last few feet, of course.'

There were some lumps of soot on the

hearthrug. Downey realized he'd heard them fall, but that hadn't been particularly extraordinary. No one could get down the chimney. There was a heavy grid firmly in place near the top of the flue.

'But there's a blocked-in fireplace behind the old library,' said Teatime, apparently reading his thoughts. 'The flues connect, under the bars. It was really a stroll, sir.'

'Really . . .'

'Oh, yes, sir.'

Downey nodded. The tendency of old buildings to be honeycombed with sealed chimney flues was a fact you learned early in your career. And then, he told himself, you forgot. It always paid to put the other fellow in awe of you, too. He had forgotten they taught *that*, too.

'The dogs seem to like you,' he said.

'I get on well with animals, sir.'

Teatime's face was young and open and friendly. Or, at least, it smiled all the time. But the effect was spoiled for most people by the fact that it had only one eye. Some unexplained accident had taken the other one, and the missing orb had been replaced by a ball of glass. The result was disconcerting. But what bothered Lord Downey far more was the man's other eye, the one that might loosely be called normal. He'd never seen such a small and sharp pupil. Teatime looked at the world through a pinhole.

He found he'd retreated behind his desk again. There was that about Teatime. You always felt happier if you had something between you and him.

'You like animals, do you?' he said. 'I have a report here that says you nailed Sir George's dog to the ceiling.'

'Couldn't have it barking while I was working, sir.'

'Some people would have drugged it.'

'Oh.' Teatime looked despondent for a moment, but then he brightened. 'But I definitely fulfilled the contract, sir. There can be no doubt about that, sir. I checked Sir George's breathing with a mirror as instructed. It's in my report.'

'Yes, indeed.' Apparently the man's head had been several feet from his body at that point. It was a terrible thought that Teatime might see nothing incongruous about this.

'And . . . the servants . . . ?' he said.

'Couldn't have them bursting in, sir.'

Downey nodded, half hypnotized by the glassy stare and the pinhole eyeball. No, you couldn't have them bursting in. And an Assassin might well face serious professional opposition, possibly even by people trained by the same teachers. But an old man and a maidservant who'd merely had the misfortune to be in the house at the time . . .

There was no actual *rule*, Downey had to admit. It was just that, over the years, the Guild had developed a certain ethos and members tended to be very neat about their work, even shutting doors behind them and generally tidying up as they went. Hurting the harmless was worse than a transgression against the moral fabric of society, it was a breach of *good manners*. It was worse even than that. It was *bad taste*. But there was no actual *rule* . . .

'That was all right, wasn't it, sir?' said Teatime, with apparent anxiety.

'It, uh . . . lacked elegance,' said Downey.

'Ah. Thank you, sir. I am always happy to be corrected. I shall remember that next time.'

Downey took a deep breath.

'It's about that I wish to talk,' he said. He held up the picture of . . . what had the thing called him? . . . the Fat Man?

'As a matter of interest,' he said, 'how would you go about inhuming this . . . gentleman?'

Anyone else, he was sure, would have burst out laughing. They would have said things like 'Is this a joke, sir?' Teatime merely leaned forward, with a curious intent expression.

'Difficult, sir.'

'Certainly,' Downey agreed.

'I would need some time to prepare a plan, sir,' Teatime went on.

'Of course, and—'

There was a knock at the door and Carter came in with another cup and saucer. He nodded respectfully to Lord Downey and crept out again.

'Right, sir,' said Teatime.

'I'm sorry?' said Downey, momentarily distracted.

'I have now thought of a plan, sir,' said Teatime, patiently.

'You have?'

'Yes, sir.'

'As quickly as that?'

'Yes, sir.'

'Ye gods!'

'Well, sir, you know we are encouraged to consider hypothetical problems . . . ?'

'Oh, yes. A very valuable exercise—' Downey stopped, and then looked shocked.

'You mean you have actually devoted time to considering how to inhume the Hogfather?' he said weakly. 'You've actually sat down and thought out how to do it? You've actually devoted your spare time to the problem?'

'Oh, yes, sir. And the Soul Cake Duck. And the Sandman. And Death.'

Downey blinked again. 'You've actually sat down and considered how to—'

'Yes, sir. I've amassed quite an interesting file. In my own time, of course.'

'I want to be quite certain about this, Mister Teatime. You . . . have . . . applied . . . yourself to a study of ways of killing *Death*?'

'Only as a hobby, sir.'

'Well, *yes*, hobbies, yes, I mean, I used to collect butterflies myself,' said Downey, recalling those first moments of awakening pleasure at the use of poison and the pin, 'but—'

'Actually, sir, the basic methodology is exactly the same as it would be for a human. Opportunity, geography, technique . . . You just have to work with the known facts about the individual concerned. Of course, with *this* one such a lot is known.'

'And you've worked it all out, have you?' said Downey, almost fascinated.

'Oh, a long time ago, sir.'

'When, may I ask?'

'I think it was when I was lying in bed one Hogswatchnight, sir.'

My gods, thought Downey, and to think that *I* just used to listen for sleigh bells.

'My word,' he said aloud.

'I may have to check some details, sir. I'd appreciate access to some of the books in the Dark Library. But, yes, I think I can see the basic shape.'

'And yet . . . this person . . . some people might say that he is technically immortal.'

'Everyone has their weak point, sir.'

'Even Death?'

'Oh, yes. Absolutely. Very much so.'

'Really?'

Downey drummed his fingers on the desk again. The boy couldn't possibly have a *real* plan, he told himself. He certainly had a skewed mind – skewed? It was a positive helix – but the Fat Man wasn't just another target in some mansion somewhere. It was reasonable to assume that people had tried to trap him before.

He felt happy about this. Teatime would fail, and possibly even fail fatally if his plan was stupid enough. And maybe the Guild would lose the gold, but maybe not.

'Very well,' he said. 'I don't need to know what your plan is.'

'That's just as well, sir.'

'What do you mean?'

'Because I don't propose to tell you, sir. You'd be obliged to disapprove of it.'

'I am amazed that you are so confident that it can work, Teatime.'

'I just think logically about the problem, sir,' said the boy. He sounded reproachful.

'Logically?' said Downey.

'I suppose I just see things differently from other people,' said Teatime.

It was a quiet day for Susan, although on the way to the park Gawain trod on a crack in the pavement. On purpose.

One of the many terrors conjured up by the previous governess's happy way with children had been the bears that waited around in the street to eat you if you stood on the cracks.

Susan had taken to carrying the poker under her respectable coat. One wallop generally did the trick. They were amazed that anyone else saw them.

'Gawain?' she said, eyeing a nervous bear who had suddenly spotted her and was now trying to edge away nonchalantly.

'Yes?'

'You meant to tread on that crack so that I'd have to thump some poor creature whose

36

only fault is wanting to tear you limb from limb.'

'I was just skipping—'

'Quite. Real children don't go hoppity-skip unless they are on drugs.'

He grinned at her.

'If I catch you being twee again I will knot your arms behind your head,' said Susan levelly.

He nodded, and went to push Twyla off the swings.

Susan relaxed, satisfied. It was her personal discovery. Ridiculous threats didn't worry them at all, but they were obeyed. Especially the ones in graphic detail.

The previous governess had used various monsters and bogeymen as a form of discipline. There was always something waiting to eat or carry off bad boys and girls for crimes like stuttering or defiantly and aggravatingly persisting in writing with their left hand. There was always a Scissor Man waiting for a little girl who sucked her thumb, always a bogeyman in the cellar. Of such bricks is the innocence of childhood constructed.

Susan's attempts at getting them to disbelieve in the things only caused the problems to get worse.

Twyla had started to wet the bed. This may have been a crude form of defence against the terrible clawed creature that she was certain lived under it.

Susan had found out about this one the first

night, when the child had woken up crying because of a bogeyman in the closet.

She'd sighed and gone to have a look. She'd been so angry that she'd pulled it out, hit it over the head with the nursery poker, dislocated its shoulder as a means of emphasis and kicked it out of the back door.

The children refused to disbelieve in the monsters because, frankly, they knew damn well the things were there.

But she'd found that they could, very firmly, also believe in the poker.

Now she sat down on a bench and read a book. She made a point of taking the children, every day, somewhere where they could meet others of the same age. If they got the hang of the playground, she thought, adult life would hold no fears. Besides, it was nice to hear the voices of little children at play, provided you took care to be far enough away not to hear what they were actually saying.

There were lessons later on. These were going a lot better now she'd got rid of the reading books about bouncy balls and dogs called Spot. She'd got Gawain on to the military campaigns of General Tacticus, which were suitably bloodthirsty but, more importantly, considered too difficult for a child. As a result his vocabulary was doubling every week and he could already use words like 'disembowelled' in everyday conversation. After all, what was the point of teaching children to be children?

They were naturally good at it.

And she was, to her mild horror, naturally good with them. She wondered suspiciously if this was a family trait. And if, to judge by the way her hair so readily knotted itself into a prim bun, she was destined for jobs like this for the rest of her life.

It was her parents' fault. They hadn't meant it to turn out like this. At least, she hoped charitably that they hadn't.

They'd wanted to protect her, to keep her away from the worlds outside this one, from what people thought of as the occult, from . . . well, from her grandfather, to put it bluntly. This had, she felt, left her a little twisted up.

Of course, to be fair, that was a parent's job. The world was so full of sharp bends that if they didn't put a few twists in you, you wouldn't stand a chance of fitting in. And they'd been conscientious and kind and given her a good home and even an education.

It had been a good education, too. But it had only been later on that she'd realized that it had been an education in, well, education. It meant that if ever anyone needed to calculate the volume of a cone, then they could confidently call on Susan Sto-Helit. Anyone at a loss to recall the campaigns of General Tacticus or the square root of 27.4 would not find her wanting. If you needed someone who could talk about household items and things to buy in the shops in five languages, then Susan was at the head of the queue. Education had been easy.

Learning things had been harder.

Getting an education was a bit like a communicable sexual disease. It made you unsuitable for a lot of jobs and then you had the urge to pass it on.

She'd become a governess. It was one of the few jobs a known lady could do. And she'd taken to it well. She'd sworn that if she did indeed ever find herself dancing on rooftops with chimney sweeps she'd beat herself to death with her own umbrella.

After tea she read them a story. They liked her stories. The one in the book was pretty awful, but the Susan version was well received. She translated as she read.

'. . . and then Jack chopped down the beanstalk, adding murder and ecological vandalism to the theft, enticement and trespass charges already mentioned, but he got away with it and lived happily ever after without so much as a guilty twinge about what he had done. Which proves that you can be excused just about anything if you're a hero, because no one asks inconvenient questions. And now,' she closed the book with a snap, 'it's time for bed.'

The previous governess had taught them a prayer which included the hope that some god or other would take their soul if they died while they were asleep and, if Susan was any judge, had the underlying message that this would be a good thing.

One day, Susan averred, she'd hunt that woman down.

'Susan,' said Twyla, from somewhere under the blankets.

'Yes?'

'You know last week we wrote letters to the Hogfather?'

'Yes?'

'Only . . . in the park Rachel says he doesn't exist and it's your father really. And everyone else said she was right.'

There was a rustle from the other bed. Twyla's brother had turned over and was listening surreptitiously.

Oh dear, thought Susan. She had hoped she could avoid this. It was going to be like that business with the Soul Cake Duck all over again.

'Does it matter if you get the presents anyway?' she said, making a direct appeal to greed.

' 'es.'

Oh dear, oh dear. Susan sat down on the bed, wondering how the hell to get through this. She patted the one visible hand.

'Look at it this way, then,' she said, and took a deep mental breath. 'Wherever people are obtuse and absurd . . . and wherever they have, by even the most generous standards, the attention span of a small chicken in a hurricane and the investigative ability of a one-legged cockroach . . . and wherever people are inanely credulous, pathetically attached to the certainties of the nursery and, in general, have as much grasp of the realities of the physical universe as an oyster has of mountaineering . . . *yes*, Twyla: there *is* a Hogfather.'

There was silence from under the bedclothes, but she sensed that the tone of voice had worked. The words had meant nothing. That, as her grandfather might have said, was humanity all over.

'G'night.'

'Good night,' said Susan.

It wasn't even a bar. It was just a room where people drank while they waited for other people with whom they had business. The business usually involved the transfer of ownership of something from one person to another, but then, what business doesn't?

Five businessmen sat round a table, lit by a candle stuck in a saucer. There was an open bottle between them. They were taking some care to keep it away from the candle flame.

' 's gone six,' said one, a huge man with dread-locks and a beard you could keep goats in. 'The clocks struck ages ago. He ain't coming. Let's go.'

'Sit *down*, will you? Assassins are always late. 'cos of style, right?'

'This one's mental.'

'Eccentric.'

'What's the difference?'

'A bag of cash.'

The three that hadn't spoken yet looked at one another.

'What's this? You never said he was an Assassin,' said Chickenwire. 'He never said the guy was an Assassin, did he, Banjo?'

There was a sound like distant thunder. It was Banjo Lilywhite clearing his throat.

'Dat's right,' said a voice from the upper slopes. 'Youse never said.'

The others waited until the rumble died away. Even Banjo's *voice* hulked.

'He's' – the first speaker waved his hands vaguely, trying to get across the point that someone was a hamper of food, several folding chairs, a tablecloth, an assortment of cooking gear and an entire colony of ants short of a picnic – '*mental*. And he's got a funny eye.'

'It's just glass, all right?' said the one known as Catseye, signalling a waiter for four beers and a glass of milk. 'And he's paying ten thousand dollars each. I don't care what kind of eye he's got.'

'I heard it was made of the same stuff they make them fortune-telling crystals out of. You can't tell *me* that's right. And he looks at you with it,' said the first speaker. He was known as Peachy, although no one had ever found out why.*

Catseye sighed. Certainly there was something

---

*Peachy was not someone you generally asked questions of, except the sort that go like: 'If-if-if-if I give you all my money could you possibly not break the other leg, thank you so much?'

odd about Mister Teatime, there was no doubt about that. But there was something weird about all Assassins. And the man paid well. Lots of Assassins used informers and locksmiths. It was against the rules, technically, but standards were going down everywhere, weren't they? Usually they paid you late and sparsely, as if *they* were doing the favour. But Teatime was OK. True, after a few minutes talking to him your eyes began to water and you felt you needed to scrub your skin even on the inside, but no one was perfect, were they?

Peachy leaned forward. 'You know what?' he said. 'I reckon he could be here already. In disguise! Laughing at us! Well, if he's in here laughing at us—' He cracked his knuckles.

Medium Dave Lilywhite, the last of the five, looked around. There were indeed a number of solitary figures in the low, dark room. Most of them wore cloaks with big hoods. They sat alone, in corners, hidden by the hoods. None of them looked very friendly.

'Don't be daft, Peachy,' Catseye murmured.

'That's the sort of thing they do,' Peachy insisted. 'They're masters of disguise!'

'With that eye of his?'

'That guy sitting by the fire has got an eye patch,' said Medium Dave. Medium Dave didn't speak much. He watched a lot.

The others turned to stare.

'He'll wait till we're off our guard then go ahahaha,' said Peachy.

'They can't kill you unless it's for money,' said Catseye. But now there was a soupçon of doubt in his voice.

They kept their eyes on the hooded man. He kept his eye on them.

If asked to describe what they did for a living, the five men around the table would have said something like 'This and that' or 'The best I can', although in Banjo's case he'd have probably said 'Dur?' They were, by the standards of an uncaring society, criminals, although they wouldn't have thought of themselves as such and couldn't even *spell* words like 'nefarious'. What they generally did was move things around. Sometimes the things were on the wrong side of a steel door, say, or in the wrong house. Sometimes the things were in fact people who were far too unimportant to trouble the Assassins' Guild with, but who were nevertheless inconveniently positioned where they were and could much better be located on, for example, a sea bed somewhere.* None of the five belonged to any formal guild and they generally found their clients among those people who, for their own

*Chickenwire had got his name from his own individual contribution to the science of this very specialized 'concrete overshoe' form of waste disposal. An unfortunate drawback of the process was the tendency for bits of the client to eventually detach and float to the surface, causing much comment in the general population. Enough chickenwire, he'd pointed out, would solve that, while also allowing the ingress of crabs and fish going about their vital recycling activities.

dark reasons, didn't want to put the guilds to any trouble, sometimes because they were guild members themselves. They had plenty of work. There was always something that needed transferring from A to B or, of course, to the bottom of the C.

'Any minute now,' said Peachy, as the waiter brought their beers.

Banjo cleared his throat. This was a sign that another thought had arrived.

'What I don' unnerstan,' he said, 'is . . .'

'Yes?' said his brother.*

'What I don' unnerstan is, how longaz diz place had waiters?'

'Good evening,' said Teatime, putting down the tray.

They stared at him in silence.

He gave them a friendly smile.

Peachy's huge hand slapped the table.

'You crept up on us, you little—' he began.

Men in their line of business develop a certain prescience. Medium Dave and Catseye, who were sitting on either side of Peachy, leaned away nonchalantly.

'Hi!' said Teatime. There was a blur, and a knife shuddered in the table between Peachy's thumb and index finger.

---

*Ankh-Morpork's underworld, which was so big that the overworld floated around on top of it like a very small hen trying to mother a nest of ostrich chicks, already had Big Dave, Fat Dave, Mad Dave, Wee Davey, and Lanky Dai. Everyone had to find their niche.

46

He looked down at it in horror.

'My name's Teatime,' said Teatime. 'Which one are you?'

' 'm . . . Peachy,' said Peachy, still staring at the vibrating knife.

'That's an interesting name,' said Teatime. 'Why are you called Peachy, Peachy?'

Medium Dave coughed.

Peachy looked up into Teatime's face. The glass eye was a mere ball of faintly glowing grey. The other eye was a little dot in a sea of white. Peachy's only contact with intelligence had been to beat it up and rob it whenever possible, but a sudden sense of self-preservation glued him to his chair.

' 'cos I don't shave,' he said.

'Peachy don't like blades, mister,' said Catseye.

'And do you have a lot of friends, Peachy?' said Teatime.

'Got a few, yeah . . .'

With a sudden whirl of movement that made the men start, Teatime spun away, grabbed a chair, swung it up to the table and sat down on it. Three of them had already got their hands on their swords.

'I don't have many,' he said, apologetically. 'Don't seem to have the knack. On the other hand . . . I don't seem to have *any* enemies at all. Not one. Isn't that nice?'

*   *   *

47

Teatime had been thinking, in the cracking, buzzing firework display that was his head. What he had been thinking about was immortality.

He might have been quite, quite insane, but he was no fool. There were, in the Assassins' Guild, a number of paintings and busts of famous members who had, in the past, put . . . no, of course, that wasn't right. There were paintings and busts of the famous *clients* of members, with a noticeably modest brass plaque screwed somewhere nearby, bearing some unassuming little comment like 'Departed this vale of tears on Grune 3, Year of the Sideways Leech, with the assistance of the Hon. K. W. Dobson (Viper House)'. Many fine old educational establishments had dignified memorials in some hall listing the Old Boys who had laid down their lives for monarch and country. The Guild's was very similar, except for the question of whose life had been laid.

Every Guild member wanted to be up there somewhere. Because getting up there represented immortality. And the bigger your client, the more incredibly discreet and restrained would be the little brass plaque, so that everyone couldn't help but notice your name.

In fact, if you were very, very renowned, they wouldn't even have to write down your name at all . . .

The men around the table watched him. It was always hard to know what Banjo was thinking, or even if he was thinking at all, but the other four were thinking along the lines of: bumptious little tit, like all Assassins. Thinks he knows it all. I could take him down one-handed, no trouble. But . . . you hear stories. Those eyes give me the creeps . . .

'So what's the job?' said Chickenwire.

'We don't do jobs,' said Teatime. 'We perform services. And the service will earn each of you ten thousand dollars.'

'That's a lot more'n Thieves' Guild rate,' said Medium Dave.

'I've never liked the Thieves' Guild,' said Teatime, without turning his head.

'Why not?'

'They ask too many questions.'

'We don't ask questions,' said Chickenwire quickly.

'We shall suit one another perfectly,' said Teatime. 'Do have another drink while we wait for the other members of our little troupe.'

Chickenwire saw Medium Dave's lips start to frame the opening letters 'Who—' These letters he deemed inauspicious at this time. He kicked Medium Dave's leg under the table.

The door opened slightly. A figure came in, but only just. It inserted itself in the gap and sidled along the wall in a manner calculated not to attract attention. Calculated, that is, by someone not good at this sort of calculation.

It looked at them over its turned-up collar.

'That's a *wizard*,' said Peachy.

The figure hurried over and dragged up a chair.

'No I'm not!' it hissed. 'I'm incognito!'

'Right, Mr Gnito,' said Medium Dave. 'You're just someone in a pointy hat. This is my brother Banjo, that's Peachy, this is Chick—'

The wizard looked desperately at Teatime.

'I didn't want to come!'

'Mr Sideney here is indeed a wizard,' said Teatime. 'A student, anyway. But down on his luck at the moment, hence his willingness to join us on this venture.'

'Exactly how far down on his luck?' said Medium Dave.

The wizard tried not to meet anyone's gaze.

'I made a misjudgement to do with a wager,' he said.

'Lost a bet, you mean?' said Chickenwire.

'I paid up on time,' said Sideney.

'Yes, but Chrysoprase the troll has this odd little thing about money that turns into lead the next day,' said Teatime cheerfully. 'So our friend needs to earn a little cash in a hurry and in a climate where arms and legs stay on.'

'No one said anything about there being magic in all this,' said Peachy.

'Our destination is . . . probably you should think of it as something like a wizard's tower, gentlemen,' said Teatime.

'It isn't an actual wizard's tower, is it?' said Medium Dave. 'They got a very odd sense of humour when it comes to booby traps.'

'No.'

'Guards?'

'I believe so. According to legend. But nothing very much.'

Medium Dave narrowed his eyes. 'There's valuable stuff in this . . . tower?'

'Oh, yes.'

'Why ain't there many guards, then?'

'The . . . person who owns the property probably does not realize the value of what . . . of what they have.'

'Locks?' said Medium Dave.

'On our way we shall be picking up a locksmith.'

'Who?'

'Mr Brown.'

They nodded. Everyone – at least, everyone in 'the business', and everyone in 'the business' knew what 'the business' was, and if you didn't know what 'the business' was you weren't a businessman – knew Mr Brown. His presence anywhere around a job gave it a certain kind of respectability. He was a neat, elderly man who'd invented most of the tools in his big leather bag. No matter what cunning you'd used to get into a place, or overcome a small army, or find the secret treasure room, sooner or later you sent for Mr Brown, who'd turn up with his leather bag and his little springy things and his little bottles of strange alchemy and his neat little boots. And he'd do nothing for ten minutes but look at the lock, and then he'd select a piece of bent metal from a ring of several hundred almost identical pieces, and under an hour later he'd be walking away with a neat ten per cent of the takings. Of course, you didn't *have* to use Mr Brown's services. You could always opt to spend the rest of your life looking at a locked door.

'All right. Where is this place?' said Peachy.

Teatime turned and smiled at him. 'If I'm paying you, why isn't it me who's asking the questions?'

Peachy didn't even try to outstare the glass eye a second time.

'Just want to be prepared, that's all,' he mumbled.

'Good reconnaissance is the essence of a successful operation,' said Teatime. He turned and looked up at the bulk that was Banjo and added, 'What is this?'

'This is Banjo,' said Medium Dave, rolling himself a cigarette.

'Does it do tricks?'

Time stood still for a moment. The other men looked at Medium Dave. He was known to Ankh-Morpork's professional underclass as a thoughtful, patient man, and considered something of an intellectual because some of his tattoos were spelled right. He was reliable in a tight spot and, above all, he was honest, because good criminals have to be honest. If he had a fault, it was a tendency to deal out terminal and definitive retribution to anyone who said anything about his brother.

If he had a virtue, it was a tendency to pick his time. Medium Dave's fingers tucked the tobacco into the paper and raised it to his lips.

'No,' he said.

Chickenwire tried to defrost the conversation. 'He's not what you'd call bright, but he's always useful. He can lift two men in each hand. By their necks.'

'Yur,' said Banjo.

'He looks like a volcano,' said Teatime.

'*Really?*' said Medium Dave Lilywhite. Chickenwire reached out hastily and pushed him back down in his seat.

Teatime turned and smiled at him.

'I do so hope we're going to be friends, Mr Medium Dave,' he said. 'It really hurts to think I might not be among friends.' He gave him another bright smile. Then he turned back to the rest of the table.

'Are we resolved, gentlemen?'

They nodded. There was some reluctance, given the consensus view that Teatime belonged in a room with soft walls, but ten thousand dollars was ten thousand dollars, possibly even more.

'Good,' said Teatime. He looked Banjo up and down. 'Then I suppose we might as well make a start.'

And he hit Banjo very hard in the mouth.

Death in person did not turn up upon the cessation of every life. It was not necessary. Governments govern, but prime ministers and

53

presidents do not personally turn up in people's homes to tell them how to run their lives, because of the mortal danger this would present. There are laws instead.

But from time to time Death checked up to see that things were functioning properly or, to put it another and more accurate way, properly *ceasing* to function in the less significant areas of his jurisdiction.

And now he walked through dark seas.

Silt rose in clouds around his feet as he strode along the trench bottom. His robes floated out around him.

There was silence, pressure and utter, utter darkness. But there was life down here, even this far below the waves. There were giant squid, and lobsters with teeth on their eyelids. There were spidery things with their stomachs on their feet, and fish that made their own light. It was a quiet, black nightmare world, but life lives everywhere that life can. Where life can't, this takes a little longer.

Death's destination was a slight rise in the trench floor. Already the water around him was getting warmer and more populated, by creatures that looked as though they had been put together from the bits left over from everything else.

Unseen but felt, a vast column of scalding hot water was welling up from a fissure. Somewhere below were rocks heated to near incandescence by the Disc's magical field.

Spires of minerals had been deposited around

this vent. And, in this tiny oasis, a type of life had grown up. It did not need air or light. It did not even need food in the way that most other species would understand the term.

It just grew at the edge of the streaming column of water, looking like a cross between a worm and a flower.

Death kneeled down and peered at it, because it was so small. But for some reason, in this world without eyes or light, it was also a brilliant red. The profligacy of life in these matters never ceased to amaze him.

He reached inside his robe and pulled out a small roll of black material, like a jeweller's toolkit. With great care he took from one of its pouches a scythe about an inch long, and held it expectantly between thumb and forefinger.

Somewhere overhead a shard of rock was dislodged by a stray current and tumbled down, raising little puffs of silt as it bounced off the tubes.

It landed just beside the living flower and then rolled, wrenching it from the rock.

Death flicked the tiny scythe just as the bloom faded . . .

The omnipotent eyesight of various supernatural entities is often remarked upon. It is said they can see the fall of every sparrow.

And this may be true. But there is only one who is always there when it hits the ground.

The soul of the tube worm was very small and

uncomplicated. It wasn't bothered about sin. It had never coveted its neighbour's polyps. It had never gambled or drunk strong liquor. It had never bothered itself with questions like 'Why am I here?' because it had no concept at all of 'here' or, for that matter, of 'I'.

Nevertheless, something was cut free under the surgical edge of the scythe and vanished in the roiling waters.

Death carefully put the instrument away and stood up. All was well, things were functioning satisfactorily, and—

—but they weren't.

In the same way that the best of engineers can hear the tiny change that signals a bearing going bad long before the finest of instruments would detect anything wrong, Death picked up a discord in the symphony of the world. It was one wrong note among billions but all the more noticeable for that, like a tiny pebble in a very large shoe.

He waved a finger in the waters. For a moment a blue, door-shaped outline appeared. He stepped through it and was gone.

The tube creatures didn't notice him go. They hadn't noticed him arrive. They never ever noticed anything.

A cart trundled through the freezing foggy streets, the driver hunched in his seat. He seemed to be all big thick brown overcoat.

A figure darted out of the swirls and was suddenly on the box next to him.

'Hi!' it said. 'My name's Teatime. What's yours?'

''ere, you get down, I ain't allowed to give li—'

The driver stopped. It was amazing how Teatime had been able to thrust a knife through four layers of thick clothing and stop it just at the point where it pricked the flesh.

'Sorry?' said Teatime, smiling brightly.

'Er – there ain't nothing valuable, y'know, nothing valuable, only a few bags of—'

'Oh, dear,' said Teatime, his face a sudden acre of concern. 'Well, we'll just have to see, won't we . . . What *is* your name, sir?'

'Ernie. Er. Ernie,' said Ernie. 'Yes. Ernie. Er . . .'

Teatime turned his head slightly.

'Come along, gentlemen. This is my friend Ernie. He's going to be our driver for tonight.'

Ernie saw half a dozen figures emerge from the fog and climb into the cart behind him. He didn't turn to look at them. By the pricking of his kidneys he knew this would not be an exemplary career move. But it seemed that one of the figures, a huge shambling mound of a creature, was carrying a long bundle over its shoulder. The bundle moved and made muffled noises.

'Do stop shaking, Ernie. We just need a lift,' said Teatime, as the cart rumbled over the cobbles.

'Where to, mister?'

'Oh, we don't mind. But first, I'd like you to

stop in Sator Square, near the second fountain.'

The knife was withdrawn. Ernie stopped trying to breathe through his ears.

'Er . . .'

'What is it? You do seem tense, Ernie. I always find a neck massage helps.'

'I ain't rightly allowed to carry passengers, see. Charlie'll give me a right telling-off . . .'

'Oh, don't you worry about *that*,' said Teatime, slapping him on the back. 'We're all friends here!'

'What're we bringing the girl for?' said a voice behind them.

' 's not right, hittin' girls,' said a deep voice. 'Our mam said no hittin' girls. Only bad boys do that, our mam said—'

'You be quiet, Banjo.'

'Our mam said—'

'Shssh! Ernie here doesn't want to listen to our troubles,' said Teatime, not taking his gaze off the driver.

'Me? Deaf as a post, me,' burbled Ernie, who in some ways was a very quick learner. 'Can't hardly see more'n a few feet, neither. Got no recollection for them faces that I do see, come to that. Bad memory? Hah! Talk about bad memory. Cor, sometimes I can be like as it were on the cart, talking to people, hah, just like I'm talking to you now, and then when they're gone, hah, try as I might, do you think I can remember anything about them or how many they were or what they were carrying or anything about any

58

girl or anything?' By this time his voice was a high-pitched wheeze. 'Hah! Sometimes I forget me own name!'

'It's *Ernie*, isn't it?' said Teatime, giving him a happy smile. 'Ah, and here we are. Oh dear. There seems to be some excitement.'

There was the sound of fighting somewhere ahead, and then a couple of masked trolls ran past with three Watchmen after them. They all ignored the cart.

'I heard the De Bris gang were going to have a go at Packley's strongroom tonight,' said a voice behind Ernie.

'Looks like Mr Brown won't be joining us, then,' said another voice. There was a snigger.

'Oh, I don't know about that, Mr Lilywhite, I don't know about that at all,' said a third voice, and this one was from the direction of the fountain. 'Could you take my bag while I climb up, please? Do be careful, it's a little heavy.'

It was a neat little voice. The owner of a voice like that kept his money in a shovel purse and always counted his change carefully. Ernie thought all this, and then tried very hard to forget that he had.

'On you go, Ernie,' said Teatime. 'Round behind the University, I think.'

As the cart rolled on, the neat little voice said, 'You grab all the money and then you get out very smartly. Am I right?'

There was a murmur of agreement.

'Learned that on my mother's knee, yeah.'

'You learned a lot of stuff across your ma's knee, Mr Lilywhite.'

'Don't you say nuffin' about our mam!' The voice was like an earthquake.

'This is *Mr Brown*, Banjo. You smarten up.'

'He dint ort to tork about our mam!'

'All right! All right! Hello, Banjo . . . I think I may have a sweet somewhere . . . Yes, there you are. Yes, your ma knew the way all right. You go in quietly, you take your time, you get what you came for and you leave smartly and in good order. You *don't* hang around at the scene to count it out and tell one another what brave lads you are, am I right?'

'You seem to have done all right, Mr Brown.' The cart rattled towards the other side of the square.

'Just a little for expenses, Mr Catseye. A little Hogswatch present, you might say. Never take the lot and run. Take a little and walk. Dress neat. That's my motto. Dress neat and walk away slowly. Never run. *Never* run. The Watch'll always chase a running man. They're like terriers for giving chase. No, you walk out slow, you walk round the corner, you wait till there's a lot of excitement, then you turn around and walk back. They can't cope with that, see. Half the time they'll stand aside to let you walk past. "Good evening, officers," you say, and then you go home for your tea.'

'Wheee! Gets you out of trouble, I can see that. If you've got the nerve.'

'Oh, no, Mr Peachy. Doesn't get you out of. *Keeps* you out of.'

It was like a very good schoolroom, Ernie thought (and immediately tried to forget). Or a back-street gym when a champion prizefighter had just strolled in.

'What's up with your mouth, Banjo?'

'He lost a tooth, Mr Brown,' said another voice, and sniggered.

'Lost a toot', Mr Brown,' said the thunder that was Banjo.

'Keep your eyes on the road, Ernie,' said Teatime beside him. 'We don't want an accident, do we . . .'

The road here was deserted, despite the bustle of the city behind them and the bulk of the University nearby. There were a few streets, but the buildings were abandoned. And something was happening to the sound. The rest of Ankh-Morpork seemed very far away, the sounds arriving as if through quite a thick wall. They were entering that scorned little corner of Ankh-Morpork that had long been the site of the University's rubbish pits and was now known as the Unreal Estate.

'Bloody wizards,' muttered Ernie, automatically.

'I beg your pardon?' said Teatime.

'My great-grandpa said we used t'own prop'ty round here. Low levels of magic, my arse! Hah, it's all right for them wizards, they got all kindsa spells to protect 'em. Bit of magic here, bit of magic there . . . Stands to reason it's got to go somewhere, right?'

'There used to be warning signs up,' said the neat voice from behind.

'Yeah, well, warning signs in Ankh-Morpork might as well have "Good firewood" written on them,' said someone else.

'I mean, stands to reason, they chuck out an old spell for exploding this, and another one for twiddlin' that, and another one for making carrots grow, they finish up interfering with one another, who knows what they'll end up doing?' said Ernie. 'Great-grandpa said sometimes they'd wake up in the morning and the cellar'd be higher than the attic. And that weren't the worst,' he added darkly.

'Yeah, I heard where it got so bad you could walk down the street and meet yourself coming the other way,' someone supplied. 'It got so's you didn't know it was bum or breakfast time, I heard.'

'The dog used to bring home all kinds of stuff,' said Ernie. 'Great-grandpa said half the time they used to dive behind the sofa if it came in with anything in its mouth. Corroded fire spells startin' to fizz, broken wands with green smoke coming out of 'em and I don't know what else . . . and if you saw the cat playing with anything, it was best not to try to find out what it was, I can tell you.'

He twitched the reins, his current predicament almost forgotten in the tide of hereditary resentment.

'I mean, they *say* all the old spell books and stuff was buried deep and they recycle the used spells now, but that don't seem much comfort when your potatoes started walkin' about,' he grumbled. 'My great-grandpa went to see the head wizard about it, and *he* said' – he put on a strangled nasal voice which was his idea of how you talked when you'd got an education – ' "Oh, there might be some temp'ry inconvenience now, my good man, but just you come back in fifty thousand years." Bloody wizards.'

The horse turned a corner.

This was a dead-end street. Half-collapsed houses, windows smashed, doors stolen, leaned against one another on either side.

'I heard they said they were going to clean up this place,' said someone.

'Oh, *yeah*,' said Ernie, and spat. When it hit the ground it ran away. 'And you know what? You get loonies coming in all the time now, poking around, pulling things about—'

'Just at the wall up ahead,' said Teatime conversationally. 'I think you generally go through just where there's a pile of rubble by the old dead tree, although you wouldn't see it unless you looked closely. But I've never seen how you *do* it . . .'

"ere, I can't take you lot through,' said Ernie. 'Lifts is one thing, but not taking people through—'

Teatime sighed. 'And we were getting on *so* well. Listen, Ernie . . . Ern . . . you will take us

63

through or, and I say this with very considerable regret, I will have to kill you. You seem a nice man. Conscientious. A very serious overcoat and sensible boots.'

'But if'n I take you through—'

'What's the worst that can happen?' said Teatime. 'You'll lose your job. Whereas if you don't, you'll die. So if you look at it like that, we're actually doing you a favour. Oh, *do* say yes.'

'Er . . .' Ernie's brain felt twisted up. The lad was definitely what Ernie thought of as a toff, and he seemed nice and friendly, but it didn't all add up. The tone and the content didn't match.

'Besides,' said Teatime, 'if you've been coerced, it's not your fault, is it? No one can blame you. No one could blame *anyone* who'd been coerced at knife point.'

'Oh, well, I s'pose, if we're talking *coerced* . . .' Ernie muttered. Going along with things seemed to be the only way.

The horse stopped and stood waiting with the patient look of an animal that probably knows the route better than the driver.

Ernie fumbled in his overcoat pocket and took out a small tin, rather like a snuff box. He opened it. There was glowing dust inside.

'What do you do with that?' said Teatime, all interest.

'Oh, you just takes a pinch and throws it in the air and it goes *twing* and it opens the soft place,' said Ernie.

64

'So . . . you don't need any special training or anything?'

'Er . . . you just chucks it at the wall there and it goes *twing*,' said Ernie.

'Really? May I try?'

Teatime took the tin from his unresisting hand and threw a pinch of dust into the air in front of the horse. It hovered for a moment and then produced a narrow, glittering arch in the air. It sparkled and went . . .

. . . *twing*.

'Aw,' said a voice behind them. 'Innat nice, eh, our Davey?'

'Yeah.'

'All pretty sparkles . . .'

'And then you just drive forward?' said Teatime.

'That's right,' said Ernie. 'Quick, mind. It only stays open for a little while.'

Teatime pocketed the little tin. 'Thank you very much, Ernie. Very much indeed.'

His other hand lashed out. There was a glint of metal. The carter blinked, and then fell sideways off his seat.

There was silence from behind, tinted with horror and possibly just a little terrible admiration.

'Wasn't he *dull*?' said Teatime, picking up the reins.

Snow began to fall. It fell on the recumbent shape of Ernie, and it also fell through several hooded grey robes that hung in the air.

There appeared to be nothing inside them. You could believe they were there merely to make a certain point in space.

Well, said one, we are frankly impressed.

Indeed, said another. We would never have thought of doing it *this* way.

He is certainly a resourceful human, said a third.

The beauty of it all, said the first – or it may have been the second, because absolutely nothing distinguished the robes – is that there is so much else we will control.

Quite, said another. It is really amazing how they think. A sort of . . . illogical logic.

Children, said another. Who would have thought it? But today the children, tomorrow the world.

Give me a child until he is seven and he's mine for life, said another.

There was a dreadful pause.

The consensus beings that called themselves the Auditors did not believe in anything, except possibly immortality. And the way to be immortal, they knew, was to avoid living. Most of all they did not believe in personality. To be a personality was to be a creature with a beginning and an end. And since they reasoned that in an infinite universe any life was by comparison unimaginably short, they died instantly. There was a flaw in their logic, of course, but by the time they found this out it was always too late. In the meantime, they scrupulously avoided any comment, action or experience that set them apart . . .

You said 'me', said one.

Ah. Yes. But, you see, we were quoting, said the other one hurriedly. Some religious person said that. About educating children. And so would logically say 'me'. But I wouldn't use that term of myself, of – *damn!*

The robe vanished in a little puff of smoke.

Let that be a lesson to us, said one of the survivors, as another and totally indistinguishable robe popped into existence where the stricken colleague had been.

Yes, said the newcomer. Well, it certainly appears—

It stopped. A dark shape was approaching through the snow.

It's *him*, it said.

They faded hurriedly – not simply vanishing, but spreading out and thinning until they were just lost in the background.

The dark figure stopped by the dead carter and reached down.

COULD I GIVE YOU A HAND?

Ernie looked up gratefully.

'Cor, yeah,' he said. He got to his feet, swaying a little. 'Here, your fingers're cold, mister!'

SORRY.

'What'd he go and do that for? I *did* what he said. He could've *killed* me.'

Ernie felt inside his overcoat and pulled out a small and, at this point, strangely transparent silver flask.

'I always keep a nip on me these cold nights,' he said. 'Keeps me spirits up.'

YES INDEED. Death looked around briefly and sniffed the air.

'How'm I going to explain all this, then, eh?' said Ernie, taking a pull.

SORRY? THAT WAS VERY RUDE OF ME. I WASN'T PAYING ATTENTION.

'I said what'm I going to tell people? Letting some blokes ride off with my cart neat as you like . . . That's gonna be the sack for sure, I'm gonna be in *big* trouble . . .'

AH. WELL. THERE AT LEAST I HAVE SOME GOOD NEWS, ERNEST. AND, THEN AGAIN, I HAVE SOME BAD NEWS.

Ernie listened. Once or twice he looked at the corpse at his feet. He looked smaller from the outside. He was bright enough not to argue. Some things are fairly obvious when it's a seven-foot skeleton with a scythe telling you them.

'So I'm dead, then,' he concluded.

CORRECT.

'Er . . . The priest said that . . . you know . . . after you're dead . . . it's like going through a door and on one side of it there's . . . He . . . well, a terrible place . . . ?'

Death looked at his worried, fading face.

THROUGH A DOOR . . .

'That's what he said . . .'

68

I EXPECT IT DEPENDS ON THE DIRECTION YOU'RE
WALKING IN.

When the street was empty again, except for
the fleshy abode of the late Ernie, the grey shapes
came back into focus.

Honestly, he gets worse and worse, said one.

He was looking for us, said another. Did you
notice? He suspects something. He gets so . . .
concerned about things.

Yes . . . but the beauty of this plan, said a third,
is that he *can't* interfere.

He can go everywhere, said one.

No, said another. Not quite *everywhere*.

And, with ineffable smugness, they faded into
the foreground.

It started to snow quite heavily.

It was the night before Hogswatch. All through
the house . . .

. . . one creature stirred. It was a mouse.

And someone, in the face of all appro-
priateness, had baited a trap. Although, because
it was the festive season, they'd used a piece of
pork crackling. The smell of it had been driving
the mouse mad all day but now, with no one
about, it was prepared to risk it.

The mouse didn't know it was a trap. Mice
aren't good at passing on information. Young
mice aren't taken up to famous trap sites and told,
'This is where your Uncle Arthur passed away.'
All it knew was that, what the hey, here was

something to eat. On a wooden board with some wire round it.

A brief scurry later and its jaw had closed on the rind.

Or, rather, passed through it.

The mouse looked around at what was now lying under the big spring, and thought, 'Oops . . .'

Then its gaze went up to the black-clad figure that had faded into view by the wainscoting.

'Squeak?' it asked.

SQUEAK, said the Death of Rats.

And that was *it*, more or less.

Afterwards, the Death of Rats looked around with interest. In the nature of things his very important job tended to take him to rickyards and dark cellars and the inside of cats and all the little dank holes where rats and mice finally found out if there was a Promised Cheese. This place was different.

It was brightly decorated, for one thing. Ivy and mistletoe hung in bunches from the bookshelves. Brightly coloured streamers festooned the walls, a feature seldom found in most holes or even quite civilized cats.

The Death of Rats took a leap onto a chair and from there on to the table and in fact right into a glass of amber liquid, which tipped over and broke. A puddle spread around four turnips and began to soak into a note which had been written rather awkwardly on pink writing paper.

It read:

Dere HogFather,

For Hogswatch I would like a drum an a dolly an a teddybear an a Gharstley Omnian Inquisision Torchure Chamber with Wind-up Rack and Nearly Real Blud You Can Use Agian, you can get it from the toyshoppe in Short Strete, it is $5.99p. I have been good an here is a glars of sherre an a pork pie for you and turnips for Gouger an Tusker an Rooter an ~~Snot~~ Snouter. I hop the Chimney is big enough but my friend Willaim Says you are your father really.   Yrs. Virginia Prood.

The Death of Rats nibbled a bit of the pork pie because when you are the personification of the death of small rodents you have to behave in certain ways. He also piddled on one of the turnips for the same reason, although only meta-phorically, because when you are a small skeleton in a black robe there are also some things you technically cannot do.

Then he leapt down from the table and left sherry-flavoured footprints all the way to the tree that stood in a pot in the corner. It was really only a bare branch of oak, but so much shiny holly and mistletoe had been wired onto it that it gleamed in the light of the candles.

There was tinsel on it, and glittering ornaments, and small bags of chocolate money.

The Death of Rats peered at his hugely distorted reflection in a glass ball, and then looked up at the mantelpiece.

He reached it in one jump, and ambled curiously through the cards that had been ranged along it. His grey whiskers twitched at messages like '*Wiſhing you Joye and all Goode Cheer at Hogswatchtime & All Through The Yeare*'. A couple of them had pictures of a big jolly fat man carrying a sack. In one of them he was riding in a sledge drawn by four enormous pigs.

The Death of Rats sniffed at a couple of long stockings that had been hung from the mantelpiece, over the fireplace in which a fire had died down to a few sullen ashes.

He was aware of a subtle tension in the air, a feeling that here was a scene that was also a stage, a round hole, as it were, waiting for a round peg—

There was a scraping noise. A few lumps of soot thumped into the ashes.

The Grim Squeaker nodded to himself.

The scraping became louder, and was followed by a moment of silence and then a clang as something landed in the ashes and knocked over a set of ornamental fire irons.

The rat watched carefully as a red-robed figure pulled itself upright and staggered across the hearthrug, rubbing its shin where it had been caught by the toasting fork.

It reached the table and read the note. The Death of Rats thought he heard a groan.

The turnips were pocketed and so, to the Death of Rats' annoyance, was the pork pie. He was pretty sure it was meant to be eaten here, not taken away.

The figure scanned the dripping note for a moment, and then turned around and approached the mantelpiece. The Death of Rats pulled back slightly behind *'Seaſon's Greetings!'*

A red-gloved hand took down a stocking. There was some creaking and rustling and it was replaced, looking a lot fatter – the larger box sticking out of the top had, just visible, the words 'Victim Figures Not Included. 3–10 yrs'.

The Death of Rats couldn't see much of the donor of this munificence. The big red hood hid all the face, apart from a long white beard.

Finally, when the figure finished, it stood back and pulled a list out of its pocket. It held it up to the hood and appeared to be consulting it. It waved its other hand vaguely at the fireplace, the sooty footprints, the empty sherry glass and the stocking. Then it bent forward, as if reading some tiny print.

AH, YES, it said. ER . . . HO. HO. HO.

With that, it ducked down and entered the chimney. There was some scrabbling before its boots gained a purchase, and then it was gone.

The Death of Rats realized he'd begun to knaw his little scythe's handle in sheer shock.

SQUEAK?

He landed in the ashes and swarmed up the sooty cave of the chimney. He emerged so fast that he shot out with his legs still scrabbling and landed in the snow on the roof.

There was a sledge hovering in the air by the gutter.

The red-hooded figure had just climbed in and appeared to be talking to someone invisible behind a pile of sacks.

HERE'S ANOTHER PORK PIE.

'Any mustard?' said the sacks. 'They're a treat with mustard.'

IT DOES NOT APPEAR SO.

'Oh, well. Pass it over anyway.'

IT LOOKS VERY BAD.

'Nah, 's just where something's nibbled it—'

I MEAN THE SITUATION. MOST OF THE LETTERS . . . THEY DON'T REALLY *BELIEVE*. THEY PRETEND TO BELIEVE, JUST IN CASE.* I FEAR IT MAY BE TOO LATE. IT HAS SPREAD SO FAST AND BACK IN TIME, TOO.

'Never say die, master. That's our motto, eh?' said the sacks, apparently with their mouth full.

I CAN'T SAY IT'S EVER REALLY BEEN MINE.

'I meant we're not going to be intimidated by

---

*This is very similar to the suggestion put forward by the Quirmian philosopher Ventre, who said, 'Possibly the gods exist, and possibly they do not. So why not believe in them in any case? If it's all true you'll go to a lovely place when you die, and if it isn't then you've lost nothing, right?' When he died he woke up in a circle of gods holding nasty-looking sticks and one of them said, 'We're going to show you what we think of Mr Clever Dick in these parts . . .'

the certain prospect of complete and utter failure, master.'

AREN'T WE? OH, GOOD. WELL, I SUPPOSE WE'D BETTER BE GOING. The figure picked up the reins. UP, GOUGER! UP, ROOTER! UP, TUSKER! UP, SNOUTER! GIDDYUP!

The four large boars harnessed to the sledge did not move.

WHY DOESN'T THAT WORK? said the figure in a puzzled, heavy voice.

'Beats me, master,' said the sacks.

IT WORKS ON HORSES.

'You could try "Pig-hooey!"'

PIG-HOOEY. They waited. NO . . . DOESN'T SEEM TO REACH THEM.

There was some whispering.

REALLY? YOU THINK THAT WOULD WORK?

'It'd bloody well work on me if I was a pig, master.'

VERY WELL, THEN.

The figure gathered up the reins again.

APPLE! SAUCE!

The pigs' legs blurred. Silver light flicked across them, and exploded outwards. They dwindled to a dot, and vanished.

SQUEAK?

The Death of Rats skipped across the snow, slid down a drainpipe and landed on the roof of a shed.

There was a raven perched there. It was staring disconsolately at something.

SQUEAK!

75

'Look at that, willya?' said the raven rhetori-cally. It waved a claw at a bird table in the garden below. 'They hangs up half a bloody coconut, a lump of bacon rind, a handful of peanuts in a bit of wire and they think they're the gods' gift to the nat'ral world. Huh. Do I see eyeballs? Do I see entrails? I think *not*. Most intelligent bird in the temperate latitudes an' I gets the cold shoulder just because I can't hang upside down and go twit, twit. Look at robins, now. Stroppy little evil buggers, fight like demons, but all they got to do is go bob-bob-bobbing along and they can't move for breadcrumbs. Whereas me myself can recite poems and repeat many hum'rous phrases—'

SQUEAK!

'Yes? What?'

The Death of Rats pointed at the roof and then the sky and jumped up and down excitedly. The raven swivelled one eye upwards.

'Oh, yes. *Him*,' he said. 'Turns up at this time of year. Tends to be associated distantly with robins, which—'

SQUEAK! SQUEE IK IK IK! The Death of Rats pantomimed a figure landing in a grate and walking around a room. SQUEAK EEK IK IK, SQUEAK 'HEEK HEEK HEEK'! IK IK *SQUEAK*!

'Been overdoing the Hogswatch cheer, have you? Been rootling around in the brandy butter?'

SQUEAK?

The raven's eyes revolved.

'Look, Death's *Death*. It's a full-time job right?

It's not as though you can run, like, a window cleaning round on the side or nip round after work cutting people's lawns.'

SQUEAK!

'Oh, please yourself.'

The raven crouched a little to allow the tiny figure to hop on to its back, and then lumbered into the air.

'Of course, they can go mental, your occult types,' it said, as it swooped over the moonlit garden. 'Look at Old Man Trouble, for one—'

SQUEAK.

'Oh, I'm not suggesting—'

Susan didn't like Biers but she went there anyway, when the pressure of being normal got too much. Biers, despite the smell and the drink and the company, had one important virtue. In Biers no one took any notice. Of anything. Hogswatch was traditionally supposed to be a time for families but the people who drank in Biers probably didn't have families; some of them looked as though they might have had litters, or clutches. Some of them looked as though they'd probably eaten their relatives, or at least *someone*'s relatives.

Biers was where the undead drank. And when Igor the barman was asked for a Bloody Mary, he didn't mix a metaphor.

The regular customers didn't ask questions, and not only because some of them found anything above a growl hard to articulate. None of them was in the answers business. Everyone in Biers drank alone, even when they were in groups. Or packs.

Despite the decorations put up inexpertly by Igor the barman to show willing,* Biers was not a family place.

Family was a subject Susan liked to avoid.

Currently she was being aided in this by a gin and tonic. In Biers, unless you weren't choosy, it paid to order a drink that was transparent because Igor also had undirected ideas about what you could stick on the end of a cocktail stick. If you saw something spherical and green, you just had to hope that it was an olive.

She felt hot breath on her ear. A bogeyman had sat down on the stool beside her.

'Woss a normo doin' in a place like this, then?' it rumbled, causing a cloud of vaporized alcohol and halitosis to engulf her. 'Hah, you fink it's *cool* comin' down here an' swannin' around in a black dress wid all the lost boys, eh? Dabblin' in a bit of designer darkness, eh?'

Susan moved her stool away a little. The bogeyman grinned.

'Want a bogeyman under yer bed, eh?'

'Now then, Shlimazel,' said Igor, without looking up from polishing a glass.

'Well, woss she down here for, eh?' said the

_____

*He'd done his best. But black and purple and vomit yellow weren't a good colour combination for paperchains, and no Hogswatch fairy doll should be nailed up by its head.

bogeyman. A huge hairy hand grabbed Susan's arm. 'O' course, maybe what she wants is—'

'I ain't telling you again, Shlimazel,' said Igor.

He saw the girl turn to face Shlimazel.

Igor wasn't in a position to see her face fully, but the bogeyman was. He shot back so quickly that he fell off his stool.

And when the girl spoke, what she said was only partly words but also a statement, written in stone, of how the future was going to be.

'GO AWAY AND STOP BOTHERING ME.'

She turned back and gave Igor a polite and slightly apologetic smile. The bogeyman struggled frantically out of the wreckage of his stool and loped towards the door.

Susan felt the drinkers turn back to their private preoccupations. It was amazing what you could get away with in Biers.

Igor put down the glass and looked up at the window. For a drinking den that relied on darkness it had rather a large one but, of course, some customers did arrive by air.

Something was tapping on it now.

Igor lurched over and opened it.

Susan looked up.

'Oh, no . . .'

The Death of Rats leapt down onto the counter, with the raven fluttering after it.

SQUEAK SQUEAK EEK! EEK! SQUEAK IK IK 'HEEK HEEK HEEK'! SQ—

'Go away,' said Susan coldly. 'I'm not interest-ed. You're just a figment of my imagination.'

79

The raven perched on a bowl behind the bar and said, 'Ah, great.'

SQUEAK!

'What're these?' said the raven, flicking something off the end of its beak. '*Onions?* Pfah!'

'Go on, go away, the pair of you,' said Susan.

'The rat says your granddad's gone mad,' said the raven. 'Says he's pretending to be the Hogfather.'

'Listen, I just don't— What?'

'Red cloak, long beard—'

HEEK! HEEK! HEEK!

'—going "Ho, ho, ho", driving around in the big sledge drawn by the four piggies, the whole thing . . .'

'Pigs? What happened to Binky?'

'Search me. O' course, it can happen, as I was telling the rat only just now—'

Susan put her hands over her ears, more for desperate theatrical effect than for the muffling they gave.

'I don't want to know! I don't *have* a grandfather!'

She had to hold on to that.

The Death of Rats squeaked at length.

'The rat says you must remember, he's tall, not what you'd call fleshy, he carries a scythe—'

'Go *away*! And take the . . . the *rat* with you!'

She waved her hand wildly and, to her horror and shame, knocked the little hooded skeleton over an ashtray.

EEK?

The raven took the rat's cowl in its beak and tried to drag him away, but a tiny skeletal fist shook its scythe.

EEK *IK* EEK SQUEAK!

'He says, you don't mess with the rat,' said the raven.

In a flurry of wings they were gone.

Igor closed the window. He didn't pass any comment.

'They weren't real,' said Susan, hurriedly. 'Well, that is . . . the raven's probably real, but he hangs around with the rat—'

'Which isn't real,' said Igor.

'That's right!' said Susan, gratefully. 'You probably didn't see a thing.'

'That's right,' said Igor. 'Not a thing.'

'Now . . . how much do I owe you?' said Susan.

Igor counted on his fingers.

'That'll be a dollar for the drinks,' he said, 'and fivepence because the raven that wasn't here messed in the pickles.'

It was the night before Hogswatch.

In the Archchancellor's new bathroom Modo wiped his hands on a piece of rag and looked proudly at his handiwork. Shining porcelain gleamed back at him. Copper and brass shone in the lamplight.

He was a little worried that he hadn't been able to test everything, but Mr Ridcully had said, 'I'll test it when I use it,' and Modo never argued with the Gentlemen, as he thought of them. He knew that they all knew a lot more than he knew, and was quite happy knowing this. *He* didn't meddle with the fabric of time and space, and *they* kept out of his greenhouses. The way he saw it, it was a partnership.

He'd been particularly careful to scrub the floors. Mr Ridcully had been very specific about that.

'Verruca Gnome,' he said to himself, giving a tap a last polish. 'What an imagination the Gentlemen do have . . .'

Far off, unheard by anyone, was a faint little noise, like the ringing of tiny silver bells.

Glingleglingleglingle . . .

And someone landed abruptly in a snowdrift and said, 'Bugger!', which is a terrible thing to say as your first word ever.

Overhead, heedless of the new and somewhat angry life that was even now dusting itself off, the sledge soared onwards through time and space.

I'M FINDING THE BEARD A BIT OF A TRIAL, said Death.

'Why've you got to have the beard?' said the voice from among the sacks. 'I thought you said people see what they expect to see.'

CHILDREN DON'T. TOO OFTEN THEY SEE WHAT'S THERE.

'Well, at least it's keeping you in the right

82

frame of mind, master. In character, sort of thing.'

BUT GOING DOWN THE CHIMNEY? WHERE'S THE
SENSE IN THAT? I CAN JUST WALK THROUGH THE
WALLS.

'Walking through the walls is not right,
neither,' said the voice from the sacks.

IT WORKS FOR ME.

'It's got to be chimneys. Same as the beard,
really.'

A head thrust itself out from the pile. It
appeared to belong to the oldest, most unpleasant
pixie in the universe. The fact that it was underneath a jolly little green hat with a bell on it did
not do anything to improve matters.

It waved a crabbed hand containing a thick
wad of letters, many of them on pastel-coloured
paper, often with bunnies and teddy bears on
them, and written mostly in crayon.

'You reckon these little buggers'd be writing to
someone who walked through walls?' it said.
'And the "Ho, ho, ho" could use some more
work, if you don't mind my saying so.'

HO. HO. HO.

'No, no, *no*!' said Albert. 'You got to put a bit
of life in it, sir, no offence intended. It's got to be
a big fat laugh. You got to . . . you got to sound
like you're pissing brandy and crapping plum
pudding, sir, excuse my Klatchian.'

REALLY? HOW DO YOU KNOW ALL THIS?

'I *was* young once, sir. Hung up my stocking
like a good boy every year. For to get it filled
with toys, just like you're doing. Mind you, in

those days basically it was sausages and black puddings if you were lucky. But you always got a pink sugar piglet in the toe. It wasn't a good Hogswatch unless you'd eaten so much you were sick as a pig, master.'

Death looked at the sacks.

It was a strange but demonstrable fact that the sacks of toys carried by the Hogfather, no matter what they really contained, always appeared to have sticking out of the top a teddy bear, a toy soldier in the kind of colourful uniform that would stand out in a disco, a drum and a red-and-white candy cane. The actual contents always turned out to be something a bit garish and costing $5.99.

Death had investigated one or two. There had been a Real Agatean Ninja, for example, with Fearsome Death Grip, and a Captain Carrot One-Man Night Watch with a complete wardrobe of toy weapons, each of which cost as much as the original wooden doll in the first place.

Mind you, the stuff for the girls was just as depressing. It seemed to be nearly all horses. Most of them were grinning. Horses, Death felt, shouldn't grin. Any horse that was grinning was planning something.

He sighed again.

Then there was this business of deciding who'd been naughty or nice. He'd never had to think about that sort of thing before. Naughty or nice, it was ultimately all the same.

Still, it had to be done *right*. Otherwise it wouldn't *work*.

The pigs pulled up alongside another chimney.

'Here we are, here we are,' said Albert. 'James Riddle, aged eight.'

HAH, YES. HE ACTUALLY SAYS IN HIS LETTER, 'I BET YOU DON'T EXIST 'COS EVERYONE KNOWS ITS YORE PARENTS.' OH *YES*, said Death, with what almost sounded like sarcasm, I'M SURE HIS PARENTS ARE JUST *IMPATIENT* TO BANG THEIR ELBOWS IN TWELVE FEET OF NARROW UNSWEPT CHIMNEY, I DON'T THINK. I SHALL TREAD EXTRA SOOT INTO HIS CARPET.

'Right, sir. Good thinking. Speaking of which – down you go, sir.'

HOW ABOUT IF I DON'T GIVE HIM ANYTHING AS A PUNISHMENT FOR NOT BELIEVING?

'Yeah, but what's that going to prove?'

Death sighed. I SUPPOSE YOU'RE RIGHT.

'Did you check the list?'

YES. TWICE. ARE YOU SURE THAT'S ENOUGH?

'Definitely.'

COULDN'T REALLY MAKE HEAD OR TAIL OF IT, TO TELL YOU THE TRUTH. HOW CAN I *TELL* IF HE'S BEEN NAUGHTY OR NICE, FOR EXAMPLE?

'Oh, well . . . I don't know . . . Has he hung his clothes up, that sort of thing . . .'

AND IF HE HAS BEEN GOOD I MAY GIVE HIM THIS KLATCHIAN WAR CHARIOT WITH REAL SPINNING SWORD BLADES?

'That's right.'

AND IF HE'S BEEN BAD?

Albert scratched his head. 'When I was a lad, you got a bag of bones. 's'mazing how kids got better behaved towards the end of the year.'

OH DEAR. AND NOW?

Albert held a package up to his ear and rustled it. 'Sounds like socks.'

SOCKS.

'Could be a woolly vest.'

SERVE HIM RIGHT, IF I MAY VENTURE TO EXPRESS AN OPINION . . .

Albert looked across the snowy rooftops and sighed. This wasn't right. He was helping because, well, Death was his master and that's all there was to it, and if the master *had* a heart it would be in the right place. But . . .

'Are you *sure* we ought to be doing this, master?'

Death stopped, halfway out of the chimney.

CAN YOU THINK OF A BETTER ALTERNATIVE, ALBERT?

And that was it. Albert couldn't.

Someone had to do it.

There were bears on the street again.

Susan ignored them and didn't even make a point of not treading on the cracks.

They just stood around, looking a bit puzzled and slightly transparent, visible only to children and Susan. News like Susan gets around. The bears had heard about the poker. Nuts and berries, their expressions seemed to say. That's what we're here for. Big sharp teeth? What big shar— Oh, *these* big sharp teeth? They're just for, er, cracking nuts. And some of these berries can be really vicious.

The city's clocks were striking six when she got back to the house. She was allowed her own key. It wasn't as if she was a servant, exactly.

You couldn't be a duchess *and* a servant. But it was all right to be a governess. It was understood that it wasn't exactly what you *were*, it was merely a way of passing the time until you did what every girl, or gel, was supposed to do in life, i.e., marry some man. It was understood that you were playing.

The parents were in awe of her. She was the daughter of a duke whereas Mr Gaiter was a man to be reckoned with in the wholesale boots and shoes business. Mrs Gaiter was bucking for a transfer into the Upper Classes, which she currently hoped to achieve by reading books on etiquette. She treated Susan with the kind of worried deference she thought was due to anyone who'd known the difference between a serviette and a napkin from *birth*.

Susan had never before come across the idea that you could rise in Society by, as it were, gaining marks, especially since such noblemen as she'd met in her father's house had used neither serviette nor napkin but a state of mind, which was 'Drop it on the floor, the dogs'll eat it.'

When Mrs Gaiter had tremulously asked her how one addressed the second cousin of a queen,

Susan had replied without thinking, 'We called him Jamie, usually,' and Mrs Gaiter had had to go and have a headache in her room.

Mr Gaiter just nodded when he met her in a passage and never said very much to her. He was pretty sure he knew where he stood in boots and shoes and that was that.

Gawain and Twyla, who'd been named by people who apparently loved them, had been put to bed by the time Susan got in, at their own insistence. It's a widely held belief at a certain age that going to bed early makes tomorrow come faster.

She went to tidy up the schoolroom and get things ready for the morning, and began to pick up the things the children had left lying around. Then something tapped at a window pane.

She peered out at the darkness, and then opened the window. A drift of snow fell down outside.

In the summer the window opened into the branches of a cherry tree. In the winter dark, they were little grey lines where the snow had settled on them.

'Who's that?' said Susan.

Something hopped through the frozen branches.

'Tweet tweet tweet, would you believe?' said the raven.

'Not *you* again?'

'You wanted maybe some dear little robin? Listen, your grand—'

'Go *away*!'

Susan slammed the window and pulled the curtains across. She put her back to them, to make sure, and tried to concentrate on the room. It helped to think about . . . *normal* things.

There was the Hogswatch tree, a rather smaller version of the grand one in the hall. She'd helped the children to make paper decorations for it. Yes. Think about that.

There were the paperchains. There were the bits of holly, thrown out from the main rooms for not having enough berries on them, and now given fake modelling clay berries and stuck in anyhow on shelves and behind pictures.

There were two stockings hanging from the mantelpiece of the small schoolroom grate. There were Twyla's paintings, all blobby blue skies and violently green grass and red houses with four square windows. There were . . .

Normal things . . .

She straightened up and stared at them, her fingernails beating a thoughtful tattoo on a wooden pencil case.

The door was pushed open. It revealed the tousled shape of Twyla, hanging onto the doorknob with one hand.

'Susan, there's a monster under my bed *again* . . .'

The click of Susan's fingernails stopped.

'. . . I can hear it moving about . . .'

Susan sighed and turned towards the child.

'All right, Twyla. I'll be along directly.'

The girl nodded and went back to her room, leaping into bed from a distance as a precaution against claws.

There was a metallic *tzing* as Susan withdrew the poker from the little brass stand it shared with the tongs and the coal shovel.

She sighed. Normality was what you made it.

She went into the children's bedroom and leaned over as if to tuck Twyla up. Then her hand darted down and under the bed. She grabbed a handful of hair. She pulled.

The bogeyman came out like a cork but before it could get its balance it found itself spread-eagled against the wall with one arm behind its back. But it did manage to turn its head, to see Susan's face glaring at it from a few inches away.

Gawain bounced up and down on his bed.

'Do the Voice on it! Do the Voice on it!' he shouted.

'Don't do the Voice, don't do the Voice!' pleaded the bogeyman urgently.

'Hit it on the head with the poker!'

'Not the poker! Not the poker!'

'It's you, isn't it,' said Susan. 'From this afternoon . . .'

'Aren't you going to poke it with the poker?' said Gawain.

'Not the poker!' whined the bogeyman.

'New in town?' whispered Susan.

'Yes!' The bogeyman's forehead wrinkled with puzzlement. 'Here, how come you can see me?'

'Then this is a friendly warning, understand? Because it's Hogswatch.'

The bogeyman tried to move. 'You call this friendly?'

'Ah, you want to try for *un*friendly?' said Susan, adjusting her grip.

'No, no, no, I *like* friendly!'

'This house is out of bounds, right?'

'You a witch or something?' moaned the bogeyman.

'I'm just . . . something. Now . . . you won't be around here again, will you? Otherwise it'll be the *blanket* next time.'

'No!'

'I mean it. We'll put your head under the blanket.'

'No!'

'It's got *fluffy bunnies* on it . . .'

'*No!*'

'Off you go, then.'

The bogeyman half fell, half ran towards the door.

''s not right,' it mumbled. 'You're not s'*posed* to see us if you ain't dead or magic . . . 's not fair . . .'

'Try number nineteen,' said Susan, relenting a little. 'The governess there doesn't believe in bogeymen.'

'Right?' said the monster hopefully.

'She believes in algebra, though.'

'Ah. Nice.' The bogeyman grinned hugely. It was amazing the sort of mischief that could be caused in a house where no one in authority thought you existed.

'I'll be off, then,' it said. 'Er. Happy Hogswatch.'

'Possibly,' said Susan, as it slunk away.

'That wasn't as much fun as the one last month,' said Gawain, getting between the sheets again. 'You know, when you kicked him in the trousers—'

'Just you two get to sleep now,' said Susan.

'Verity said the sooner we got to sleep the sooner the Hogfather would come,' said Twyla conversationally.

'Yes,' said Susan. 'Unfortunately, that might be the case.'

The remark passed right over their heads. She wasn't sure why it had gone through hers, but she knew enough to trust her senses.

She *hated* that kind of sense. It ruined your life. But it was the sense she had been born with.

The children were tucked in, and she closed the door quietly and went back to the schoolroom.

Something had changed.

She glared at the stockings, but they were unfulfilled. A paperchain rustled.

She stared at the tree. Tinsel had been twined around it, badly pasted-together decorations had been hung on it. And on top was the fairy made of—

She crossed her arms, looked up at the ceiling, and sighed theatrically.

'It's you, isn't it?' she said.

SQUEAK?

'Yes, it *is*. You're sticking out your arms like a scarecrow and you've stuck a little star on your scythe, haven't you . . . ?'

The Death of Rats hung his head guiltily.

SQUEAK.

'You're not fooling *anyone*.'

SQUEAK.

'Get down from there this minute!'

SQUEAK.

'And *what* did you do with the fairy?'

'It's shoved under a cushion on the chair,' said a voice from the shelves on the other side of the room. There was a clicking noise and the raven's voice added, 'These damn eyeballs are hard, aren't they?'

Susan raced across the room and snatched the bowl away so fast that the raven somersaulted and landed on its back.

'They're *walnuts*!' she shouted, as they bounced around her. '*Not* eyeballs! This is a *schoolroom*! And the difference between a school and a-a-a raven delicatessen is that they hardly *ever* have eyeballs lying around in bowls in case a raven drops in for a quick snack! Understand? *No* eyeballs! The world is full of small round things that *aren't* eyeballs! OK?'

The raven's own eyes revolved.

' 'n' I suppose a bit of warm liver's out of the question—'

'Shut up! I want both of you out of here

right now! I don't know how you got in here—'

'There's a law against coming down the chimney on Hogswatchnight?'

'—but I *don't* want you back in my life, understand?'

'The rat said you ought to be warned even if you *were* crazy,' said the raven sulkily. '*I* didn't want to come, there's a donkey dropped dead just outside the city gates, I'll be lucky now if I get a hoof—'

'Warned?' said Susan.

There it was again. The change in the weather of the mind, a sensation of tangible time . . .

The Death of Rats nodded.

There was a scrabbling sound far overhead. A few flakes of soot dropped down the chimney.

SQUEAK, said the rat, but very quietly.

Susan was aware of a new sensation, as a fish might be aware of a new tide, a spring of fresh water flowing into the sea. Time was pouring into the world.

She glanced up at the clock. It was just on half past six.

The raven scratched its beak.

'The rat says . . . The rat says: you'd better watch out . . .'

There were others at work on this shining Hogswatch Eve. The Sandman was out and about, dragging his sack from bed to bed. Jack Frost wandered from window pane to window pane, making icy patterns.

And one tiny hunched shape slid and slithered along the gutter, squelching its feet in slush and swearing under its breath.

It wore a stained black suit and, on its head, the type of hat known in various parts of the multiverse as 'bowler', 'derby' or 'the one that makes you look a bit of a tit'. The hat had been pressed down very firmly and, since the creature had long pointy ears, these had been forced out sideways and gave it the look of a small malignant wing-nut.

The thing was a gnome by shape but a fairy by profession. Fairies aren't necessarily little twinkly creatures. It's purely a job description, and the commonest ones aren't even visible.* A fairy is simply any creature currently employed under supernatural laws to take things away or, as in the case of the small creature presently climbing up the inside of a drainpipe and swearing, to bring things.

Oh, yes. He does. Someone has to do it, and he looks the right gnome for the job.

Oh, yes.

Sideney was worried. He didn't like violence, and there had been a lot of it in the last few days, if days passed in this place. The men . . . well, they

---

*Such as the Electric Drill Chuck Key Fairy.

only seemed to find life interesting when they were doing something sharp to someone else and, while they didn't bother him much in the same way that lions don't trouble themselves with ants, they certainly worried him.

But not as much as Teatime did. Even the brute called Chickenwire treated Teatime with caution, if not respect, and the monster called Banjo just followed him around like a puppy.

The enormous man was watching him now.

He reminded Sideney too much of Ronnie Jenks, the bully who'd made his life miserable at Gammer Wimblestone's dame school. Ronnie hadn't been a pupil. He was the old woman's grandson or nephew or something, which gave him a licence to hang around the place and beat up any kid smaller or weaker or brighter than he was, which more or less meant he had the whole world to choose from. In those circumstances, it was particularly unfair that he always chose Sideney.

Sideney hadn't hated Ronnie. He'd been too frightened. He'd wanted to be his friend. Oh, so much. Because that way, just possibly, he wouldn't have his head trodden on such a lot and would actually get to eat his lunch instead of having it thrown in the privy. And it had been a *good* day when it had been his lunch.

And then, despite all Ronnie's best efforts, Sideney had grown up and gone to university. Occasionally his mother told him how Ronnie was getting on (she assumed, in the way of mothers, that because they had been small boys at school together they had been friends). Apparently he ran a fruit stall and was married to a girl called Angie.* This was not enough punishment, Sideney considered.

Banjo even *breathed* like Ronnie, who had to concentrate on such an intellectual exercise and always had one blocked nostril. And his mouth open all the time. He looked as though he was living on invisible plankton.

He tried to keep his mind on what he was doing and ignore the laboured gurgling behind him. A change in its tone made him look up.

'Fascinating,' said Teatime. 'You make it look so *easy*.'

Sideney sat back, nervously.

'Um . . . it should be fine now, sir,' he said. 'It just got a bit scuffed when we were piling up the . . .' He couldn't bring himself to say it, he even had to avert his eyes from the heap, it was the *sound* they'd made. '. . . the things,' he finished.

'We don't need to repeat the spell?' said Teatime.

'Oh, it'll keep going for ever,' said Sideney.

---

*Who was (according to Sideney's mother) a bit of a catch since her father owned a half-share in an eel pie shop in Gleam Street, you must know her, got all her own teeth and a wooden leg you'd hardly notice, got a sister called Continence, lovely girl, why didn't she invite her along for tea next time he was over, not that she hardly saw her son the big wizard at all these days, but you never knew and if the magic thing didn't work out then a quarter-share in a thriving eel pie business was not to be sneezed at . . .

'The simple ones do. It's just a state change, powered by the . . . the . . . it just keeps going . . .'

He swallowed.

'So,' he said, 'I was thinking . . . since you don't actually *need* me, sir, perhaps . . .'

'Mr Brown seems to be having some trouble with the locks on the top floor,' said Teatime. 'That door we couldn't open, remember? I'm sure you'll want to help.'

Sideney's face fell.

'Um, I'm not a locksmith . . .'

'They appear to be magical.'

Sideney opened his mouth to say, 'But I'm very bad at magical locks,' and then thought much better of it. He had already fathomed that if Teatime wanted you to do something, and you weren't very good at it, then your best plan, in fact quite possibly your *only* plan, was to learn to be good at it very quickly. Sideney was not a fool. He'd seen the way the others reacted around Teatime, and *they* were men who did things he'd only dreamed of.*

At which point he was relieved to see Medium Dave walk down the stairs, and it said a lot for the effect of Teatime's stare that anyone could be relieved to have it punctuated by someone like Medium Dave.

---

*Not, that is, things that he wanted to do, or wanted done to him. Just things that he dreamed of, in the armpit of a bad night.

'We've found another guard, sir. Up on the sixth floor. He's been hiding.'

Teatime stood up. 'Oh dear,' he said. 'Not trying to be heroic, was he?'

'He's just scared. Shall we let him go?'

'Let him go?' said Teatime. 'Far too messy. I'll go up there. Come along, Mr Wizard.'

Sideney followed him reluctantly up the stairs.

The tower – if that's what it was, he thought; he was used to the odd architecture at Unseen University and this made UU look normal – was a hollow tube. No fewer than four spiral staircases climbed the inside, criss-crossing on landings and occasionally passing through one another in defiance of generally accepted physics. But that was practically normal for an alumnus of Unseen University, although technically Sideney had not alumed. What threw the eye was the absence of shadows. You didn't notice shadows, how they delineated things, how they gave texture to the world, until they weren't there. The white marble, if that's what it was, seemed to glow from the inside. Even when the impossible sun shone through a window it barely caused faint grey smudges where honest shadows should be. The tower seemed to avoid darkness.

That was even more frightening than the times when, after a complicated landing, you found yourself walking *up* by stepping *down* the underside of a stair and the distant floor now hung overhead like a ceiling. He'd noticed that even the other men shut their eyes when that happened. Teatime, though, took those stairs three at a time, laughing like a kid with a new toy.

They reached an upper landing and followed a corridor. The others were gathered by a closed door.

'He's barricaded himself in,' said Chickenwire.

Teatime tapped on it. 'You in there,' he said. 'Come on out. You have my word you won't be harmed.'

'No!'

Teatime stood back. 'Banjo, knock it down,' he said.

Banjo lumbered forward. The door withstood a couple of massive kicks and then burst open.

The guard was cowering behind an overturned cabinet. He cringed back as Teatime stepped over it. 'What're you doing here?' he shouted. 'Who *are* you?'

'Ah, I'm glad you asked. I'm your worst nightmare!' said Teatime cheerfully.

The man shuddered.

'You mean . . . the one with the giant cabbage and the sort of whirring knife thing?'

'Sorry?' Teatime looked momentarily nonplussed.

'Then you're the one about where I'm falling, only instead of ground underneath it's all—'

'No, in fact I'm—'

The guard sagged. 'Awww, *not* the one where there's all this kind of, you know, mud and then everything goes blue—'

'No, I'm—'

'Oh, *shit*, then you're the one where there's this door only there's no floor beyond it and then there's these claws—'

'No,' said Teatime. 'Not that one.' He withdrew a dagger from his sleeve. 'I'm the one where this man comes out of nowhere and kills you stone dead.'

The guard grinned with relief. 'Oh, *that* one,' he said. 'But that one's not very—'

He crumpled around Teatime's suddenly outthrust fist. And then, just like the others had done, he faded.

'Rather a charitable act there, I feel,' Teatime said as the man vanished. 'But it *is* nearly Hogswatch, after all.'

Death, pillow slipping gently under his red robe, stood in the middle of the nursery carpet . . .

It was an old one. Things ended up in the nursery when they had seen a complete tour of duty in the rest of the house. Long ago, someone had made it by carefully knotting long bits of brightly coloured rag into a sacking base, giving it the look of a deflated Rastafarian hedgehog. Things lived among the rags. There were old rusks, bits of toy, buckets of dust. It had seen life. It may even have evolved some.

Now the occasional lump of grubby melting snow dropped onto it.

Susan was crimson with anger.

'I mean, *why*?' she demanded, walking around the figure. 'This is *Hogswatch*! It's supposed to be jolly, with mistletoe and holly, and – and other things ending in olly! It's a time when people want to feel good about things and eat until they explode! It's a time when they want to see all their relatives—'

She stopped *that* sentence.

'I mean it's a time when humans are really human,' she said. 'And they *don't* want a . . . a skeleton at the feast! Especially one, I might add, who's wearing a false beard and has got a damn cushion shoved up his robe! I mean, *why*?'

Death looked nervous.

ALBERT SAID IT WOULD HELP ME GET INTO THE SPIRIT OF THE THING. ER . . . IT'S GOOD TO SEE YOU AGAIN—

There was a small squelchy noise.

Susan spun around, grateful right now for any distraction.

'Don't think I can't hear you! They're *grapes*, understand? And the other things are satsumas! Get *out* of the fruit bowl!'

'Can't blame a bird for trying,' said the raven sulkily, from the table.

'And you, you leave those nuts alone! They're for tomorrow!'

SKQUEAF, said the Death of Rats, swallowing hurriedly.

Susan turned back to Death. The Hogfather's artificial stomach was now at groin level.

'This is a *nice* house,' she said. 'And this is a

good job. And it's real, with normal people. And I was looking forward to a real life, where normal things happen! And suddenly the old circus comes to town. Look at yourselves. Three Stooges, No Waiting! Well, I don't know what's going on, but you can all leave again, right? This is *my* life. It doesn't belong to any of you. It's not going to—'

There was a muffled curse, a rush of soot, and a skinny old man landed in the grate.

'Bum!' he said.

'Good *grief*!' raged Susan. 'And here is Pixie Albert! Well, well, well! Come along in, do! If the real Hogfather doesn't come soon there's not going to be *room*.'

HE WON'T BE JOINING US, said Death. The pillow slid softly on to the rug.

'Oh, and why not? Both of the children did letters to him,' said Susan. 'There's *rules*, you know.'

YES. THERE ARE RULES. AND THEY'RE ON THE LIST. I CHECKED IT.

Albert pulled the pointy hat off his head and spat out some soot.

'Right. He did. Twice,' he said. 'Anything to drink around here?'

'So what have *you* turned up for?' Susan demanded. 'And if it's for business reasons, I will add, then that outfit is in extremely poor taste—'

THE HOGFATHER IS . . . UNAVAILABLE.

'Unavailable? At Hogswatch?'

YES.

'Why?'

HE IS . . . LET ME SEE . . . THERE ISN'T AN
ENTIRELY APPROPRIATE HUMAN WORD, SO . . . LET'S
SETTLE FOR . . . DEAD. YES. HE IS DEAD.

Susan had never hung up a stocking. She'd never
looked for eggs laid by the Soul Cake Duck. She'd
never put a tooth under her pillow in the serious
expectation that a dentally inclined fairy would
turn up.

It wasn't that her parents didn't believe in such
things. They didn't *need* to believe in them. They
knew they existed. They just wished they didn't.

Oh, there had been presents, at the right time,
with a careful label saying who they were from.
And a superb egg on Soul Cake Morning, filled
with sweets. Juvenile teeth earned no less than a
dollar each from her father, without argument.*
But it was all *straightforward*.

She knew now that they'd been trying to
protect her. She hadn't known then that her
father had been Death's apprentice for a
while, and that her mother was Death's adopted
daughter. She'd had very dim recollections of

---

*In fact, when she was eight she'd found a collection of
animal skulls in an attic, relict of some former duke of an
enquiring turn of mind. Her father had been a bit pre-
occupied with affairs of state and she'd made twenty-seven
dollars before being found out. The hippopotamus molar
had, with hindsight, been a mistake.

Skulls never frightened her, even then.

being taken a few times to see someone who'd been quite, well, jolly, in a strange, thin way. And the visits had suddenly stopped. And she'd met him later and, yes, he had his good side, and for a while she'd wondered why her parents had been so unfeeling and—

She knew now why they'd tried to keep her away. There was far more to genetics than little squirmy spirals.

She could walk through walls when she really had to. She could use a tone of voice that was more like actions than words, that somehow reached inside people and operated all the right switches. And her hair . . .

That had only happened recently, though. It used to be unmanageable, but at around the age of seventeen she had found it more or less managed itself.

That had lost her several young men. Someone's hair rearranging itself into a new style, the tresses curling around themselves like a nest of kittens, could definitely put the crimp on any relationship.

She'd been making good progress, though. She could go for *days* now without feeling anything other than entirely human.

But it was always the case, wasn't it? You could go out into the world, succeed on your own terms, and sooner or later some embarrassing old relative was bound to turn up.

*   *   *

Grunting and swearing, the gnome clambered out of another drainpipe, jammed its hat firmly on its head, threw its sack onto a snowdrift and jumped down after it.

' 's a good one,' he said. 'Ha, take 'im *weeks* to get rid of *that* one!'

He took a crumpled piece of paper out of a pocket and examined it closely. Then he looked at an elderly figure working away quietly at the next house.

It was standing by a window, drawing with great concentration on the glass.

The gnome wandered up, interested, and watched critically.

'Why just fern patterns?' he said, after a while. 'Pretty, yeah, but you wouldn't catch me puttin' a penny in your hat for fern patterns.'

The figure turned, brush in hand.

'I happen to like fern patterns,' said Jack Frost coldly.

'It's just that people expect, you know, sad big-eyed kids, kittens lookin' out of boots, little doggies, that sort of thing.'

'I do ferns.'

'Or big pots of sunflowers, happy seaside scenes . . .'

'And ferns.'

'I mean, s'posing some big high priest wanted you to paint the temple ceiling with gods 'n' angels and suchlike, what'd you do then?'

'He could have as many gods and angels as he liked, provided they—'

'—looked like ferns?'

'I resent the implication that I am solely fern-fixated,' said Jack Frost. 'I can also do a very nice paisley pattern.'

'What's that look like, then?'

'Well . . . it does, admittedly, have a certain ferny quality to the uninitiated eye.' Frost leaned forward. 'Who're you?'

The gnome took a step backwards.

'You're not a tooth fairy, are you? I see more and more of them about these days. Nice girls.'

'Nah. Nah. Not teeth,' said the gnome, clutching his sack.

'What, then?'

The gnome told him.

'Really?' said Jack Frost. 'I thought they just turned up.'

'Well, come to *that*, I thought frost on the windows just happened all by itself,' said the gnome. ' 'ere, you don't half look spiky. I bet you go through a lot of bedsheets.'

'I don't sleep,' said Frost icily, turning away. 'And now, if you'll excuse me, I have a large number of windows to do. Ferns aren't easy. You need a steady hand.'

'What do you mean dead?' Susan demanded. 'How can the Hogfather be *dead*? He's . . . isn't he what you are? An—'

ANTHROPOMORPHIC PERSONIFICATION. YES. HE HAS BECOME SO. THE SPIRIT OF HOGSWATCH.

'But . . . how? How can anyone kill the Hog-father? Poisoned sherry? Spikes in the chimney?'

THERE ARE . . . MORE SUBTLE WAYS.

'Coff. Coff. Coff. Oh dear, this soot,' said Albert loudly. 'Chokes me up something cruel.'

'And you've taken over?' said Susan, ignoring him. 'That's *sick*!'

Death contrived to look hurt.

'I'll just go and have a look somewhere,' said Albert, brushing past her and opening the door.

She pushed it shut quickly.

'And what are you doing here, Albert?' she said, clutching at the straw. 'I thought you'd die if you ever came back to the world!'

AH, BUT WE ARE NOT IN THE WORLD, said Death. WE ARE IN THE SPECIAL CONGRUENT REALITY CREATED FOR THE HOGFATHER. NORMAL RULES HAVE TO BE SUSPENDED. HOW ELSE COULD ANY-ONE GET AROUND THE ENTIRE WORLD IN ONE NIGHT?

''s right,' said Albert, leering. 'One of the Hogfather's Little Helpers, me. Official. Got the pointy green hat and everything.' He spotted the glass of sherry and couple of turnips that the children had left on the table, and bore down on them.

Susan looked shocked. A couple of days earlier she'd taken the children to the Hogfather's Grotto in one of the big shops in The Maul. Of course, it wasn't the real one, but it had turned out to be a fairly good actor in a red suit. There had been people dressed up as pixies, and a picket outside the shop by the Campaign for Equal Heights.*

None of the pixies had looked anything like Albert. If they had, people would have only gone into the grotto armed.

'Been good, 'ave yer?' said Albert, and spat into the fireplace.

Susan stared at him.

Death leaned down. She stared up into the blue glow of his eyes.

YOU ARE KEEPING WELL? he said.

'Yes.'

SELF-RELIANT? MAKING YOUR OWN WAY IN THE WORLD?

'Yes!'

GOOD. WELL, COME, ALBERT. WE WILL LOAD THE STOCKINGS AND GET ON WITH THINGS.

A couple of letters appeared in Death's hand.

SOMEONE CHRISTENED THE CHILD TWYLA?

'I'm afraid so, but why—'

AND THE OTHER ONE GAWAIN?

'Yes. But look, how—'

*The CEH was always ready to fight for the rights of the differently tall, and was not put off by the fact that most pixies and gnomes weren't the least interested in dressing up in little pointy hats with bells on when there were other far more interesting things to do. All that tinkly-wee stuff was for the old folks back home in the forest – when a tiny man hit Ankh-Morpork he preferred to get drunk, kick some serious ankle, and search for tiny women. In fact the CEH now had to spend so much time explaining to people that they hadn't got enough rights that they barely had any time left to fight for them.

WHY GAWAIN?

'I . . . suppose it's a good strong name for a fighter . . .'

A SELF-FULFILLING PROPHECY, I SUSPECT. I SEE THE GIRL WRITES IN GREEN CRAYON ON PINK PAPER WITH A MOUSE IN THE CORNER. THE MOUSE IS WEARING A DRESS.

'I ought to point out that she decided to do that so the Hogfather would think she was sweet,' said Susan. 'Including the deliberate bad spelling. But look, why are *you*—'

SHE SAYS SHE IS FIVE YEARS OLD.

'In years, yes. In cynicism, she's about thirty-five. Why are *you* doing the—'

BUT SHE BELIEVES IN THE HOGFATHER?

'She'd believe in anything if there was a dolly in it for her. But you're *not* going to leave without telling me—'

Death hung the stockings back on the mantel-piece.

NOW WE MUST BE GOING. HAPPY HOGSWATCH. ER . . . OH, YES: HO. HO. HO.

'Nice sherry,' said Albert, wiping his mouth.

Rage overtook Susan's curiosity. It had to travel quite fast.

'You've actually been drinking the actual drinks little children leave out for the actual Hog-father?' she said.

'Yeah, why not? *He* ain't drinking 'em. Not where *he's* gone.'

'And how many have you had, may I ask?'

'Dunno, ain't counted,' said Albert happily.

ONE MILLION, EIGHT HUNDRED THOUSAND, SEVEN HUNDRED AND SIX, said Death. AND SIXTY-EIGHT THOUSAND, THREE HUNDRED AND NINE-TEEN PORK PIES. AND ONE TURNIP.

'It looked pork-pie shaped,' said Albert. 'Everything does, after a while.'

'Then why haven't you exploded?'

'Dunno. Always had a good digestion.'

TO THE HOGFATHER, ALL PORK PIES ARE AS ONE PORK PIE. EXCEPT THE ONE LIKE A TURNIP. COME, ALBERT. WE HAVE TRESPASSED ON SUSAN'S TIME.

'*Why are you doing this?*' Susan screamed.

I AM SORRY. I CANNOT TELL YOU. FORGET YOU SAW ME. IT'S NOT YOUR BUSINESS.

'Not my business? How can—'

AND NOW . . . WE MUST BE GOING . . .

'Nighty-night,' said Albert.

The clock struck, twice, for the half-hour. It was still half past six.

And they were gone.

The sledge hurtled across the sky.

'She'll try to find out what this is all about, you know,' said Albert.

OH DEAR.

'Especially after you told her not to.'

YOU THINK SO?

'Yeah,' said Albert.

DEAR ME. I STILL HAVE A LOT TO LEARN ABOUT HUMANS, DON'T I?

'Oh . . . I dunno . . . ' said Albert.

OBVIOUSLY IT WOULD BE QUITE WRONG TO IN-
VOLVE A HUMAN IN ALL THIS. THAT IS WHY, YOU
WILL RECALL, I CLEARLY FORBADE HER TO TAKE AN
INTEREST.

'Yeah . . . you did . . .'

BESIDES, IT'S AGAINST THE RULES.

'You said them little grey buggers had already
broken the rules.'

YES, BUT I CAN'T JUST WAVE A MAGIC WAND AND
MAKE IT ALL BETTER. THERE MUST BE PROCEDURES.
Death stared ahead for a moment and then
shrugged. AND WE HAVE SO MUCH TO DO. WE HAVE
PROMISES TO KEEP.

'Well, the night is young,' said Albert, sitting
back in the sacks.

THE NIGHT IS OLD. THE NIGHT IS ALWAYS OLD.

The pigs galloped on. Then, 'No, it ain't.'

I'M SORRY?

'The night isn't any older than the day, master.
It stands to reason. There must have been a day
before anyone knew what the night was.'

YES, BUT IT'S MORE DRAMATIC.

'Oh. Right, then.'

Susan stood by the fireplace.

It wasn't as though she *disliked* Death. Death
considered as an individual rather than life's final
curtain was someone she couldn't help liking, in
a strange kind of way.

Even so . . .

The idea of the Grim Reaper filling the

112

Hogswatch stockings of the world didn't fit well in her head, no matter which way she twisted it. It was like trying to imagine Old Man Trouble as the Tooth Fairy. Oh, yes. Old Man Trouble . . . now *there* was a nasty one for you . . .

But *honestly*, what kind of *sick* person went round creeping into little children's bedrooms all night?

Well, the Hogfather, of course, but . . .

There was a little tinkling sound from somewhere near the base of the Hogswatch tree.

The raven backed away from the shards of one of the glittering balls.

'Sorry,' it mumbled. 'Bit of a species reaction there. You know . . . round, glittering . . . sometimes you just gotta peck—'

'That chocolate money belongs to the children!'

SQUEAK? said the Death of Rats, backing away from the shiny coins.

'Why's he doing this?'

SQUEAK.

'You don't know either?'

SQUEAK.

'Is there some kind of trouble? Did he *do* something to the real Hogfather?'

SQUEAK.

'Why won't he tell me?'

SQUEAK.

'Thank you. You've been very helpful.'

Something ripped, behind her. She turned and saw the raven carefully removing a strip of red wrapping paper from a package.

113

'Stop that this minute!'

It looked up guiltily.

'It's only a little bit,' it said. 'No one's going to miss it.'

'What do you want it for, anyway?'

'We're attracted to bright colours, right? Automatic reaction.'

'That's jackdaws!'

'Damn. Is it?'

The Death of Rats nodded. SQUEAK.

'Oh, so suddenly you're Mr Ornithologist, are you?' snapped the raven.

Susan sat down and held out her hand.

The Death of Rats leapt onto it. She could feel its claws, like tiny pins.

It was just like those scenes where the sweet and pretty heroine sings a little duet with Mr Bluebird.

Similar, anyway.

In general outline, at least. But with more of a PG rating.

'*Has* he gone funny in the head?'

SQUEAK. The rat shrugged.

'But it could happen, couldn't it? He's very old, and I suppose he sees a lot of terrible things.'

SQUEAK.

'All the trouble in the world,' the raven translated.

'I understood,' said Susan. That was a talent, too. She didn't understand what the rat said. She just understood what it meant.

'There's something wrong and he won't tell me?' said Susan.

That made her even more angry.

'But Albert is in on it too,' she added.

She thought: thousands, *millions* of years in the same job. Not a nice one. It isn't always cheerful old men passing away at a great age. Sooner or later, it was bound to get anyone down.

Someone had to do something. It was like that time when Twyla's grandmother had started telling everyone that she was the Empress of Krull and had stopped wearing clothes.

And Susan was bright enough to know that the phrase 'Someone ought to do something' was not, by itself, a helpful one. People who used it *never* added the rider 'and that someone is me'. But someone ought to do something, and right now the whole pool of someones consisted of her, and no one else.

Twyla's grandmother had ended up in a nursing home overlooking the sea at Quirm. That sort of option probably didn't apply here. Besides, he'd be unpopular with the other residents.

She concentrated. *This* was the simplest talent of them all. She was amazed that other people couldn't do it. She shut her eyes, placed her hands palm down in front of her at shoulder height, spread her fingers and lowered her hands.

When they were halfway down she heard

the clock stop ticking. The last tick was long-drawn-out, like a death rattle.

Time stopped.

But *duration* continued.

She'd always wondered, when she was small, why visits to her grandfather could go on for days and yet, when they got back, the calendar was still plodding along as if they'd never been away.

Now she knew the why, although probably no human being would ever really understand the how. Sometimes, somewhere, somehow, the numbers on the clock did not count.

Between every rational moment were a billion irrational ones. Somewhere behind the hours there was a place where the Hogfather rode, the tooth fairies climbed their ladders, Jack Frost drew his pictures, the Soul Cake Duck laid her chocolate eggs. In the endless spaces between the clumsy seconds Death moved like a witch dancing through raindrops, never getting wet.

Humans could liv— No, humans couldn't *live* here, no, because even when you diluted a glass of wine with a bathful of water you might have more liquid but you still have the same amount of wine. A rubber band was still the same rubber band no matter how far it was stretched.

Humans could *exist* here, though.

It was never too cold, although the air did prickle like winter air on a sunny day. But out of human habit Susan got her cloak out of the closet.

SQUEAK.

116

'Haven't you got some mice and rats to see to, then?'

'Nah, 's pretty quiet just before Hogswatch,' said the raven, who was trying to fold the red paper between his claws. 'You get a lot of gerbils and hamsters and that in a few days, mind. When the kids forget to feed them or try to find out what makes them go.'

Of course, she'd be leaving the children. But it wasn't as if anything could happen to them. There wasn't any time for it to happen to them in.

She hurried down the stairs and let herself out of the front door.

Snow hung in the air. It was not a poetic description. It hovered like the stars. When flakes touched Susan they melted with little electric flashes.

There was a lot of traffic in the street, but it was fossilized in Time. She walked carefully between it until she reached the entrance to the park.

The snow had done what even wizards and the Watch couldn't do, which was clean up Ankh-Morpork. It hadn't had time to get dirty. In the morning it'd probably look as though the city had been covered in coffee meringue, but for now it mounded the bushes and trees in pure white.

There was no noise. The curtains of snow shut out the city lights. A few yards into the park and she might as well be in the country.

She stuck her fingers into her mouth and whistled.

'Y'know, that could've been done with a bit more ceremony,' said the raven, who'd perched on a snow-encrusted twig.

'Shut up.'

''s good, though. Better than most women could do.'

'Shut up.'

They waited.

'Why have you stolen that piece of red paper from a little girl's present?' said Susan.

'I've got plans,' said the raven darkly.

They waited again.

She wondered what would happen if it didn't work. She wondered if the rat would snigger. It had the most annoying snigger in the world.

Then there were hoofbeats and the floating snow burst open and the horse was there.

Binky trotted round in a circle, and then stood and steamed.

He wasn't saddled. Death's horse didn't let you fall.

If I get on, Susan thought, it'll all start again. I'll be out of the light and into the world beyond this one. I'll fall off the tightrope.

But a voice inside her said, *You want to, though . . . don't you . . . ?*

Ten seconds later, there was only the snow.

The raven turned to the Death of Rats.

'Any idea where I can get some string?'

SQUEAK.

She was watched.

One said, Who is she?

One said, Do we remember that Death adopted a daughter? The young woman is *her* daughter.

One said, She is human?

One said, Mostly.

One said, Can she be killed?

One said, Oh, yes.

One said, Well, that's all right, then.

One said, Er . . . we don't think we're going to get into trouble over this, do we? All this is not exactly . . . authorized. We don't want questions asked.

One said, We have a duty to rid the universe of sloppy thinking.

One said, Everyone will be grateful when they find out.

Binky touched down lightly on Death's lawn.

Susan didn't bother with the front door but went round the back, which was never locked.

There had been changes. One significant change, at least.

There was a cat-flap in the door.

She stared at it.

After a second or two a ginger cat came through the flap, gave her an I'm-not-hungry-and-you're-not-interesting look, and padded off into the gardens.

Susan pushed open the door into the kitchen.

Cats of every size and colour covered every surface. Hundreds of eyes swivelled to watch her.

It was Mrs Gammage all over again, she thought. The old woman was a regular in Biers for the company and was quite gaga, and one of the symptoms of those going completely yoyo was that they broke out in chronic cats. Usually cats who'd mastered every detail of feline existence except the whereabouts of the dirt box.

Several of them had their noses in a bowl of cream.

Susan had never been able to see the attraction in cats. They were owned by the kind of people who liked puddings. There were actual people in the world whose idea of heaven would be a chocolate cat.

'Push off, the lot of you,' she said. 'I've never known him have *pets*.'

The cats gave her a look to indicate that they were intending to go somewhere else in any case and strolled off, licking their chops.

The bowl slowly filled up again.

They were obviously living cats. Only life had colour here. Everything else was created by Death. Colour, along with plumbing and music, were arts that escaped the grasp of his genius.

She left them in the kitchen and wandered along to the study.

There were changes here, too. By the look of it, he'd been trying to learn to play the violin again. He'd never been able to understand why he couldn't play music.

The desk was a mess. Books lay open, piled on one another. They were the ones Susan had never learned to read. Some of the characters hovered above the pages or moved in complicated little patterns as they read you while you read them.

Intricate devices had been scattered across the top. They looked vaguely navigational, but on what oceans and under which stars?

Several pages of parchment had been filled up with Death's own handwriting. It was immediately recognizable. No one else Susan had ever met had handwriting with serifs.

It looked as though he'd been trying to work something out.

NOT KLATCH. NOT HOWONDALAND. NOT THE
   EMPIRE.
LET US SAY 20 MILLION CHILDREN AT 2LB OF
   TOYS PER CHILD.
EQUALS 17,857 TONS. 1,785 TONS PER HOUR.
MEMO: DON'T FORGET THE SOOTY FOOTPRINTS.
   MORE PRACTICE ON THE HO HO HO.
CUSHION.

She put the paper back carefully.

Sooner or later it'd get to you. Death was fascinated by humans, and study was never a one-way thing. A man might spend his life peering at the private life of elementary particles and then find he either knew who he was or where he was, but not both. Death had picked up . . . humanity. Not the real thing, but something that might pass for it until you examined it closely.

The house even imitated human houses. Death had created a bedroom for himself, despite the fact that he never slept. If he really picked things up from humans, had he tried insanity? It was very popular, after all.

Perhaps, after all these millennia, he wanted to be nice.

She let herself into the Room of Lifetimers. She'd liked the sound of it, when she was a little girl. But now the hiss of sand from millions of hourglasses, and the little *pings* and *pops* as full ones vanished and new empty ones appeared, was not so enjoyable. *Now* she knew what was going on. Of course, everyone died sooner or later. It just wasn't right to be listening to it happening.

She was about to leave when she noticed the open door in a place where she had never seen a door before.

It was disguised. A whole section of shelving, complete with its whispering glasses, had swung out.

Susan pushed it back and forth with a finger. When it was shut, you'd have to look hard to see the crack.

There was a much smaller room on the other side. It was merely the size of, say, a cathedral. And it was lined floor to ceiling with more hourglasses that Susan could just see dimly in the light from the big room. She stepped inside and snapped her fingers.

'Light,' she commanded. A couple of candles sprang into life.

The hourglasses were . . . wrong.

The ones in the main room, however metaphorical they might be, were solid-looking things of wood and brass and glass. But *these* looked as though they were made of highlights and shadows with no real substance at all.

She peered at a large one.

The name in it was: OFFLER.

'The crocodile god?' she thought.

Well, gods had a life, presumably. But they never actually died, as far as she knew. They just dwindled away to a voice on the wind and a footnote in some textbook on religion.

There were other gods lined up. She recognized a few of them.

But there were smaller lifetimers on the shelf. When she saw the labels she nearly burst out laughing.

'The Tooth Fairy? The Sandman? John Barleycorn? The Soul Cake Duck? The God of – *what*?'

She stepped back, and something crunched under her feet.

There were shards of glass on the floor. She reached down and picked up the biggest. Only a few letters remained of the name etched into the glass—

HOGFA . . .

'Oh, *no* . . . it's *true*. Granddad, what have you *done*?'

When she left, the candles winked out. Darkness sprang back.

And in the darkness, among the spilled sand, a faint sizzle and a tiny spark of light . . .

Mustrum Ridcully adjusted the towel around his waist.

'How're we doing, Mr Modo?'

The University gardener saluted.

'The tanks are full, Mr Archchancellor sir!' he said brightly. 'And I've been stoking the hot-water boilers all day!'

The other senior wizards clustered in the doorway.

'Really, Mustrum, I really think this is *most* unwise,' said the Lecturer in Recent Runes. 'It was surely sealed up for a purpose.'

'Remember what it said on the door,' said the Dean.

'Oh, they just wrote that on it to keep people out,' said Ridcully, opening a fresh bar of soap.

'Well, yes,' said the Chair of Indefinite Studies. 'That's right. That's what people do.'

'It's a *bathroom*,' said Ridcully. 'You are all acting as if it's some kind of a torture chamber.'

'A bathroom,' said the Dean, 'designed by Bloody Stupid Johnson. Archchancellor Weatherwax only used it once and then had it sealed up! Mustrum, I beg you to reconsider! It's a *Johnson*!'

There was something of a pause, because even Ridcully had to adjust his mind around this.

The late (or at least severely delayed) Bergholt Stuttley Johnson was generally recognized as the worst inventor in the world, yet in a very specialized sense. Merely *bad* inventors made things that failed to operate. He wasn't among these small fry. Any fool could make something that did absolutely nothing when you pressed the button. He scorned such fumble-fingered amateurs. Everything he built worked. It just didn't do what it said on the box. If you wanted a small ground-to-air missile, you asked Johnson to design an ornamental fountain. It amounted to pretty much the same thing. But this never discouraged him, or the morbid curiosity of his clients. Music, landscape gardening, architecture – there was no start to his talents.

Nevertheless, it was a little bit surprising to find that Bloody Stupid had turned to bathroom design. But, as Ridcully said, it was known that he had designed and built several large musical organs and, when you got right down to it, it was all just plumbing, wasn't it?

The other wizards, who'd been there longer than the Archchancellor, took the view that if Bloody Stupid Johnson had built a fully functional bathroom he'd actually meant it to be something else.

'Y'know, I've always felt that Mr Johnson was a much maligned man,' said Ridcully, eventually.

'Well, yes, of *course* he was,' said the Lecturer

in Recent Runes, clearly exasperated. 'That's like saying that jam attracts wasps, you see.'

'Not everything he made worked badly,' said Ridcully stoutly, flourishing his scrubbing brush. 'Look at that thing they use down in the kitchens for peelin' the potatoes, for example.'

'Ah, you mean the thing with the brass plate on it saying "Improved Manicure Device", Archchancellor?'

'Listen, it's just water,' snapped Ridcully. 'Even Johnson couldn't do much harm with water. Modo, open the sluices!'

The rest of the wizards backed away as the gardener turned a couple of ornate brass wheels.

'I'm fed up with groping around for the soap like you fellows!' shouted the Archchancellor, as water gushed through hidden channels. 'Hygiene. That's the ticket!'

'Don't say we didn't warn you,' said the Dean, shutting the door.

'Er, I still haven't worked out where all the pipes lead, sir,' Modo ventured.

'We'll find out, never you fear,' said Ridcully happily. He removed his hat and put on a shower cap of his own design. In deference to his profession, it was pointy. He picked up a yellow rubber duck.

'Man the pumps, Mr Modo. Or dwarf them, of course, in your case.'

'Yes, Archchancellor.'

Modo hauled on a lever. The pipes started a

hammering noise and steam leaked out of a few joints.

Ridcully took a last look around the bathroom.

It was a hidden treasure, no doubt about it. Say what you like, old Johnson must sometimes have got it right, even if it was only by accident. The entire room, including the floor and ceiling, had been tiled in white, blue and green. In the centre, under its crown of pipes, was Johnson's Patent 'Typhoon' Superior Indoor Ablutorium with Automatic Soap Dish, a sanitary poem in mahogany, rosewood and copper.

He'd got Modo to polish every pipe and brass tap until they gleamed. It had taken ages.

Ridcully shut the frosted door behind him.

The inventor of the ablutionary marvel had decided to make a mere shower a fully controllable experience, and one wall of the large cubicle held a marvellous panel covered with brass taps cast in the shape of mermaids and shells and, for some reason, pomegranates. There were separate feeds for salt water, hard water and soft water and huge wheels for accurate control of temperature. Ridcully inspected them with care.

Then he stood back, looked around at the tiles and sang, 'Mi, mi, mi!'

His voice reverberated back at him.

'A perfect echo!' said Ridcully, one of nature's bathroom baritones.

He picked up a speaking tube that had been

installed to allow the bather to communicate with the engineer.

'All cisterns go, Mr Modo!'

'Aye, aye, sir!'

Ridcully opened the tap marked 'Spray' and leapt aside, because part of him was still well aware that Johnson's inventiveness didn't just push the edge of the envelope but often went across the room and out through the wall of the sorting office.

A gentle shower of warm water, almost a caressing mist, enveloped him.

'My word!' he exclaimed, and tried another tap.

'Shower' turned out to be a little more invigorating. 'Torrent' made him gasp for breath and 'Deluge' sent him groping to the panel because the top of his head felt that it was being removed. 'Wave' sloshed a wall of warm salt water from one side of the cubicle to the other before it disappeared into the grating that was set into the middle of the floor.

'Are you all right, sir?' Modo called out.

'Marvellous! And there's a dozen knobs I haven't tried yet!'

Modo nodded, and tapped a valve. Ridcully's voice, raised in what he considered to be song, boomed out through the thick clouds of steam.

'Oh, IIIIIII knew a . . . er . . . an agricultural worker of some description, possibly a thatcher,
And I knew him well, and he – he was a farmer, now I come to think of it – and he had a daughter and her name I can't recall at the moment,

And . . . Where was I? Ah yes. Chorus:

Something something, a humorously shaped vegetable, a turnip, I believe, something something and the sweet nightingaleeeeaarggooooooh-ARRGHH oh oh oh—'

The song shut off suddenly. All Modo could hear was a ferocious gushing noise.

'Archchancellor?'

After a moment a voice answered from near the ceiling. It sounded somewhat high and hesitant.

'Er . . . I wonder if you would be so very good as to shut the water off from out there, my dear chap? Er . . . quite gently, if you wouldn't mind . . .'

Modo carefully spun a wheel. The gushing sound gradually subsided.

'Ah. Well done,' said the voice, but now from somewhere nearer floor level. 'Well. Jolly good job. I think we can definitely call it a success. Yes, indeed. Er. I wonder if you could help me walk for a moment. I inexplicably feel a little unsteady on my feet . . .'

Modo pushed open the door and helped Ridcully out and onto a bench. He looked rather pale.

'Yes, indeed,' said the Archchancellor, his eyes a little glazed. 'Astoundingly successful. Er. Just a minor point, Modo—'

'Yes, sir?'

'There's a tap in there we perhaps should leave alone for now,' said Ridcully. 'I'd esteem it a service if you could go and make a little sign to hang on it.'

'Yes, sir?'

'Saying "Do not touch at all", or something like that.'

'Right, sir.'

'Hang it on the one marked "Old Faithful".'

'Yes, sir.'

'No need to mention it to the other fellows.'

'Yes, sir.'

'Ye gods, I've never felt so *clean*.'

From a vantage point among some ornamental tilework near the ceiling a small gnome in a bowler hat watched Ridcully carefully.

When Modo had gone the Archchancellor slowly began to dry himself on a big fluffy towel. As he got his composure back, so another song wormed its way under his breath.

'*On the second day of Hogswatch I . . . sent my true love back*
A nasty little letter, hah, yes indeed, and a partridge in a pear tree—'

The gnome slid down onto the tiles and crept up behind the briskly shaking shape.

Ridcully, after a few more trial runs, settled on a song which evolves somewhere on every planet where there are winters. It's often dragooned into the service of some local religion and a few words are changed, but it's really about things that have to do with gods only in the same way that roots have to do with leaves.

'*—the rising of the sun, and the running of the deer—*'

Ridcully spun. A corner of wet towel caught

130

the gnome on the ear and flicked it onto its back.

'I saw you creeping up!' roared the Archchancellor. 'What's the game, then? Small-time thief, are you?'

The gnome slid backwards on the soapy surface.

' 'ere, what's *your* game, mister, you ain't supposed to be able to see me!'

'I'm a wizard! We can see things that are really there, you know,' said Ridcully. 'And in the case of the Bursar, things that aren't there, too. What's in this bag?'

'You don't wanna open the bag, mister! You really don't wanna open the bag!'

'Why? What have you got in it?'

The gnome sagged. 'It ain't what's in it, mister. It's what'll come out. I has to let 'em out one at a time, no knowin' what'd happen if they all gets out at once!'

Ridcully looked interested, and started to undo the string.

'You'll really wish you hadn't, mister!' the gnome pleaded.

'Will I? What're you doing here, young man?'

The gnome gave up.

'Well . . . you know the Tooth Fairy?'

'Yes. Of course,' said Ridcully.

'Well . . . I ain't her. But . . . it's sort of like the same business . . .'

'What? You take things away?'

131

'Er . . . not take away, as such. More sort of . . . bring . . .'

'Ah . . . like new teeth?'

'Er . . . like new verrucas,' said the gnome.

Death threw the sack into the back of the sledge and climbed in after it.

'You're doing well, master,' said Albert.

THIS CUSHION IS STILL UNCOMFORTABLE, said Death, hitching his belt. I AM NOT USED TO A BIG FAT STOMACH.

'Just *a* stomach's the best I could do, master. You're starting off with a handicap, sort of thing.'

Albert unscrewed the top off a bottle of cold tea. All the sherry had made him thirsty.

'Doing well, master,' he repeated, taking a pull. 'All the soot in the fireplace, the footprints, them swigged sherries, the sleigh tracks all over the roofs . . . it's got to work.'

YOU THINK SO?

'Sure.'

AND I MADE SURE SOME OF THEM SAW ME. I KNOW IF THEY ARE PEEPING, Death added proudly.

'Well done, sir.'

YES.

'Though here's a tip, though. *Just* "Ho. Ho. Ho," will do. Don't say, "Cower, brief mortals" unless you want them to grow up to be money-lenders or some such.'

HO. HO. HO.

132

'Yes, you're really getting the hang of it.' Albert looked down hurriedly at his notebook so that Death wouldn't see his face. 'Now, I got to tell you, master, what'll *really* do some good is a public appearance. Really.'

OH. I DON'T NORMALLY DO THEM.

'The Hogfather's more've a public figure, master. And one good public appearance'll do more good than any amount of letting kids see you by accident. Good for the old belief muscles.'

REALLY? HO. HO. HO.

'Right, right, that's really *good*, master. Where was I . . . yes . . . the shops'll be open late. Lots of kiddies get taken to see the Hogfather, you see. Not the *real* one, of course. Just some ole geezer with a pillow up his jumper, saving yer presence, master.'

NOT REAL? HO. HO. HO.

'Oh, no. And you don't need—'

THE CHILDREN KNOW THIS? HO. HO. HO.

Albert scratched his nose. 'S'pose so, master.'

THIS SHOULD NOT BE. NO WONDER THERE HAS BEEN . . . THIS DIFFICULTY. BELIEF WAS COMPROMISED? HO. HO. HO.

'Could be, master. Er, the "ho, ho—"'

WHERE DOES THIS TRAVESTY TAKE PLACE? HO. HO. HO.

Albert gave up. 'Well, Crumley's in The Maul, for one. Very popular, the Hogfather Grotto. They always have a good Hogfather, apparently.'

LET'S GET THERE AND SLEIGH THEM. HO. HO. HO.

'Right you are, master.'

THAT WAS A PUNE OR PLAY ON WORDS, ALBERT.
I DON'T KNOW IF YOU NOTICED.

'I'm laughing like hell deep down, sir.'

HO. HO. HO.

Archchancellor Ridcully grinned.

He often grinned. He was one of those men who grinned even when they were annoyed, but right now he grinned because he was proud. A little sore still, perhaps, but still proud.

'Amazing bathroom, ain't it?' he said. 'They had it walled up, you know. Damn silly thing to do. I mean, perhaps there were a few teething troubles,' he shifted gingerly, 'but that's only to be expected. It's got everything, d'you see? Foot baths in the shape of clam shells, look. A whole wardrobe for dressing gowns. And that tub over there's got a big blower thingy so's you get bubbly water without even havin' to eat starchy food. And this thingy here with the mermaids holdin' it up's a special pot for your toenail clippings. It's got everything, this place.'

'A special pot for nail clippings?' said the Verruca Gnome.

'Oh, can't be too careful,' said Ridcully, lifting the lid of an ornate jar marked BATH SALTS and pulling out a bottle of wine. 'Get hold of something like someone's nail clipping and you've got 'em under your control. That's real old magic. Dawn of time stuff.'

He held the wine bottle up to the light.

'Should be cooled nicely by now,' he said, extracting the cork. 'Verrucas, eh?'

'Wish I knew why,' said the gnome.

'You mean you don't know?'

'Nope. Suddenly I wake up and I'm the Verruca Gnome.'

'Puzzling, that,' said Ridcully. 'My dad used to say the Verruca Gnome turned up if you walked around in bare feet but I never knew you *existed*. I thought he just made it up. I mean, tooth fairies, yes, and them little buggers that live in flowers, used to collect 'em myself as a lad, but can't recall anything about verrucas.' He drank thoughtfully. 'Got a distant cousin called Verruca, as a matter of fact. It's quite a nice sound, when you come to think of it.'

He looked at the gnome over the top of his glass.

You didn't become Archchancellor without a feeling for subtle wrongness in a situation. Well, that wasn't quite true. It was more accurate to say that you didn't *remain* Archchancellor for very long.

'Good job, is it?' he said thoughtfully.

'Dandruff'd be better,' said the gnome. 'At least I'd be out in the fresh air.'

'I think we'd better check up on this,' said Ridcully. 'Of course, it might be nothing.'

'Oh, thank you,' said the Verruca Gnome, gloomily.

*   *   *

It was a magnificent Grotto this year, Vernon Crumley told himself. The staff had worked really hard. The Hogfather's sleigh was a work of art in itself, and the pigs looked really real and a *wonderful* shade of pink.

The Grotto took up nearly all of the first floor. One of the pixies had been Disciplined for smoking behind the Magic Tinkling Waterfall and the clockwork Dolls of All Nations showing how We Could All Get Along were a bit jerky and giving trouble but all in all, he told himself, it was a display to Delight the Hearts of Kiddies everywhere.

The kiddies were queueing up with their parents and watching the display owlishly.

And the money was coming in. Oh, how the money was coming in.

So that the staff would not be Tempted, Mr Crumley had set up an arrangement of overhead wires across the ceilings of the store. In the middle of each floor was a cashier in a little cage. Staff took money from customers, put it in a little clockwork cable car, sent it whizzing overhead to the cashier, who'd make change and start it rattling back again. Thus there was no possibility of Temptation, and the little trolleys were shooting back and forth like fireworks.

Mr Crumley loved Hogswatch. It was for the Kiddies, after all.

He tucked his fingers in the pockets of his waistcoat and beamed.

'Everything going well, Miss Harding?'

'Yes, Mr Crumley,' said the cashier, meekly.

'*Jolly* good.' He looked at the pile of coins.

A bright little zig-zag crackled off them and earthed itself on the metal grille.

Mr Crumley blinked. In front of him sparks flashed off the steel rims of Miss Harding's spectacles.

The Grotto display changed. For just a fraction of a second Mr Crumley had the sensation of speed, as though what appeared had screeched to a halt. Which was *ridiculous*.

The four pink papier-mâché pigs exploded. A cardboard snout bounced off Mr Crumley's head.

There, sweating and grunting in the place where the little piggies had been, were . . . well, he assumed they were pigs, because hippopotamuses didn't have pointy ears and rings through their noses. But the creatures were huge and grey and bristly and a cloud of acrid mist hung over each one.

And they didn't look sweet. There was nothing charming about them. One turned to look at him with small, red eyes, and didn't go 'oink', which was the sound that Mr Crumley, born and raised in the city, had always associated with pigs.

It went '*Ghnaaarrrwnnkh?*'

The sleigh had changed, too. He'd been very pleased with that sleigh. It had delicate silver curly bits on it. He'd personally supervised the gluing on of every twinkling star. But the splendour of it was lying in glittering shards around a sledge that looked as though it had been

137

built of crudely sawn tree trunks laid on two massive wooden runners. It looked ancient and there were faces carved on the wood, nasty crude grinning faces that looked quite out of place.

Parents were yelling and trying to pull their children away, but they weren't having much luck. The children were gravitating towards it like flies to jam.

Mr Crumley ran towards the terrible thing, waving his hands.

'Stop that! Stop that!' he screamed. 'You'll frighten the Kiddies!'

He heard a small boy behind him say, 'They've got tusks! *Cool!*'

His sister said, 'Hey, look, that one's doing a wee!' A tremendous cloud of yellow steam arose. 'Look, it's going all the way to the stairs! All those who can't swim hold onto the banisters!'

'They eat you if you're bad, you know,' said a small girl with obvious approval. 'All up. Even the bones. They *crunch* them.'

Another, older, child opined: 'Don't be childish. They're not real. They've just got a wizard in to do the magic. Or it's all done by clockwork. Everyone knows they're not really r—'

One of the boars turned to look at him. The boy moved behind his mother.

Mr Crumley, tears of anger streaming down his face, fought through the milling crowd until he reached the Hogfather's Grotto. He grabbed a frightened pixie.

'It's the Campaign for Equal Heights that've done this, isn't it!' he shouted. 'They're out to ruin me! And they're ruining it for all the Kiddies! Look at the lovely dolls!'

The pixie hesitated. Children were clustering around the pigs, despite the continued efforts of their mothers. The small girl was giving one of them an orange.

But the animated display of Dolls of All Nations was definitely in trouble. The musical box underneath was still playing 'Wouldn't It Be Nice If Everyone Was Nice' but the rods that animated the figures had got twisted out of shape, so that the Klatchian boy was rhythmically hitting the Omnian girl over the head with his ceremonial spear, while the girl in Agatean national costume was kicking a small Llamedosian druid repeatedly in the ear. A chorus of small children was cheering them on indiscriminately.

'There's, er, there's more trouble in the Grotto, Mr Crum—' the pixie began.

A red and white figure pushed its way through the crush and rammed a false beard into Mr Crumley's hands.

'That's *it*,' said the old man in the Hogfather costume. 'I don't mind the smell of oranges and the damp trousers but I ain't putting up with *this*.'

He stamped off through the queue. Mr Crumley heard him add, 'And he's not even doin' it right!'

Mr Crumley forced his way onward.

Someone was sitting in the big chair. There was a child on his knee. The figure was . . . strange.

139

It was definitely in something like a Hogfather costume but Mr Crumley's eye kept slipping, it wouldn't focus, it skittered away and tried to put the figure on the very edge of vision. It was like trying to look at your own ear.

'What's going on here? What's going on here?' Crumley demanded.

A hand took his shoulder firmly. He turned round and looked into the face of a Grotto Pixie. At least, it was wearing the costume of a Grotto Pixie, although somewhat askew, as if it had been put on in a hurry.

'Who are *you*?'

The pixie took the soggy cigarette end out of its mouth and leered at him.

'Call me Uncle Heavy,' he said.

'You're not a pixie!'

'Nah, I'm a fairy cobbler, mister.'

Behind Crumley, a voice said:

AND WHAT DO YOU WANT FOR HOGSWATCH, SMALL HUMAN?

Mr Crumley turned in horror.

In front of – well, he had to think of it as the usurping Hogfather – was a small child of indeterminate sex who seemed to be mostly woollen bobble hat.

Mr Crumley knew how it was supposed to go. It was supposed to go like this: the child was always struck dumb and the attendant mother would lean forward and catch the Hogfather's eye and say very pointedly, in that voice adults use when they're conspiring against children:

140

'You want a Baby Tinkler Doll, don't you, Doreen? And the Just Like Mummy Cookery Set you've got in the window. And the Cut-Out Kitchen Range Book. And what do you say?'

And the stunned child would murmur ''nk you' and get given a balloon or an orange.

This time, though, it didn't work like that.

Mother got as far as 'You want a—'

WHY ARE YOUR HANDS ON BITS OF STRING, CHILD?

The child looked down the length of its arms to the dangling mittens affixed to its sleeves. It held them up for inspection.

'Glubs,' it said.

I SEE. VERY PRACTICAL.

'Are you weal?' said the bobble hat.

WHAT DO *YOU* THINK?

The bobble hat sniggered. 'I saw your piggie do a wee!' it said, and implicit in the tone was the suggestion that this was unlikely to be dethroned as the most enthralling thing the bobble hat had ever seen.

OH. ER . . . GOOD.

'It had a gwate big—'

WHAT DO YOU WANT FOR HOGSWATCH? said the Hogfather hurriedly.

Mother took her economic cue again, and said briskly: 'She wants a—'

The Hogfather snapped his fingers impatiently. The mother's mouth slammed shut.

The child seemed to sense that here was a once-in-a-lifetime opportunity and spoke quickly.

'I wanta narmy. Anna big castle wif pointy bits,' said the child. 'Anna swored.'

WHAT DO YOU SAY? prompted the Hogfather.

'A *big* swored?' said the child, after a pause for deep cogitation.

THAT'S RIGHT.

Uncle Heavy nudged the Hogfather.

'They're supposed to *thank* you,' he said.

ARE YOU SURE? PEOPLE DON'T, NORMALLY.

'I meant they thank the *Hogfather*,' Albert hissed. 'Which is you, right?'

YES, OF COURSE. AHEM. YOU'RE SUPPOSED TO SAY THANK YOU.

' 'nk you.'

AND BE GOOD. THIS IS PART OF THE ARRANGEMENT.

' 'es.'

THEN WE HAVE A CONTRACT. The Hogfather reached into his sack and produced—

—a very large model castle with, as correctly interpreted, pointy blue cone roofs on turrets suitable for princesses to be locked in—

—a box of several hundred assorted knights and warriors—

—and a sword. It was four feet long and glinted along the blade.

The mother took a deep breath.

'You can't give her that!' she screamed. 'It's not safe!'

IT'S A SWORD, said the Hogfather. THEY'RE NOT *MEANT* TO BE SAFE.

'She's a child!' shouted Crumley.

IT'S EDUCATIONAL.

'What if she cuts herself?'

THAT WILL BE AN IMPORTANT LESSON.

Uncle Heavy whispered urgently.

REALLY? OH, WELL. IT'S NOT FOR ME TO ARGUE, I SUPPOSE.

The blade went wooden.

'And she doesn't want all that other stuff!' said Doreen's mother, in the face of previous testimony. 'She's a girl! Anyway, I can't afford big posh stuff like that!'

I THOUGHT I GAVE IT AWAY, said the Hogfather, sounding bewildered.

'You do?' said the mother.

'You *do*?' said Crumley, who'd been listening in horror. 'You *don't*! That's our Merchandise! You can't give it away! Hogswatch isn't about giving it all away! I mean . . . yes, of course, of *course* things are given away,' he corrected himself, aware that people were watching, 'but first they have to be bought, d'you see, I mean . . . haha.' He laughed nervously, increasingly aware of the strangeness around him and the rangy look of Uncle Heavy. 'It's not as though the toys are made by little elves at the Hub, ahaha . . .'

'Damn right,' said Uncle Heavy sagely. 'You'd have to be a maniac even to think of giving an elf a chisel, less'n you want their initials carved on your forehead.'

'You mean this is all free?' said Doreen's mother sharply, not to be budged from what she saw as the central point.

Mr Crumley looked helplessly at the toys. They certainly didn't look like any of his stock.

Then he tried to look hard at the new Hogfather. Every cell in his brain was telling him that here was a fat jolly man in a red and white suit.

Well . . . nearly every cell. A few of the sparkier ones were saying that his eyes were reporting something else, but they couldn't agree on what. A couple had shut down completely.

The words escaped through his teeth.

'It . . . seems to be,' he said.

Although it was Hogswatch the University buildings were bustling. Wizards didn't go to bed early in any case,* and of course there was the Hogswatchnight Feast to look forward to at midnight.

It would give some idea of the scale of the Hogswatchnight Feast that a light snack at UU

---

*Often they lived to a timescale to suit themselves. Many of the senior ones, of course, lived entirely in the past, but several were like the Professor of Anthropics, who had invented an entire temporal system based on the belief that all the other ones were a mere illusion.

Many people are aware of the Weak and Strong Anthropic Principles. The Weak One says, basically, that it was jolly amazing of the universe to be constructed in such a way that humans could evolve to a point where they make a living in, for example, universities, while the Strong One says that, on the contrary, the whole point of the universe was that humans should not only work in universities but also write for huge sums books with words like 'Cosmic' and 'Chaos' in the titles.†

consisted of a mere three or four courses, not counting the cheese and nuts.

Some of the wizards had been practising for weeks. The Dean in particular could now lift a twenty-pound turkey on one fork. Having to wait until midnight merely put a healthy edge on appetites already professionally honed.

There was a general air of pleasant expectancy about the place, a general sizzling of salivary glands, a general careful assembling of the pills and powders against the time, many hours ahead, when eighteen courses would gang up somewhere below the ribcage and mount a counter-attack.

Ridcully stepped out into the snow and turned up his collar. The lights were all on in the High Energy Magic Building.

'I don't know, I don't know,' he muttered. 'Hogswatchnight and they're *still* working. It's just not natural. When *I* was a student I'd have been sick twice by now—'

In fact Ponder Stibbons and his group of

The UU Professor of Anthropics had developed the Special and Inevitable Anthropic Principle, which was that the entire reason for the existence of the universe was the eventual evolution of the UU Professor of Anthropics. But this was only a formal statement of the theory which absolutely everyone, with only some minor details of a 'Fill in name here' nature, secretly believes to be true.

†And they are correct. The universe clearly operates for the benefit of humanity. This can be readily seen from the convenient way the sun comes up in the morning, when people are ready to start the day.

research students *had* made a concession to Hogs-watchnight. They'd draped holly over Hex and put a paper hat on the big glass dome containing the main ant heap.

Every time he came in here, it seemed to Ridcully, something more had been done to the . . . engine, or thinking machine, or whatever it was. Sometimes stuff turned up overnight. Occasionally, according to Stibbons, Hex hims—*it*self would draw plans for extra bits that he – *it* needed. It all gave Ridcully the willies, and an additional willy was engendered right now when he saw the Bursar sitting in front of the thing. For a moment, he forgot all about verrucas.

'What're you doing here, old chap?' he said. 'You should be inside, jumping up and down to make more room for tonight.'

'Hooray for the pink, grey and green,' said the Bursar.

'Er . . . we thought Hex might be of . . . you know . . . help, sir,' said Ponder Stibbons, who liked to think of himself as the University's token sane person. 'With the Bursar's problem. We thought it might be a nice Hogswatch present for him.'

'Ye gods, Bursar's got no problems,' said Ridcully, and patted the aimlessly smiling man on the head while mouthing the words 'mad as a spoon'. 'Mind just wanders a bit, that's all. I said MIND WANDERS A BIT, eh? Only to be expected, spends far too much time addin' up numbers. Doesn't get out in the fresh air. I said,

YOU DON'T GET OUT IN THE FRESH AIR, OLD CHAP!'

'We thought, er, he might like someone to talk to,' said Ponder.

'What? What? But I talk to him all the time! I'm always trying to take him out of himself,' said Ridcully. 'It's important to stop him mopin' around the place.'

'Er . . . yes . . . certainly,' said Ponder diplomatically. He recalled the Bursar as a man whose idea of an exciting time had once been a soft-boiled egg. 'So . . . er . . . well, let's give it another try, shall we? Are you ready, Mr Dinwiddie?'

'Yes, thank you, a green one with cinnamon if it's not too much trouble.'

'Can't see how he can talk to a machine,' said Ridcully, in a sullen voice. 'The thing's got no damn ears.'

'Ah, well, in fact we made it *one* ear,' said Ponder. 'Er . . .'

He pointed to a large drum in a maze of tubes.

'Isn't that old Windle Poons' ear trumpet sticking out of the end?' said Ridcully suspiciously.

'Yes, Archchancellor.' Ponder cleared his throat. 'Sound, you see, comes in waves—'

He stopped. Wizardly premonitions rose in his mind. He just *knew* Ridcully was going to assume he was talking about the sea. There was going to be one of those huge bottomless misunderstandings that always occurred whenever anyone tried to explain anything to the

Archchancellor. Words like 'surf', and probably 'ice cream' and 'sand' were just . . .

'It's all done by magic, Archchancellor,' he said, giving up.

'Ah. Right,' said Ridcully. He sounded a little disappointed. 'None of that complicated business with springs and cogwheels and tubes and stuff, then.'

'That's right, sir,' said Ponder. 'Just magic. Sufficiently *advanced* magic.'

'Fair enough. What's it do?'

'Hex can hear what you say.'

'Interesting. Saves all that punching holes in bits of cards and hitting keys you lads are forever doing, then—'

'Watch this, sir,' said Ponder. 'All right, Adrian, initialize the GBL.'

'How do you do that, then?' said Ridcully, behind him.

'It . . . it means pull the great big lever,' Ponder said, reluctantly.

'Ah. Takes less time to say.'

Ponder sighed. 'Yes, that's right, Archchancellor.'

He nodded to one of the students, who pulled a large red lever marked 'Do Not Pull'. Gears spun, somewhere inside Hex. Little trap-doors opened in the ant farms and millions of ants began to scurry along the networks of glass tubing. Ponder tapped at the huge wooden keyboard.

'Beats me how you fellows remember how to

do all this stuff,' said Ridcully, still watching him with what Ponder considered to be amused interest.

'Oh, it's largely intuitive, Archchancellor,' said Ponder. 'Obviously you have to spend a lot of time learning it first, though. Now, then, Bursar,' he added. 'If you'd just like to say something . . .'

'He says, SAY SOMETHING, BURSAAAR!' yelled Ridcully helpfully, into the Bursar's ear.

'Corkscrew? It's a tickler, that's what Nanny says,' said the Bursar.

Things started to spin inside Hex. At the back of the room a huge converted waterwheel covered with sheep skulls began to turn, ponderously.

And the quill pen in its network of springs and guiding arms started to write:

+++ Why Do You Think You Are A Tickler? +++

For a moment the Bursar hesitated. Then he said, 'I've got a spoon of my own, you know.'

+++ Tell Me About Your Spoon +++

'Er . . . it's a little spoon . . .'

+++ Does Your Spoon Worry You? +++

The Bursar frowned. Then he seemed to rally. 'Whoops, here comes Mr Jelly,' he said, but he didn't sound as though his heart was in it.

+++ How Long Have You Been Mr Jelly? +++

The Bursar glared. 'Are you making *fun* of me?' he said.

'Amazin'!' said Ridcully. 'It's got him stumped!

's better than dried frog pills! How did you work it out?'

'Er . . .' said Ponder. 'It sort of just happened . . .'

'Amazin',' said Ridcully. He knocked the ashes out of his pipe on Hex's 'Anthill Inside' sticker, causing Ponder to wince. 'This thing's a kind of big artificial brain, then?'

'You *could* think of it like that,' said Ponder, carefully. 'Of course, Hex doesn't actually think. Not as such. It just *appears* to be thinking.'

'Ah. Like the Dean,' said Ridcully. 'Any chance of fitting a brain like this into the Dean's head?'

'It does weigh ten tons, Archchancellor.'

'Ah. Really? Oh. Quite a large crowbar would be in order, then.' He paused, and then reached into his pocket. 'I knew I'd come here for something,' he added. 'This here chappie is the Verruca Gnome—'

'Hello,' said the Verruca Gnome shyly.

'—who seems to have popped into existence to be with us here tonight. And, you know, I thought: this is a bit odd. Of course, there's always something a *bit* unreal about Hogswatchnight,' said Ridcully. 'Last night of the year and so on. The Hogfather whizzin' around and so forth. Time of the darkest shadows and so on. All the old year's occult rubbish pilin' up. Anythin' could happen. I just thought you fellows might check up on this. Probably nothing to worry about.'

'A *Verruca* Gnome?' said Ponder.

The gnome clutched his sack protectively.

'Makes about as much sense as a lot of things, I suppose,' said Ridcully. 'After all, there's a Tooth Fairy, ain' there? You might as well wonder why we have a God of Wine and not a God of Hangovers—'

He stopped.

'Anyone else hear that noise just then?' he said.

'Sorry, Archchancellor?'

'Sort of *glingleglingleglingle*? Like little tinkly bells?'

'Didn't hear anything like that, sir.'

'Oh.' Ridcully shrugged. 'Anyway . . . what was I saying . . . yes . . . no one's ever *heard* of a Verruca Gnome until tonight.'

'That's right,' said the gnome. 'Even I've never heard of me until tonight, and I'm *me*.'

'We'll see what we can find out, Archchancellor,' said Ponder diplomatically.

'Good man.' Ridcully put the gnome back in his pocket and looked up at Hex.

'Amazin',' he said again. 'He just *looks* as though he's thinking, right?'

'Er . . . yes.'

'But he's not actually thinking?'

'Er . . . no.'

'So . . . he just gives the *impression* of thinking but really it's just a show?'

'Er . . . yes.'

'Just like everyone else, then, really,' said Ridcully.

*   *   *

The boy gave the Hogfather an appraising stare as he sat down on the official knee.

'Let's be absolutely clear. I know you're just someone dressed up,' he said. 'The Hogfather is a biological and temporal impossibility. I hope we understand one another.'

AH. SO I DON'T EXIST?

'Correct. This is just a bit of seasonal frippery and, I may say, rampantly commercial. My mother's already bought my presents. I instructed her as to the right ones, of course. She often gets things wrong.'

The Hogfather glanced briefly at the smiling, worried image of maternal ineffectiveness hovering nearby.

HOW OLD ARE YOU, BOY?

The child rolled his eyes. 'You're not supposed to say that,' he said. 'I *have* done this before, you know. You have to start by asking me my name.'

AARON FIDGET, 'THE PINES', EDGEWAY ROAD, ANKH-MORPORK.

'I expect someone told you,' said Aaron. 'I expect these people dressed up as pixies get the information from the mothers.'

AND YOU ARE EIGHT, GOING ON . . . OH, ABOUT FORTY-FIVE, said the Hogfather.

'There's forms to fill in when they pay, I expect,' said Aaron.

AND YOU WANT WALNUT'S *INOFFENSIVE REPTILES OF THE STO PLAINS*, A DISPLAY CABINET, A COLLECTOR'S ALBUM, A KILLING JAR AND A LIZARD PRESS. WHAT IS A LIZARD PRESS?

'You can't glue them in when they're still fat, or didn't you know that? I expect she told you about them when I was momentarily distracted by the display of pencils. Look, shall we end this charade? Just give me my orange and we'll say no more about it.'

I CAN GIVE FAR MORE THAN ORANGES.

'Yes, yes, I saw all that. Probably done in collusion with accomplices to attract gullible customers. Oh dear, you've even got a false beard. By the way, old chap, did you know that your pig—'

YES.

'All done by mirrors and string and pipes, I expect. It all looked very artificial to *me*.'

The Hogfather snapped his fingers.

'That's probably a signal, I expect,' said the boy, getting down. 'Thank you very much.'

HAPPY HOGSWATCH, said the Hogfather as the boy walked away.

Uncle Heavy patted him on the shoulder.

'Well done, master,' he said. 'Very patient. I'd have given him a clonk athwart the earhole, myself.'

OH, I'M SURE HE'LL SEE THE ERROR OF HIS WAYS. The red hood turned so that only Albert could see into its depths. RIGHT AROUND THE TIME HE OPENS THOSE BOXES HIS MOTHER WAS CARRYING . . .

HO. HO. HO.

*   *   *

'Don't tie it so tight! Don't tie it so *tight*!'

SQUEAK.

There was a bickering behind Susan as she sought along the shelves in the canyons of Death's huge library, which was so big that clouds would form in it if they dared.

'Right, right,' said the voice she was trying to ignore. 'That's about right. I've got to be able to move my wings, right?'

SQUEAK.

'Ah,' said Susan, under her breath. 'The Hogfather . . .'

He had several shelves, not just one book. The first volume seemed to be written on a roll of animal skin. The Hogfather was *old*.

'OK, OK. How does it look?'

SQUEAK.

'Miss?' said the raven, seeking a second opinion.

Susan looked up. The raven bounced past, its breast bright red.

'Twit, twit,' it said. 'Bobbly bobbly bob. Hop hop hopping along . . .'

'You're fooling no one but yourself,' said Susan. 'I can see the string.'

She unrolled the scroll.

'Maybe I should sit on a snowy log,' mumbled the raven behind her. 'That's probably the trick, right enough.'

'I can't read this!' said Susan. 'The letters are all . . . odd . . .'

'Ethereal runes,' said the raven. 'The Hogfather ain't human, after all.'

Susan ran her hands over the thin leather. The . . . shapes flowed around her fingers.

She couldn't read them but she could *feel* them. There was the sharp smell of snow, so vivid that her breath condensed in the air. There were sounds, hooves, the snap of branches in a freezing forest—

A bright shining ball . . .

Susan jerked awake and thrust the scroll aside. She unrolled the next one, which looked as though it was made of strips of bark. Characters hovered over the surface. Whatever they were, they had never been designed to be read by the eye; you could believe they were a Braille for the touching mind. Images ribboned across her senses – wet fur, sweat, pine, soot, iced air, the tang of damp ash, pig . . . manure, her governess mind hastily corrected. There was blood . . . and the taste of . . . beans? It was all images without words. Almost . . . animal.

'But none of this is right! Everyone knows he's a jolly old fat man who hands out presents to kids!' she said aloud.

'*Is. Is*. Not *was*. You know how it is,' said the raven.

'Do I?'

'It's like, you know, industrial re-training,' said the bird. 'Even gods have to move with the times, am I right? He was probably quite different thousands of years ago. Stands to reason. No one wore stockings, for one thing.' He scratched at his beak.

155

'Yersss,' he continued expansively, 'he was probably just your basic winter demi-urge. You know . . . blood on the snow, making the sun come up. Starts off with animal sacrifice, y'know, hunt some big hairy animal to death, that kind of stuff. You know there's some people up on the Ramtops who kill a wren at Hogswatch and walk around from house to house singing about it? With a whack-fol-oh-diddle-dildo. Very folkloric, very myffic.'

'A *wren*? Why?'

'I dunno. Maybe someone said, hey, how'd you like to hunt this evil bastard of an eagle with his big sharp beak and great ripping talons, sort of thing, or how about instead you hunt this wren, which is basically about the size of a pea and goes "twit"? Go on, *you* choose. Anyway, then later on it sinks to the level of religion and then they start this business where some poor bugger finds a special bean in his tucker, oho, everyone says, you're *king*, mate, and he thinks "This is a bit of all right" only they don't say it wouldn't be a good idea to start any long books, 'cos next thing he's legging it over the snow with a dozen other buggers chasing him with holy sickles so's the earth'll come to life again and all this snow'll go away. Very, you know . . . *ethnic*. Then some bright spark thought, hey, looks like that damn sun comes up *anyway*, so how come we're giving those druids all this free grub? Next thing you know, there's a job vacancy. That's the

156

thing about gods. They'll always find a way to, you know . . . hang on.'

'The damn sun comes up anyway,' Susan repeated. 'How do you know that?'

'Oh, observation. It happens every morning. I *seen* it.'

'I meant all that stuff about holy sickles and things.'

The raven contrived to look smug.

'Very occult bird, your basic raven,' he said. 'Blind Io the Thunder God used to have these myffic ravens that flew everywhere and told him everything that was going on.'

'Used to?'

'Weeelll . . . you know how he's not got eyes in his face, just these, like, you know, free-floating eyeballs that go and zoom around . . .' The raven coughed in species embarrassment. 'Bit of an accident waiting to happen, really.'

'Do you ever think of *anything* except eyeballs?'

'Well . . . there's entrails.'

SQUEAK.

'He's right, though,' said Susan. 'Gods don't die. Never completely die . . .'

There's always somewhere, she told herself. Inside some stone, perhaps, or the words of a song, or riding the mind of some animal, or maybe in a whisper on the wind. They never entirely go, they hang on to the world by the tip of a fingernail, always fighting to find a way back. Once a god, always a god. Dead, perhaps, but only like the world in winter—

'All right,' she said. 'Let's see what happened to him . . .'

She reached out for the last book and tried to open it at random . . .

The feeling lashed at her out of the book, like a whip . . .

. . . *hooves, fear, blood, snow, cold, night* . . .

She dropped the scroll. It slammed shut.

SQUEAK?

'I'm . . . all right.'

She looked down at the book and knew that she'd been given a friendly warning, such as a pet animal might give when it was crazed with pain but just still tame enough not to claw and bite the hand that fed it – this time. Wherever the Hogfather was – dead, alive, *somewhere* – he wanted to be left alone . . .

She eyed the Death of Rats. His little eye sockets flared blue in a disconcertingly familiar way.

SQUEAK. EEK?

'The rat says, if *he* wanted to find out about the Hogfather, he'd go to the Castle of Bones.'

'Oh, that's just a nursery tale,' said Susan. 'That's where the letters are supposed to go that are posted up the chimney. That's just an old story.'

She turned. The rat and the raven were staring at her. And she realized that she'd been too normal.

SQUEAK?

'The rat says, "What d'you mean, *just*?" ' said the raven.

Chickenwire sidled towards Medium Dave in the garden. If you could call it a garden. It was the land round the . . . house. If you could call it a house. No one said much about it, but every so often you just had to get out. It didn't feel right, inside.

He shivered. 'Where's *himself*?' he said.

'Oh, up at the top,' said Medium Dave. 'Still trying to open that room.'

'The one with all the locks?'

'Yeah.'

Medium Dave was rolling a cigarette. Inside the house . . . or tower, or both, or whatever . . . you couldn't smoke, not properly. When you smoked inside it tasted horrible and you felt sick.

'What for? We done what we came to do, didn't we? Stood there like a bunch of kids and watched that wet wizard do all his chanting, it was all I could do to keep a straight face. What's he after now?'

'He just said if it was locked that bad he wanted to see inside.'

'I thought we were supposed to do what we came for and go!'

'Yeah? You tell him. Want a roll-up?'

Chickenwire took the bag of tobacco and relaxed. 'I've seen some bad places in my time, but this takes the serious biscuit.'

159

'Yeah.'

'It's the cute that wears you down. And there's got to be something else to eat than apples.'

'Yeah.'

'And that damn sky. That damn sky is really getting on my nerves.'

'Yeah.'

They kept their eyes averted from that damn sky. For some reason, it made you feel that it was about to fall on you. And it was worse if you let your eyes stray to the gap where a gap shouldn't be. The effect was like getting toothache in your eyeballs.

In the distance Banjo was swinging on a swing. Odd, that, Dave thought. Banjo seemed perfectly happy here.

'He found a tree that grows lollipops yesterday,' he said moodily. 'Well, I say *yesterday*, but how can you tell? And he follows the man around like a dog. *No one* ever laid a punch on Banjo since our mam died. He's just like a little boy, you know. Inside. Always has been. Looks to me for everything. Used to be, if I told him "punch someone", he'd do it.'

'And they stayed punched.'

'Yeah. Now he follows him around everywhere. It makes me sick.'

'What are you doing here, then?'

'Ten thousand dollars. And *he* says there's more, you know. More than we can imagine.'

He was always Teatime.

'He ain't just after money.'

'Yeah, well, I didn't sign up for world domination,' said Medium Dave. 'That sort of thing gets you into trouble.'

'I remember your mam saying that sort of thing,' said Chickenwire. Medium Dave rolled his eyes. Everyone remembered Ma Lilywhite. 'Very straight lady, was your ma. Tough but fair.'

'Yeah . . . tough.'

'I recall that time she strangled Glossy Ron with his own leg,' Chickenwire went on. 'She had a *wicked* right arm on her, your mam.'

'Yeah. Wicked.'

'She wouldn't have stood for someone like Teatime.'

'Yeah,' said Medium Dave.

'That was a lovely funeral you boys gave her. Most of the Shades turned up. Very respectful. All them flowers. An' everyone looking so . . .' Chickenwire floundered '. . . happy. In a sad way, o' course.'

'Yeah.'

'Have you got any idea how to get back home?'

Medium Dave shook his head.

'Me neither. Find the place again, I suppose.' Chickenwire shivered. 'I mean, what he did to that carter . . . I mean, well, I wouldn't even act like that to me own dad—'

'Yeah.'

'Ordinary mental, yes, I can deal with that. But he can be talking quite normal, and then—'

'Yeah.'

'Maybe the both of us could creep up on him and—'

'Yeah, yeah. And how long'll we live? In seconds.'

'We could get lucky—' Chickenwire began.

'Yeah? You've seen him. This isn't one of those blokes who threatens you. This is one of those blokes who'd kill you soon as look at you. Easier, too. We got to hang on, right? It's like that saying about riding a tiger.'

'What saying about riding a tiger?' said Chickenwire suspiciously.

'Well . . .' Medium Dave hesitated. 'You . . . well, you get branches slapping you in the face, fleas, that sort of thing. So you got to hang on. Think of the money. There's bags of it in there. You saw it.'

'I keep thinking of that glass eye watching me. I keep thinking it can see right in my head.'

'Don't worry, he doesn't suspect you of anything.'

'How d'you know?'

'You're still alive, yeah?'

In the Grotto of the Hogfather, a round-eyed child.

HAPPY HOGSWATCH. HO. HO. HO. AND YOUR NAME IS . . . EUPHRASIA GOAT, CORRECT?

'Go on, dear, answer the nice man.'

' 's.'

AND YOU ARE SIX YEARS OLD.

'Go on, dear. They're all the same at this age, aren't they . . .'

' 's.'

AND YOU WANT A PONY—

' 's.' A small hand pulled the Hogfather's hood down to mouth level. Heavy Uncle Albert heard a ferocious whispering. Then the Hogfather leaned back.

YES, I KNOW. WHAT A NAUGHTY PIG IT WAS, INDEED.

His shape flickered for a moment, and then a hand went into the sack.

HERE IS A BRIDLE FOR YOUR PONY, AND A SADDLE, AND A RATHER STRANGE HARD HAT AND A PAIR OF THOSE TROUSERS THAT MAKE YOU LOOK AS THOUGH YOU HAVE A LARGE RABBIT IN EACH POCKET.

'But we can't have a pony, can we, Euffie, because we live on the third floor . . .'

OH, YES. IT'S IN THE KITCHEN.

'I'm sure you're making a little joke, Hogfather,' said Mother, sharply.

HO. HO. YES. WHAT A JOLLY FAT MAN I AM. IN THE KITCHEN? WHAT A JOKE. DOLLIES AND SO ON WILL BE DELIVERED LATER AS PER YOUR LETTER.

'What do you say, Euffie?'

' 'nk you.'

' 'ere, you didn't really put a pony in their kitchen, did you?' said Heavy Uncle Albert as the line moved on.

DON'T BE FOOLISH, ALBERT. I SAID THAT TO BE JOLLY.

'Oh, right. Hah, for a minute—'

IT'S IN THE BEDROOM.

'Ah . . .'

MORE HYGIENIC.

'Well, it'll make sure of one thing,' said Albert. 'Third floor? They're going to believe all right.'

YES. YOU KNOW, I THINK I'M GETTING THE HANG OF THIS. HO. HO. HO.

At the Hub of the Discworld, the snow burned blue and green. The Aurora Corealis hung in the sky, curtains of pale cold fire that circled the central mountains and cast their spectral light over the ice.

They billowed, swirled and then trailed a ragged arm on the end of which was a tiny dot that became, when the eye of imagination drew nearer, Binky.

He trotted to a halt and stood on the air. Susan looked down.

And then found what she was looking for. At the end of a valley of snow-mounded trees something gleamed brightly, reflecting the sky.

The Castle of Bones.

Her parents had sat her down one day when she was about six or seven and explained how such things as the Hogfather did not *really* exist, how they were pleasant little stories that it was fun to know, how they were not *real*. And she had believed it. All the fairies and bogeymen, all those stories from the blood and bone of humanity, were not really *real*.

They'd lied. A seven-foot skeleton had turned out to be her grandfather. Not a flesh and blood grandfather, obviously. But a grandfather, you could say, in the bone.

Binky touched down and trotted over the snow.

Was the Hogfather a god? Why not? thought Susan. There were sacrifices, after all. All that sherry and pork pie. And he made commandments and rewarded the good and he knew what you were doing. If you believed, nice things happened to you. Sometimes you found him in a grotto, and sometimes he was up there in the sky . . .

The Castle of Bones loomed over her now. It certainly deserved the capital letters, up this close.

She'd seen a picture of it in one of the children's books. Despite its name, the woodcut artist had endeavoured to make it look . . . sort of jolly.

It wasn't jolly. The pillars at the entrance were hundreds of feet high. Each of the steps leading up was taller than a man. They were the grey-green of old ice.

Ice. Not bone. There were faintly familiar shapes to the pillars, possibly a suggestion of femur or skull, but it was made of ice.

Binky was not challenged by the high stairs. It wasn't that he flew. It was simply that he walked on a ground level of his own devising.

Snow had blown over the ice. Susan looked down at the drifts. Death left no tracks, but there were the faint outlines of booted footprints. She'd be prepared to bet they belonged to Albert. And . . . yes, half obscured by the snow . . . it looked as though a sledge had stood here. Animals had milled around. But the snow was covering everything.

She dismounted. This was certainly the place described, but it still wasn't right. It was supposed to be a blaze of light and abuzz with activity, but it looked like a giant mausoleum.

A little way beyond the pillars was a very large slab of ice, cracked into pieces. Far above, stars were visible through the hole it had left in the roof. Even as she stared up, a few small lumps of ice thumped into a snowdrift.

The raven popped into existence and fluttered wearily on to a stump of ice beside her.

'This place is a morgue,' said Susan.

' 's goin' to be mine, if I do . . . any more flyin' tonight,' panted the raven, as the Death of Rats got off its back. 'I never signed up for all this long-distance, faster'n time stuff. I should be back in a forest somewhere, making excitingly decorated constructions to attract females.'

'That's bower birds,' said Susan. 'Ravens don't do that.'

'Oh, so it's type-casting now, is it?' said the raven. 'I'm missing meals here, you do know that?'

It swivelled its independently sprung eyes.

'So where's all the lights?' it said. 'Where's all the noise? Where's all the jolly little buggers in

166

pointy hats and red and green suits, hitting wooden toys unconvincingly yet rhythmically with hammers?'

'This is more like the temple of some old thunder god,' said Susan.

SQUEAK.

'No, I read the map right. Anyway, Albert's been here too. There's fag ash all over the place.'

The rat jumped down and walked around for a moment, bony snout near the ground. After a few moments of snuffling it gave a squeak and hurried off into the gloom.

Susan followed. As her eyes grew more accustomed to the faint blue-green light she made out something rising out of the floor. It was a pyramid of steps, with a big chair on top.

Behind her, a pillar groaned and twisted slightly.

SQUEAK.

'That rat says this place reminds him of some old mine,' said the raven. 'You know, after it's been deserted and no one's been paying attention to the roof supports and so on? We see a lot of them.'

At least these steps were human sized, Susan thought, ignoring the chatter. Snow had come in through another gap in the roof. Albert's footprints had stamped around quite a lot here.

'Maybe the old Hogfather crashed his sleigh,' the raven suggested.

SQUEAK?

'Well, it *could've* happened. Pigs are not notably

167

aerodynamic, are they? And with all this snow, you know, poor visibility, big cloud ahead turns out too late to be a mountain, there's buggers in saffron robes looking down at you, poor devil tries to remember whether you're supposed to shove someone's head between your legs, then WHAM, and it's all over bar some lucky mountaineers making an awful lot of sausages and finding the flight recorder.'

SQUEAK!

'Yes, but he's an old man. Probably shouldn't be in the sky at his time of life.'

Susan pulled at something half buried in the snow.

It was a red-and-white-striped candy cane.

She kicked the snow aside elsewhere and found a wooden toy soldier in the kind of uniform that would only be inconspicuous if you wore it in a nightclub for chameleons on hard drugs. Some further probing found a broken trumpet.

There was some more groaning in the darkness.

The raven cleared its throat.

'What the rat meant about this place being like a mine,' he said, 'was that abandoned mines tend to creak and groan in the same way, see? No one looking after the pit props. Things fall in. Next thing you know you're a squiggle in the sandstone. We shouldn't hang around is what I'm saying.'

Susan walked further in, lost in thought.

This was all wrong. The place looked as though

it had been deserted for years, which couldn't be true.

The column nearest her creaked and twisted slightly. A fine haze of ice crystals dropped from the roof.

Of course, this wasn't exactly a normal place. You couldn't build an ice palace this big. It was a bit like Death's house. If he abandoned it for too long all those things that had been suspended, like time and physics, would roll over it. It would be like a dam bursting.

She turned to leave and heard the groan again. It wasn't dissimilar to the tortured sounds being made by the ice, except that ice, afterwards, didn't moan. 'Oh, *me* . . .'

There was a figure lying in a snowdrift. She'd almost missed it because it was wearing a long white robe. It was spreadeagled, as though it had planned to make snow angels and had then decided against it.

And it wore a little crown, apparently of vine leaves.

And it kept groaning.

She looked up. The roof was open here, too. But no one could have fallen that far and survived.

No one human, anyway.

He *looked* human and, in theory, quite young. But it was only in theory because, even by the second-hand light of the glowing snow, his face looked like someone had been sick with it.

'Are you all right?' she ventured.

The recumbent figure opened its eyes and stared straight up.

'I wish I was dead . . .' it moaned. A piece of ice the size of a house fell down in the far depths of the building and exploded in a shower of sharp little shards.

'You may have come to the right place,' said Susan. She grabbed the boy under his arms and hauled him out of the snow. 'I think leaving would be a very good idea around now, don't you? This place is going to fall apart.'

'Oh, *me* . . .'

She managed to get one of his arms around her neck.

'Can you walk?'

'Oh, *me* . . .'

'It might help if you stopped saying that and tried walking.'

'I'm sorry, but I seem to have . . . too many legs. Ow.'

Susan did her best to prop him up as, swaying and slipping, they made their way back to the exit.

'My head,' said the boy. 'My head. My head. My head. Feels awful. My head. Feels like someone's hitting it. My head. With a hammer.'

Someone was. There was a small green and purple imp sitting amid the damp curls and holding a very large mallet. It gave Susan a friendly nod and brought the hammer down again.

'Oh, *me* . . .'

'That wasn't necessary!' said Susan.

'You telling me my job?' said the imp. 'I suppose you could do it better, could you?'

'I wouldn't do it at all!'

'Well, *someone*'s got to do it,' said the imp.

'He's part. Of the. Arrangement,' said the boy.

'Yeah, see?' said the imp. 'Can you hold the hammer while I go and coat his tongue with yellow gunk?'

'Get down right now!'

Susan made a grab for the creature. It leapt away, still clutching the hammer, and grabbed a pillar.

'I'm part of the arrangement, I am!' it yelled.

The boy clutched his head.

'I feel awful,' he said. 'Have you got any ice?'

Whereupon, because there are conventions stronger than mere physics, the building fell in.

The collapse of the Castle of Bones was stately and impressive and seemed to go on for a long time. Pillars fell in, the slabs of the roof slid down, the ice crackled and splintered. The air above the tumbling wreckage filled with a haze of snow and ice crystals.

Susan watched from the trees. The boy, who she'd leaned against a handy trunk, opened his eyes.

'That was amazing,' he managed.

'Why, you mean the way it's all turning back into snow?'

'The way you just picked me up and ran. Ouch!'

'Oh, *that*.'

The grinding of the ice continued. The fallen pillars didn't stop moving when they collapsed, but went on tearing themselves apart.

When the fog of ice settled there was nothing but drifted snow.

'As though it was never there,' said Susan, aloud. She turned to the groaning figure.

'All right, what were you doing there?'

'I don't know. I just opened my. Eyes and there I was.'

'Who *are* you?'

'I . . . *think* my name is Bilious. I'm the . . . I'm the oh God of Hangovers.'

'There's a God of Hangovers?'

'An *oh god*,' he corrected. 'When people witness me, you see, they clutch their head and say, "*Oh God . . .*" How many of you are standing here?'

'What? There's just me!'

'Ah. Fine. Fine.'

'I've never heard of a God of Hangovers . . .'

'You've heard of Bibulous, the God of Wine? Ouch.'

'Oh, yes.'

'Big fat man, wears vine leaves round his head, always pictured with a glass in his hand . . . Ow. Well, you know *why* he's so cheerful? Him and his big face? It's because he knows he's going to feel good in the morning! It's because it's *me* that—'

'—gets the hangovers?' said Susan.

'I don't even drink! Ow! But who is it who ends up head down in the privy every morning? Arrgh.' He stopped and clutched at his head. 'Should your skull feel like it's lined with dog hair?'

'I don't think so.'

'Ah.' Bilious swayed. 'You know when people say "I had fifteen lagers last night and when I woke up my head was clear as a bell"?'

'Oh, yes.'

'Bastards! That's because *I* was the one who woke up groaning in a pile of recycled chilli. Just once, I mean just *once*, I'd like to open my eyes in the morning without my head sticking to something.' He paused. 'Are there any giraffes in this wood?'

'Up here? I shouldn't think so.'

He looked nervously past Susan's head.

'Not even indigo-coloured ones which are sort of stretched and keep flashing on and off?'

'Very unlikely.'

'Thank goodness for that.' He swayed back and forth. 'Excuse me, I think I'm about to throw up my breakfast.'

'It's the middle of the evening!'

'Is it? In that case, I think I'm about to throw up my dinner.'

He folded up gently in the snow behind the tree.

'He's a long streak of widdle, isn't he?' said a

voice from a branch. It was the raven. 'Got a neck with a knee in it.'

The oh god reappeared after a noisy interlude.

'I *know* I must eat,' he mumbled. 'It's just that the only time I remember seeing my food it's always going the other way . . .'

'What were you doing in there?' said Susan.

'Ouch! Search me,' said the oh god. 'It's only a mercy I wasn't holding a traffic sign and wearing a—' he winced and paused '—having some kind of women's underwear about my person.' He sighed. 'Someone somewhere has a lot of fun,' he said wistfully. 'I wish it was me.'

'Get a drink inside you, that's my advice,' said the raven. 'Have a hair of the dog that bit someone else.'

'But why *there*?' Susan insisted.

The oh god stopped trying to glare at the raven. 'I don't know, where was *there* exactly?'

Susan looked back at where the castle had been. It was entirely gone.

'There was a very important building there a moment ago,' she said.

The oh god nodded carefully.

'I often see things that weren't there a moment ago,' he said. 'And they often aren't there a moment later. Which is a blessing in most cases, let me tell you. So I don't usually take a lot of notice.'

He folded up and landed in the snow again.

There's just snow now, Susan thought. Noth-

ing but snow and the wind. There's not even a
ruin.

The certainty stole over her again that the
Hogfather's castle wasn't *simply* not there any
more. No . . . it had never been there. There was
no ruin, no trace.

It had been an odd enough place. It was where
the Hogfather lived, according to the legends.
Which was odd, when you thought about it. It
didn't look like the kind of place a cheery old
toymaker would live in.

The wind soughed in the trees behind them.
Snow slid off branches. Somewhere in the dark
there was a flurry of hooves.

A spidery little figure leapt off a snowdrift and
landed on the oh god's head. It turned a beady
eye up towards Susan.

'All right by you, is it?' said the imp, producing
its huge hammer. 'Some of us have a job to do,
you know, even if we are of a metaphorical, nay,
folkloric persuasion.'

'Oh, go *away*.'

'If you think *I'm* bad, wait until you see the
little pink elephants,' said the imp.

'I don't believe you.'

'They come out of his ears and fly around his
head making tweeting noises.'

'Ah,' said the raven, sagely. 'That sounds more
like robins. I wouldn't put anything past *them*.'

The oh god grunted.

Susan suddenly felt that she didn't want to
leave him. He was human. Well, human shaped.

Well, at least he had two arms and legs. He'd freeze to death here. Of course, gods, or even oh gods, probably couldn't, but humans didn't think like that. You couldn't just *leave* someone. She prided herself on this bit of normal thinking.

Besides, he might have some answers, if she could make him stay awake enough to understand the questions.

From the edge of the frozen forest, animal eyes watched them go.

Mr Crumley sat on the damp stairs and sobbed. He couldn't get any nearer to the toy department. Every time he tried he got lifted off his feet by the mob and dumped at the edge of the crowd by the current of people.

Someone said, 'Top of the evenin', squire,' and he looked up blearily at the small yet irregularly formed figure that had addressed him thusly.

'Are you one of the pixies?' he said, after mentally exhausting all the other possibilities.

'No, sir. I am not in fact a pixie, sir, I am in fact Corporal Nobbs of the Watch. And this is Constable Visit, sir.' The creature looked at a piece of paper in its paw. 'You Mr Crummy?'

'Crumley!'

'Yeah, right. You sent a runner to the Watch House and we have hereby responded with commendable speed, sir,' said Corporal Nobbs. 'Despite it being Hogswatchnight and there being a lot of strange things happening and most importantly it being the occasion of our Hogs-watchly piss-up, sir. But this is all right because Washpot, that's Constable Visit here, he doesn't drink, sir, it being against his religion, and although I *do* drink, sir, I volunteered to come because it is my civic duty, sir.' Nobby tore off a salute, or what he liked to believe was a salute. He did *not* add, 'And turning out for a rich bugger such as your good self is bound to put the officer concerned in the way of a seasonal bottle or two or some other tangible evidence of gratitude,' because his entire stance said it for him. Even Nobby's ears could look suggestive.

Unfortunately, Mr Crumley wasn't in the right receptive frame of mind. He stood up and waved a shaking finger towards the top of the stairs.

'I want you to go up there,' he said, 'and arrest him!'

'Arrest who, sir?' said Corporal Nobbs.

'The Hogfather!'

'What for, sir?'

'Because he's sitting up there as bold as brass in his Grotto, giving away presents!'

Corporal Nobbs thought about this.

'You haven't been having a festive drink, have you, sir?' he said hopefully.

'I do not drink!'

'Very wise, sir,' said Constable Visit. 'Alcohol is the tarnish of the soul. Ossory, Book Two, Verse Twenty-four.'

'Not quite up to speed here, sir,' said Corporal Nobbs, looking perplexed. 'I thought the

177

Hogfather is s'*posed* to give away stuff, isn't he?'

This time Mr Crumley had to stop and think. Up until now he hadn't quite sorted things out in his head, other than recognizing their essential wrongness.

'This one is an Impostor!' he declared. 'Yes, that's right! He smashed his way into here!'

'Y'know, I always thought that,' said Nobby. 'I thought, every year, the Hogfather spends a fortnight sitting in a wooden grotto in a shop in Ankh-Morpork? At his busy time, too? Hah! Not likely! Probably just some old man in a beard, I thought.'

'I meant . . . he's not the Hogfather we usually have,' said Crumley, struggling for firmer ground. 'He just barged in here!'

'Oh, a *different* impostor? Not the real impostor at all?'

'Well . . . yes . . . no . . .'

'And started giving stuff away?' said Corporal Nobbs.

'That's what I said! That's got to be a Crime, hasn't it?'

Corporal Nobbs rubbed his nose.

'Well, *nearly*,' he conceded, not wishing to totally relinquish the chance of any festive re-muneration. Realization dawned. 'He's giving away *your* stuff, sir?'

'No! No, he brought it in with him!'

'Ah? Giving away *your* stuff, now, if he was doing that, yes, I could see the problem. That's a sure sign of crime, stuff going missing. Stuff turning up, weerlll, that's a tricky one. Unless it's stuff like arms and legs, o' course. We'd be on safer ground if he was nicking stuff, sir, to tell you the truth.'

'This is a *shop*,' said Mr Crumley, finally getting to the root of the problem. 'We do *not* give Merchandise *away*. How can we expect people to buy things if some Person is *giving* them away? Now please go and get him out of here.'

'Arrest the Hogfather, style of thing?'

'Yes!'

'On Hogswatchnight?'

'Yes!'

'In your shop?'

'*Yes!*'

'In front of all those kiddies?'

'Y—' Mr Crumley hesitated. To his horror, he realized that Corporal Nobbs, against all expectation, had a point. 'You think that will look bad?' he said.

'Hard to see how it could look good, sir.'

'Could you not do it surreptitiously?' he said.

'Ah, well, surreption, yes, we could give that a try,' said Corporal Nobbs. The sentence hung in the air with its hand out.

'You won't find me ungrateful,' said Mr Crumley, at last.

'Just you leave it to us,' said Corporal Nobbs, magnanimous in victory. 'You just nip down to your office and treat yourself to a nice cup of tea and we'll sort this out in no time. You'll be ever so grateful.'

179

Crumley gave him a look of a man in the grip of serious doubt, but staggered away nonetheless. Corporal Nobbs rubbed his hands together.

'You don't have Hogswatch back where you come from, do you, Washpot?' he said, as they climbed the stairs to the first floor. 'Look at this carpet, you'd think a pig'd pissed on it . . .'

'We call it the Fast of St Ossory,' said Visit, who was from Omnia. 'But it is not an occasion for superstition and crass commercialism. We simply get together in family groups for a prayer meeting and a fast.'

'What, turkey and chicken and that?'

'A *fast*, Corporal Nobbs. We don't eat *anything*.'

'Oh, right. Well, each to his own, I s'pose. And at least you don't have to get up early in the morning and find that the nothing you've got is too big to fit in the oven. No presents neither?'

They stood aside hurriedly as two children scuttled down the stairs carrying a large toy boat between them.

'It is sometimes appropriate to exchange new religious pamphlets, and of course there are usually copies of the *Book of Ossory* for the children,' said Constable Visit. 'Sometimes with *illustrations*,' he added, in the guarded way of a man hinting at licentious pleasures.

A small girl went past carrying a teddy bear larger than herself. It was pink.

'They always gives *me* bath salts,' complained Nobby. 'And bath soap and bubble bath and herbal bath lumps and tons of bath stuff and I

180

can't think why, 'cos it's not as if I hardly ever *has* a bath. You'd think they'd take the hint, wouldn't you?'

'Abominable, I call it,' said Constable Visit.

The first floor was a mob.

'Huh, look at them. Mr Hogfather never brought *me* anything when I was a kid,' said Corporal Nobbs, eyeing the children gloomily. 'I used to hang up my stocking every Hogswatch, regular. All that ever happened was my dad was sick in it once.' He removed his helmet.

Nobby was not by any measure a hero, but there was the sudden gleam in his eye of someone who'd seen altogether too many empty stockings plus one rather full and dripping one. A scab had been knocked off some wound in the corrugated little organ of his soul.

'I'm going in,' he said.

In between the University's Great Hall and its main door is a rather smaller circular hall or vestibule known as Archchancellor Bowell's Remembrance, although no one now knows why, or why an extant bequest pays for one small currant bun and one copper penny to be placed on a high stone shelf on one wall every second Wednesday.* Ridcully stood in the middle of the floor, looking upwards.

*The ceremony still carries on, of course. If you left off traditions because you didn't know why they started you'd be no better than a foreigner.

'Tell me, Senior Wrangler, we never invited any *women* to the Hogswatchnight Feast, did we?'

'Of course not, Archchancellor,' said the Senior Wrangler. He looked up in the dust-covered rafters, wondering what had caught Ridcully's eye. 'Good heavens, no. They'd spoil everything. I've always said so.'

'And all the maids have got the evening off until midnight?'

'A very generous custom, I've always said,' said the Senior Wrangler, feeling his neck crick.

'So why, every year, do we hang a damn great bunch of mistletoe up there?'

The Senior Wrangler turned in a circle, still staring upwards.

'Well, er . . . it's . . . well, it's . . . it's symbolic, Archchancellor.'

'Ah?'

The Senior Wrangler felt that something more was expected. He groped around in the dusty attics of his education.

'Of . . . the leaves, d'y'see . . . they're symbolic of . . . of green, d'y'see, whereas the berries, in fact, yes, the berries symbolize . . . symbolize white. Yes. White and green. Very . . . symbolic.'

He waited. He was not, unfortunately, disappointed.

'What of?'

The Senior Wrangler coughed.

'I'm not sure there *has* to *be* an *of*,' he said.

'Ah? So,' said the Archchancellor, thoughtfully,

'it could be said that the white and green symbolize a small parasitic plant?'

'Yes, indeed,' said the Senior Wrangler.

'So mistletoe, in fact, symbolizes mistletoe?'

'Exactly, Archchancellor,' said the Senior Wrangler, who was now just hanging on.

'Funny thing, that,' said Ridcully, in the same thoughtful tone of voice. 'That statement is either so deep it would take a lifetime to fully comprehend every particle of its meaning, or it is a load of absolute tosh. Which is it, I wonder?'

'It could be both,' said the Senior Wrangler desperately.

'And *that* comment,' said Ridcully, 'is either very perceptive, or very trite.'

'It might be bo—'

'Don't push it, Senior Wrangler.'

There was a hammering on the outer door.

'Ah, that'll be the wassailers,' said the Senior Wrangler, happy for the distraction. 'They call on us first every year. I personally have always liked "The Lily-white Boys", you know.'

The Archchancellor glanced up at the mistletoe, gave the beaming man a sharp look, and opened the little hatch in the door.

'Well, now, wassailing you fellows—' he began. 'Oh. Well, I must say you might've picked a better time . . .'

A hooded figure stepped through the wood of the door, carrying a limp bundle over its shoulder.

183

The Senior Wrangler stepped backwards quickly.

'Oh . . . no, not *tonight* . . .'

And then he noticed that what he had taken for a robe had lace around the bottom, and the hood, while quite definitely a hood, was nevertheless rather more stylish than the one he had first mistaken it for.

'Putting down or taking away?' said Ridcully.

Susan pushed back her hood.

'I need your help, Mr Ridcully,' she said.

'You're . . . aren't you Death's granddaughter?' said Ridcully. 'Didn't I meet you a few—'

'Yes,' sighed Susan.

'And . . . are you helping out?' said Ridcully. His waggling eyebrows indicated the slumbering figure over her shoulder.

'I need you to wake him up,' said Susan.

'Some sort of miracle, you mean?' said the Senior Wrangler, who was a little behind.

'He's not dead,' said Susan. 'He's just resting.'

'That's what they all say,' the Senior Wrangler quavered.

Ridcully, who was somewhat more practical, lifted the oh god's head. There was a groan.

'Looks a bit under the weather,' he said.

'He's the God of Hangovers,' said Susan. 'The *Oh* God of Hangovers.'

'Really?' said Ridcully. 'Never had one of those myself. Funny thing, I can drink all night and feel as fresh as a daisy in the morning.'

The oh god's eyes opened. Then he soared

towards Ridcully and started beating him on the chest with both fists.

'You utter, utter bastard! I hate you hate you hate you hate you—'

His eyes shut, and he slid down to the floor.

'What was all that about?' said Ridcully.

'I think it was some kind of nervous reaction,' said Susan diplomatically. 'Something nasty's happening tonight. I'm hoping he can tell me what it is. But he's got to be able to think straight first.'

'And you brought him *here*?' said Ridcully.

HO. HO. HO. YES INDEED, HELLO, SMALL CHILD CALLED VERRUCA LUMPY, WHAT A LOVELY NAME, AGED SEVEN, I BELIEVE? GOOD. YES, I KNOW IT DID. ALL OVER THE NICE CLEAN FLOOR, YES. THEY DO, YOU KNOW. THAT'S ONE OF THE THINGS ABOUT REAL PIGS. HERE WE ARE, DON'T MENTION IT. HAPPY HOGSWATCH AND BE GOOD. I WILL KNOW IF YOU'RE GOOD OR BAD, YOU KNOW. HO. HO. HO.

'Well, you brought some magic into *that* little life,' said Albert, as the next child was hurried away.

IT'S THE EXPRESSION ON THEIR LITTLE FACES I LIKE, said the Hogfather.

'You mean sort of fear and awe and not knowing whether to laugh or cry or wet their pants?'

YES. NOW *THAT* IS WHAT I CALL BELIEF.

*   *   *

The oh god was carried into the Great Hall and laid out on a bench. The senior wizards gathered round, ready to help those less fortunate than themselves remain that way.

'I know what's good for a hangover,' said the Dean, who was feeling in a party mood.

They looked at him expectantly.

'Drinking heavily the previous night!' he said. He beamed at them.

'That was a good word joke,' he said, to break the silence.

The silence came back.

'Most amusing,' said Ridcully. He turned back and stared thoughtfully at the oh god.

'Raw eggs are said to be good—' he glared at the Dean '—I mean *bad* for a hangover,' he said. 'And fresh orange juice.'

'Klatchian coffee,' said the Lecturer in Recent Runes, firmly.

'But this fellow hasn't just got *his* hangover, he's got *everyone*'s hangover,' said Ridcully.

'I've tried it,' mumbled the oh god. 'It just makes me feel suicidal *and* sick.'

'A mixture of mustard and horseradish?' said the Chair of Indefinite Studies. 'In cream, for preference. With anchovies.'

'Yoghurt,' said the Bursar.

Ridcully looked at him, surprised.

'That sounded almost relevant,' he said. 'Well done. I should leave it at that if I were you, Bursar. Hmm. Of course, my uncle always used to swear at Wow-Wow Sauce,' he added.

'You mean swear *by*, surely?' said the Lecturer in Recent Runes.

'Possibly both,' said Ridcully. 'I know he once drank a whole bottle of it as a hangover cure and it certainly seemed to cure him. He looked very peaceful when they came to lay him out.'

'Willow bark,' said the Bursar.

'That's a good idea,' said the Lecturer in Recent Runes. 'It's an analgesic.'

'Really? Well, possibly, though it's probably better to give it to him by mouth,' said Ridcully. 'I say, are you feeling yourself, Bursar? You seem somewhat coherent.'

The oh god opened his crusted eyes.

'Will all that stuff help?' he mumbled.

'It'll probably kill you,' said Susan.

'Oh. Good.'

'We could add Englebert's Enhancer,' said the Dean. 'Remember when Modo put some on his peas? We could only manage one each!'

'Can't you do something more, well, magical?' said Susan. 'Magic the alcohol out of him or something?'

'Yes, but it's not alcohol by this time, is it?' said Ridcully. 'It'll have turned into a lot of nasty little poisons all dancin' round on his liver.'

'Spold's Unstirring Divisor would do it,' said the Lecturer in Recent Runes. 'Very simply, too. You'd end up with a large beaker full of all the nastiness. Not difficult at all, if you don't mind the side effects.'

'Tell me about the side effects,' said Susan, who had met wizards before.

'The main one is that the rest of him would end up in a somewhat larger beaker,' said the Lecturer in Recent Runes.

'Alive?'

The Lecturer in Recent Runes screwed up his face and waggled his hands. '*Broadly*, yes,' he said. 'Living tissue, certainly. And definitely sober.'

'I think we had in mind something that would leave him the same shape and still breathing,' said Susan.

'Well, you might've *said* . . .'

Then the Dean repeated the mantra that has had such a marked effect on the progress of knowledge throughout the ages.

'Why don't we just mix up absolutely everything and see what happens?' he said.

And Ridcully responded with the traditional response.

'It's got to be worth a try,' he said.

The big glass beaker for the cure had been placed on a pedestal in the middle of the floor. The wizards liked to make a ceremony of everything in any case, but felt instinctively that if they were going to cure the biggest hangover in the world it needed to be done with style.

Susan and Bilious watched as the ingredients were added. Round about halfway the mixture, which was an orange-brown colour, went *gloop*.

'Not a lot of improvement, I feel,' said the Lecturer in Recent Runes.

Englebert's Enhancer was the penultimate ingredient. The Dean dropped in a greenish ball of light that sank under the surface. The only apparent effect was that it caused purple bubbles to creep over the sides of the beaker and drip onto the floor.

'That's *it*?' said the oh god.

'I think the yoghurt probably wasn't a good idea,' said the Dean.

'I'm not drinking *that*,' said Bilious firmly, and then clutched at his head.

'But gods are practically unkillable, aren't they?' said the Dean.

'Oh, *good*,' muttered Bilious. 'Why not stick my legs in a meat grinder, then?'

'Well, if you think it might help—'

'I anticipated a certain amount of resistance from the patient,' said the Archchancellor. He removed his hat and fished out a small crystal ball from a pocket in the lining. 'Let's see what the God of Wine is up to at the moment, shall we? Shouldn't be too difficult to locate a fun-loving god like him on an evening like this . . .'

He blew on the glass and polished it. Then he brightened up.

'Why, here he is, the little rascal! On Dunmanifestin, I do believe. Yes . . . yes . . . reclining on his couch, surrounded by naked maenads.'

'What? Maniacs?' said the Dean.

'He means . . . excitable young women,' said Susan. And it seemed to her that there was a general ripple of movement among the wizards, a sort of nonchalant drawing towards the glittering ball.

'Can't quite see what he's doing . . .' said Ridcully.

'Let me see if I can make it out,' said the Chair of Indefinite Studies hopefully. Ridcully half turned to keep the ball out of his reach.

'Ah, yes,' he said. 'It looks like he's drinking . . . yes, could very well be lager and blackcurrant, if I'm any judge . . .'

'Oh, *me* . . .' moaned the oh god.

'These young women, now—' the Lecturer in Recent Runes began.

'I can see there's some bottles on the table,' Ridcully continued. 'That one, hmm, yes, could be scumble which, as you know, is made from apples—

'*Mainly* apples,' the Dean volunteered. 'Now, about these poor mad girls—'

The oh god slumped to his knees.

'. . . and there's . . . that drink, you know, there's a worm in the bottle . . .'

'Oh, *me* . . .'

'. . . and . . . there's an empty glass, a big one, can't quite see what it contained, but there's a paper umbrella in it. And some cherries on a stick. Oh, and an amusing little monkey.'

'. . . *ooohhh* . . .'

'. . . of course, there's a lot of other bottles too,'

said Ridcully, cheerfully. 'Different coloured drinks, mainly. The sort made from melons and coconuts and chocolate and suchlike, don'tcher-know. Funny thing is, all the glasses on the table are pint mugs . . .'

Bilious fell forward.

'All right,' he murmured. 'I'll drink the wretched stuff.'

'It's not quite ready yet,' said Ridcully. 'Ah, thank you, Modo.'

Modo tiptoed in, pushing a trolley. There was a large metal bowl on it, in which a small bottle stood in the middle of a heap of crushed ice.

'Only just made this for Hogswatch dinner,' said Ridcully. 'Hasn't had much time to mature yet.'

He put down the crystal and fished a pair of heavy gloves out of his hat.

The wizards spread like an opening flower. One moment they were gathered around Rid-cully, the next they were standing close to various items of heavy furniture.

Susan felt she was present at a ceremony and hadn't been told the rules.

'What's that?' she said, as Ridcully carefully lifted up the bottle.

'Wow-Wow Sauce,' said Ridcully. 'Finest con-diment known to man. A happy accompaniment to meat, fish, fowl, eggs and many types of vegetable dishes. It's not safe to drink it when sweat's still condensing on the bottle, though.' He peered at the bottle, and then rubbed at it, causing a glassy, squeaky noise. 'On the other hand,' he said brightly, 'if it's a kill-or-cure remedy then we are, given that the patient is practically immortal, probably on to a winner.'

He placed a thumb over the cork and shook the bottle vigorously. There was a crash as the Chair of Indefinite Studies and the Senior Wrangler tried to get under the same table.

'And these fellows seem to have taken against it for some reason,' he said, approaching the beaker.

'I prefer a sauce that doesn't mean you mustn't make any jolting movements for half an hour after using it,' muttered the Dean.

'And that can't be used for breaking up small rocks,' said the Senior Wrangler.

'Or getting rid of tree roots,' said the Chair of Indefinite Studies.

'And which isn't actually outlawed in three cities,' said the Lecturer in Recent Runes.

Ridcully cautiously uncorked the bottle. There was a brief hiss of indrawn air.

He allowed a few drops to splash into the beaker. Nothing happened.

A more generous helping was allowed to fall. The mixture remained irredeemably inert.

Ridcully sniffed suspiciously at the bottle.

'I wonder if I added enough grated wahooni?' he said, and then upturned the sauce and let most of it slide into the mixture.

It merely went *gloop*.

The wizards began to stand up and brush themselves off, giving one another the rather embarrassed grins of people who know that they've just been part of a synchronized making-a-fool-of-yourself team.

'I know we've had that asafoetida rather a long time,' said Ridcully. He turned the bottle round, peering at it sadly.

Finally he tipped it up for the last time and thumped it hard on the base.

A trickle of sauce arrived on the lip of the bottle and glistened there for a moment. Then it began to form a bead.

As if drawn by invisible strings, the heads of the wizards turned to look at it.

Wizards wouldn't be wizards if they couldn't see a *little* way into the future.

As the bead swelled and started to go pear-shaped they turned and, with a surprising turn of speed for men so wealthy in years and waist-line, began to dive for the floor.

The drop fell.

It went *gloop*.

And that was all.

Ridcully, who'd been standing like a statue, sagged in relief.

'I don't know,' he said, turning away, 'I wish you fellows would show some backbone—'

The fireball lifted him off his feet. Then it rose to the ceiling, where it spread out widely and vanished with a pop, leaving a perfect chrysanthemum of scorched plaster.

Pure white light filled the room. And there was a sound.

TINKLE. TINKLE.

FIZZ.

The wizards risked looking around.

The beaker gleamed. It was filled with a liquid glow, which bubbled gently and sent out sparkles like a spinning diamond.

'My word . . .' breathed the Lecturer in Recent Runes.

Ridcully picked himself up off the floor. Wizards tended to roll well, or in any case are well padded enough to bounce.

Slowly, the flickering brilliance casting their long shadows on the walls, the wizards gravitated towards the beaker.

'Well, what *is* it?' said the Dean.

'I remember my father tellin' me some very valuable advice about drinks,' said Ridcully. 'He said, "Son, never drink any drink with a paper umbrella in it, never drink any drink with a humorous name, and never drink any drink that changes colour when the last ingredient goes in. And never, ever, do this—" '

He dipped his finger into the beaker.

It came out with one glistening drop on the end.

'Careful, Archchancellor,' warned the Dean. 'What you have there might represent pure sobriety.'

Ridcully paused with the finger halfway to his lips.

'Good point,' he said. 'I don't want to start being sober at my time of life.' He looked around. 'How do we usually test stuff?'

'Generally we ask for student volunteers,' said the Dean.

'What happens if we don't get any?'

'We give it to them anyway.'

'Isn't that a bit unethical?'

'Not if we don't tell them, Archchancellor.'

'Ah, good point.'

'I'll try it,' the oh god mumbled.

'Something these clo— gentlemen have cooked up?' said Susan. 'It might kill you!'

'You've never *had* a hangover, I expect,' said the oh god. 'Otherwise you wouldn't talk such rot.'

He staggered up to the beaker, managed to grip it on the second go, and drank the lot.

'There'll be fireworks now,' said the raven, from Susan's shoulder. 'Flames coming out of the mouth, screams, clutching at the throat, lying down under the cold tap, that sort of thing—'

Death found, to his amazement, that dealing with the queue was very enjoyable. Hardly anyone had ever been pleased to see him before.

NEXT! AND WHAT'S YOUR NAME, LITTLE . . . He hesitated, but rallied, and continued . . . PERSON?

'Nobby Nobbs, Hogfather,' said Nobby. Was it him, or was this knee he was sitting on a lot bonier than it should be? His buttocks argued with his brain, and were sat on.

AND HAVE YOU BEEN A GOOD BO . . . A GOOD DWA . . . A GOOD GNO . . . A GOOD INDIVIDUAL?

And suddenly Nobby found he had no control at all of his tongue. Of its own accord, gripped by a terrible compulsion, it said:

'′s.′

He struggled for self-possession as the great voice went on: SO I EXPECT YOU'LL WANT A PRESENT FOR A GOOD MON . . . A GOOD HUM . . . A GOOD MALE?

Aha, got you bang to rights, you'll be coming along with *me*, my old chummy, I bet you don't remember the cellar at the back of the shoelace maker's in Old Cobblers, eh, all those Hogswatch mornings with a little hole in my world, eh?

The words rose in Nobby's throat but were overridden by something ancient before they reached his voice box, and to his amazement were translated into:

'′s.′

SOMETHING NICE?

'′s.′

There was hardly anything left of Nobby's conscious will now. The world consisted of nothing but his naked soul and the Hogfather, who filled the universe.

AND YOU WILL OF COURSE BE GOOD FOR ANOTHER YEAR?

The tiny remnant of basic Nobbyness wanted to say, 'Er, how exactly do you define "good", mister? Like, suppose there was just some stuff that no one'd miss, say? Or, f'r instance, say a friend of mine was on patrol, sort of thing, and found a shopkeeper had left his door unlocked at night. I mean, anyone could walk in, right, but suppose this friend took one or two things, sort of like, you know, a *gratuity*, and then called the shopkeeper out and got him to lock up, that counts as "good", does it?'

Good and bad were, to Nobby's way of thinking, entirely relative terms. Most of his relatives, for example, were criminals. But, again, this invitation to philosophical debate was ambushed somewhere in his head by sheer dread of the big beard in the sky.

' 's,' he squeaked.

NOW, I WONDER WHAT YOU WOULD LIKE?

Nobby gave up, and sat mute. Whatever was going to happen next was going to happen, and there was not a thing he could do about it . . . Right now, the light at the end of his mental tunnel showed only more tunnel.

AH, YES . . .

The Hogfather reached into his sack and pulled out an awkwardly shaped present wrapped in festive Hogswatch paper which, owing to some slight confusion on the current Hogfather's part, had merry ravens on it. Corporal Nobbs took it in nervous hands.

WHAT DO YOU SAY?

' 'nk you.'

OFF YOU GO.

Corporal Nobbs slid down gratefully and barged his way through the crowds, stopping only when he was fielded by Constable Visit.

'What happened? What happened? I couldn't see!'

'I dunno,' mumbled Nobby. 'He gave me *this*.'

'What is it.'

'I dunno . . .'

He clawed at the raven-bedecked paper.

'This is disgusting, this whole business,' said Constable Visit. 'It's the worship of idols—'

'It's a genuine Burleigh and Stronginthearm double-action triple-cantilever crossbow with a polished walnut stock and engraved silver facings!'

'—a crass commercialization of a date which is purely of astronomical significance,' said Visit, who seldom paid attention when he was in mid-denounce. 'If it is to be celebrated at all, then—'

'I saw this in Bows and Ammo*! It got Editor's Choice in the "What to Buy When Rich Uncle Sidney Dies" category! They had to break both the reviewer's arms to get him to let go of it!'*

'—ought to be commemorated in a small service of—'

'It must cost more'n a year's salary! They only make 'em to order! You have to wait ages!'

'—religious significance.' It dawned on Constable Visit that something behind him was amiss.

'Aren't we going to arrest this impostor, corporal?' he said.

Corporal Nobbs looked blearily at him through the mists of possessive pride.

'You're foreign, Washpot,' he said. 'I can't

expect you to know the real meaning of Hogs-watch.'

The oh god blinked.

'Ah,' he said. 'That's better. Oh, *yes*. That's a lot better. Thank you.'

The wizards, who shared the raven's belief in the essential narrative conventions of life, watched him cautiously.

'Any minute now,' said the Lecturer in Recent Runes confidently, 'it'll probably start with some kind of amusing yell—'

'You know,' said the oh god, 'I think I could just possibly eat a soft-boiled egg.'

'—or maybe the ears spinning round—'

'And perhaps drink a glass of milk,' said the oh god.

Ridcully looked nonplussed.

'You really feel better?' he said.

'Oh, yes,' said the oh god. 'I really think I could risk a smile without the top of my head falling off.'

'No, no, no,' said the Dean. 'This can't be right. Everyone knows that a good hangover cure has got to involve a lot of humorous shouting, ekcetra.'

'I could possibly tell you a joke,' said the oh god carefully.

'You don't have this pressing urge to run outside and stick your head in a water butt?' said Ridcully.

'Er . . . not really,' said the oh god. 'But I'd like some toast, if that helps.'

The Dean took off his hat and pulled a thaumameter out of the point. '*Something* happened,' he said. 'There was a massive thaumic surge.'

'Didn't it even taste a bit . . . well, spicy?' said Ridcully.

'It didn't taste of anything, really,' said the oh god.

'Oh, look, it's obvious,' said Susan. 'When the God of Wine drinks, Bilious here gets the after-effects, so when the God of Hangovers drinks a hangover cure then the effects must jump back across the same link.'

'That could be right,' said the Dean. 'He is, after all, basically a conduit.'

'I've always thought of myself as more of a tube,' said the oh god.

'No, no, she's right,' said Ridcully. 'When he drinks, this lad here gets the nasty result. So, logically, when our friend here takes a hangover cure the side effects should head back the same way—'

'Someone mentioned a crystal ball just now,' said the oh god in a voice suddenly clanging with vengeance. 'I want to *see* this—'

It was a big drink. A very big and a very long drink. It was one of those special cocktails where each very sticky, very strong ingredient is poured in very slowly, so that they layer on top of one another. Drinks like this tend to get called Traffic Lights or Rainbow's Revenge or, in places where truth is more highly valued, Hello and Goodbye, Mr Brain Cell.

In addition, this drink had some lettuce floating in it. And a slice of lemon *and* a piece of pineapple hooked coquettishly on the side of the glass, which had sugar frosted round the rim. There were *two* paper umbrellas, one pink and one blue, and they each had a cherry on the end.

And someone had taken the trouble to freeze ice cubes in the shape of little elephants. After that, there's no hope. You might as well be drinking in a place called the Cococobana.

The God of Wine picked it up lovingly. It was his kind of drink.

There was a rumba going on in the background. There were also a couple of young ladies snuggling up to him. It was going to be a good night. It was always a good night.

'Happy Hogswatch, everyone!' he said, and raised the glass.

And then: 'Can anyone hear something?'

Someone blew a paper squeaker at him.

'No, seriously . . . like a sort of descending note . . . ?'

Since no one paid this any attention he shrugged, and nudged one of his fellow drinkers.

'How about we have a couple more and go to this club I know?' he said.

And then—

*　　*　　*

The wizards leaned back, and one or two of them grimaced.

Only the oh god stayed glued to the glass, face contorted in a vicious smile.

'We have eructation!' he shouted, and punched the air. 'Yes! Yes! *Yes!* The worm is on the other boot now, eh? Hah! How do you like *them* apples, huh?'

'Well, *mainly* apples—' said the Dean.

'Looked like a lot of other things to me,' said Ridcully. 'It seems we have reversed the cause-effect flow . . .'

'Will it be permanent?' said the oh god hopefully.

'I shouldn't think so. After all, you *are* the God of Hangovers. It'll probably just reverse itself again when the potion wears off.'

'Then I may not have much time. Bring me . . . let's see . . . twenty pints of lager, some pepper vodka and a bottle of coffee liqueur! With an umbrella in it! Let's see how he enjoys that, Mr You've Got Room For Another One In There!'

Susan grabbed his hand and pulled him over to a bench.

'I didn't have you sobered up just so you could go on a binge!' she said.

He blinked at her. 'You didn't?'

'I want you to help me!'

'Help you what?'

'You said you'd never been human before, didn't you?'

'Er . . .' The oh god looked down at himself. 'That's right,' he said. 'Never.'

'You've never incarnated?' said Ridcully.

'Surely that's a rather personal question, isn't it?' said the Chair of Indefinite Studies.

'That's . . . right,' said the oh god. 'Odd, that. I remember always having headaches . . . but never having a head. That can't be right, can it?'

'You existed in potentia?' said Ridcully.

'Did I?'

'Did he?' said Susan.

Ridcully paused. 'Oh dear,' he said. 'I think *I* did it, didn't I? I said something to young Stibbons about drinking and hangovers, didn't I . . . ?'

'And you created him just like that?' said the Dean. 'I find that *very* hard to believe, Mustrum. Hah! Out of thin air? I suppose we can *all* do that, can we? Anyone care to think up some new pixie?'

'Like the Hair Loss Fairy?' said the Lecturer in Recent Runes. The other wizards laughed.

'I am *not* losing my hair!' snapped the Dean. 'It is just very finely spaced.'

'Half on your head and half on your hairbrush,' said the Lecturer in Recent Runes.

'No sense in bein' bashful about goin' bald,' said Ridcully evenly. 'Anyway, you know what they say about bald men, Dean.'

'Yes, they say, "Look at him, he's got no hair,"' said the Lecturer in Recent Runes. The Dean had been annoying him lately.

'For the last time,' shouted the Dean, 'I am *not*—'

He stopped.

There was a *glingleglingleglingle* noise.

'I wish I knew where that was coming from,' said Ridcully.

'Er . . .' the Dean began. 'Is there . . . something on my head?'

The other wizards stared.

Something was moving under his hat.

Very carefully, he reached up and removed it.

The very small gnome sitting on his head had a clump of the Dean's hair in each hand. It blinked guiltily in the light.

'Is there a problem?' it said.

'Get it off me!' the Dean yelled.

The wizards hesitated. They were all vaguely aware of the theory that very small creatures could pass on diseases, and while the gnome was larger than such creatures were generally thought to be, no one wanted to catch Expanding Scalp Sickness.

Susan grabbed it.

'Are you the Hair Loss Fairy?' she said.

'Apparently,' said the gnome, wriggling in her grip.

The Dean ran his hands desperately through his hair.

'What have you been doing with my hair?' he demanded.

'Well, some of it I think I have to put on hairbrushes,' said the gnome, 'but sometimes I think I weave it into little mats to block up the bath with.'

'What do you mean, you *think*?' said Ridcully.

'Just a minute,' said Susan. She turned to the oh god. 'Where exactly *were* you before I found you in the snow?'

'Er . . . sort of . . . everywhere, I think,' said the oh god. 'Anywhere where drink had been consumed in beastly quantities some time previously, you could say.'

'Ah-*ha*,' said Ridcully. 'You were an immanent vital force, yes?'

'I suppose I could have been,' the oh god conceded.

'And when we joked about the Hair Loss Fairy it suddenly focused on the Dean's head,' said Ridcully, 'where its operations have been noticeable to all of us in recent months although of course we have been far too polite to pass comment on the subject.'

'You're calling things into being,' said Susan.

'Things like the Give the Dean a Huge Bag of Money Goblin?' said the Dean, who could think very quickly at times. He looked around hopefully. 'Anyone hear any fairy tinkling?'

'Do you often get given huge bags of money, sir?' said Susan.

'Not on what you'd call a daily basis, no,' said the Dean. 'But if—'

'Then there probably isn't any occult room for a Huge Bags of Money Goblin,' said Susan.

'I personally have always wondered what

happens to my socks,' said the Bursar cheerfully. 'You know how there's always one missing? When I was a lad I always thought that something was taking them . . .'

The wizards gave this some thought. Then they all heard it – the little crinkly tinkling noise of magic taking place.

The Archchancellor pointed dramatically skywards.

'To the laundry!' he said.

'It's downstairs, Ridcully,' said the Dean.

'*Down* to the laundry!'

'And you know Mrs Whitlow doesn't like us going in there,' said the Chair of Indefinite Studies.

'And who is Archchancellor of this University, may I ask?' said Ridcully. 'Is it Mrs Whitlow? I don't think so! Is it me? Why, how amazing, I do believe it is!'

'Yes, but you know what she can be like,' said the Chair.

'Er, yes, that's true—' Ridcully began.

'I believe she's gone to her sister's for the holiday,' said the Bursar.

'We certainly don't have to take orders from any kind of housekeeper!' said the Archchancellor. 'To the laundry!'

The wizards surged out excitedly, leaving Susan, the oh god, the Verruca Gnome and the Hair Loss Fairy.

'Tell me again who those people were,' said the oh god.

'Some of the cleverest men in the world,' said Susan.

'And I'm sober, am I?'

'Clever isn't the same as sensible,' said Susan, 'and they do say that if you wish to walk the path to wisdom then for your first step you must become as a small child.'

'Do you think they've heard about the second step?'

Susan sighed. 'Probably not, but sometimes they fall over it while they're running around shouting.'

'Ah.' The oh god looked around. 'Do you think they have any soft drinks here?' he said.

The path to wisdom does, in fact, begin with a single step.

Where people go wrong is in ignoring all the thousands of other steps that come after it. They make the single step of deciding to become one with the universe, and for some reason forget to take the logical next step of living for seventy years on a mountain and a daily bowl of rice and yak-butter tea that would give it any kind of meaning. While evidence says that the road to Hell is paved with good intentions, they're probably all on first steps.

The Dean was always at his best at times like this. He led the way between the huge, ancient copper vats, prodding with his staff into dark corners and going 'Hut! Hut!' under his breath.

'Why would it turn up here?' whispered the Lecturer in Recent Runes.

'Point of reality instability,' said Ridcully, standing on tip-toe to look into a bleaching cauldron. 'Every damn thing turns up here. You should know that by now.'

'But why *now*?' said the Chair of Indefinite Studies.

'No talking!' hissed the Dean, and leapt out into the next alleyway, staff held protectively in front of him.

'Hah!' he screamed, and then looked disappointed.

'Er, how big would this sock-stealing thing be?' said the Senior Wrangler.

'Don't know,' said Ridcully. He peered behind a stack of washboards. 'Come to think of it, I must've lost a ton of socks over the years.'

'Me too,' said the Lecturer in Recent Runes.

'So . . . should we be looking in small places or very *large* places?' the Senior Wrangler went on, in the voice of one whose train of thought has just entered a long dark tunnel.

'Good point,' said Ridcully. 'Dean, why do you keep referring to sheds all the time?'

'It's "hut", Mustrum,' said the Dean. 'It means . . . it means . . .'

'Small wooden building?' Ridcully suggested.

'Well, sometimes, agreed, but other times . . . well, you just have to say "hut".'

'This sock creature . . . does it just steal them,

or does it *eat* them?' said the Senior Wrangler.

'Valuable contribution, that man,' said Ridcully, giving up on the Dean. 'Right, pass the word along: no one is to look like a sock, understand?'

'How can you—' the Dean began, and stopped. They all heard it.

. . . *grnf, grnf, grnf* . . .

It was a busy sound, the sound of something with a serious appetite to satisfy.

'The Eater of Socks,' moaned the Senior Wrangler, with his eyes shut.

'How many tentacles would you expect it to have?' said the Lecturer in Recent Runes. 'I mean, roughly speaking?'

'It's a very *large* sort of noise, isn't it?' said the Bursar.

'To the nearest dozen, say,' said the Lecturer in Recent Runes, edging backwards.

. . . *grnf, grnf, grnf* . . .

'It'd probably tear our socks off as soon as look at us . . .' wailed the Senior Wrangler.

'Ah. So at least five or six tentacles, then, would you say?' said the Lecturer in Recent Runes.

'Seems to me it's coming from one of the washing engines,' said the Dean.

The engines were each two storeys high, and usually only used when the University's population soared during term time. A huge treadmill connected to a couple of big bleached wooden paddles in each vat, which were heated via the fireboxes underneath. In full production the washing engines needed at least half a dozen people to manhandle the loads, maintain the fires and oil the scrubbing arms. Ridcully had seen them at work once, when it had looked like a picture of a very clean and hygienic Hell, the kind of place soap might go to when it died.

The Dean stopped by the door to the boiler area.

'Something's in here,' he whispered. 'Listen!'

. . . grnf . . .

'It's stopped! It knows we're here!' he hissed. 'All right? Ready? Hut!'

'No!' squeaked the Lecturer in Recent Runes.

'I'll open the door and you be ready to stop it! One . . . two . . . *three*! Oh . . .'

The sleigh soared into the snowy sky.

ON THE WHOLE, I THINK THAT WENT VERY WELL, DON'T YOU?

'Yes, master,' said Albert.

I WAS RATHER PUZZLED BY THE LITTLE BOY IN THE CHAIN MAIL, THOUGH.

'I think that was a Watchman, master.'

REALLY? WELL, HE WENT AWAY HAPPY, AND THAT'S THE MAIN THING.

'Is it, master?' There was worry in Albert's voice. Death's osmotic nature tended to pick up new ideas altogether too quickly. Of course, Albert understood why they had to do all this, but the master . . . well, sometimes the master lacked the necessary mental equipment to work out what should be true and what shouldn't . . .

AND I THINK I'VE GOT THE LAUGH WORKING REALLY WELL NOW. HO. HO. HO.

'Yeah, sir, very jolly,' said Albert. He looked down at the list. 'Still, work goes on, eh? The next one's pretty close, master, so I should keep them down low if I was you.'

JOLLY GOOD. HO. HO. HO.

'Sarah the little match girl, doorway of Thimble's Pipe and Tobacco Shop, Money Trap Lane, it says here.'

AND WHAT DOES *SHE* WANT FOR HOGSWATCH? HO. HO. HO.

'Dunno. Never sent a letter. By the way, just a tip, you don't have to say "Ho, ho, ho," *all* the time, master. Let's see . . . It says here . . .' Albert's lips moved as he read.

I EXPECT A DOLL IS ALWAYS ACCEPTABLE. OR A SOFT TOY OF SOME DESCRIPTION. THE SACK SEEMS TO KNOW. WHAT'VE WE GOT FOR HER, ALBERT? HO. HO. HO.

Something small was dropped into his hand.

'This,' said Albert.

OH.

There was a moment of horrible silence as they both stared at the lifetimer.

'You're for life, not just for Hogswatch,' prompted Albert. 'Life goes on, master. In a manner of speaking.'

BUT THIS IS *HOGSWATCHNIGHT.*

211

'Very traditional time for this sort of thing, I understand,' said Albert.

I THOUGHT IT WAS THE SEASON TO BE JOLLY, said Death.

'Ah, well, yes, you see, one of the things that makes folks even more jolly is knowing there're people who ain't,' said Albert, in a matter-of-fact voice. 'That's how it goes, master. Master?'

NO. Death stood up. THIS IS HOW IT SHOULDN'T GO.

The University's Great Hall had been set for the Hogswatchnight Feast. The tables were already groaning under the weight of the cutlery, and it would be hours before any real food was put on them. It was hard to see where there would be space for any among the drifts of ornamental fruit bowls and forests of wine glasses.

The oh god picked up a menu and turned to the fourth page.

'Course four: molluscs and crustaceans. A medley of lobster, crab, king crab, prawn, shrimp, oyster, clam, giant mussel, green-lipped mussel, thin-lipped mussel and Fighting Tiger Limpet. With a herb and butter dipping sauce. Wine: "Three Wizards" Chardonnay, Year of the Talking Frog. Beer: Winkles' Old Peculiar.' He put it down. 'That's *one* course?' he said.

'They're big men in the food department,' said Susan.

He turned the menu over. On the cover was the University's coat of arms and, over it, three large letters in ancient script:

η β π

'Is this some sort of magic word?'

'No.' Susan sighed. 'They put it on all their menus. You might call it the unofficial motto of the University.'

'What's it mean?'

'Eta Beta Pi.'

Bilious gave her an expectant look.

'Yes . . . ?'

'Er . . . like, Eat a Better Pie?' said Susan.

'That's what you just said, yes,' said the oh god.

'Um. No. You see, the letters are Ephebian characters which just *sound* a bit like "eat a better pie".'

'Ah.' Bilious nodded wisely. 'I can see that might cause confusion.'

Susan felt a bit helpless in the face of the look of helpful puzzlement. 'No,' she said, 'in fact they are *supposed* to cause a little bit of confusion, and then you laugh. It's called a pune or play on words. Eta Beta Pi.' She eyed him carefully. 'You laugh,' she said. 'With your mouth. Only, in *fact*, you don't laugh, because you're not supposed to laugh at things like this.'

'Perhaps I could find that glass of milk,' said the oh god helplessly, peering at the huge array of jugs and bottles. He'd clearly given up on sense of humour.

'I gather the Archchancellor won't have milk

213

in the University,' said Susan. 'He says he knows where it comes from and it's unhygienic. And that's a man who eats three eggs for breakfast every day, mark you. How do you know about milk, by the way?'

'I've got . . . memories,' said the oh god. 'Not exactly of anything, er, specific. Just, you know, memories. Like, I know trees usually grow green-end up . . . that sort of thing. I suppose gods just know things.'

'Any special god-like powers?'

'I might be able to turn water into an ener-vescent drink.' He pinched the bridge of his nose. 'Is that any help? And it's just possible I can give people a blinding headache.'

'I need to find out why my grandfather is . . . acting strange.'

'Can't you ask him?'

'He won't tell me!'

'Does he throw up a lot?'

'I shouldn't think so. He doesn't often eat. The occasional curry, once or twice a month.'

'He must be pretty thin.'

'You've no idea.'

'Well, then . . . Does he often stare at himself in the mirror and say "Arrgh"? Or stick out his tongue and wonder why it's gone yellow? You see, it's possible I might have some measure of influence over people who are hung over. If he's been drinking a lot, I might be able to find him.'

'I can't see him doing any of those things. I

think I'd better tell you . . . My grandfather is Death.'

'Oh, I'm sorry to hear that.'

'I said *Death*.'

'Sorry?'

'Death. You know . . . Death?'

'You mean the robes, the—'

'—scythe, white horse, bones . . . yes. Death.'

'I just want to make sure I've got this clear,' said the oh god in a reasonable tone of voice. 'You think your grandfather is Death and you think *he's* acting strange?'

The Eater of Socks looked up at the wizards, cautiously. Then its jaws started to work again.

. . . grnf, grnf . . .

'Here, that's one of mine!' said the Chair of Indefinite Studies, making a grab. The Eater of Socks backed away hurriedly.

It looked like a very small elephant with a very wide, flared trunk, up which one of the Chair's socks was disappearing.

'Funny lookin' little thing, ain't it?' said Ridcully, leaning his staff against the wall.

'Let go, you wretched creature!' said the Chair, making a grab for the sock. 'Shoo!'

The sock eater tried to get away while remaining where it was. This should be impossible, but it is in fact a move attempted by many small animals when they are caught eating something forbidden. The legs scrabble hurriedly but the

215

neck and feverishly working jaws merely stretch and pivot around the food. Finally the last of the sock disappeared up the snout with a faint sucking noise and the creature lumbered off behind one of the boilers. After a while it poked one suspicious eye around the corner to watch them.

'They're expensive, you know, with the flax-reinforced heel,' muttered the Chair of Indefinite Studies.

Ridcully pulled open a drawer in his hat and extracted his pipe and a pouch of herbal tobacco. He struck a match on the side of the washing engine. This was turning out to be a far more interesting evening than he had anticipated.

'We've got to get this sorted out,' he said, as the first few puffs filled the washing hall with the scent of autumn bonfires. 'Can't have creatures just popping into existence because someone's thought about them. It's unhygienic.'

The sleigh slewed around at the end of Money Trap Lane.

COME ON, ALBERT.

'You know you're not supposed to do this sort of thing, master. You know what happened last time.'

THE HOGFATHER CAN DO IT, THOUGH.

'But . . . little match girls dying in the snow is part of what the Hogswatch spirit is all *about*, master,' said Albert desperately. 'I mean, people hear about it and say, "We may be poorer than a disabled banana and only have mud and old boots to eat, but at least we're better off than the poor little match girl," master. It makes them feel happy and grateful for what they've got, see.'

I KNOW WHAT THE SPIRIT OF HOGSWATCH IS, ALBERT.

'Sorry, master. But, look, it's all right, anyway, because she wakes up and it's all bright and shining and tinkling music and there's angels, master.'

Death stopped.

AH. THEY TURN UP AT THE LAST MINUTE WITH WARM CLOTHES AND A HOT DRINK?

Oh dear, thought Albert. The master's really in one of his funny moods now.

'Er. No. Not exactly at the *last* minute, master. Not as such.'

WELL?

'More sort of just *after* the last minute.' Albert coughed nervously.

YOU MEAN *AFTER* SHE'S—

'Yes. That's how the story goes, master, 's not my fault.'

WHY NOT TURN UP BEFORE? AN ANGEL HAS QUITE A LARGE CARRYING CAPACITY.

'Couldn't say, master. I suppose people think it's more . . . satisfying the other way . . .' Albert hesitated, and then frowned. 'You know, now that I come to tell someone . . .'

Death looked down at the shape under the falling snow. Then he set the lifetimer on the air and touched it with a finger. A spark flashed across.

'You ain't really allowed to do that,' said Albert, feeling wretched.

THE HOGFATHER CAN. THE HOGFATHER GIVES PRESENTS. THERE'S NO BETTER PRESENT THAN A FUTURE.

'Yeah, but—'

ALBERT.

'All right, master.'

Death scooped up the girl and strode to the end of the alley.

The snowflakes fell like angel's feathers. Death stepped out into the street and accosted two figures who were tramping through the drifts.

TAKE HER SOMEWHERE WARM AND GIVE HER A GOOD DINNER, he commanded, pushing the bundle into the arms of one of them. AND I MAY WELL BE CHECKING UP LATER.

Then he turned and disappeared into the swirling snow.

Constable Visit looked down at the little girl in his arms, and then at Corporal Nobbs.

'What's all this about, corporal?'

Nobby pulled aside the blanket.

'Search me,' he said. 'Looks like we've been chosen to do a bit of charity.'

'*I* don't call it very charitable, just dumping someone on people like this.'

'Come on, there'll still be some grub left in the Watch-house,' said Nobby. He'd got a very deep and certain feeling that this was expected of him. He remembered a big man in a grotto, although he couldn't quite remember the face. And he couldn't quite remember the face of the person who had handed over the girl, so that meant it must be the same one.

Shortly afterwards there was some tinkling music and a very bright light and two rather affronted angels appeared at the other end of the alley, but Albert threw snowballs at them until they went away.

Hex worried Ponder Stibbons. He didn't know how it worked, but everyone else assumed that he did. Oh, he had a good idea about *some* parts, and he was pretty certain that Hex thought about things by turning them all into numbers and crunching them (a clothes wringer from the laundry, or CWL, had been plumbed in for this very purpose), but why did it need a lot of small religious pictures? And there was the mouse. It didn't seem to do much, but whenever they forgot to give it its cheese Hex stopped working. There were all those ram skulls. The ants wandered over to them occasionally but they didn't seem to *do* anything.

What Ponder was worried about was the fear that he was simply engaged in a cargo cult. He'd

read about them. Ignorant* and credulous†
people, whose island might once have been
visited by some itinerant merchant vessel that
traded pearls and coconuts for such fruits of
civilization as glass beads, mirrors, axes and
sexual diseases, would later make big model
ships out of bamboo in the hope of once again
attracting this magical cargo. Of course, they
were far too ignorant and credulous to know that
just because you built the shape you didn't get
the substance . . .

He'd built the shape of Hex and, it occurred
to him, he'd built it in a magical university
where the border between the real and 'not
real' was stretched so thin you could almost see
through it. He got the horrible suspicion that,
somehow, they were merely making solid a

*Ignorant: a state of not knowing what a pronoun is, or
how to find the square root of 27.4, and merely knowing
childish and useless things like which of the seventy almost
identical-looking species of the purple sea snake are the
deadly ones, how to treat the poisonous pith of the Sago-
sago tree to make a nourishing gruel, how to foretell the
weather by the movements of the tree-climbing Burglar
Crab, how to navigate across a thousand miles of featureless
ocean by means of a piece of string and a small clay model
of your grandfather, how to get essential vitamins from the
liver of the ferocious Ice Bear, and other such trivial matters.
It's a strange thing that when everyone becomes educated,
everyone knows about the pronoun but no one knows about
the Sago-sago.

†Credulous: having views about the world, the universe
and humanity's place in it that are shared only by very
unsophisticated people and the most intelligent and
advanced mathematicians and physicists.

sketch that was hidden somewhere in the air.

Hex knew what it ought to be.

All that business about the electricity, for example. Hex had raised the subject one night, not long after it'd asked for the mouse.

Ponder prided himself that he knew pretty much all there was to know about electricity. But they'd tried rubbing balloons and glass rods until they'd been able to stick Adrian onto the ceiling, and it hadn't had any effect on Hex. Then they'd tried tying a lot of cats to a wheel which, when revolved against some beads of amber, caused any amount of electricity all over the place. The wretched stuff hung around for *days*, but there didn't seem any way of ladling it into Hex and anyway no one could stand the noise.

So far the Archchancellor had vetoed the lightning rod idea.

All this depressed Ponder. He was certain that the world ought to work in a more efficient way.

And now even the things that he thought were going right were going wrong.

He stared glumly at Hex's quill pen in its tangle of springs and wire.

The door was thrown open. Only one person could make a door bang on its hinges like that. Ponder didn't even turn round.

'Hello again, Archchancellor.'

'That thinking engine of yours working?' said Ridcully. 'Only there's an interesting little—'

'It's not working,' said Ponder.

'It ain't. What's this, a half-holiday for Hogs-watch?'

'Look,' said Ponder.

Hex wrote: +++ Whoops! Here Comes The Cheese! +++ MELON MELON MELON +++ Error At Address: 14, Treacle Mine Road, Ankh-Morpork +++ !!!!! +++ Oneoneoneoneoneone +++ Redo From Start +++

'What's going on?' said Ridcully, as the others pushed in behind them.

'I know it sounds stupid, Archchancellor, but we think it might have caught something off the Bursar.'

'Daftness, you mean?'

'That's ridiculous, boy!' said the Dean. 'Idiocy is *not* a communicable disease.'

Ridcully puffed his pipe.

'I used to think that, too,' he said. 'Now I'm not so sure. Anyway, you can catch wisdom, can't you?'

'No, you can't,' snapped the Dean. 'It's not like 'flu, Ridcully. Wisdom is . . . well, instilled.'

'We bring students here and hope they catch wisdom off us, don't we?' said Ridcully.

'Well, *metaphorically*,' said the Dean.

'And if you hang around with a bunch of idiots you're bound to become pretty daft yourself,' Ridcully went on.

'I suppose in a manner of speaking . . .'

'And you've only got to talk to the poor old Bursar for five minutes and you think you're going a bit potty yourself, am I right?'

The wizards nodded glumly. The Bursar's company, although quite harmless, had a habit of making one's brain squeak.

'So Hex here has caught daftness off the Bursar,' said Ridcully. 'Simple. Real stupidity beats artificial intelligence every time.' He banged his pipe on the side of Hex's listening tube and shouted: 'FEELING ALL RIGHT, OLD CHAP?'

Hex wrote: +++ Hi Mum Is Testing +++ MELON MELON MELON +++ Out Of Cheese Error +++ !!!!! +++ Mr Jelly! Mr Jelly! +++

'Hex seems perfectly able to work out anything purely to do with numbers but when it tries anything else it does this,' said Ponder.

'See? Bursar Disease,' said Ridcully. 'The bee's knees when it comes to adding up, the pig's ear at everything else. Try giving him dried frog pills?'

'Sorry, sir, but that is a very uninformed suggestion,' said Ponder. 'You can't give medicine to machines.'

'Don't see why not,' said Ridcully. He banged on the tube again and bellowed, 'SOON HAVE YOU BACK ON YOUR . . . your . . . yes, indeed, old chap! Where's that board with all the letter and number buttons, Mr Stibbons? Ah, good.' He sat down and typed, with one finger, as slowly as a company chairman:

D-R-Y-D-F-R-O-R-G-½P-I-L-L-S

Hex's pipes jangled.

'That can't possibly work, sir,' said Ponder.

'It ought to,' said Ridcully. 'If he can get the

idea of being ill, he can get the idea of being cured.'

He typed: L-O-T-S-O-F-D-R-Y-D-F-R-O-R-G-P-¼-L-L-S

'Seems to me,' he said, 'that this thing believes what it's told, right?'

'Well, it's true that Hex has, if you want to put it that way, no idea of an untruth.'

'Right. Well, I've just told the thing it's had a lot of dried frog pills. It's not going to call me a liar, is it?'

There was some clickings and whirrings within the structure of Hex.

Then it wrote: +++ Good Evening, Archchancellor. I Am Fully Recovered And Enthusiastic About My Tasks +++

'Not mad, then?'

+++ I Assure You I Am As Sane As The Next Man +++

'Bursar, just move away from the machine, will you?' said Ridcully. 'Oh well, I expect it's the best we're going to get. Right, let's get all this sorted out. We want to find out what's going on.'

'Anywhere specific or just everywhere?' said Ponder, a shade sarcastically.

There was a scratching noise from Hex's pen. Ridcully glanced down at the paper.

'Says here "Implied Creation Of Anthropomorphic Personification",' he said. 'What's that mean?'

'Er . . . I think Hex has tried to work out the answer,' said Ponder.

'Has it, bigods? *I* hadn't even worked out what the question was yet . . .'

'It heard you talking, sir.'

Ridcully raised his eyebrows. Then he leaned down towards the speaking tube.

'CAN YOU HEAR ME IN THERE?'

The pen scratched.

+++ Yes +++

'LOOKIN' AFTER YOU ALL RIGHT, ARE THEY?'

'You don't have to shout, Archchancellor,' said Ponder.

'What's this Implied Creation, then?' said Ridcully.

'Er, I think I've heard of it, Archchancellor,' said Ponder. 'It means the existence of some things automatically brings into existence other things. If some things exist, certain other things have to exist as well.'

'Like . . . crime and punishment, say?' said Ridcully. 'Drinking and hangovers . . . of course . . .'

'*Something* like that, sir, yes.'

'So . . . if there's a Tooth Fairy there has to be a Verruca Gnome?' Ridcully stroked his beard. 'Makes a sort of sense, I suppose. But why not a Wisdom Tooth Goblin? You know, bringing them extra ones? Some little devil with a bag of big teeth?'

There was silence. But in the depths of the silence there was a little tingly fairy bell sound.

'Er . . . do you think I might have—' Ridcully began.

'Sounds logical to me,' said the Senior Wrangler. 'I remember the agony I had when *my* wisdom teeth came through.'

'Last week?' said the Dean, and smirked.

'Ah,' said Ridcully. He didn't look embarrassed because people like Ridcully are never, ever embarrassed about anything, although often people are embarrassed on their behalf. He bent down to the ear trumpet again.

'YOU STILL IN THERE?'

Ponder Stibbons rolled his eyes.

'MIND TELLING US WHAT THE REALITY IS LIKE ROUND HERE?'

The pen wrote: +++ On A Scale Of One To Ten – Query +++

'FINE,' Ridcully shouted.

+++ Divide By Cucumber Error. Please Re-install Universe And Reboot +++

'Interestin',' said Ridcully. 'Anyone know what that means?'

'Damn,' said Ponder. 'It's crashed again.'

Ridcully looked mystified. 'Has it? I never even saw it take off.'

'I mean it's . . . it's sort of gone a little bit mad,' said Ponder.

'Ah,' said Ridcully. 'Well, we're experts at that around here.'

He thumped on the drum again.

'WANT SOME MORE DRIED FROG PILLS, OLD CHAP?' he shouted.

'Er, I should let us sort it out, Archchancellor,' said Ponder, trying to steer him away.

'What does "divide by cucumber" mean?' said Ridcully.

'Oh, Hex just says that if it comes up with an answer that it knows can't possibly be real,' said Ponder.

'And this "rebooting" business? Give it a good kicking, do you?'

'Oh, no, of course, we . . . that is . . . well, yes, in fact,' said Ponder. 'Adrian goes round the back and . . . er . . . prods it with his foot. But in a *technical* way,' he added.

'Ah. I think I'm getting the hang of this thinkin' engine business,' said Ridcully cheerfully. 'So it reckons the universe needs a kicking, does it?'

Hex's pen was scratching across the paper. Ponder glanced at the figures.

'It must do. These figures can't be right!'

Ridcully grinned again. 'You mean either the whole world has gone wrong or your machine is wrong?'

'Yes!'

'Then I'd imagine the answer's pretty easy, wouldn't you?' said Ridcully.

'Yes. It certainly is. Hex gets thoroughly tested every day,' said Ponder Stibbons.

'Good point, that man,' said Ridcully. He banged on Hex's listening tube once more.

'YOU DOWN THERE—'

'You really *don't* need to shout, Archchancellor,' said Ponder.

—what's this *Anthropomorphic* Personification, then?'

+++ Humans Have Always Ascribed Random, Seasonal, Natural Or Inexplicable Actions To Human-Shaped Entities. Such Examples Are Jack Frost, The Hogfather, The Tooth Fairy And Death +++

'Oh, *them*. Yes, but they exist,' said Ridcully. 'Met a couple of 'em myself.'

+++ Humans Are Not Always Wrong +++

'All right, but I'm damn sure there's never been an Eater of Socks or God of Hangovers.'

+++ But There Is No Reason Why There Should Not Be +++

'The thing's right, you know,' said the Lecturer in Recent Runes. 'A little man who carries verrucas around is no more ridiculous than someone who takes away children's teeth for money, when you come to think about it.'

'Yes, but what about the Eater of Socks?' said the Chair of Indefinite Studies. 'Bursar just said he always thought something was eating his socks and, bingo, there it was.'

'But we all believed him, didn't we? I know *I* did. Seems like the best possible explanation for all the socks *I've* lost over the years. I mean, if they'd just fallen down the back of the drawer or something there'd be a mountain of the things by now.'

'I know what you mean,' said Ponder. 'It's like pencils. I must have bought hundreds of pencils over the years, but how many have I ever actually worn down to the stub? Even I've caught myself thinking that something's creeping up and eating them—'

There was a faint *glingleglingle* noise. He froze.

'What was that?' he said. 'Should I look round? Will I see something horrible?'

'Looks like a very puzzled bird,' said Ridcully.

'With a very odd-shaped beak,' said the Lecturer in Recent Runes.

'I wish I knew who's making that bloody tinkling noise,' said the Archchancellor.

The oh god listened attentively. Susan was amazed. He didn't seem to disbelieve anything. She'd never been able to talk like this before, and said so.

'I think that's because I haven't got any pre-conceived ideas,' said the oh god. 'It comes of not having been conceived, probably.'

'Well, that's how it is, anyway,' said Susan. 'Obviously I haven't inherited . . . physical characteristics. I suppose I just look at the world in a certain way.'

'What way?'

'It . . . doesn't always present barriers. Like this, for example.'

She closed her eyes. She felt better if she didn't see what she was doing. Part of her would keep on insisting it was impossible.

All she felt was a faintly cold, prickling sensation.

'What did I just do?' she said, her eyes still shut.

'Er . . . you waved your hand through the table,' said the oh god.

'You see?'

'Um . . . I assume that most humans can't do that?'

'No!'

'You don't have to shout. I'm not very experienced about humans, am I? Apart from around the point the sun shines through the gap in the curtains. And then they're mainly wishing that the ground would open up and swallow them. I mean the humans, not the curtains.'

Susan leaned back in her chair – and knew that a tiny part of her brain was saying, yes, there is a chair here, it's a real thing, you can sit on it.

'There's other things,' she said. 'I can remember things. Things that haven't happened yet.'

'Isn't that useful?'

'No! Because I never know what they – look, it's like looking at the future through a keyhole. You see bits of things but you never really know what they mean until you arrive where they are and see where the bit fits in.'

'That could be a problem,' said the oh god politely.

'Believe me. It's the waiting that's the worst part. You keep watching out for one of the bits to go past. I mean I don't usually remember anything *useful* about the future, just twisted little clues that don't make sense until it's too late. Are you *sure* you don't know why you turned up at the Hogfather's castle?'

'No. I just remember being a . . . well, can you

understand what I mean by a disembodied mind?'

'Oh, yes.'

'Good. Now can you understand what I mean by a disembodied headache? And then, next moment, I was lying on a back I didn't used to have in a lot of cold white stuff I'd never seen before. But I suppose if you're going to pop into existence, you've got to do it *somewhere*.'

'Somewhere where someone else, who should have existed, didn't,' said Susan, half to herself.

'Pardon?'

'The Hogfather wasn't there,' said Susan. 'He shouldn't have been there *anyway*, not tonight, but this time he wasn't there not because he was somewhere else but because he wasn't anywhere any more. Even his castle was vanishing.'

'I expect I shall get the hang of this incarnation business as I go along,' said the oh god.

'Most people—' Susan began. A shudder ran through her body. 'Oh, no. What's he doing? WHAT'S HE DOING?'

A JOB WELL DONE, I FANCY.

The sleigh thundered across the night. Frozen fields passed underneath.

'Hmph,' said Albert. He sniffed.

WHAT DO YOU CALL THAT WARM FEELING YOU GET INSIDE?

'Heartburn!' Albert snapped.

DO I DETECT A NOTE OF UNSEASONAL

GRUMPINESS? said Death. NO SUGAR PIGGYWIGGY FOR *YOU*, ALBERT.

'I don't want any present, master.' Albert sighed. 'Except maybe to wake up and find it's all back to normal. Look, you know it always goes wrong when you start changing things . . .'

BUT THE HOGFATHER *CAN* CHANGE THINGS. LITTLE MIRACLES ALL OVER THE PLACE, WITH MANY A MERRY HO, HO, HO. TEACHING PEOPLE THE REAL MEANING OF HOGSWATCH, ALBERT.

'What, you mean that the pigs and cattle have all been slaughtered and with any luck everyone's got enough food for the winter?'

WELL, WHEN I SAY THE *REAL* MEANING—

'Some wretched devil's had his head chopped off in a wood somewhere 'cos he found a bean in his dinner and now the summer's going to come back?'

NOT EXACTLY THAT, BUT—

'Oh, you mean that they've chased down some poor beast and shot arrows up into their apple trees and now the shadows are going to go away?'

THAT IS DEFINITELY A MEANING, BUT I—

'Ah, then you're talking about the one where they light a bloody big bonfire to give the sun a hint and tell it to stop lurking under the horizon and do a proper day's work?'

Death paused, while the hogs hurtled over a range of hills.

YOU'RE NOT HELPING, ALBERT.

'Well, they're all the real meanings that *I* know.'

I THINK YOU COULD WORK WITH ME ON THIS.

'It's all about the sun, master. White snow and red blood and the sun. Always has been.'

VERY WELL, THEN. THE HOGFATHER CAN TEACH PEOPLE THE *UNREAL* MEANING OF HOGSWATCH.

Albert spat over the side of the sleigh. 'Hah! "Wouldn't It Be Nice If Everyone Was Nice", eh?'

THERE ARE WORSE BATTLE CRIES.

'Oh dear, oh dear, oh dear . . .'

EXCUSE ME . . .

Death reached into his robe and pulled out an hourglass.

TURN THE SLEIGH AROUND, ALBERT. DUTY CALLS.

'Which one?'

A MORE POSITIVE ATTITUDE WOULD ASSIST AT THIS POINT, THANK YOU SO VERY MUCH.

'Fascinatin'. Anyone got another pencil?' said Ridcully.

'It's had four already,' said the Lecturer in Recent Runes. 'Right down to the stub, Archchancellor. And you *know* we buy our own these days.'

It was a sore point. Like most people with no grasp whatsoever of real economics, Mustrum Ridcully equated 'proper financial control' with the counting of paperclips. Even senior wizards had to produce a pencil stub to him before they were allowed a new one out of the locked cupboard below his desk. Since of course hardly anyone retained a half-used pencil, the wizards had been reduced to sneaking out and buying new ones with their own money.

The reason for the dearth of short pencils was perched in front of them, whirring away as it chewed an HB down to the eraser on the end, which it spat at the Bursar.

Ponder Stibbons had been making notes.

'I think it works like this,' he said. 'What we're getting is the personification of forces, just like Hex said. But it only works if the thing is . . . well, logical.' He swallowed. Ponder was a great believer in logic, in the face of all the local evidence, and he hated having to use the word in this way. 'I don't mean it's *logical* that there's a creature that eats socks, but it . . . a . . . it makes a sort of sense . . . I mean it's a working hypothesis.'

'Bit like the Hogfather,' said Ridcully. 'When you're a kiddie, he's as good an explanation as any, right?'

'What's not logical about there being a goblin that brings me huge bags of money?' said the Dean sulkily. Ridcully fed the Stealer of Pencils another pencil.

'Well, sir . . . firstly, you've never mysteriously received huge bags of money and needed to find a hypothesis to explain them, and secondly, no one else would think it at all likely.'

'Huh!'

'Why's it happening now?' said Ridcully. 'Look, it's hopped onto my finger! Anyone got another pencil?'

'Well, these . . . forces have always been here,' said Ponder. 'I mean, socks and pencils have always inexplicably gone missing, haven't they? But why they're suddenly getting personified like this . . . I'm afraid I don't know.'

'Well, we'd better find out, hadn't we?' said Ridcully. 'Can't have this sort of thing going on. Daft anti-gods and miscellaneous whatnots being created just because people've thought about 'em? We could have anything turn up, anyway. Supposing some idiot says there must be a god of indigestion, eh?'

Glingleglingleglingle.

'Er . . . I think someone just did, sir,' said Ponder.

'What's the matter? What's the matter?' said the oh god. He took Susan by the shoulders.

They felt bony under his hands.

'DAMN,' said Susan. She pushed him away and steadied herself on the table, taking care that he didn't see her face.

Finally, with a measure of the self-control she'd taught herself over the last few years, she managed to get her own voice back.

'He's slipping out of character,' she muttered, to the hall in general. 'I can *feel* him doing it. And *that* drags *me* in. What's he doing it all *for*?'

'Search me,' said the oh god, who'd backed away hurriedly. 'Er . . . just then . . . before you turned your face away . . . it looked as though you were wearing *very* dark eye shadow . . . only you weren't . . .'

'Look, it's very simple,' said Susan, spinning round. She could feel her hair restyling itself, which it always did when it was anxious. 'You know how stuff runs in families? Blue eyes, buck teeth, that sort of thing? Well, Death runs in *my* family.'

'Er . . . in everybody's family, doesn't it?' said the oh god.

'Just shut up, please, don't gabble,' said Susan. 'I didn't mean death, I meant Death with a capital D. I remember things that haven't happened yet and I can TALK THAT TALK and stalk that stalk and . . . if he gets sidetracked, then I'll have to do it. And he *does* get sidetracked. I don't know what's really happened to the real Hogfather or why Grandfather's doing his job, but I know a bit about how he thinks and he's got no . . . no mental shields like we have. He doesn't know how to forget things or ignore things. He takes everything literally and logically and doesn't understand why that doesn't always work—'

She saw his bemused expression.

'Look . . . how would you make sure everyone in the world was well fed?' she demanded.

'Me? Oh, well, I . . .' The oh god spluttered for a moment. 'I suppose you'd have to think about the prevalent political systems, and the proper division and cultivation of arable land, and—'

'Yes, yes. But *he'd* just give everyone a good meal,' said Susan.

236

'Oh, I see. Very impractical. Hah, it's as silly as saying you could clothe the naked by, well, giving them some clothes.'

'Yes! I mean, no. Of course not! I mean, *obviously* you'd give— oh, you *know* what I mean!'

'Yes, I suppose so.'

'But *he* wouldn't.'

There was a crash beside them.

A burning wheel always rolls out of flaming wreckage. Two men carrying a large sheet of glass always cross the road in front of any comedy actor involved in a crazy car chase. Some narrative conventions are so strong that equivalents happen even on planets where the rocks boil at noon. And when a fully laden table collapses, one miraculously unbroken plate always rolls across the floor and spins to a halt.

Susan and the oh god watched it, and then turned their attention to the huge figure now lying in what remained of an enormous centre-piece made of fruit.

'He just . . . came right out of the air,' whispered the oh god.

'Really? Don't just stand there. Give me a hand to help him up, will you?' said Susan, pulling at a large melon.

'Er, that's a bunch of grapes behind his ear—'

'Well?'

'I don't like even to *think* about grapes—'

'Oh, come *on*.'

Together they managed to get the newcomer on to his feet.

'Toga, sandals . . . he looks a bit like you,' said Susan, as the fruit victim swayed heavily.

'Was I that green colour?'

'Close.'

'Is . . . is there a privy nearby?' mumbled their burden, through clammy lips.

'I believe it's through that arch over there,' said Susan. 'I've heard it's not very pleasant, though.'

'That's not a rumour, that's a forecast,' said the fat figure, and lurched off. 'And then can I please have a glass of water and one charcoal biscuit . . .'

They watched him go.

'Friend of yours?' said Susan.

'God of Indigestion, I think. Look . . . I . . . er . . . I think I *do* remember *something*,' said the oh god. 'Just before I, um, incarnated. But it sounds stupid . . .'

'Well?'

'Teeth,' said the oh god.

Susan hesitated.

'You don't mean something attacking you, do you?' she said flatly.

'No. Just . . . a sensation of toothiness. Probably doesn't mean much. As God of Hangovers I see a lot worse, I can tell you.'

'Just teeth. Lots of teeth. But not horrible teeth. Just lots and lots of little teeth. Almost . . . sad?'

'Yes! How did you know?'

'Oh, I . . . maybe I remember you telling me

before you told me. I don't know. How about a big shiny red globe?'

The oh god looked thoughtful for a moment and then said, 'No, can't help you there, I'm afraid. It's just teeth. Rows and rows of teeth.'

'I don't remember rows,' said Susan. 'I just felt . . . teeth were important.'

'Nah, it's amazing what you can do with a beak,' said the raven, who'd been investigating the laden table and had succeeded in levering a lid off a jar.

'What have you got there?' said Susan wearily.

'Eyeballs,' said the raven. 'Hah, wizards know how to live all right, eh? They don't want for nothing around here, I can tell you.'

'They're olives,' said Susan.

'Tough luck,' said the raven. 'They're mine now.'

'They're a kind of fruit! Or a vegetable or something!'

'You sure?' The raven swivelled one doubtful eye on the jar and the other on her.

'Yes!'

The eyes swivelled again.

'So you're an eyeball expert all of a sudden?'

'Look, they're *green*, you stupid bird!'

'They could be very *old* eyeballs,' said the raven defiantly. 'Sometimes they go like that—'

SQUEAK, said the Death of Rats, who was halfway through a cheese.

'And not so much of the stupid,' said the raven. 'Corvids are exceptionally bright with reasoning

239

and, in the case of some forest species, tool-using abilities!'

'Oh, so *you* are an expert on ravens, are you?' said Susan.

'Madam, I happen to *be* a—'

SQUEAK, said the Death of Rats again.

They both turned. It was pointing at its grey teeth.

'The Tooth Fairy?' said Susan. 'What about her?'

SQUEAK.

'Rows of teeth,' said the oh god again. 'Like . . . rows, you know? What's the Tooth Fairy?'

'Oh, you see her around a lot these days,' said Susan. 'Or them, rather. It's a sort of franchise operation. You get the ladder, the moneybelt and the pliers and you're set up.'

'Pliers?'

'If she can't make change she has to take an extra tooth on account. But, look, the tooth fairies are harmless enough. I've met one or two of them. They're just working girls. They don't *menace* anyone.'

SQUEAK.

'I just hope Grandfather doesn't take it into his head to do *their* job as well. Good grief, the thought of it—'

'They collect teeth?'

'Yes. Obviously.'

'Why?'

'Why? It's their *job*.'

'I meant why, where do they take the teeth after they collect them?'

'*I* don't know! They just . . . well, they just take the teeth and leave the money,' said Susan. 'What sort of question is that – "Where do they take the teeth?"?'

'I just wondered, that's all. Probably all humans know, I'm probably very silly for asking, it's probably a well-known fact.'

Susan looked thoughtfully at the Death of Rats.

'Actually . . . where *do* they take the teeth?'

SQUEAK?

'He says search him,' said the raven. 'Maybe they sell 'em?' It pecked at another jar. 'How about these, these look nice and wrinkl—'

'Pickled walnuts,' said Susan absently. 'What do they do with the teeth? What use is there for a lot of teeth? But . . . what harm can a tooth fairy do?'

'Have we got time to find one and ask her?' said the oh god.

'Time isn't the problem,' said Susan.

There are those who believe knowledge is something that is acquired – a precious ore hacked, as it were, from the grey strata of ignorance.

There are those who believe that knowledge can only be recalled, that there was some Golden Age in the distant past when everything was known and the stones fitted together so you could hardly put a knife between them, you know, and it's obvious they had flying machines, right, because of the way the earthworks can only be seen from above, yeah? and there's this museum I read about where they found a pocket calculator under the altar of this ancient temple, you know what I'm saying? but the government hushed it up . . .*

Mustrum Ridcully believed that knowledge could be acquired by shouting at people, and was endeavouring to do so. The wizards were sitting around the Uncommon Room table, which was piled high with books.

'It *is* Hogswatch, Archchancellor,' said the Dean reproachfully, thumbing through an ancient volume.

---

*It's amazing how good governments are, given their track record in almost every other field, at hushing up things like alien encounters.

One reason may be that the aliens themselves are too embarrassed to talk about it.

It's not known why most of the space-going races of the universe want to undertake rummaging in Earthling underwear as a prelude to formal contact. But representatives of several hundred races have taken to hanging out, unsuspected by one another, in rural corners of the planet and, as a result of this, keep on abducting other would-be abductees. Some have been in fact abducted while waiting to carry out an abduction on a couple of other aliens trying to abduct the aliens who were, as a result of misunderstood instructions, trying to form cattle into circles and mutilate crops.

The planet Earth is now banned to all alien races until they can compare notes and find out how many, if any, real humans they have actually got. It is gloomily suspected that there is only one – who is big, hairy and has very large feet.

The truth may be out there, but lies are inside your head.

'Not until midnight,' said Ridcully. 'Sortin' this out will give you fellows an appetite for your dinner.'

'I think I might have something, Archchancellor,' said the Chair of Indefinite Studies. 'This is *Woddeley's Basic Gods*. There's some stuff here about lares and penates that seems to fit the bill.'

'Lares and penates? What were they when they were at home?' said Ridcully.

'Hahaha,' said the Chair.

'What?' said Ridcully.

'I thought you were making a rather good joke, Archchancellor,' said the Chair.

'Was I? I didn't *mean* to,' said Ridcully.

'Nothing new there,' said the Dean, under his breath.

'What was that, Dean?'

'Nothing, Archchancellor.'

'I thought you made the reference "at home" because they are, in fact, household gods. Or were, rather. They seemed to have faded away long ago. They were . . . little spirits of the house, like, for example—'

Three of the other wizards, thinking quite fast for wizards, clapped their hands over his mouth.

'Careful!' said Ridcully. 'Careless talk creates lives! That's why we've got a big fat God of Indigestion being ill in the privy. By the way, where's the Bursar?'

'He was in the privy, Archchancellor,' said the Lecturer in Recent Runes.

243

'What, when the—?'

'*Yes*, Archchancellor.'

'Oh, well, I'm sure he'll be all right,' said Ridcully, in the matter-of-fact voice of someone contemplating something nasty that was happening to someone else out of earshot. 'But we don't want any more of these . . . what're they, Chair?'

'Lares and penates, Archchancellor, but I wasn't suggesting—'

'Seems clear to me. Something's gone wrong and these little devils are coming back. All we have to do is find out what's gone wrong and put it right.'

'Oh, well, I'm glad that's all sorted out,' said the Dean.

'Household gods,' said Ridcully. 'That's what they are, Chair?' He opened the drawer in his hat and took out his pipe.

'Yes, Archchancellor. It says here they used to be the . . . local spirits, I suppose. They saw to it that the bread rose and the butter churned properly.'

'Did they eat pencils? What was their attitude in the socks department?'

'This was back in the time of the First Empire,' said the Chair of Indefinite Studies. 'Sandals and togas and so on.'

'Ah. Not noticeably socked?'

'Not excessively so, no. And it was nine hundred years before Osric Pencillium first discovered, in the graphite-rich sands of the remote island of Sumtri, the small bush which, by dint

244

of careful cultivation, he induced to produce the long—'

'Yes, we can all see you've got the encyclopaedia open under the table, Chair,' said Ridcully. 'But I daresay things have changed a bit. Moved with the times. Bound to have been a few developments. Once they looked after the bread rising, now we have things that eat pencils and socks and see to it that you can never find a clean towel when you want one—'

There was a distant tinkling.

He stopped.

'I just said that, didn't I?' he said.

The wizards nodded glumly.

'And this is the first time anyone's mentioned it?'

The wizards nodded again.

'Well, dammit, it's amazing, you *can* never find a clean towel when—'

There was a rising *wheeee* noise. A towel went by at shoulder height. There was a suggestion of many small wings.

'That was mine,' said the Lecturer in Recent Runes reproachfully. The towel disappeared in the direction of the Great Hall.

'Towel Wasps,' said the Dean. 'Well done, Archchancellor.'

'Well, I mean, *dammit*, it's human nature, isn't it?' said Ridcully hotly. 'Things go wrong, things get lost, it's *natural* to invent little creatures that – All right, all right, I'll be careful. I'm just saying man is naturally a mythopoeic creature.'

'What's that mean?' said the Senior Wrangler.

'Means we make things up as we go along,' said the Dean, not looking up.

'Um . . . excuse me, gentlemen,' said Ponder Stibbons, who had been scribbling thoughtfully at the end of the table. 'Are we suggesting that things are coming back? Do we think that's a viable hypothesis?'

The wizards looked at one another around the table.

'Definitely viable.'

'Viable, right enough.'

'Yes, that's the stuff to give the troops.'

'What is? What's the stuff to give the troops?'

'Well . . . tinned rations? Decent weapons, good boots . . . that sort of thing.'

'What's that got to do with anything?'

'Don't ask *me*. *He* was the one who started talking about giving stuff to the troops.'

'Will you lot shut up? No one's giving anything to the troops!'

'Oh, shouldn't they have something? It's Hogswatch, after all.'

'Look, it was just a figure of speech, all right? I just meant I was fully in agreement. It's just colourful language. Good grief, you surely can't think I'm actually suggesting giving stuff to the troops, at Hogswatch or any other time!'

'You weren't?'

'No!'

'That's a bit mean, isn't it?'

Ponder just let it happen. It's because their

minds are so often involved with deep and problematic matters, he told himself, that their mouths are allowed to wander around making a nuisance of themselves.

'I don't hold with using that thinking machine,' said the Dean. 'I've said this before. It's meddling with the Cult. The occult has always been good enough for me, thank you very much.'

'On the other hand it's the only person round here who can think straight and it does what it's told,' said Ridcully.

The sleigh roared through the snow, leaving rolling trails in the sky.

'Oh, what fun,' muttered Albert, hanging on tightly.

The runners hit a roof near the University and the pigs trotted to a halt.

Death looked at the hourglass again.

ODD, he said.

'It's a scythe job, then?' said Albert. 'You won't be wanting the false beard and the jolly laugh?' He looked around, and puzzlement replaced sarcasm. 'Hey . . . how could anyone be dead up here?'

Someone was. A corpse lay in the snow.

It was clear that the man had only just died. Albert squinted up at the sky.

'There's nowhere to fall from and there's no footprints in the snow,' he said, as Death swung his scythe. 'So where did he come from? Looks like someone's personal guard. Been stabbed to death. Nasty knife wound there, see?'

'It's not good,' agreed the spirit of the man, looking down at himself.

Then he stared from himself to Albert to Death and his phantom expression went from shock to concern.

'They got the teeth! All of them! They just walked in . . . and . . . they . . . no, wait . . .'

He faded and was gone.

'Well, what was *that* all about?' said Albert.

I HAVE MY SUSPICIONS.

'See that badge on his shirt? Looks like a drawing of a tooth.'

YES. IT DOES.

'Where's that come from?'

A PLACE I CANNOT GO.

Albert looked down at the mysterious corpse and then back up at Death's impassive skull.

'I keep thinking it was a funny thing, us bumping into your grand-daughter like that,' he said.

YES.

Albert put his head on one side. 'Given the large number of chimneys and kids in the world, ekcetra.'

INDEED.

'Amazing coincidence, really.'

IT JUST GOES TO SHOW.

'Hard to believe, you might say.'

LIFE CERTAINLY SPRINGS A FEW SURPRISES.

'Not just life, I reckon,' said Albert. 'And she

got *real* worked up, didn't she? Flew right off the ole handle. Wouldn't be surprised if she started asking questions.'

THAT'S PEOPLE FOR YOU.

'But Rat is hanging around, ain't he? He'll probably keep an eye socket on her. Guide her path, prob'ly.'

HE IS A LITTLE SCAMP, ISN'T HE?

Albert knew he couldn't win. Death had the ultimate poker face.

I'M SURE SHE'LL ACT SENSIBLY.

'Oh, yeah,' said Albert, as they walked back to the sleigh. 'It runs in the family, acting sensibly.'

Like many barmen, Igor kept a club under the bar to deal with those little upsets that occurred around closing time, although in fact Biers never closed and no one could ever remember not seeing Igor behind the bar. Nevertheless, things sometimes got out of hand. Or paw. Or talon.

Igor's weapon of choice was a little different. It was tipped with silver (for werewolves), hung with garlic (for vampires) and wrapped around with a strip of blanket (for bogeymen). For everyone else the fact that it was two feet of solid bog-oak usually sufficed.

He'd been watching the window. The frost was creeping across it. For some reason the creeping fingers were forming into a pattern of three little dogs looking out of a boot.

Then someone had tapped him on the

shoulder. He spun around, club already in his hand, and relaxed.

'Oh . . . it's you, miss. I didn't hear the door.'

There hadn't been the door. Susan was in a hurry.

'Have you seen Violet lately, Igor?'

'The tooth girl?' Igor's one eyebrow writhed in concentration. 'Nah, haven't seen her for a week or two.'

The eyebrow furrowed into a V of annoyance as he spotted the raven, which tried to shuffle behind a half-empty display card of beer nuts.

'You can get that out of here, miss,' he said. 'You *know* the rule 'bout pets and familiars. If it can't turn back into human on demand, it's out.'

'Yeah, well, some of us have more brain cells than fingers,' muttered a voice from behind the beer nuts.

'Where does she live?'

'Now, miss, you know I never answers questions like that—'

'WHERE DOES SHE LIVE, IGOR?'

'Shamlegger Street, next to the picture framers,' said Igor automatically. The eyebrow knotted in anger as he realized what he'd said.

'Now, *miss*, you *know* the rules! I don't get bitten, I don't get me froat torn out and no one hides behind me door! And *you* don't try your granddad's voice on me! I could ban you for messin' me about like that!'

'Sorry, it's important,' said Susan. Out of the corner of her eye she could see that the raven had crept on to the shelves and was pecking the top off a jar.

'Yeah, well, suppose one of the vampires decides it's important he's missed his tea?' grumbled Igor, putting the club away.

There was a *plink* from the direction of the pickled egg jar. Susan tried hard not to look.

'Can we go?' said the oh god. 'All this alcohol makes me nervous.'

Susan nodded and hurried out.

Igor grunted. Then he went back to watching the frost, because Igor never demanded much out of life. After a while he heard a muffled voice say:

'I 'ot 'un! I *'ot* 'un!'

It was indistinct because the raven had speared a pickled egg with its beak.

Igor sighed, and picked up his club. And it would have gone very hard for the raven if the Death of Rats hadn't chosen that moment to bite Igor on the ear.

DOWN THERE, said Death.

The reins were hauled so sharply so quickly that the hogs ended up facing the other way.

Albert fought his way out of a drift of teddy bears, where he'd been dozing.

'What's up? What's up? Did we hit something?' he said.

Death pointed downwards. An endless white snowfield lay below, only the occasional glow of a window candle or a half-covered hut indicating the presence on this world of brief mortality.

Albert squinted, and then saw what Death had spotted.

' 's some old bugger trudging through the snow,' he said. 'Been gathering wood, by the look of it. A bad night to be out,' he said. 'And I'm out in it too, come to that. Look, master, I'm sure you've done enough now to make sure—'

SOMETHING'S HAPPENING DOWN THERE. HO. HO. HO.

'Look, he's all *right*,' said Albert, hanging on as the sleigh tumbled downwards. There was a brief wedge of light below as the wood-gatherer opened the door of a snow-drifted hovel. 'See, over there, there's a couple of blokes catching him up, look, they're weighed down with parcels and stuff, see? He's going to have a decent Hogswatch after all, no problem there. *Now* can we go—'

Death's glowing eye sockets took in the scene in minute detail.

IT'S WRONG.

'Oh, no . . . here we go *again*.'

The oh god hesitated.

'What do you mean, you can't walk through the door?' said Susan. 'You walked through the door in the bar.'

'That was different. I have certain god-like powers in the presence of alcohol. Anyway, we've knocked and she hasn't answered and whatever happened to Mr Manners?'

Susan shrugged, and walked through the cheap woodwork. She knew she probably shouldn't. Every time she did something like this she used up a certain amount of, well, *normal*. And sooner or later she'd forget what doorknobs were for, just like Grandfather.

Come to think of it, he'd never found *out* what doorknobs were for.

She opened the door from the inside. The oh god stepped in and looked around. This did not take long. It was not a large room. It had been subdivided from a room that itself hadn't been all that big to start with.

'*This* is where the Tooth Fairy lives?' Bilious said. 'It's a bit . . . poky, isn't it? Stuff all over the floor . . . What're these things hanging from this line?'

'They're . . . women's clothes,' said Susan, rummaging through the paperwork on a small rickety table.

'They're not very big,' said the oh god. 'And a bit thin . . .'

'Tell me,' said Susan, without looking up. 'These memories you arrived here with . . . They weren't very complicated, were they . . . ? Ah . . .'

He looked over her shoulder as she opened a small red notebook.

'I've only talked to Violet a few times,' she said. 'I think she delivers the teeth somewhere and gets a percentage of the money. It's not a highly paid

253

line of work. You know, they say you can Earn
$$$ in Your Spare Time but she says really she
could earn more money waiting on tables – Ah,
this looks right . . .'

'What's that?'

'She said she gets given the names every week.'

'What, of the children who're going to lose
teeth?'

'Yes. Names and addresses,' said Susan, flick-
ing through the pages.

'That doesn't sound very likely.'

'Pardon me, but are you the God of Hang-
overs? Oh, look, here's Twyla's tooth last month.'
She smiled at the neat grey writing. 'She practi-
cally hammered it out because she needed the
half-dollar.'

'Do you *like* children?' said the oh god.

She gave him a look. 'Not raw,' she said.
'Other people's are OK. Hold on . . .'

She flicked some pages back and forth.

'There's just blank days,' she said. 'Look, the
last few days, all unticked. No names. But if you
go back a week or two, look, they're all properly
marked off and the money added up at the
bottom of the page, see? And . . . *this* can't be
right, can it?'

There were only five names entered on the first
unticked night, for the previous week. Most
children instinctively knew when to push their
luck and only the greedy or dentally improvident
called out the Tooth Fairy around Hogswatch.

'Read the names,' said Susan.

'William Wittles, a.k.a. Willy (home), Tosser (school),
    2nd flr bck bdrm, 68 Kicklebury Street;
Sophie Langtree, a.k.a. Daddy's Princess, attic bdrm,
    5 The Hippo;
The Hon. Jeffrey Bibbleton, a.k.a. Trouble in Trousers
    (home), Foureyes (school), 1st flr bck, Scrote
    Manor, Park Lane—'

He stopped. 'I say, this is a bit intrusive, isn't
it?'

'It's a whole new world,' said Susan. 'You
haven't got there yet. Keep going.'

'Nuhakme Icta, a.k.a. Little Jewel, basement, The
    Laughing Falafel, Klatchistan Take-Away and All-
    Nite Grocery, cnr. Soake and Dimwell;
Reginald Lilywhite, a.k.a. Banjo, The Park Lane Bully,
    Have You Seen This Man?, The Goose Gate
    Grabber, The Nap Hill Lurker, Rm 17, YMPA.'

'YMPA?'

'It's what we generally call the Young-Men's-
Reformed-Cultists-of-the-Ichor-God-Bel-Shamha-
roth-Association,' said Susan. 'Does that sound to
you like someone who'd expect a visit from a
tooth fairy?'

'No.'

'Me neither. He sounds like someone who'd
expect a visit from the Watch.'

Susan looked around. It really was a crummy
room, the sort rented by someone who probably
took it never intending to stay long, the sort
where walking across the floor in the middle of
the night would be accompanied by the crack
of cockroaches in a death flamenco. It was

amazing how many people spent their whole lives in places where they never intended to stay.

Cheap, narrow bed, crumbling plaster, tiny window—

She opened the window and fished around below the ledge, and felt satisfied when her questing fingers closed on a piece of string which was attached to an oilcloth bag. She hauled it in.

'What's that?' said the oh god, as she opened it on the table.

'Oh, you see them a lot,' said Susan, taking out some packages wrapped in second-hand waxed paper. 'You live alone, mice and roaches eat everything, there's nowhere to store food – but outside the window it's cold and safe. More or less safe. It's an old trick. Now . . . look at this. Leathery bacon, a green loaf and a bit of cheese you could shave. She hasn't been back home for some time, believe me.'

'Oh dear. What now?'

'Where would she take the teeth?' said Susan, to the world in general but mainly to herself. 'What the hell does the Tooth Fairy *do* with—'

There was a knock at the door. Susan opened it.

Outside was a small bald man in a long brown coat. He was holding a clipboard and blinked nervously at the sight of her.

'Er . . .' he began.

'Can I help you?' said Susan.

'Er, I saw the light, see. I thought Violet was

in,' said the little man. He twiddled the pencil that was attached to his clipboard by a piece of string. 'Only she's a bit behind with the teeth and there's a bit of money owing and Ernie's cart ain't come back and it's got to go in my report and I come round in case . . . in case she was ill or something, it not being nice being alone and ill at Hogswatch—'

'She's not here,' said Susan.

The man gave her a worried look and shook his head sadly.

'There's nearly thirteen dollars in pillow money, see. I'll have to report it.'

'Who to?'

'It has to go higher up, see. I just hope it's not going to be like that business in Quirm where the girl started robbing houses. We never heard the end of that one—'

'Report to who?'

'And there's the ladder and the pliers,' the man went on, in a litany against a world that had no understanding of what it meant to have to fill in an AF17 report in triplicate. 'How can I keep track of stocktaking if people go around taking stock?' He shook his head. 'I dunno, they get the job, they think it's all nice sunny nights, they get a bit of sharp weather and suddenly it's goodbye Charlie I'm off to be a waitress in the warm. And then there's Ernie. I know him. It's a nip to keep out the cold, and then another one to keep it company, and then a third in case the other two get lost . . . It's all going to have to go down in

257

my report, you know, and who's going to get the blame? I'll tell you—'

'It's going to be you, isn't it?' said Susan. She was almost hypnotized. The man even had a fringe of worried hair and a small, worried moustache. And the voice suggested exactly that here was a man who, at the end of the world, would worry that it would be blamed on him.

'That's *right*,' he said, but in a slightly grudging voice. He was not about to allow a bit of understanding to lighten his day. 'And the girls all go on about the job but I tell them they've got it easy, it's just basic'ly ladder work, they don't have to spend their evenings knee-deep in paper *and* making shortfalls good out of their own money, I might add—'

'You employ the tooth fairies?' said Susan quickly. The oh god was still vertical but his eyes had glazed over.

The little man preened slightly. '*Sort* of,' he said. 'Basic'ly I run Bulk Collection and Despatch—'

'Where to?'

He stared at her. Sharp, direct questions weren't his forte.

'I just sees to it they gets on the cart,' he mumbled. 'When they're on the cart and Ernie's signed the GV19 for 'em, that's it done and finished, only like I said he ain't turned up this week and—'

'A whole cart for a handful of teeth?'

'Well, there's the food for the guards, and –

'ere, who are you, anyway? What're you doing here?'

Susan straightened up. 'I don't have to put up with this,' she said sweetly, to no one in particular. She leaned forward again.

'WHAT CART ARE WE TALKING ABOUT HERE, CHARLIE?' The oh god jolted away. The man in the brown coat shot backwards and splayed against the corridor wall as Susan advanced.

'Comes Tuesdays,' he panted. ' 'ere, what—'

'AND WHERE DOES IT GO?'

'Dunno! Like I said, when he's—'

'Signed the GV19 for them it's you done and finished,' said Susan, in her normal voice. 'Yes. You said. What's Violet's full name? She never mentioned it.'

The man hesitated.

'I SAID—'

'Violet Bottler!'

'Thank you.'

'An' Ernie's gorn too,' said Charlie, continuing more or less on auto-pilot. 'I call that suspicious. I mean, he's got a wife and everything. Won't be the first man to get his head turned by thirteen dollars and a pretty ankle and, o' course, no one thinks about muggins who has to carry the can, I mean, supposing we was all to get it in our heads to run off with young wimmin?'

He gave Susan the stern look of one who, if it was not for the fact that the world needed him, would even now be tiring of painting naked young ladies on some tropical island somewhere.

259

'What happens to the teeth?' said Susan.

He blinked at her. A bully, thought Susan. A very small, weak, very *dull* bully, who doesn't manage any real bullying because there's hardly anyone smaller and weaker than him, so he just makes everyone's lives just that little bit more difficult . . .

'What sort of question is that?' he managed, in the face of her stare.

'You never wondered?' said Susan, and added to herself, *I didn't. Did anyone?*

'Well, 's not my job, I just—'

'Oh, yes. You said,' said Susan. 'Thank you. You've been very helpful. Thank you very much.'

The man stared at her, and then turned and ran down the stairs.

'Drat,' said Susan.

'That's a very unusual swearword,' said the oh god nervously.

'It's *so* easy,' said Susan. 'If I want to, I can find *anybody*. It's a family trait.'

'Oh. Good.'

'No. Have you any *idea* how hard it is to be normal? The things you have to remember? How to go to sleep? How to forget things? What doorknobs are for?'

Why ask him, she thought, as she looked at his shocked face. All that's normal for *him* is remembering to throw up what someone else drank.

'Oh, come on,' she said, and hurried towards the stairs.

It was so easy to slip into immortality, to ride

the horse, to know everything. And every time you did, it brought closer the day when you could never get off and never forget.

Death *was* hereditary.

You got it from your ancestors.

'Where are we going now?' said the oh god.

'Down to the YMPA,' said Susan.

The old man in the hovel looked uncertainly at the feast spread in front of him. He sat on his stool as curled up on himself as a spider in a flame.

'I'd got a bit of a mess of beans cooking,' he mumbled, looking at his visitors through filmy eyes.

'Good heavens, you can't eat *beans* at Hogswatch,' said the king, smiling hugely. 'That's terribly unlucky, eating beans at Hogswatch. My word, yes!'

'Di'nt know that,' the old man said, looking down desperately at his lap.

'*We've* brought you this *magnificent* spread. Don't you think so?'

'I bet you're incredibly grateful for it, too,' said the page, sharply.

'Yes, well, o' course, it's very kind of you gennelmen,' said the old man, in a voice the size of a mouse. He blinked, uncertain of what to do next.

'The turkey's hardly been touched, still *plenty* of meat on it,' said the king. 'And do have some of this *cracking* good widgeon stuffed with swan's liver.'

'—only I'm partial to a bowl of beans and I've never been beholden to no one nor nobody,' the old man said, still staring at his lap.

'Good heavens, man, you don't need to worry about *that*,' said the king heartily. 'It's Hogswatch! I was only just now looking out of the window and I saw you plodding through the snow and I said to young Jermain here, I said, "Who's that chappie?" and he said, "Oh, he's some peasant fellow who lives up by the forest," and I said, "Well, I couldn't eat another thing and it's Hogswatch, after all," and so we just bundled everything up and here we are!'

'And I expect you're pathetically thankful,' said the page. 'I expect we've brought a ray of light into your dark tunnel of a life, hmm?'

'—yes, well, o' course, only I'd been savin' 'em for weeks, see, and there's some bakin' potatoes under the fire, I found 'em in the cellar 'n' the mice'd hardly touched 'em.' The old man never raised his eyes from knee level. ' 'n' our dad brought me up never to ask for—'

'Listen,' said the king, raising his voice a little, 'I've walked *miles* tonight and I bet you've never seen food like this in your whole life, eh?'

Tears of humiliated embarrassment were rolling down the old man's face.

'—well, I'm sure it's very kind of you fine gennelmen but I ain't sure I knows how to eat swans and suchlike, but if you want a bit o' my beans you've only got to say—'

'Let me make myself *absolutely* clear,' said the king sharply. 'This is some genuine Hogswatch charity, d'you understand? And we're going to sit here and watch the smile on your grubby but honest face, is that understood?'

'And what do you say to the good king?' the page prompted.

The peasant hung his head.

' 'nk you.'

'Right,' said the king, sitting back. 'Now, pick up your fork—'

The door burst open. An indistinct figure strode into the room, snow swirling around it in a cloud.

WHAT'S GOING ON HERE?

The page started to stand up, drawing his sword. He never worked out how the *other* figure could have got behind him, but there it was, pressing him gently down again.

'Hello, son, my name is Albert,' said a voice by his ear. 'Why don't you put that sword back very slowly? People might get hurt.'

A finger prodded the king, who had been too shocked to move.

WHAT DO YOU THINK YOU ARE DOING, SIRE?

The king tried to focus on the figure. There was an impression of red and white, but black, too.

To Albert's secret amazement, the man managed to get to his feet and draw himself up as regally as he could.

'What is going on here, whoever you are, is some fine old Hogswatch charity! And who—'

NO, IT'S NOT.

'What? How dare you—'

WERE YOU HERE LAST MONTH? WILL YOU BE HERE NEXT WEEK? NO. BUT TONIGHT YOU WANTED TO FEEL ALL WARM INSIDE. TONIGHT YOU WILL WANT THEM TO SAY: WHAT A GOOD KING HE IS.

'Oh, no, he's going too far again—' muttered Albert under his breath. He pushed the page down again. 'No, you stay still, sonny. Else you'll just be a paragraph.'

'Whatever it is, it's more than he's got!' snapped the king. 'And all we've had from him is ingratitude—'

YES, THAT DOES SPOIL IT, DOESN'T IT? Death leaned forward. GO AWAY.

To the king's own surprise his body took over and marched him out of the door.

Albert patted the page on the shoulder. 'And you can run along too,' he said.

'—I didn't mean to go upsetting anyone, it's just that I never asked no one for nothing—' mumbled the old man, in a small humble world of his own, his hands tangling themselves together out of nervousness.

'Best if you leave this one to me, master, if you don't mind,' said Albert. 'I'll be back in just a tick.' Loose ends, he thought, that's my job. Tying up loose ends. The master never thinks things through.

He caught up with the king outside.

'Ah, there you are, your sire,' he said. 'Just before you go, won't keep you a minute, just a minor point—' Albert leaned close to the stunned monarch. 'If anyone was thinking about making a mistake, you know, like maybe sending the guards down here tomorrow, tipping the old man out of his hovel, chuckin' him in prison, anything like that . . . werrlll . . . that's the kind of mistake he ought to treasure on account of it being the last mistake he'll ever make. A word to the wise men, right?' He tapped the side of his nose conspiratorially. 'Happy Hogswatch.'

Then he hurried back into the hovel.

The feast had vanished. The old man was looking blearily at the bare table.

HALF-EATEN LEAVINGS, said Death. WE COULD CERTAINLY DO BETTER THAN THIS. He reached into the sack.

Albert grabbed his arm before he could withdraw his hand.

'Mind taking a bit of advice, master? I was brung up in a place like this.'

DOES IT BRING TEARS TO YOUR EYES?

'A box of matches to me hand, more like. Listen . . .'

The old man was only dimly aware of some whispering. He sat hunched up, staring at nothing.

WELL, IF YOU ARE SURE . . .

'Been there, done that, chewed the bones,' said Albert. 'Charity ain't giving people what you wants to give, it's giving people what they need to get.'

VERY WELL.

Death reached into the sack again.

HAPPY HOGSWATCH. HO. HO. HO.

There was a string of sausages. There was a side of bacon. And a small tub of salt pork. And a mass of chitterlings wrapped up in greased paper. There was a black pudding. There were several other tubs of disgusting yet savoury pork-adjacent items highly prized in any pig-based economy. And, laid on the table with a soft thump, there was—

'A pig's head,' breathed the old man. 'A *whole* one! Ain't had brawn in years! And a basin of pig knuckles! And a bowl of pork dripping!'

HO. HO. HO.

'Amazing,' said Albert. 'How did you get the head's expression to look like the king?'

I THINK THAT'S ACCIDENTAL.

Albert patted the old man on the back.

'Have yourself a ball,' he said. 'In fact, have two. Now I think we ought to be going, master.'

They left the old man staring at the laden board.

WASN'T THAT NICE? said Death, as the hogs accelerated.

'Oh, yes,' said Albert, shaking his head. 'Poor old devil. Beans at Hogswatch? Unlucky, that. Not a night for a man to find a bean in his bowl.'

I FEEL I WAS CUT OUT FOR THIS SORT OF THING, YOU KNOW.

'Really, master?'

IT'S NICE TO DO A JOB WHERE PEOPLE LOOK FORWARD TO SEEING YOU.

'Ah,' said Albert glumly.

THEY DON'T NORMALLY LOOK FORWARD TO SEEING ME.

'Yes, I expect so.'

EXCEPT IN SPECIAL AND RATHER UNFORTUNATE CIRCUMSTANCES.

'Right, right.'

AND THEY SELDOM LEAVE A GLASS OF SHERRY OUT.

'I expect they don't, no.'

I COULD GET INTO THE HABIT OF DOING THIS, IN FACT.

'But you won't need to, will you, master?' said Albert hurriedly, with the horrible prospect of being a permanent Pixie Albert looming in his mind again. 'Because we'll get the Hogfather back, right? That's what you *said* we were going to do, right? And young Susan's probably bustling around . . .'

YES. OF COURSE.

'Not that you asked her to, of course.'

Albert's jittery ears didn't detect any enthusiasm.

Oh dear, he thought.

I HAVE ALWAYS CHOSEN THE PATH OF DUTY.

'Right, master.'

The sleigh sped on.

I AM THOROUGHLY IN CONTROL AND FIRM OF PURPOSE.

'No problem there, then, master,' said Albert.

NO NEED TO WORRY AT ALL.

'Pleased to hear it, master.'

IF I HAD A FIRST NAME, 'DUTY' WOULD BE MY MIDDLE NAME.

'Good.'

NEVERTHELESS . . .

Albert strained his ears and thought he heard, just on the edge of hearing, a voice whisper sadly.

HO. HO. HO.

There was a party going on. It seemed to occupy the entire building.

'Certainly very energetic young men,' said the oh god carefully, stepping over a wet towel. 'Are women allowed in here?'

'No,' said Susan. She stepped through a wall into the superintendent's office.

A group of young men went past, man-handling a barrel of beer.

'You'll feel bad about it in the morning,' said Bilious. 'Strong drink is a mocker, you know.'

They set it up on a table and knocked out the bung.

'Someone's going to have to be sick after all that,' he said, raising his voice above the hubbub. 'I hope you realize that. You think it's clever, do you, reducing yourself to the level of the beasts of the field . . . er . . . or the level they'd sink to if they drank, I mean.'

They moved away, leaving one mug of beer by the barrel.

The oh god glanced at it, and picked it up and sniffed at it.

'Ugh.'

Susan stepped out of the wall.

'He hasn't been back for— What're you doing?'

'I thought I'd see what beer tastes like,' said the oh god guiltily.

'*You* don't know what beer tastes like?'

'Not on the way *down*, no. It's . . . quite different by the time it gets to me,' he said sourly. He took another sip, and then a longer one. 'I can't see what all the fuss is about,' he added.

He tipped up the empty pot.

'I suppose it comes out of this tap here,' he said. 'You know, for once in my existence I'd like to get drunk.'

'Aren't you always?' said Susan, who wasn't really paying attention.

'No. I've always *been* drunk. I'm sure I explained.'

'He's been gone a couple of days,' said Susan. 'That's odd. And he didn't say where he was going. The last night he was here was the night he was on Violet's list. But he paid for his room for the week, and I've got the number.'

'And the key?' said the oh god.

'What a strange idea.'

Mr Lilywhite's room was small. That wasn't surprising. What was surprising was how neat it was, how carefully the little bed had been made, how well the floor had been swept. It was hard to imagine anyone living in it, but there were a few signs. On the simple table by the bed was a small, rather crude portrait of a bulldog in a wig, although on closer inspection it might have been a woman. This tentative hypothesis was borne out by the inscription 'To a Good Boy, from his Mother' on the back.

A book lay next to it. Susan wondered what kind of reading someone with Mr Banjo's background would buy.

It turned out to be a book of six pages, one of those that were supposed to enthral children with the magic of the printed word by pointing out that they could See Spot Run.

There were no more than ten words on each page and yet, carefully placed between pages four and five, was a bookmark.

She turned back to the cover. The book was called *Happy Tales*. There was a blue sky and trees and a couple of impossibly pink children playing with a jolly-looking dog.

It looked as though it had been read frequently, if slowly.

And that was it.

A dead end.

No. Perhaps not . . .

On the floor by the bed, as if it had been accidentally dropped, was a small, silvery half-dollar piece.

Susan picked it up and tossed it idly. She looked the oh god up and down. He was swilling a mouthful of beer from cheek to cheek and looking thoughtfully at the ceiling.

She wondered about his likelihood of survival incarnate in Ankh-Morpork at Hogswatch, especially if the cure wore off. After all, the only purpose of his existence was to have a headache and throw up. There were not a great many post-graduate jobs for which these were the main qualifications.

'Tell me,' she said. 'Have you ever ridden a horse?'

'I don't know. What's a horse?'

In the depths of the library of Death, a squeaking noise.

It was not loud, but it appeared louder than mere decibels would suggest in the furtive, scribbling hush of the books.

Everyone, it is said, has a book inside them. In this library, everyone was inside a book.

The squeaking got louder. It had a rhythmical, circular quality.

Book on book, shelf on shelf . . . and in every one, at the page of the ever-moving now, a scribble of handwriting following the narrative of every life . . .

The squeaking came round the corner.

It was issuing from what looked like a very rickety edifice, several storeys high. It looked rather like a siege tower, open at the sides. At the base, between the wheels, was a pair of geared treadles which moved the whole thing.

Susan clung to the railing of the topmost platform.

'Can't you hurry up?' she said. 'We're only at the Bi's at the moment.'

'I've been pedalling for ages!' panted the oh god.

'Well, "A" is a very popular letter.'

Susan stared up at the shelves. A was for Anon, among other things. All those people who, for one reason or another, never officially got a name.

They tended to be short books.

'Ah . . . Bo . . . Bod . . . Bog . . . turn left . . .'

The library tower squeaked ponderously around the next corner.

'Ah, Bo . . . blast, the Bots are at least twenty shelves up.'

'Oh, how nice,' said the oh god grimly.

He heaved on the lever that moved the drive chain from one sprocket to another, and started to pedal again.

Very ponderously, the creaking tower began to telescope upwards.

'Right, we're there,' Susan shouted down, after a few minutes of slow rise. 'Here's . . . let's see . . . Aabana Bottler . . .'

'I expect Violet will be a lot further,' said the oh god, trying out irony.

'Onwards!'

Swaying a little, the tower headed down the Bs until:

'Stop!'

It rocked as the oh god kicked the brake block against a wheel.

'I think this is her,' said a voice from above. 'OK, you can lower away.'

A big wheel with ponderous lead weights on it spun slowly as the tower concertina'd back, creaking and grinding. Susan climbed down the last few feet.

'*Everyone*'s in here?' said the oh god, as she thumbed through the pages.

'Yes.'

'Even gods?'

'Anything that's alive and self-aware,' said Susan, not looking up. 'This is . . . odd. It looks as though she's in some sort of . . . prison. Who'd want to lock up a tooth fairy?'

'Someone with very sensitive teeth?'

Susan flicked back a few pages. 'It's all . . . hoods over her head and people carrying her and so on. But . . .' she turned a page '. . . it says the last job she did was on Banjo and . . . yes, she got the tooth . . . and then she felt as though someone was behind her and . . . there's a ride on a cart . . . and the hood's come off . . . and there's a causeway . . . and . . .'

'All that's in a *book*?'

'The autobiography. Everyone has one. It writes down your life as you go along.'

'I've got one?'

'I expect so.'

'Oh, dear. "Got up, was sick, wanted to die." Not a gripping read, really.'

Susan turned the page.

'A tower,' she said. 'She's in a tower. From

273

what she saw, it was tall and white inside . . . but not outside? It didn't look real. There were apple trees around it, but the trees, the trees didn't look right. And a river, but that wasn't right either. There were goldfish in it . . . but they were on *top* of the water.'

'Ah. Pollution,' said the oh god.

'I don't think so. It says here she saw them swimming.'

'Swimming on top of the water?'

'That's how she thinks she saw it.'

'Really? You don't think she'd been eating any of that mouldy cheese, do you?'

'And there was blue sky but . . . she must have got this wrong . . . it says here there was only blue sky *above* . . .'

'Yep. Best place for the sky,' said the oh god. 'Sky underneath you, that probably means trouble.'

Susan flicked a page back and forth. 'She means . . . sky overhead but not around the edges, I think. No sky on the horizon.'

'Excuse me,' said the oh god. 'I'm not long in this world, I appreciate that, but I think you have to have sky on the horizon. That's how you can tell it's the horizon.'

A sense of familiarity was creeping up on Susan, but surreptitiously, dodging behind things whenever she tried to concentrate on it.

'I've *seen* this place,' she said, tapping the page. 'If only she'd looked harder at the trees . . . She says they've got brown trunks and green leaves

and it says here she thought they were odd. And
. . .' She concentrated on the next paragraph.
'Flowers. Growing in the grass. With big round
petals.'

She stared unseeing at the oh god again.

'This isn't a proper landscape,' she said.

'It doesn't sound too unreal to me,' said the oh
god. 'Sky. Trees. Flowers. Dead fish.'

'*Brown* tree trunks? Really they're mostly a sort
of greyish mossy colour. You only ever see brown
tree trunks in one place,' said Susan. 'And it's the
same place where the sky is only ever overhead.
The blue never comes down to the ground.'

She looked up. At the far end of the corridor
was one of the very tall, very thin windows. It
looked out on to the black gardens. Black bushes,
black grass, black trees. Skeletal fish cruising in
the black waters of a pool, under black water
lilies.

There was colour, in a sense, but it was
the kind of colour you'd get if you could shine
a beam of black through a prism. There were
hints of tints, here and there a black you
might persuade yourself was a very deep purple
or a midnight blue. But it was basically black,
under a black sky, because this was the world
belonging to Death and that was all there was
to it.

The shape of Death was the shape people had
created for him, over the centuries. Why bony?
Because bones were associated with death. He'd
got a scythe because agricultural people could

spot a decent metaphor. And he lived in a sombre land because the human imagination would be rather stretched to let him live somewhere nice with flowers.

People like Death lived in the human imagination, and got their shape there, too. He wasn't the only one . . .

. . . but he didn't like the script, did he? He'd started to take an interest in people. Was that a thought, or just a memory of something that hadn't happened yet?

The oh god followed her gaze.

'Can we go after her?' said the oh god. 'I say *we*, I think I've just got drafted in because I was in the wrong place.'

'She's alive. That means she is mortal,' said Susan. 'That means I can find her, too.' She turned and started to walk out of the library.

'If she says the sky is just blue overhead, what's between it and the horizon?' said the oh god, running to keep up.

'You don't *have* to come,' said Susan. 'It's not your problem.'

'Yes, but given that my problem is that my whole purpose in life is to feel rotten, anything's an improvement.'

'It could be dangerous. I don't think she's there of her own free will. Would you be any good in a fight?'

'Yes. I could be sick on people.'

*   *   *

It was a shack, somewhere out on the outskirts of the Plains town of Scrote. Scrote had a lot of outskirts, spread so widely – a busted cart here, a dead dog there – that often people went through it without even knowing it was there, and really it only appeared on the maps because cartographers get embarrassed about big empty spaces.

Hogswatch came after the excitement of the cabbage harvest when it was pretty quiet in Scrote and there was nothing much to look forward to until the fun of the sprout festival.

This shack had an iron stove, with a pipe that went up through the thick cabbage-leaf thatch.

Voices echoed faintly within the pipe.

THIS IS REALLY, REALLY STUPID.

'I think the tradition got started when everyone had them big chimneys, master.' *This* voice sounded as though it was coming from someone standing on the roof and shouting down the pipe.

INDEED? IT'S ONLY A MERCY IT'S UNLIT.

There was some muffled scratching and banging, and then a thump from within the pot belly of the stove.

DAMN.

'What's up, master?'

THE DOOR HAS NO HANDLE ON THE INSIDE. I CALL THAT INCONSIDERATE.

There were some more bumps, and then a scrape as the stove lid was lifted up and pushed sideways. An arm came out and felt around the front of the stove until it found the handle.

It played with it for a while, but it was obvious that the hand did not belong to a person used to opening things.

In short, Death came out of the stove. Exactly how would be difficult to describe without folding the page. Time and space were, from Death's point of view, merely things that he'd heard described. When it came to Death, they ticked the box marked Not Applicable. It might help to think of the universe as a rubber sheet, or perhaps not.

'Let us in, master,' a pitiful voice echoed down from the roof. 'It's brass monkeys out here.'

Death went over to the door. Snow was blowing underneath it. He peered nervously at the woodwork. There was a thump outside and Albert's voice sounded a lot closer.

'What's up, master?'

Death stuck his head through the wood of the door.

THERE'S THESE METAL THINGS—

'Bolts, master. You slide them,' said Albert, sticking his hands under his armpits to keep them warm.

AH.

Death's head disappeared. Albert stamped his feet and watched his breath cloud in the air while he listened to the pathetic scrabbling on the other side of the door.

Death's head appeared again.

ER . . .

'It's the latch, master,' said Albert wearily.

RIGHT. RIGHT.

'You put your thumb on it and push it down.'

RIGHT.

The head disappeared. Albert jumped up and down a bit, and waited.

The head appeared.

ER . . . I WAS WITH YOU UP TO THE THUMB . . .

Albert sighed. 'And then you press down and pull, master.'

AH. RIGHT. GOT YOU.

The head disappeared.

Oh dear, thought Albert. He just can't get the hang of them, can he . . . ?

The door jerked open. Death stood behind it, beaming proudly, as Albert staggered in, snow blowing in with him.

'Blimey, it's getting really parky,' said Albert. 'Any sherry?' he added hopefully.

IT APPEARS NOT.

Death looked at the sock hooked on to the side of the stove. It had a hole in it.

A letter, in erratic handwriting, was attached to it. Death picked it up.

THE BOY WANTS A PAIR OF TROUSERS THAT HE DOESN'T HAVE TO SHARE, A HUGE MEAT PIE, A SUGAR MOUSE, 'A LOT OF TOYS' AND A PUPPY CALLED SCRUFF.

'Ah, sweet,' said Albert. 'I shall wipe away a tear, 'cos what he's *gettin'*, see, is this little wooden toy and an apple.' He held them out.

BUT THE LETTER CLEARLY—

'Yes, well, it's socio-economic factors again,

right?' said Albert. 'The world'd be in a right mess if everyone got what they asked for, eh?'

I GAVE THEM WHAT THEY WANTED IN THE STORE . . .

'Yeah, and that's gonna cause a *lot* of trouble, master. All them "toy pigs that really work". I didn't say nothing 'cos it was getting the job done but you can't go on like that. What good's a god who gives you everything you want?'

YOU HAVE ME THERE.

'It's the *hope* that's important. Big part of belief, hope. Give people jam today and they'll just sit and eat it. Jam tomorrow, now – that'll keep them going for ever.'

AND YOU MEAN THAT BECAUSE OF THIS THE POOR GET POOR THINGS AND THE RICH GET RICH THINGS?

' 's right,' said Albert. 'That's the meaning of Hogswatch.'

Death nearly wailed.

BUT I'M THE HOGFATHER! He looked embarrassed. AT THE MOMENT, I MEAN.

'Makes no difference,' said Albert, shrugging. 'I remember when I was a nipper, one Hogswatch I had my heart set on this huge model horse they had in the shop . . .' His face creased for a moment in a grim smile of recollection. 'I remember I spent *hours* one day, cold as charity the weather was, I spent *hours* with my nose pressed up against the window . . . until they heard me callin', and unfroze me. I saw them take it out of the window, someone was in there buying it, and, y'know, just for a second I thought it really was going to be for me . . . Oh. I *dreamed* of that toy horse. It were red and white with a real saddle and everything. And rockers. I'd've *killed* for that horse.' He shrugged again. 'Not a chance, of course, 'cos we didn't have a pot to piss in and we even 'ad to spit on the bread to make it soft enough to eat—'

PLEASE ENLIGHTEN ME. WHAT IS SO IMPORTANT ABOUT HAVING A POT TO PISS IN?

'It's . . . it's more like a figure of speech, master. It means you're as poor as a church mouse.'

ARE THEY POOR?

'Well . . . yeah.'

BUT SURELY NOT MORE POOR THAN ANY OTHER MOUSE? AND, AFTER ALL, THERE TEND TO BE LOTS OF CANDLES AND THINGS THEY COULD EAT.

'Figure of speech again, master. It doesn't have to make sense.'

OH. I SEE. DO CARRY ON.

'O' course, I still hung up my stocking on Hogswatch Eve, and in the morning, you know, you know what? Our dad had put in this little horse he'd carved his very own self . . .'

AH, said Death. AND THAT WAS WORTH MORE THAN ALL THE EXPENSIVE TOY HORSES IN THE WORLD, EH?

Albert gave him a beady look. 'No!' he said. 'It *weren't*. All I could think of was it wasn't the big horse in the window.'

Death looked shocked.

BUT HOW MUCH BETTER TO HAVE A TOY CARVED WITH—

'No. Only grown-ups think like that,' said

Albert. 'You're a selfish little bugger when you're seven. Anyway, Dad got ratted after lunch and trod on it.'

LUNCH?

'All right, mebbe we had a bit of pork dripping for the bread . . .'

EVEN SO, THE SPIRIT OF HOGSWATCH—

Albert sighed. 'If you like, master. If you like.' Death looked perturbed.

BUT SUPPOSING THE HOGFATHER HAD BROUGHT YOU THE WONDERFUL HORSE—

'Oh, Dad would've flogged it for a couple of bottles,' said Albert.

BUT WE HAVE BEEN INTO HOUSES WHERE THE CHILDREN HAD MANY TOYS AND BROUGHT THEM EVEN *MORE* TOYS, AND IN HOUSES LIKE THIS THE CHILDREN GET PRACTICALLY NOTHING.

'Huh, we'd have given *anything* to get *practically* nothing when I were a lad,' said Albert.

BE HAPPY WITH WHAT YOU'VE GOT, IS THAT THE IDEA?

'That's about the size of it, master. A good god line, that. Don't give 'em too much and tell 'em to be happy with it. Jam tomorrow, see.'

THIS IS WRONG. Death hesitated. I MEAN . . . IT'S *RIGHT* TO BE HAPPY WITH WHAT YOU'VE GOT. BUT YOU'VE GOT TO HAVE SOMETHING TO BE HAPPY ABOUT HAVING. THERE'S NO POINT IN BEING HAPPY ABOUT HAVING NOTHING.

Albert felt a bit out of his depth in this new tide of social philosophy.

'Dunno,' he said. 'I suppose people'd say

they've got the moon and the stars and suchlike.'

I'M SURE THEY WOULDN'T BE ABLE TO PRODUCE THE PAPERWORK.

'All I know is, if Dad'd caught *us* with a big bag of pricey toys we'd just have got a ding round the earhole for nicking 'em.'

IT IS . . . UNFAIR.

'That's life, master.'

BUT I'M NOT.

'I meant this is how it's supposed to go, master,' said Albert.

NO. YOU MEAN THIS IS HOW IT GOES.

Albert leaned against the stove and rolled himself one of his horrible thin cigarettes. It was best to let the master work his own way through these things. He got over them eventually. It was like that business with the violin. For three days there was nothing but twangs and broken strings, and then he'd never touched the thing again. That was the trouble, really. Everything the master did *was* a bit like that. When things got into his head you just had to wait until they leaked out again.

He'd thought that Hogswatch was all . . . plum pudding and brandy and ho ho ho and he didn't have the kind of mind that could ignore all the other stuff. And so it hurt him.

IT IS HOGSWATCH, said Death, AND PEOPLE DIE ON THE STREETS. PEOPLE FEAST BEHIND LIGHTED WINDOWS AND OTHER PEOPLE HAVE NO HOMES. IS THIS FAIR?

'Well, of course, that's the big issue—' Albert began.

THE PEASANT HAD A HANDFUL OF BEANS AND THE KING HAD SO MUCH HE WOULD NOT EVEN NOTICE THAT WHICH HE GAVE AWAY. IS THIS FAIR?

'Yeah, but if you gave it all to the peasant then in a year or two he'd be just as snooty as the king—' began Albert, jaundiced observer of human nature.

NAUGHTY AND NICE? said Death. BUT IT'S *EASY* TO BE NICE IF YOU'RE RICH. IS THIS FAIR?

Albert wanted to argue. He wanted to say, Really? In that case, how come so many of the rich buggers is bastards? And being poor don't mean being naughty, neither. We was poor when I were a kid, but we was honest. Well, more stupid than honest, to tell the truth. But basically honest.

He didn't argue, though. The master wasn't in any mood for it. He always did what needed to be done.

'You *did* say we just had to do this so's people'd believe—' he began, and then stopped and started again. 'When it comes to *fair*, master, you yourself—'

I AM EVEN-HANDED TO RICH AND POOR ALIKE, snapped Death. BUT THIS SHOULD NOT BE A SAD TIME. THIS IS SUPPOSED TO BE THE SEASON TO BE JOLLY. He wrapped his red robe around him. AND OTHER THINGS ENDING IN OLLY, he added.

'There's no blade,' said the oh god. 'It's just a sword hilt.'

Susan stepped out of the light and her wrist moved. A sparkling blue line flashed in the air, for a moment outlining an edge too thin to be seen.

The oh god backed away.

'What's *that*?'

'Oh, it cuts tiny bits of the air in half. It can cut the soul away from the body, so stand back, please.'

'Oh, I will, I will.'

Susan fished the black scabbard out of the umbrella stand.

Umbrella stand! It never rained here, but Death had an umbrella stand. Practically no one else Susan knew had an umbrella stand. In any list of useful furniture, the one found at the bottom would be the umbrella stand.

Death lived in a black world, where nothing was alive and everything was dark and his great library only had dust and cobwebs because he'd created them for effect and there was never any sun in the sky and the air never moved and he had an umbrella stand. And a pair of silver-backed hairbrushes by his bed. He wanted to be something more than just a bony apparition. He tried to create these flashes of personality but somehow they betrayed themselves, they tried too hard, like an adolescent boy going out wearing an aftershave called 'Rampant'.

Grandfather *always* got things wrong. He saw life from outside and never quite understood.

'That looks dangerous,' said the oh god.

285

Susan sheathed the sword.

'I hope so,' she said.

'Er . . . where are we going? Exactly?'

'Somewhere under an overhead sky,' said Susan. 'And . . . I've seen it before. Recently. I *know* the place.'

They walked out to the stable yard. Binky was waiting.

'I said you don't have to come,' said Susan, grasping the saddle. 'I mean, you're a . . . an innocent bystander.'

'But I'm a god of hangovers who's been cured of hangovers,' said the oh god. 'I haven't really got any function at all.'

He looked so forlorn when he said this that she relented.

'All right. Come on, then.'

She pulled him up behind her.

'Just hang on,' she said. And then she said, 'Hang on somewhere differently, I mean.'

'I'm sorry, was that a problem?' said the oh god, shifting his grip.

'It might take too long to explain and you probably don't know all the words. Around the *waist*, please.'

Susan took out Violet's hourglass and held it up. There was a lot of sand left to run, but she couldn't be certain that was a good sign.

All she could be certain of was that the horse of Death could go anywhere.

* * *

The sound of Hex's quill as it scrabbled across the paper was like a frantic spider trapped in a matchbox.

Despite his dislike of what was going on, there was a part of Ponder Stibbons that was very, very impressed.

In the past, when Hex had been recalcitrant about its calculations, when it had got into a mechanical sulk and had started writing things like '+++ Out of Cheese Error +++' and '+++ Redo From Start +++' Ponder had tried to sort things out calmly and logically.

It had never, ever occurred to him to contemplate hitting Hex with a mallet. But this was, in fact, what Ridcully was threatening to do.

What was *impressive*, and also more than a little worrying, was that Hex seemed to understand the concept.

'Right,' said Ridcully, putting the mallet aside. 'Let's have no more of this "Insufficient dates" business, shall we? There's boxes of the damn things back in the Great Hall. You can have the lot as far as I'm concerned—'

'It's *data*, not dates,' said Ponder helpfully.

'What? You mean like . . . more than dates? Extra sticky?'

'No, no, data is Hex's word for . . . well, facts,' said Ponder.

'Ridiculous way to behave,' said Ridcully brusquely. 'If he's stumped for an answer, why can't he write "You've got me there" or "Damned if I know" or "That's a bit of a puzzler and no mistake"? All this "Insufficient data" business is just pure contrariness, to my mind. It's just swank.' He turned back to Hex. 'Right, you. Hazard a guess.'

The quill started to write '+++ Insuff' and then stopped. After quivering for a moment it went down a line and started again.

+++ This Is Just Calculating Aloud, You Understand +++

'Fair enough,' said Ridcully.

+++ The Amount Of Belief In The World Must Be Subject To An Upper Limit +++

'What an odd question,' said the Dean.

'Sounds sensible,' said Ridcully. 'I suppose people just . . . believe in stuff. Obviously there's a limit to what you can believe in. I've always said so. So what?'

+++ Creatures Have Appeared That Were Once Believed In +++

'Yes. Yes, you could put it like that.'

+++ They Disappeared Because They Were Not Believed In +++

'Seems reasonable,' said Ridcully.

+++ People Were Believing In Something Else – Query? +++

Ridcully looked at the other wizards. They shrugged.

'Could be,' he said guardedly. 'People can only believe in so many things.'

+++ It Follows That If A Major Focus Of Belief Is Removed, There Will Be Spare Belief +++

Ridcully stared at the words.

'You mean . . . sloshing around?'

The big wheel with the ram skulls on it began to turn ponderously. The scurrying ants in the glass tubes took on a new urgency.

'What's happening?' said Ridcully, in a loud whisper.

'I think Hex is looking up the word "sloshing",' said Ponder. 'It may be in long-term storage.'

A large hourglass came down on the spring.

'What's that for?' said Ridcully.

'Er . . . it shows Hex is working things out.'

'Oh. And that buzzing noise? Seems to be coming from the other side of the wall.'

Ponder coughed.

'That *is* the long-term storage, Archchancellor.'

'And how does that work?'

'Er . . . well, if you think of memory as a series of little shelves or, or, or holes, Archchancellor, in which you can put things, well, we found a way of making a sort of memory which, er, interfaces neatly with the ants, in fact, but more importantly can expand its size depending on how much we give it to remember and, er, is possibly a bit slow but—'

'It's a very *loud* buzzing,' said the Dean. 'Is it going wrong?'

'No, that shows it's working,' said Ponder. 'It's, er, beehives.'

He coughed.

'Different types of pollen, different thicknesses of honey, placement of the eggs . . . It's actually

289

amazing how much information you can store on one honeycomb.'

He looked at their faces. 'And it's very secure because anyone trying to tamper with it will get stung to death and Adrian believes that when we shut it down in the summer holidays we should get a nice lot of honey, too.' He coughed again. 'For our . . . sand . . . wiches,' he said.

He felt himself getting smaller and hotter under their gazes.

Hex came to his rescue. The hourglass bounced away and the quill pen was jerked in and out of its inkwell.

+++ Yes. Sloshing Around. Accreting +++

'That means forming around new centres, Archchancellor,' said Ponder helpfully.

'I know *that*,' said Ridcully. 'Blast. Remember when we had all that life force all over the place? A man couldn't call his trousers his own! So . . . there's spare belief sloshing around, thank you, and these little devils are taking advantage of it? Coming back? Household gods?'

+++ This Is Possible +++

'All right, then, so what are people *not* believing in all of a sudden?'

+++ Out Of Cheese Error +++ MELON MELON MELON +++ Redo From Start +++

'Thank you. A simple "I don't know" would have been sufficient,' said Ridcully, sitting back.

'One of the major gods?' said the Chair of Indefinite Studies.

'Hah, we'd soon know about it if one of *those* vanished.'

'It's Hogswatch,' said the Dean. 'I *suppose* the Hogfather is around, is he?'

'You believe in him?' said Ridcully.

'Well, he's for kids, isn't he?' said the Dean. 'But I'm sure *they* all believe in him. *I* certainly did. It wouldn't be Hogswatch when I was a kid without a pillowcase hanging by the fire—'

'A pillowcase?' said the Senior Wrangler, sharply.

'Well, you can't get much in a stocking,' said the Dean.

'Yes, but a whole pillowcase?' the Senior Wrangler insisted.

'Yes. What of it?'

'Is it just me, or is that a rather greedy and selfish way to behave? In *my* family we just hung up very small socks,' said the Senior Wrangler. 'A sugar pig, a toy soldier, a couple of oranges and that was it. Hah, turns out people with whole pillowcases were cornering the market, eh?'

'Shut up and stop squabbling, both of you,' said Ridcully. 'There must be a simple way to check up. How can you tell if the Hogfather exists?'

'Someone's drunk the sherry, there's sooty footprints on the carpet, sleigh tracks on the roof and your pillowcase is full of presents,' said the Dean.

'Hah, *pillowcase*,' said the Senior Wrangler darkly. 'Hah. I expect *your* family were the stuck-up sort that didn't even open their presents until after Hogswatch dinner, eh? One of them with a big snooty Hogswatch tree in the hall?'

'What if—' Ridcully began, but he was too late.

'Well?' said the Dean. 'Of course we waited until after lunch—'

'You know, it really used to wind me *right* up, people with big snooty Hogswatch trees. And I just bet you had one of those swanky fancy nutcrackers like a big thumbscrew,' said the Senior Wrangler. '*Some* people had to make do with the coal hammer out of the outhouse, of course. *And* had dinner in the middle of the day instead of lah-di-dah posh dinner in the evening.'

'I can't help it if my family had money,' said the Dean, and that might have defused things a bit had he not added, 'and standards.'

'And big pillowcases!' shouted the Senior Wrangler, bouncing up and down in rage. '*And* I bet you *bought* your holly, eh?'

The Dean raised his eyebrows. 'Of course! We didn't go creeping around the country pinching it out of other people's hedges, like *some* people did,' he snapped.

'That's traditional! That's part of the fun!'

'Celebrating Hogswatch with stolen greenery?' Ridcully put his hand over his eyes.

The word for this, he had heard, was 'cabin fever'. When people had been cooped up for too long in the dark days of the winter, they always tended to get on one another's nerves, although there was probably a school of thought that would hold that spending your time in a university with more than five thousand known rooms, a huge library, the best kitchens in the city, its own brewery, dairy, extensive wine cellar, laundry, barber shop, cloisters and skittle alley was testing the definition of 'cooped up' a little. Mind you, wizards could get on one another's nerves in opposite corners of a very large field.

'Just shut up, will you?' he said. 'It's Hogswatch! That's *not* the time for silly arguments, all right?'

'Oh, yes it is,' said the Chair of Indefinite Studies glumly. 'It's exactly the time for silly arguments. In our family we were lucky to get through dinner without a reprise of What A Shame Henry Didn't Go Into Business With Our Ron. Or Why Hasn't Anyone Taught Those Kids To Use A Knife? That was another favourite.'

'And the sulks,' said Ponder Stibbons.

'Oh, the sulks,' said the Chair of Indefinite Studies. 'Not a proper Hogswatch without everyone sitting staring at different walls.'

'The games were worse,' said Ponder.

'Worse than the kids hitting one another with their toys, d'you think? Not a proper Hogswatch afternoon without wheels and bits of broken dolly everywhere and everyone whining. Assault and battery included.'

'We had a game called Hunt the Slipper,' said Ponder. 'Someone hid a slipper. And then we had to find it. And then we had a row.'

'It's not *really* bad,' said the Lecturer in Recent

Runes. 'I mean, not proper *Hogswatch* bad, unless everyone's wearing a paper hat. There's always that bit, isn't there, when someone's horrible great-aunt puts on a paper hat and smirks at everyone because she's being so bohemian.'

'I'd forgotten about the paper hats,' said the Chair of Indefinite Studies. 'Oh, dear.'

'And then later on someone'll suggest a board game,' said Ponder.

'That's right. Where no one exactly remembers all the rules.'

'Which doesn't stop someone suggesting that you play for pennies.'

'And five minutes later there's two people not speaking to one another for the rest of their lives because of tuppence.'

'And some horrible little kid—'

'I know, I know! Some little kid who's been allowed to stay up wins everyone's money by being a nasty little cut-throat swot!'

'Right!'

'Er . . .' said Ponder, who rather suspected that he had *been* that child.

'And don't forget the presents,' said the Chair of Indefinite Studies, as if reading off some internal list of gloom. 'How . . . how full of potential they seem in all that paper, how pregnant with possibilities . . . and then you open them and basically the wrapping paper was *more* interesting and you have to say "How thoughtful, that *will* come in handy." It's not better to give than to receive, in my opinion, it's just less embarrassing.'

'I've worked out,' said the Senior Wrangler, 'that over the years I have been a net exporter of Hogswatch presents—'

'Oh, everyone is,' said the Chair. 'You spend a fortune on other people and what you get when all the paper is cleared away is one slipper that's the wrong colour and a book about earwax.'

Ridcully sat in horrified amazement. He'd always enjoyed Hogswatch, every bit of it. He'd enjoyed seeing ancient relatives, he'd enjoyed the food, he'd been *good* at games like Chase My Neighbour Up The Passage and Hooray Jolly Tinker. He was always the first to don a paper hat. He felt that paper hats lent a special festive air to the occasion. And he always very carefully read the messages on Hogswatch cards and found time for a few kind thoughts about the sender.

Listening to his wizards was like watching someone kick apart a doll's house.

'At least the Hogswatch cracker mottoes are fun . . . ?' he ventured.

They all turned to look at him, and then turned away again.

'If you have the sense of humour of a wire coathanger,' said the Senior Wrangler.

'Oh dear,' said Ridcully. 'Then perhaps there *isn't* a Hogfather if all you chaps are sitting around with long faces. He's not the sort to let people go around being miserable!'

'Ridcully, he's just some old winter god,' said the Senior Wrangler wearily. 'He's not the Cheerful Fairy or anything.'

The Lecturer in Recent Runes raised his chin from his hands. 'What Cheerful Fairy?'

'Oh, it's just something my granny used to go on about if it was a wet afternoon and we were getting on her nerves,' said the Senior Wrangler. 'She'd say "I'll call the Cheerful Fairy if you're . . ." ' He stopped, looking guilty.

The Archchancellor held a hand to his ear in a theatrical gesture denoting 'Hush. What was that I heard?'

'Someone tinkled,' he said. 'Thank you, Senior Wrangler.'

'Oh no,' the Senior Wrangler moaned. 'No, no, no!'

They listened for a moment.

'We might have got away with it,' said Ponder. '*I* didn't hear anything . . .'

'Yes, but you can just imagine her, can't you?' said the Dean. 'The moment you said it, I had this picture in my mind. She's going to have a whole bag of word games, for one thing. Or she'll suggest we go outdoors for our health.'

The wizards shuddered. They weren't against the outdoors, it was simply their place in it they objected to.

'Cheerfulness has always got me down,' said the Dean.

'Well, if some wretched little ball of cheerfulness turns up I shan't have it for one,' said the Senior Wrangler, folding his arms. 'I've put up with monsters and trolls and big green things with teeth, so I'm not sitting still for any kind of—'

'Hello!! Hello!!'

The voice was the kind of voice that reads suitable stories to children. Every vowel was beautifully rounded. And they could hear the extra exclamation marks, born of a sort of desperate despairing jollity, slot into place. They turned.

The Cheerful Fairy was quite short and plump in a tweed skirt and shoes so sensible they could do their own tax returns, and was pretty much like the first teacher you get at school, the one who has special training in dealing with nervous incontinence and little boys whose contribution to the wonderful world of sharing consists largely of hitting a small girl repeatedly over the head with a wooden horse. In fact, this picture was helped by the whistle on a string around her neck and a general impression that at any moment she would clap her hands.

The tiny gauzy wings just visible on her back were probably just for show, but the wizards kept on staring at her shoulder.

'Hello—' she said again, but a lot more uncertainly. She gave them a suspicious look. 'You're rather *big* boys,' she said, as if they'd become so in order to spite her. She blinked. 'It's my job to chase those blues away,' she added, apparently following a memorized script. Then she seemed to rally a bit and went on. 'So chins up, everyone, and let's see a lot of bright shining faces!!'

Her gaze met that of the Senior Wrangler, who had probably never had a bright shining face in his entire life. He specialized in dull, sullen ones. The one he was wearing now would have won prizes.

'Excuse me, madam,' said Ridcully. 'But is that a chicken on your shoulder?'

'It's, er, it's, er, it's the Blue Bird of Happiness,' said the Cheerful Fairy. Her voice now had the slightly shaking tone of someone who doesn't quite believe what she has just said but is going to go on saying it anyway, just in case saying it will eventually make it true.

'I beg your pardon, but it is a chicken. A live chicken,' said Ridcully. 'It just went cluck.'

'It *is* blue,' she said hopelessly.

'Well, that at least is true,' Ridcully conceded, as kindly as he could manage. 'Left to myself, I expect I'd have imagined a slightly more *stream-lined* Blue Bird of Happiness, but I can't actually fault you there.'

The Cheerful Fairy coughed nervously and fiddled with the buttons on her sensible woolly jumper.

'How about a nice game to get us all in the mood?' she said. 'A guessing game, perhaps? Or a painting competition? There may be a small prize for the winner.'

'Madam, we're wizards,' said the Senior Wrangler. 'We don't do cheerful.'

'Charades?' said the Cheerful Fairy. 'Or per-haps you've been playing them already? How about a sing-song? Who knows "Row Row Row Your Boat"?'

Her bright little smile hit the group scowl of the assembled wizards. 'We don't want to be Mr Grumpy, do we?' she added hopefully.

'Yes,' said the Senior Wrangler.

The Cheerful Fairy sagged, and then patted frantically at her shapeless sleeves until she tugged out a balled-up handkerchief. She dabbed at her eyes.

'It's all going wrong again, isn't it?' she said, her chin trembling. 'No one ever wants to be cheerful these days, and I really *do* try. I've made a Joke Book and I've got three boxes of clothes for charades and . . . and . . . and whenever I try to cheer people up they all look embarrassed . . . and really I *do* make an effort . . .'

She blew her nose loudly.

Even the Senior Wrangler had the grace to look embarrassed.

'Er . . .' he began.

'Would it hurt anyone just *occasionally* to try to be a *little* bit cheerful?' said the Cheerful Fairy.

'Er . . . in what way?' said the Senior Wrangler, feeling wretched.

'Well, there's so many nice things to be cheerful about,' said the Cheerful Fairy, blowing her nose again.

'Er . . . raindrops and sunsets and that sort of thing?' said the Senior Wrangler, managing some sarcasm, but they could tell his heart wasn't in it. 'Er, would you like to borrow my handkerchief? It's nearly fresh.'

'Why don't you get the lady a nice sherry?'

said Ridcully. 'And some corn for her chicken . . .'

'Oh, I *never* drink alcohol,' said the Cheerful Fairy, horrified.

'Really?' said Ridcully. 'We find it's something to be cheerful about. Mr Stibbons . . . would you be so kind as to step over here for a moment?'

He beckoned him up close.

'There's got to be a lot of belief sloshing around to let *her* be created,' he said. 'She's a good fourteen stone, if I'm any judge. If we wanted to contact the Hogfather, how would we go about it? Letter up chimney?'

'Yes, but not *tonight*, sir,' said Ponder. 'He'll be out delivering.'

'No telling where he'll be, then,' said Ridcully. 'Blast.'

'Of course, he might not have come *here* yet,' said Ponder.

'Why should he come here?' said Ridcully.

The Librarian pulled the blankets over himself and curled up.

As an orang-utan he hankered for the warmth of the rainforest. The problem was that he'd never even *seen* a rainforest, having been turned into an orang-utan when he was already a fully grown human. Something in his bones knew about it, though, and didn't like the cold of winter at all. But he was also a librarian in those same bones and he flatly refused to allow fires to be lit in the library. As a result, pillows and blankets went missing everywhere else in the University and ended up in a sort of cocoon in the reference section, in which the ape lurked during the worst of the winter.

He turned over and wrapped himself in the Bursar's curtains.

There was a creaking outside his nest, and some whispering.

'No, don't light the lamp.'

'I wondered why I hadn't seen him all evening.'

'Oh, he goes to bed early on Hogswatch Eve, sir. Here we are . . .'

There was some rustling.

'We're in luck. It hasn't been filled,' said Ponder. 'Looks like he's used one of the Bursar's.'

'He puts it up every year?'

'Apparently.'

'But it's not as though he's a child. A certain child-like simplicity, perhaps.'

'It might be different for orang-utans, Archchancellor.'

'Do they do it in the jungle, d'you think?'

'I don't imagine so, sir. No chimneys, for one thing.'

'And quite short legs, of course. Extremely under-funded in the sock area, orang-utans. They'd be quids in if they could hang up gloves, of course. Hogfather'd be on double shifts if they could hang up their gloves. On account of the length of their arms.'

'Very good, Archchancellor.'

301

'I say, what's this on the . . . my word, a glass of sherry. Well, waste not, want not.' There was a damp glugging noise in the darkness.

'I think that was supposed to be for the Hogfather, sir.'

'And the banana?'

'I *imagine* that's been left out for the pigs, sir.'

'Pigs?'

'Oh, *you* know, sir. Tusker and Snouter and Gouger and Rooter. I mean,' Ponder stopped, conscious that a grown man shouldn't be able to remember this sort of thing, 'that's what children believe.'

'Bananas for pigs? That's not traditional, is it? I'd have thought acorns, perhaps. Or apples or swedes.'

'Yes, sir, but the Librarian likes bananas, sir.'

'Very nourishin' fruit, Mr Stibbons.'

'Yes, sir. Although, funnily enough it's not actually a fruit, sir.'

'Really?'

'Yes, sir. Botanically, it's a type of fish, sir. According to my theory it's cladistically associated with the Krullian pipefish, sir, which of course is also yellow and goes around in bunches or shoals.'

'And lives in trees?'

'Well, not usually, sir. The banana is obviously exploiting a new niche.'

'Good heavens, really? It's a funny thing, but I've never much liked bananas and I've always been a bit suspicious of fish, too. That'd explain it.'

'Yes, sir.'

'Do they attack swimmers?'

'Not that I've heard, sir. Of course, they may be clever enough to only attack swimmers who're far from land.'

'What, you mean sort of . . . high up? In the trees, as it were?'

'Possibly, sir.'

'Cunning, eh?'

'Yes, sir.'

'Well, we might as well make ourselves comfortable, Mr Stibbons.'

'Yes, sir.'

A match flared in the darkness as Ridcully lit his pipe.

The Ankh-Morpork wassailers had practised for weeks.

The custom was referred to by Anaglypta Huggs, organizer of the best and most select group of the city's singers, as an occasion for fellowship and good cheer.

One should always be wary of people who talk unashamedly of 'fellowship and good cheer' as if it were something that can be applied to life like a poultice. Turn your back for a moment and they may well organize a Maypole dance and, frankly, there's no option then but to try and make it to the treeline.

The singers were halfway down Park Lane now, and halfway through 'The Red Rosy Hen' in marvellous harmony.* Their collecting tins were already full of donations for the poor of the city, or at least those sections of the poor who in Mrs Huggs' opinion were suitably picturesque and not too smelly and could be relied upon to say thank you. People had come to their doors to listen. Orange light spilled on to the snow. Candle lanterns glowed among the tumbling flakes. If you could have taken the lid off the scene, there would have been chocolates inside. Or at least an interesting biscuit assortment.

Mrs Huggs had heard that wassailing was an ancient ritual, and you didn't need anyone to tell you what *that* meant, but she felt she'd carefully removed all those elements that would affront the refined ear.

And it was only gradually that the singers became aware of the discord.

Around the corner, slipping and sliding on the ice, came another band of singers.

Some people march to a different drummer. The drummer in question here must have been trained elsewhere, possibly by a different species on another planet.

---

*'The red rosy hen greets the dawn of the day'. In fact the hen is not the bird traditionally associated with heralding a new sunrise, but Mrs Huggs, while collecting many old folk songs for posterity, has taken care to rewrite them where necessary to avoid, as she put it, 'offending those of a refined disposition with unwarranted coarseness'. Much to her surprise, people often couldn't spot the unwarranted coarseness until it had been pointed out to them.
Sometimes a chicken is nothing but a bird.

In front of the group was a legless man on a small wheeled trolley, who was singing at the top of his voice and banging two saucepans together. His name was Arnold Sideways. Pushing him along was Coffin Henry, whose croaking progress through an entirely different song was punctuated by bouts of off-the-beat coughing. He was accompanied by a perfectly ordinary-looking man in torn, dirty and yet expensive clothing, whose pleasant tenor voice was drowned out by the quacking of a duck on his head. He answered to the name of Duck Man, although he never seemed to understand why, or why he was always surrounded by people who seemed to see ducks where no ducks could be. And finally, being towed along by a small grey dog on a string, was Foul Ole Ron, generally regarded in Ankh-Morpork as the deranged beggars' deranged beggar. He was probably incapable of singing, but at least he was attempting to swear in time to the beat, or beats.

The wassailers stopped and watched them in horror.

Neither party noticed, as the beggars oozed and ambled up the street, that little smears of black and grey were spiralling out of drains and squeezing out from under tiles and buzzing off into the night. People have always had the urge to sing and clang things at the dark stub of the year, when all sorts of psychic nastiness has taken advantage of the long grey days and the deep shadows to lurk and breed. Lately people had taken to singing harmoniously, which rather lost the effect. Those who really understood just clanged something and shouted.

The beggars were not in fact this well versed in folkloric practice. They were just making a din in the well-founded hope that people would give them money to stop.

It was just possible to make out a consensus song in there somewhere.

'Hogswatch is coming,
The pig is getting fat,
Please put a dollar in the old man's hat
If you ain't got a dollar a penny will do—'

'And if you ain't got a penny,' Foul Ole Ron yodelled, solo, 'then – fghfgh yffg mfmfmf . . .'

The Duck Man had, with great presence of mind, clamped a hand over Ron's mouth.

'So sorry about this,' he said, 'but *this* time I'd like people not to slam their doors on us. And it doesn't scan, anyway.'

The nearby doors slammed regardless. The other wassailers fled hastily to a more salubrious location. Goodwill to all men was a phrase coined by someone who hadn't met Foul Ole Ron.

The beggars stopped singing, except for Arnold Sideways, who tended to live in his own small world.

'—nobody knows how good we can live, on boots three times a day . . .'

Then the change in the air penetrated even his consciousness.

Snow thumped off the trees as a contrary wind brushed them. There was a whirl of flakes and it was just possible, since the beggars did not always have their mental compasses pointing due Real, that they heard a brief snatch of conversation.

'It just ain't that simple, master, that's all I'm saying—'

IT IS BETTER TO GIVE THAN TO RECEIVE, ALBERT.

'No, master, it's just a lot more expensive. You can't just go around—'

Things rained down on the snow.

The beggars looked at them. Arnold Sideways carefully picked up a sugar pig and bit its nose off. Foul Ole Ron peered suspiciously into a cracker that had bounced off his hat, and then shook it against his ear.

The Duck Man opened a bag of sweets.

'Ah, humbugs?' he said.

Coffin Henry unlooped a string of sausages from around his neck.

'Buggrit?' said Foul Ole Ron.

'It's a cracker,' said the dog, scratching its ear. 'You pull it.'

Ron waved the cracker aimlessly by one end.

'Oh, give it here,' said the dog, and gripped the other end in its teeth.

'My word,' said the Duck Man, fishing in a snowdrift. 'Here's a whole roast pig! *And* a big dish of roast potatoes, miraculously uncracked!

And . . . look . . . isn't this caviar in the jar? Asparagus! Potted shrimp! My goodness! What were we going to have for Hogswatch dinner, Arnold?'

'Old boots,' said Arnold. He opened a fallen box of cigars and licked them.

'Just old boots?'

'Oh, no. Stuffed with mud, and with roast mud. 's good mud, too. I bin saving it up.'

'Now we can have a merry feast of goose!'

'All right. Can we stuff it with old boots?'

There was a pop from the direction of the cracker. They heard Foul Ole Ron's thinking-brain dog growl.

'No, no, no, you put the *hat* on your *head* and you *read* the hum'rous *mottar.*'

'Millennium hand and shrimp?' said Ron, pass-ing the scrap of paper to the Duck Man. The Duck Man was regarded as the intellectual of the group.

He peered at the motto.

'Ah, yes, let's see now . . . It says "Help Help Help Ive Fallen in the Crakker Machine I Cant Keep Runin on this Roller Please Get me Ou—".' He turned the paper over a few times. 'That appears to be it, except for the stains.'

'Always the same ole mottars,' said the dog. 'Someone slap Ron on the back, will you? If he laughs any more he'll – oh, he has. Oh well, nothing new about that.'

The beggars spent a few more minutes picking

up hams, jars and bottles that had settled on the snow. They packed them around Arnold on his trolley and set off down the street.

'How come we got all this?'

' 's Hogswatch, right?'

'Yeah, but who hung up their stocking?'

'I don't think we've got any, have we?'

'I hung up an old boot.'

'Does that count?'

'Dunno. Ron ate it.'

I'm waiting for the Hogfather, thought Ponder Stibbons. I'm in the dark waiting for the Hogfather. Me. A believer in Natural Philosophy. I can find the square root of 27.4 in my head.* I shouldn't be doing this.

It's not as if I've hung a stocking up. There'd be some *point* if . . .

He sat rigid for a moment, and then pulled off his pointy sandal and rolled down a sock. It helped if you thought of it as the scientific testing of an interesting hypothesis.

From out of the darkness Ridcully said, 'How long, do you think?'

'It's generally believed that all deliveries are completed well before midnight,' said Ponder, and tugged hard.

'Are you all right, Mr Stibbons?'

---

*He'd have to admit that the answer would be 'five and a bit', but at least he could come up with it.

'Fine, sir. Fine. Er . . . do you happen to have a drawing pin about you? Or a small nail, perhaps?'

'I don't believe so.'

'Oh, it's all right. I've found a penknife.'

After a while Ridcully heard a faint scratching noise in the dark.

'How do you spell "electricity", sir?'

Ridcully thought for a while. 'You know, I don't think I ever do.'

There was silence again, and then a clang. The Librarian grunted in his sleep.

'What are you doing?'

'I just knocked over the coal shovel.'

'Why are you feeling around on the mantelpiece?'

'Oh, just . . . you know, just . . . just looking. A little . . . experiment. After all, you never know.'

'You never know what?'

'Just . . . never know, you know.'

'*Sometimes* you know,' said Ridcully. 'I think I know quite a lot that I didn't used to know. It's amazing what you *do* end up knowing, I sometimes think. I often wonder what new stuff I'll know.'

'Well, you never know.'

'That's a fact.'

High over the city Albert turned to Death, who seemed to be trying to avoid his gaze.

'You didn't get *that* stuff out of the sack! Not cigars and peaches in brandy and grub with fancy foreign names!'

YES, IT CAME OUT OF THE SACK.

Albert gave him a suspicious look.

'But you put it in the sack in the first place, didn't you?'

NO.

'You did, didn't you?' Albert stated.

NO.

'You put all those things in the sack.'

NO.

'You got them from somewhere and put them in the sack.'

NO.

'You *did* put them in the sack, didn't you?'

NO.

'You put them in the sack.'

YES.

'I *knew* you put them in the sack. Where did you get them?'

THEY WERE JUST LYING AROUND.

'Whole roast pig does not, in my experience, just lie around.'

NO ONE SEEMED TO BE USING THEM, ALBERT.

'Couple of chimneys ago we were over that big posh restaurant . . .'

REALLY? I DON'T REMEMBER.

'And it seemed to me you were down there a bit longer than usual, if you don't mind me saying so.'

REALLY.

311

'How exactly were they just inverted comma lying around inverted comma?'

JUST . . . LYING AROUND. YOU KNOW. RECUMBENT.

'In a kitchen?'

THERE WAS A CERTAIN CULINARINESS ABOUT THE PLACE, I RECALL.

Albert pointed a trembling finger.

'You nicked someone's Hogswatch dinner, master!'

IT'S GOING TO BE EATEN, said Death defensively. ANYWAY, YOU THOUGHT IT WAS A GOOD IDEA WHEN I SHOWED THAT KING THE DOOR.

'Yeah, well, that was a bit different,' said Albert, lowering his voice. 'But, I mean, the Hogfather doesn't drop down the chimney and pinch people's grub!'

THE BEGGARS WILL ENJOY IT, ALBERT.

'Well, yes, but—'

IT WASN'T STEALING. IT WAS JUST . . . REDISTRIBUTION. IT WILL BE A GOOD DEED IN A NAUGHTY WORLD.

'No, it won't!'

THEN IT WILL BE A NAUGHTY DEED IN A NAUGHTY WORLD AND WILL PASS COMPLETELY UNNOTICED.

'Yeah, but you might at least have thought about the people whose grub you pinched.'

THEY HAVE BEEN PROVIDED FOR, OF COURSE. I AM NOT *COMPLETELY* HEARTLESS. IN A METAPHORICAL SENSE. AND NOW — ONWARDS AND UPWARDS.

'We're heading down, master.'

There were . . . swirls. Binky galloped easily through them, except that he did not seem to move. He might have been hanging in the air.

'Oh, me,' said the oh god weakly.

'What?' said Susan.

'Try shutting your eyes—'

Susan shut her eyes. Then she reached up to touch her face.

'I'm still seeing . . .'

'I thought it was just me. It's usually just me.'

The swirls vanished.

There was greenery below.

And *that* was odd. It *was* greenery. Susan had flown a few times over countryside, even swamps and jungles, and there had never been a green as green as this. If green could be a primary colour, this was it.

And that wiggly thing—

'That's not a river!' she said.

'Isn't it?'

'It's blue!'

The oh god risked a look down.

'Water's blue,' he said.

'Of course it's not!'

'Grass is green, water's blue . . . I can remember that. It's some of the stuff I just know.'

'Well, in a *way* . . .' Susan hesitated. Everyone *knew* grass was green and water was blue. Quite often it wasn't true, but everyone knew it in the same way they knew the sky was blue, too.

She made the mistake of looking up as she thought that.

There was the sky. It was, indeed, blue. And down there was the land. It was green.

And in between was nothing. Not white space. Not black night. Just . . . nothing, all round the edges of the world. Where the brain said there should be, well, sky and land, meeting neatly at the horizon, there was simply a void that sucked at the eyeball like a loose tooth.

And there was the sun.

It was *under* the sky, floating above the land.

And it was yellow.

Buttercup yellow.

Binky landed on the grass beside the river. Or at least on the green. It felt more like sponge, or moss. He nuzzled it.

Susan slid off, trying to keep her gaze low. That meant she was looking at the vivid blue of the water.

There were orange fish in it. They didn't look quite right, as if they'd been created by someone who really *did* think a fish was two curved lines and a dot and a triangular tail. They reminded her of the skeletal fish in Death's quiet pool. Fish that were . . . appropriate to their surroundings. And she could see them, even though the water was just a block of colour which part of her insisted ought to be opaque . . .

She knelt down and dipped her hand in. It felt

like water, but what poured through her fingers was liquid blue.

And now she knew where she was. The last piece clicked into place and the knowledge bloomed inside her. She knew if she saw a house just how its windows would be placed, and just how the smoke would come out of the chimney.

There would almost certainly be apples on the trees. And they would be red, because everyone knew that apples were red. And the sun was yellow. And the sky was blue. And the grass was green.

But there was *another* world, called the real world by the people who believed in it, where the sky could be anything from off-white to sunset red to thunderstorm yellow. And the trees would be anything from bare branches, mere scribbles against the sky, to red flames before the frost. And the sun was white or yellow or orange. And water was brown and grey and green . . .

The colours *here* were springtime colours, and not the springtime of the world. They were the colours of the springtime of the eye.

'This is a child's painting,' she said.

The oh god slumped onto the green.

'Every time I look at the gap my eyes water,' he mumbled. 'I feel awful.'

'I said this is a child's painting,' said Susan.

'Oh, *me* . . . I think the wizards' potion is wearing off . . .'

'I've seen dozens of pictures of it,' said Susan,

ignoring him. 'You put the sky overhead because the sky's above you and when you are a couple of feet high there's not a lot of sideways to the sky in any case. And everyone tells you grass is green and water is blue. *This* is the landscape you paint. Twyla paints like that. *I* painted like that. Grandfather saved some of—'

She stopped.

'All children do it, anyway,' she muttered. 'Come on, let's find the house.'

'What house?' the oh god moaned. 'And can you speak quieter, please?'

'There'll be a house,' said Susan, standing up. 'There's *always* a house. With four windows. And the smoke coming out of the chimney all curly like a spring. Look, this is a place like gr— Death's country. It's not really geography.'

The oh god walked over to the nearest tree and banged his head on it as if he hoped it was going to hurt.

'Feels like geo'fy,' he muttered.

'But have you ever seen a tree like that? A big green blob on a brown stick? It looks like a lollipop!' said Susan, pulling him along.

'Dunno. Firs' time I ever saw a tree. Arrgh. Somethin' dropped on m'head.' He blinked owlishly at the ground. ''s red.'

'It's an apple,' she said. She sighed. 'Everyone knows apples are red.'

There were no bushes. But there were flowers, each with a couple of green leaves. They grew individually, dotted around the rolling green.

And then they were out of the trees and there, by a bend in the river, was the house.

It didn't look very big. There were four windows and a door. Corkscrew smoke curled out of the chimney.

'You know, it's a funny thing,' said Susan, staring at it. 'Twyla draws houses like that. And she practically lives in a mansion. I drew houses like that. And I was born in a palace. Why?'

'P'raps it's all this house,' muttered the oh god miserably.

'What? You really think so? Kids' paintings are all of this place? It's in our heads?'

'Don't ask me, I was just making conversation,' said the oh god.

Susan hesitated. The words What Now? loomed. Should she just go and knock?

And she realized that was *normal* thinking . . .

In the glittering, clattering, chattering atmosphere a head waiter was having a difficult time. There were a lot of people in, and the staff should have been fully stretched, putting bicarbonate of soda in the white wine to make very expensive bubbles and cutting the vegetables very small to make them cost more.

Instead they were standing in a dejected group in the kitchen.

'Where did it all go?' screamed the manager. 'Someone's been through the cellar, too!'

'William said he felt a cold wind,' said the

317

waiter. He'd been backed up against a hot plate, and now *knew* why it was called a hot plate in a way he hadn't fully comprehended before.

'I'll give him a cold wind! Haven't we got *anything*?'

'There's odds and ends . . .'

'You don't mean odds and ends, you mean *des curieux et des bouts*,' corrected the manager.

'Yeah, right, yeah. And, er, and, er . . .'

'There's nothing else?'

'Er . . . old boots. Muddy old boots.'

'Old—?'

'Boots. Lots of 'em,' said the waiter. He felt he was beginning to singe.

'How come we've got . . . vintage footwear?'

'Dunno. They just turned up, sir. The oven's full of old boots. So's the pantry.'

'There's a hundred people booked in! All the shops'll be shut! Where's Chef?'

'William's trying to get him to come out of the privy, sir. He's locked himself in and is having one of his Moments.'

'*Something*'s cooking. What's that I can smell?'

'Me, sir.'

'Old boots . . .' muttered the manager. 'Old boots . . . old boots . . . Leather, are they? Not clogs or rubber or anything?'

'Looks like . . . just boots. And lots of mud, sir.'

The manager took off his jacket. 'All right. Got any cream, have we? Onions? Garlic? Butter? Some old beef bones? A bit of pastry?'

'Er, yes . . .'

The manager rubbed his hands together. '*Right,*' he said, taking an apron off a hook. 'You there, get some water boiling! Lots of water! And find a really large hammer! And *you*, chop some onions! The rest of you, start sorting out the boots. I want the tongues out and the soles off. We'll do them . . . let's see . . . *Mousse de la Boue dans une Panier de la Pâte de Chaussures* . . .'

'Where're we going to get that from, sir?'

'Mud mousse in a basket of shoe pastry. Get the idea? It's not our fault if even Quirmians don't understand restaurant Quirmian. It's not like lying, after all.'

'Well, it's a *bit* like—' the waiter began. He'd been cursed with honesty at an early stage.

'Then there's *Brodequin rôti Façon Ombres* . . .' The manager sighed at the head waiter's panicky expression. 'Soldier's boot done in the Shades fashion,' he translated.

'Er . . . Shades fashion?'

'In mud. But if we cook the tongues separately we can put on *Languette braisée*, too.'

'There's some ladies' shoes, sir,' said an under-chef.

'Right. Add to the menu . . . Let's see now . . . *Sole d'une Bonne Femme* . . . and . . . yes . . . *Servis dans un Coulis de Terre en l'Eau*. That's mud, to you.'

'What about the laces, sir?' said another under-chef.

'Good thinking. Dig out that recipe for Spaghetti Carbonara.'

'Sir?' said the head waiter.

'I started off as a chef,' said the manager, picking up a knife. 'How do you think I was able to afford this place? I know how it's done. Get the look and the sauce right and you're three-quarters there.'

'But it's all going to be old boots!' said the waiter.

'Prime aged beef,' the manager corrected him. 'It'll tenderize in no time.'

'Anyway . . . anyway . . . we haven't got any soup—'

'Mud. And a lot of onions.'

'There's the puddings—'

'Mud. Let's see if we can get it to caramelize, you never know.'

'I can't even find the coffee . . . Still, they probably won't last till the coffee . . .'

'Mud. *Café de Terre*,' said the manager firmly. 'Genuine ground coffee.'

'Oh, they'll spot that, sir!'

'They haven't up till now,' said the manager darkly.

'We'll never get away with it, sir. Never.'

In the country of the sky on top, Medium Dave Lilywhite hauled another bag of money down the stairs.

'There must be thousands here,' said Chicken-wire.

'Hundreds of thousands,' said Medium Dave.

'And what's all this stuff?' said Catseye, opening a box. ''s just paper.' He tossed it aside.

Medium Dave sighed. He was all for class solidarity, but sometimes Catseye got on his nerves.

'They're title deeds,' he said. 'And they're better than money.'

'Paper's better'n money?' said Catseye. 'Hah, if you can burn it you can't spend it, that's what I say.'

'Hang on,' said Chickenwire. 'I know about them. The Tooth Fairy owns property?'

'Got to raise money somehow,' said Medium Dave. 'All those half-dollars under the pillow.'

'If we steal them, do they become ours?'

'Is that a trick question?' said Catseye, smirking.

'Yeah, but . . . ten thousand each doesn't sound such a lot, when you see all this.'

'He won't miss a—'

'*Gentlemen . . .*'

They turned. Teatime was in the doorway.

'We were just . . . we were just piling up the stuff,' said Chickenwire.

'Yes. I know. I told you to.'

'Right. That's right. You did,' said Chickenwire gratefully.

'And there's such a lot,' said Teatime. He gave them a smile. Catseye coughed.

''s got to be thousands,' said Medium Dave. 'And what about all these deeds and so on? Look, this one's for that pipe shop in Honey Trap Lane!

321

In Ankh-Morpork! I buy my tobacco there! Old Thimble is always moaning about the rent, too!'

'Ah. So you opened the strongboxes,' said Teatime pleasantly.

'Well . . . yes . . .'

'Fine. Fine,' said Teatime. 'I didn't ask you to, but . . . fine, fine. And how did you think the Tooth Fairy made her money? Little gnomes in some mine somewhere? Fairy gold? But *that* turns to trash in the morning!'

He laughed. Chickenwire laughed. Even Medium Dave laughed. And then Teatime was on him, pushing him irresistibly backwards until he hit the wall.

There was a blur and he tried to blink and his left eyelid was suddenly a rose of pain.

Teatime's good eye was close to him, if you could call it good. The pupil was a dot. Medium Dave could just make out his hand, right by Medium Dave's face.

It was holding a knife. The point of the blade could only be the merest fraction of an inch from Medium Dave's right eye.

'I know people say I'd kill them as soon as look at them,' whispered Teatime. 'And in fact I'd *much* rather kill you than look at you, Mr Lily-white. You stand in a castle of gold and plot to steal pennies. Oh, dear. What am I to do with you?'

He relaxed a little, but his hand still held the knife to Medium Dave's unblinking eye.

'You're thinking that Banjo is going to help

322

you,' he said. 'That's how it's always been, isn't it? But Banjo likes me. He really does. Banjo is *my* friend.'

Medium Dave managed to focus beyond Teatime's ear. His brother was just standing there, with the blank face he had while he waited for another order or a new thought to turn up.

'If I thought you were feeling bad thoughts about me I would be so downcast,' said Teatime. 'I do not have many friends left, Mr Medium Dave.'

He stood back and smiled happily. 'All friends now?' he said, as Medium Dave slumped down. 'Help him, Banjo.'

On cue, Banjo lumbered forward.

'Banjo has the heart of a little child,' said Teatime, the knife disappearing somewhere about his clothing. 'I believe I have, too.'

The others were frozen in place. They hadn't moved since the attack. Medium Dave was a heavy-set man and Teatime was a matchstick model, but he'd lifted Medium Dave off his feet like a feather.

'As far as the money goes, in fact, I really have no use for it,' said Teatime, sitting down on a sack of silver. 'It is small change. You may share it out amongst yourselves, and no doubt you'll squabble and double-cross one another more tiresomely. Oh, dear. It is so awful when friends fall out.'

He kicked the sack. It split. Silver and copper fell in an expensive trickle.

'And you'll swagger and spend it on drink and women,' he said, as they watched the coins roll into every corner of the room. 'The thought of *investment* will never cross your scarred little minds—'

There was a rumble from Banjo. Even Teatime waited patiently until the huge man had assembled a sentence. The result was:

'I gotta piggy bank.'

'And what would you do with a million dollars, Banjo?' said Teatime.

Another rumble. Banjo's face twisted up.

'Buy . . . a . . . bigger piggy bank?'

'Well done.' The Assassin stood up. 'Let's go and see how our wizard is getting on, shall we?'

He walked out of the room without looking back. After a moment Banjo followed.

The others tried not to look at one another's faces. Then Chickenwire said, 'Was he saying we could take the money and go?'

'Don't be bloody stupid, we wouldn't get ten yards,' said Medium Dave, still clutching his face. 'Ugh, this *hurts*. I think he cut the eyelid . . . he cut the damn *eyelid* . . .'

'Then let's just leave the stuff and go! I never joined up to ride on tigers!'

'And what'll you do when he comes after you?'

'Why'd he bother with the likes of us?'

'He's got time for his friends,' said Medium Dave bitterly. 'For gods' sakes, someone get me a clean rag or something . . .'

'OK, but . . . but he can't look everywhere.'

Medium Dave shook his head. He'd been through Ankh-Morpork's very own university of the streets and had graduated with his life and an intelligence made all the keener by constant friction. You only had to look into Teatime's mismatched eyes to know one thing, which was this: that if Teatime wanted to find you he would *not* look everywhere. He'd look in only one place, which would be the place where you were hiding.

'How come your brother likes him so much?'

Medium Dave grimaced. Banjo had always done what he was told, simply because Medium Dave had told him. Up to now, anyway.

It must have been that punch in the bar. Medium Dave didn't like to think about it. He'd always promised their mother that he'd look after Banjo,* and Banjo had gone back like a falling tree. And when Medium Dave had risen from his seat to punch Teatime's unbalanced lights out he'd suddenly found the Assassin already behind him, holding a knife. In front of everyone. It was humiliating, that's what it was—

And then Banjo had sat up, looking puzzled, and spat out a tooth—

'If it wasn't for Banjo going around with him all the time we could gang up on him,' said Catseye.

---

*It had been Ma Lilywhite's dying wish, although she hadn't known it at the time. Her last words to her son were 'You try and get to the horses, I'll try to hold 'em off on the stairs, and if anything happens to me, take care of the dummy!'

Medium Dave looked up, one hand clamping a handkerchief to his eye.

'*Gang up on him?*' he said.

'Yeah, it's all your fault,' Chickenwire went on.

'Oh, yeah? So it wasn't you who said, wow, ten thousand dollars, count me in?'

Chickenwire backed away. 'I didn't know there was going to be all this creepy stuff! I want to go home!'

Medium Dave hesitated, despite his pain and rage. This wasn't normal talk for Chickenwire, for all that he whined and grumbled. This was a strange place, no lie about that, and all that business with the teeth had been very . . . odd, but he'd been out with Chickenwire when jobs had gone wrong and both the Watch *and* the Thieves' Guild had been after them and he'd been as cool as anyone. And if the Guild had been the ones to catch them they'd have nailed their ears to their ankles and thrown them in the river. In Medium Dave's book, which was a simple book and largely written in mental crayon, things didn't get creepier than that.

'What's up with you?' he said. 'All of you – you're acting like little kids!'

'Would he deliver to apes *earlier* than humans?'

'Interesting point, sir. Possibly you're referring to my theory that humans may have in fact descended from apes, of course,' said Ponder. 'A bold hypothesis which ought to sweep away the ignorance of centuries if the grants committee could just see their way clear to letting me hire a boat and sail around to the islands of—'

'I just thought he might deliver alphabetically,' said Ridcully.

There was a patter of soot in the cold fireplace.

'That's presumably him now, do you think?' Ridcully went on. 'Oh, well, I thought we should check—'

Something landed in the ashes. The two wizards stood quietly in the darkness while the figure picked itself up. There was a rustle of paper.

LET ME SEE NOW—

There was a click as Ridcully's pipe fell out of his mouth.

'Who the hell are you?' he said. 'Mr Stibbons, light a candle!'

Death backed away.

I'M THE HOGFATHER, OF COURSE. ER. HO. HO. HO. WHO WOULD YOU *EXPECT* to COME DOWN A CHIMNEY ON A NIGHT LIKE THIS, MAY I ASK?

'No, you're not!'

I AM. LOOK, I'VE GOT THE BEARD AND THE PILLOW AND EVERYTHING!

'You look *extremely* thin in the face!'

I'M . . . I . . . I'M NOT WELL. IT'S ALL . . . YES, IT'S ALL THIS SHERRY. AND RUSHING AROUND. I AM A BIT ILL.

'Terminally, I should say.' Ridcully grabbed the beard. There was a twang as the string gave way.

'It's a false beard!'

NO IT'S NOT, said Death desperately.

'Here's the hooks for the ears, which must have given *you* a bit of trouble, I must say!'

Ridcully flourished the incriminating evidence.

'What were you doing coming down the chimney?' he continued. 'Not in marvellous taste, I think.'

Death waved a small grubby scrap of paper defensively.

OFFICIAL LETTER TO THE HOGFATHER. SAYS HERE . . . he began, and then looked at the paper again. WELL, QUITE A LOT, IN FACT. IT'S A LONG LIST. LIBRARY STAMPS, REFERENCE BOOKS, PENCILS, BANANAS . . .

'The Librarian asked the Hogfather for those things?' said Ridcully. 'Why?'

I DON'T KNOW, said Death. This was a diplomatic answer. He kept his finger over a reference to the Archchancellor. The orang-utan for 'duck's bottom' was quite an interesting squiggle.

'I've got plenty in my desk drawer,' mused Ridcully. 'I'm quite happy to give them out to any chap provided he can prove he's used up the old one.'

THEY MUST SHOW YOU AN ABSENCE OF PENCIL?

'Of course. If he needed essential materials he need only have come to me. No man can tell you I'm an unreasonable chap.'

Death checked the list carefully.

THAT IS PRECISELY CORRECT, he confirmed, with anthropological exactitude.

'Except for the bananas, of course. I wouldn't keep fish in my desk.'

Death looked down at the list and then back up at Ridcully.

GOOD? he said, in the hope that this was the right response.

Wizards know when they are going to die.* Ridcully had no such premonitions, and to Ponder's horror prodded Death in the cushion.

'Why *you*?' he said. 'What's happened to the other fellow?'

I SUPPOSE I MUST TELL YOU.

In the house of Death, a whisper of shifting sand and the faintest chink of moving glass, some-where in the darkness of the floor . . .

And, in the dry shadows, the sharp smell of snow and a thud of hooves.

Sideney almost swallowed his tongue when Tea-time appeared beside him.

'Are we making progress?'

'Gnk—'

'I'm sorry?' said Teatime.

Sideney recovered himself. 'Er . . . some,' he said. 'We think we've worked out . . . er . . . one lock.'

---

*They generally know in time to have their best robe cleaned, do some serious damage to the wine cellar and have a really good last meal. It's a nicer version of Death Row, with the bonus of no lawyers.

Light gleamed off Teatime's eye.

'I believe there are seven of them?' said the Assassin.

'Yes, but . . . they're half magic and half real and half not there . . . I mean . . . there's parts of them that don't exist all the time—'

Mr Brown, who had been working at one of the locks, laid down his pick.

' 't's no good, mister,' he said. 'Can't even get a purchase with a crowbar. Maybe if I went back to the city and got a couple of dragons we could do something. You can melt through steel with them if you twist their necks right and feed 'em carbon.'

'I was told you were the best locksmith in the city,' said Teatime.

Behind him, Banjo shifted position.

Mr Brown looked annoyed . . .

'Well, *yes*,' he said. 'But locks don't generally alter 'emselves while you're working on 'em, that's what I'm saying.'

'And *I* thought you could open any lock anyone ever made,' said Teatime.

'Made by humans,' said Mr Brown sharply. 'And most dwarfs. I dunno *what* made these. You never said anything about magic.'

'That's a shame,' said Teatime. 'Then really I have no more need of your services. You may as well go back home.'

'I won't be sorry.' Mr Brown started putting things back into his tool bag. 'What about my money?'

'Do I owe you any?'

'I came along with you. I don't see it's my fault that this is all magic business. I should get *something.*'

'Ah, yes, I see your point,' said Teatime. 'Of course, you should get what you deserve. Banjo?'

Banjo lumbered forward, and then stopped.

Mr Brown's hand had come out of the bag holding a crowbar.

'You must think I was born yesterday, you slimy little bugger,' he said. 'I know your type. You think it's all some kind of game. You make little jokes to yourself and you think no one else notices and you think you're so smart. Well, Mr Teacup, I'm leaving, right? Right now. With what's coming to me. And you ain't stopping me. And Banjo certainly ain't. I knew old Ma Lily-white back in the good old days. You think you're nasty? You think *you're* mean? Ma Lilywhite'd tear your ears off and spit 'em in your eye, you cocky little devil. And I worked with her, so you don't scare me and nor does little Banjo, poor sod that he is.'

Mr Brown glared at each of them in turn, flourishing the crowbar. Sideney cowered in front of the doors.

He saw Teatime nod gracefully, as if the man had made a small speech of thanks.

'I appreciate your point of view,' said Teatime. 'And, I have to repeat, it's Teh-ah-tim-eh. Now, please, Banjo.'

Banjo loomed over Mr Brown, reached down and lifted him up by the crowbar so sharply that his feet came out of his boots.

'Here, you know me, Banjo!' the locksmith croaked, struggling in mid-air. 'I remembers you when you was little, I used to sit you on my knees, I often used to work for your ma—'

'D'you like apples?' Banjo rumbled.

Brown struggled.

'You got to say yes,' Banjo said.

'Yes!'

'D'you like pears? You got to say yes.'

'All right, yes!'

'D'you like falling down the stairs?'

Medium Dave held up his hands for quiet.

He glared at the gang.

'This place is getting to you, right? But we've all been in bad places before, right?'

'Not this bad,' said Chickenwire. 'I've never been anywhere where it hurts to look at the sky. It give me the creeps.'

'Chick's a little baby, nyer nyer nyer,' sang Catseye.

They looked at him. He coughed nervously.

'Sorry . . . don't know why I said that . . .'

'If we stick together we'll be fine—'

'Eeeny meeny miney mo . . .' mumbled Catseye.

'What? What are you talking about?'

'Sorry . . . it just sort of slipped out . . .'

'What I'm trying to say,' said Medium Dave, 'is that if—'

'Peachy keeps making faces at me!'

'I didn't!'

'Liar, liar, pants on fire!'

Two things happened at this point. Medium Dave lost his temper, and Peachy screamed.

A small wisp of smoke was rising from his trousers.

He hopped around, beating desperately at himself.

'Who did that? Who did that?' demanded Medium Dave.

'I didn't see anyone,' said Chickenwire. 'I mean, no one was *near* him. Catseye said "pants on fire" and next minute—'

'Now he's sucking his thumb!' Catseye jeered. 'Nyer nyer nyer! Crying for Mummy! You know what happens to kids who suck their thumbs, there's this big monster with scissors all—'

'*Will you stop talking like that!*' shouted Medium Dave. 'Blimey, it *is* like dealing with a bunch of—'

Someone screamed, high above. It went on for a while and seemed to be getting nearer, but then it stopped and was replaced by a rush of thumping and an occasional sound like a coconut being bounced on a stone floor.

Medium Dave got to the door just in time to see the body of Mr Brown the locksmith tumble past, moving quite fast and not at all neatly. A moment later his bag somersaulted around the curve of the stairs. It split as it bounced and there was a jangle as tools and lockpicks bounced out and followed their late owner.

He'd been moving quite fast. He'd probably roll all the way to the bottom.

Medium Dave looked up. Two turns above him, on the opposite side of the huge shaft, Banjo was watching him.

Banjo didn't know right from wrong. He'd always left that sort of thing to his brother.

'Er . . . poor guy must've slipped,' Medium Dave mumbled.

'Oh, yeah . . . slipped,' said Peachy.

He looked up, too.

It was funny. He hadn't noticed them before. The white tower had seemed to glow from within. But now there were shadows, moving across the stone. *In* the stone.

'What was that?' he said. 'That sound . . .'

'What sound?'

'It sounded . . . like knives scraping,' said Peachy. 'Really close.'

'There's only us here!' said Medium Dave. 'What're you afraid of? Attack by daisies? Come on . . . let's go and help him . . .'

She *couldn't* walk through the door. It simply resisted any such effort. She ended up merely bruised. So Susan turned the doorknob instead.

She heard the oh god gasp. But she was used to the idea of buildings that were bigger on the

334

inside. Her grandfather had never been able to get a handle on dimensions.

The second thing the eye was drawn to were the staircases. They started opposite one another in what was now a big round tower, its ceiling lost in the haze. The spirals circled into infinity.

Susan's eyes went back to the first thing.

It was a large conical heap in the middle of the floor.

It was white. It glistened in the cool light that shone down from the mists.

'It's teeth,' she said.

'I think I'm going to throw up,' said the oh god miserably.

'There's nothing that scary about teeth,' said Susan. She didn't mean it. The heap was very horrible indeed.

'Did I say I was scared? I'm just hung over again . . . Oh, *me* . . .'

Susan advanced on the heap, moving warily.

They were *small* teeth. Children's teeth. Whoever had piled them up hadn't been very careful about it, either. A few had been scattered across the floor. She knew because she trod on one, and the slippery little crunching sound made her desperate not to tread on any more.

Whoever had piled them up had presumably been the one who'd drawn the chalk marks around the obscene heap.

'There're so *many*,' whispered Bilious.

'At least twenty million, given the size of the

average milk tooth,' said Susan. She was shocked to find that it came almost automatically.

'How can you possibly know that?'

'Volume of a cone,' said Susan. 'Pi times the square of the radius times the height divided by three. I bet Miss Butts never thought it'd come in handy in a place like this.'

'That's amazing. You did it in your head?'

'This isn't right,' said Susan quietly. 'I don't think this is what the Tooth Fairy is all about. All that effort to get the teeth, and then just to dump them like this? No. Anyway, there's a cigarette end on the floor. I don't see the Tooth Fairy as someone who rolls her own.'

She stared down at the chalk marks.

Voices high above her made her look up. She thought she saw a head look over the stair rail, and then draw back again. She didn't see much of the face, but what she saw didn't look fairylike.

She glanced back at the circle of chalk around the teeth. Someone had wanted all the teeth in one place and had drawn a circle to show people where they had to go.

There were a few symbols scrawled around the circle.

She had a good memory for small details. It was another family trait. And a small detail stirred in her memory like a sleepy bee.

'Oh, no,' she breathed. 'Surely no one would try to—'

Someone shouted, someone up in the whiteness. A body rolled down the stairs nearest her. It had been a skinny, middle-aged man. Technically it still was, but the long spiral staircase had not been kind.

It tumbled across the white marble and slid to a boneless halt.

Then, as she hurried towards the body, it faded away, leaving nothing behind but a smear of blood.

A jingle noise made her look back up the stairs. Spinning over and over, making salmon leaps in the air, a crowbar bounded over the last dozen steps and landed point first on a flagstone, staying upright and vibrating.

Chickenwire reached the top of the stairs, panting.

'There's people down there, Mister Teatime!' he wheezed. 'Dave and the others've gone down to catch them, Mister Teatime!'

'Teh-ah-tim-eh,' said Teatime, without taking his eyes off the wizard.

'That's right, sir!'

'Well?' said Teatime. 'Just . . . do away with them.'

'Er . . . one of them's a girl, sir.'

Teatime still didn't look round. He waved a hand vaguely.

'Then do away with them *politely*.'

'Yes, Mister . . . yes, right . . .' Chickenwire coughed. 'Don't you want to find out why they're here, sir?'

'Good heavens, no. Why should I want to do that? Now go away.'

Chickenwire stood there for a moment, and then hurried off.

As he scurried down the stairs he thought he heard a creak, as of an ancient wooden door.

He went pale.

It was just a door, said the sensible bit in front of his brain. There were hundreds of them in this place, although, come to think of it, none of them had creaked.

The other bit, the bit that hung around in dark places nearly at the top of his spinal column, said: But it's not one of them, and you know it, because you know which door it really is . . .

He hadn't heard that creak for thirty years.

He gave a little yelp and started to take the stairs four at a time.

In the hollows and corners, the shadows grew darker.

Susan ran up a flight of stairs, dragging the oh god behind her.

'Do you know what they've been doing?' she said. 'You know why they've got all those teeth in a circle? The *power* . . . oh my . . .'

'I'm not going to,' said the head waiter, firmly.

'Look, I'll buy you a better pair after Hogs-watch—'

'There's two more Shoe Pastry, one for *Purée de la Terre* and three more *Tourte à la Boue*,' said a waiter, hurrying in.

'Mud pies!' moaned the waiter. 'I can't believe we're selling mud pies. And now you want *my* boots!'

'With cream and sugar, mind you. A real taste of Ankh-Morpork. And we can get at least four helpings off those boots. Fair's fair. We're all in our socks—'

'Table seven says the steaks were lovely but a bit tough,' said a waiter, rushing past.

'Right. Use a larger hammer next time and boil them for longer.' The manager turned back to the suffering head waiter. 'Look, Bill,' he said, taking him by the shoulder. 'This isn't food. No one expects it to be food. If people wanted food they'd stay at home, isn't that so? They come here for ambience. For the experience. This isn't cookery, Bill. This is *cuisine*. See? And they're coming back for more.'

'Yeah, but *old boots* . . .'

'Dwarfs eats rats,' said the manager. 'And trolls eat rocks. There's folks in Howondaland that eat insects and folks on the Counterweight Continent eat soup made out of bird spit. At least the boots have been on a cow.'

'And mud?' said the head waiter, gloomily.

'Isn't there an old proverb that says a man must eat a bushel of dirt before he dies?'

'Yes, but not all at once.'

'Bill?' said the manager, kindly, picking up a spatula.

'Yes, boss?'

'Get those damn boots off right now, will you?'

When Chickenwire reached the bottom of the tower he was trembling, and not just from the effort. He headed straight for the door until Medium Dave grabbed him.

'Let me out! It's after me!'

'Look at his *face*,' said Catseye. 'Looks like he's seen a ghost!'

'Yeah, well, it *ain't* a ghost,' muttered Chickenwire. 'It's *worse'n* a ghost—'

Medium Dave slapped him across the face.

'Pull yourself together! Look around! Nothing's chasing you! Anyway, it's not as though we couldn't put up a fight, right?'

Terror had had time to drain away a little. Chickenwire looked back up the stairs. There was nothing there.

'Good,' said Medium Dave, watching his face. 'Now . . . What happened?'

Chickenwire looked at his feet.

'I thought it was the wardrobe,' he muttered. 'Go on, laugh . . .'

They didn't laugh.

'What wardrobe?' said Catseye.

'Oh, when I was a kid . . .' Chickenwire waved his arms vaguely. 'We had this big ole wardrobe, if you must know. Oak. It had this . . . this . . .

on the door there was this . . . sort of . . . *face*.'
He looked at their faces, which were equally
wooden. 'I mean, not an actual face, there was
. . . all this . . . decoration round the keyhole, sort
of flowers and leaves and stuff, but if you looked
at it in the . . . right way . . . it was a face and
they put it in my room 'cos it was so big and in
the night . . . in the night . . . in the night—'

They were grown men or at least had lived for
several decades, which in some societies is considered the same thing. But you had to stare at a
man so creased up with dread.

'Yes?' said Catseye hoarsely.

'. . . it whispered things,' said Chickenwire, in
a quiet little voice, like a vole in a dungeon.

They looked at one another.

'What things?' said Medium Dave.

'I don't *know*! I always had my head under the
pillow! Anyway, it's just something from when I
was a kid, all right? Our dad got rid of it in the
finish. Burned it. And I *watched*.'

They mentally shook themselves, as people do
when their minds emerge back into the light.

'It's like me and the dark,' said Catseye.

'Oh, don't you start,' said Medium Dave. 'Anyway, you *ain't* afraid of the dark. You're famed
for it. I been working with you in all kinds of
cellars and stuff. I mean, that's how you got your
name. Catseye. Sees like a cat.'

'Yeah, well . . . you try an' make up for it,
don't you?' said Catseye. ' 'Cos when you're
grown you know it's just shadows and stuff.

Besides, it ain't like the dark we used to have in the cellar.'

'Oh, they had a special kind of a dark when you was a lad, did they?' said Medium Dave. 'Not like the kind of dark you get these days, eh?'

Sarcasm didn't work.

'No,' said Catseye, simply. 'It wasn't. In our cellar, it wasn't.'

'Our mam used to wallop us if we went down to the cellar,' said Medium Dave. 'She had her still down there.'

'Yeah?' said Catseye, from somewhere far off. 'Well, *our* dad used to wallop us if we tried to get out. Now shut up talking about it.'

They reached the bottom of the stairs.

There was an absence of anybody. And any body.

'He couldn't have survived that, could he?' said Medium Dave.

'I saw him as he went past,' said Catseye. 'Necks aren't supposed to bend that way—'

He squinted upwards.

'Who's that moving up there?'

'How are their *necks* moving?' quavered Chickenwire.

'Split up!' said Medium Dave. 'And this time all take a stairway. Then they can't come back down!'

'Who're they? Why're they here?'

'Why're *we* here?' said Peachy. He started, and looked behind him.

'Taking our money? After us putting up with *him*?'

'Yeah . . .' said Peachy distantly, trailing after the others. 'Er . . . did you hear that noise just then?'

'What noise?'

'A sort of clipping, snipping . . . ?'

'No.'

'No.'

'No. You must have imagined it.'

Peachy nodded miserably.

As he walked up the stairs, little shadows raced through the stone and followed his feet.

Susan darted off the stairs and dragged the oh god along a corridor lined with white doors.

'I think they saw us,' she said. 'And if they're tooth fairies there's been a really *stupid* equal opportunities policy . . .'

She pushed open a door.

There were no windows to the room, but it was lit perfectly well by the walls themselves. Down the middle of the room was something like a display case, its lid gaping open. Bits of card littered the floor.

She reached down and picked one up and read: 'Thomas Ague, aged 4 and nearly three quarters, 9 Castle View, Sto Lat'. The writing was in a meticulous rounded script.

She crossed the passage to another room, where there was the same scene of devastation.

'So now we know where the teeth were,' she

said. 'They must've taken them out of every-where and carried them downstairs.'

'What for?'

She sighed. 'It's such old magic it isn't even magic any more,' she said. 'If you've got a piece of someone's hair, or a nail clipping, or a tooth – you can control them.'

The oh god tried to focus.

'That heap's controlling millions of children?'

'Yes. Adults too, by now.'

'And you . . . you could make them think things and do things?'

She nodded. 'Yes.'

'You could get them to open Dad's wallet and post the contents to some address?'

'Well, I hadn't thought of *that*, but yes, I suppose you could . . .'

'Or go downstairs and smash all the bottles in the drinks cabinet and promise never to take a drink when they grow up?' said the oh god hopefully.

'What are you talking about?'

'It's all right for you. You don't wake up every morning and see your whole life flush before your eyes.'

Medium Dave and Catseye ran down the passage and stopped where it forked.

'You go that way, I'll—'

'Why don't we stick together?' said Catseye.

'What's got into everyone? I saw you bite the

throats out of a coupla guard dogs when we did that job in Quirm! Want me to hold your hand? You check the doors down there, I'll check them along here.'

He walked off.

Catseye peered down the other passage.

There weren't many doors down there. It wasn't very long. And, as Teatime had said, there was nothing dangerous here that they hadn't brought with them.

He heard voices coming from a doorway and sagged with relief.

He could *deal* with humans.

As he approached, a sound made him look round.

Shadows were racing down the passage behind him. They cascaded down the walls and flowed over the ceiling.

Where shadows met they became darker. And darker.

And rose. And leapt.

'What was that?' said Susan.

'Sounded like the start of a scream,' said Bilious.

Susan threw open the door.

There was no one outside.

There was movement, though. She saw a patch of darkness in the corner of a wall shrink and fade, and another shadow slid around the bend of the corridor.

And there was a pair of boots in the centre of the corridor.

She hadn't remembered any boots there before.

She sniffed. The air tasted of rats, and damp, and mould.

'Let's get out of here,' she said.

'How're we going to find this Violet in all these rooms?'

'I don't know. I should be able to . . . sense her, but I can't.' Susan peered around the end of the corridor. She could hear men shouting, some way off.

They slipped out on to the stairs again and managed another flight. There were more rooms here, and in each one a cabinet that had been broken open.

Shadows moved in the corners. The effect was as though some invisible light source was gently shifting.

'This reminds me a lot of your . . . um . . . of your grandfather's place,' said the oh god.

'I know,' said Susan. 'There aren't any rules except the ones he makes up as he goes along. I can't see *him* being very happy if someone got in and started pulling the library apart—'

She stopped. When she spoke again her voice had a different tone.

'This is a children's place,' she said. 'The rules are what children believe.'

'Well, that's a relief.'

'You think so? Things aren't going to be *right*. In the Soul Cake Duck's country ducks *can* lay chocolate eggs, in the same way that Death's country is black and sombre because that's what people believe. He's very conventional about that sort of thing. Skull and bone decorations all over the place. And *this* place—'

'Pretty flowers and an odd sky.'

'I think it's going to be a lot worse than that. And very odd, too.'

'More odd than it is now?'

'I don't think it's possible to die here.'

'That man who fell down the stairs looked pretty dead to *me*.'

'Oh, you die. But not here. You . . . let's see . . . yes . . . you go somewhere else. Away. You're just not seen any more. That's about all you understand when you're three. Grandfather said it wasn't like that fifty years ago. He said you often couldn't see the bed for everyone having a good cry. Now they just tell the child that Grandma's gone. For three weeks Twyla thought her uncle'd been buried in the sad patch behind the garden shed along with Buster and Meepo and all three Bulgies.'

'Three Bulgies?'

'Gerbils. They tend to die a lot,' said Susan. 'The trick is to replace them when she's not looking. You really don't know *anything*, do you?'

'Er . . . hello?'

The voice came from the corridor.

They worked their way round to the next room. There, sitting on the floor and tied to the leg of

347

a white display case, was Violet. She looked up in apprehension, and then in bewilderment, and finally in growing recognition.

'Aren't you—?'

'Yes, yes, we see each other sometimes in Biers, and when you came for Twyla's last tooth you were so shocked that I could see you I had to give you a drink to get your nerves back,' said Susan, fumbling with the ropes. 'I don't think we've got a lot of time.'

'And who's he?'

The oh god tried to push his lank hair into place.

'Oh, he's just a god,' said Susan. 'His name's Bilious.'

'Do you drink at all?' said the oh god.

'What sort of quest—'

'He needs to know before he decides whether he hates you or not,' said Susan. 'It's a god thing.'

'No, I don't,' said Violet. 'What an idea. I've got the blue ribbon!'

The oh god raised his eyebrows at Susan.

'That means she's a member of Offler's League of Temperance,' said Susan. 'They sign a pledge not to touch alcohol. I can't think why. Of course, Offler's a crocodile. They don't go in bars much. They're into water.'

'Not touch alcohol at all?' said the oh god.

'Never!' said Violet. 'My dad's very strict about that sort of thing!'

After a moment Susan felt forced to wave a hand across their locked gaze.

'Can we get on?' she said. 'Good. Who brought you here, Violet?'

'I don't know! I was doing the collection as usual, and then I thought I heard someone following me, and then it all went dark, and when I came to we were . . . Have you seen what it's like outside?'

'Yes.'

'Well, we were there. The big one was carrying me. The one they call Banjo. He's not bad, just a bit . . . odd. Sort of . . . slow. He just watches me. The others are thugs. Watch out for the one with the glass eye. They're all afraid of him. Except Banjo.'

'Glass eye?'

'He's dressed like an Assassin. He's called Teatime. I think they're trying to steal something . . . They spent *ages* carting the teeth out. Little teeth everywhere . . . It was horrible! Thank you,' she added to the oh god, who had helped her on to her feet.

'They've piled them up in a magic circle downstairs,' said Susan.

Violet's eyes and mouth formed three Os. It was like looking at a pink bowling ball.

'What for?'

'I think they're using them to control the children. By magic.'

Violet's mouth opened wider.

'That's *horrid*.'

Horrible, thought Susan. The word is 'horrible'. 'Horrid' is a childish word selected to impress

349

nearby males with one's fragility, if I'm any judge. She knew it was unkind and counter-productive of her to think like that. She also knew it was probably an accurate observation, which only made it worse.

'Yes,' she said.

'There was a wizard! He's got a pointy hat!'

'I think we should get her out of here,' said the oh god, in a tone of voice that Susan considered was altogether too dramatic.

'Good idea,' she conceded. 'Let's go.'

Catseye's boots had snapped their laces. It was as if he'd been pulled upwards so fast they simply couldn't keep up.

That worried Medium Dave. So did the smell. There was no smell at all in the rest of the tower, but just here there was a lingering odour of mushrooms.

His forehead wrinkled. Medium Dave was a thief and a murderer and therefore had a highly developed moral sense. He preferred not to steal from poor people, and not only because they never had anything worth stealing. If it was necessary to hurt anyone, he tried to leave wounds that would heal. And when in the course of his activities he had to kill people then he made some effort to see that they did not suffer much or at least made as few noises as possible.

This whole business was getting on his nerves. Usually, he didn't even notice that he had any.

There was a wrongness to everything that grated on his bones.

And a pair of boots was all that remained of old Catseye.

He drew his sword.

Above him, the creeping shadows moved and flowed away.

Susan edged up to the entrance to the stairways and peered around into the point of a crossbow.

'Now, all of you step out where I can see you,' said Peachy conversationally. 'And don't touch that sword, lady. You'll probably hurt yourself.'

Susan tried to make herself unseen, and failed. Usually it was so easy to do that that it happened automatically, usually with embarrassing results. She could be idly reading a book while people searched the room for her. But here, despite every effort, she seemed to remain obstinately visible.

'You don't own this place,' she said, stepping back.

'No, but you see this crossbow? I own this crossbow. So you just walk ahead of me, right, and we'll all go and see Mister Teatime.'

'Excuse me, I just want to check something,' said Bilious. To Susan's amazement he leaned over and touched the point of the arrow.

'Here! What did you do that for?' said Peachy, stepping back.

'I felt it, but of course a certain amount of pain sensation would be part of normal sensory response,' said the oh god. 'I warn you, there's a very good chance that I might be immortal.'

'Yes, but we probably aren't,' said Susan.

'Immortal, eh?' said Peachy. 'So if I was to shoot you inna head, you wouldn't die?'

'I suppose when you put it like that . . . I do know I feel pain . . .'

'Right. You just keep moving, then.'

'When something happens,' said Susan, out of the corner of her mouth, 'you two try to get downstairs and out, all right? If the worst comes to the worst, the horse will take you out of here.'

'If something happens,' whispered the oh god.

'When,' said Susan.

Behind them, Peachy looked around. He knew he'd feel a lot better when any of the others turned up. It was almost a relief to have prisoners.

Out of the corner of her eye Susan saw something move on the stairs on the opposite side of the shaft. For a moment she thought she saw several flashes like metal blades catching the light.

She heard a gasp behind her.

The man with the crossbow was standing very still and staring at the opposite stairs.

'Oh, noooo,' he said, under his breath.

'What is it?' said Susan.

He stared at her. 'You can see it too?'

'The thing like a lot of blades clicking together?' said Susan.

'Oh, *noooo* . . .'

'It was only there for a moment,' said Susan.

352

'It's gone now,' she said. 'Somewhere else,' she added.

'It's the Scissor Man . . .'

'Who's he?' said the oh god.

'No one!' snapped Peachy, trying to pull himself together. 'There's no such thing as the Scissor Man, all right?'

'Ah . . . *yes*. When you were little, did you suck your thumb?' said Susan. 'Because the only Scissor Man I know is the one people used to frighten children with. They said he'd turn up and—'

'Shutupshutupshutup!' said Peachy, prodding her with the crossbow. 'Kids believe all kinds of crap! But I'm grown up now, right, and I can open beer bottles with other people's teeth an— oh, *gods* . . .'

Susan heard the snip, snip. It sounded very close now.

Peachy had his eyes shut.

'Is there anything behind me?' he quavered.

Susan pushed the others aside and waved frantically towards the bottom of the stairs.

'No,' she said, as they hurried away.

'Is there anything standing on the stairs at all?'

'No.'

'Right! If you see that one-eyed bastard you tell him he can keep the money!'

He turned and ran.

When Susan turned to go up the stairs the Scissor Man was there.

It wasn't man-shaped. It was something like an

ostrich, and something like a lizard on its hind legs, but almost entirely like something made out of blades. Every time it moved a thousand blades went snip, snip.

Its long silver neck curved and a head made of shears stared down at her.

'You're not looking for me,' she said. 'You're not *my* nightmare.'

The blades tilted this way and that. The Scissor Man was trying to think.

'I remember you came for Twyla,' said Susan, stepping forward. 'That damn governess had told her what happens to little girls who suck their thumbs, remember? Remember the *poker*? I bet you needed a hell of a lot of sharpening afterwards . . .'

The creature lowered its head, stepped carefully around her in as polite a way as it could manage, and clanked on down the stairs after Peachy.

Susan ran on towards the top of the tower.

Sideney put a green filter over his lantern and pressed down with a small silver rod that had an emerald set on its tip. A piece of the lock moved. There was a whirring from inside the door and something went click.

He sagged with relief. It is said that the prospect of hanging concentrates the mind wonderfully, but it was Valium compared to being watched by Mister Teatime.

'I, er, think that's the third lock,' he said. 'Green light is what opens it. I remember the fabulous lock of the Hall of Murgle, which could only be opened by the Hubward wind, although that was—'

'I commend your expertise,' said Teatime. 'And the other four?'

Sideney looked up nervously at the silent bulk of Banjo, and licked his lips.

'Well, of course, if I'm right, and the locks depend on certain conditions, well, we could be here for years . . .' he ventured. 'Supposing they can only be opened by, say, a small blond child holding a mouse? On a Tuesday? In the rain?'

'You can find out what the nature of the spell is?' said Teatime.

'Yes, yes, of course, yes.' Sideney waved his hands urgently. 'That's how I worked out this one. Reverse thaumaturgy, yes, certainly. Er. In time.'

'We have lots of time,' said Teatime.

'Perhaps a *little* more time than that,' Sideney quavered. 'The processes are very, very, very . . . difficult.'

'Oh, dear. If it's too much for you, you've only got to say,' said Teatime.

'No!' Sideney yipped, and then managed to get some self-control. 'No. No. No, I can . . . I'm sure I shall work them out soon—'

'*Jolly* good,' said Teatime.

The student wizard looked down. A wisp of vapour oozed from the crack between the doors.

'Do you know what's in here, Mister Teatime?'

'No.'

'Ah. Right.' Sideney stared mournfully at the fourth lock. It was amazing how much you remembered when someone like Teatime was around.

He gave him a nervous look. 'There's not going to be any more violent deaths, are there?' he said. 'I just can't *stand* the sight of violent deaths!'

Teatime put a comforting arm around his shoulders. 'Don't *worry*,' he said. 'I'm on *your* side. A violent death is the last thing that'll happen to you.'

'Mister Teatime?'

He turned. Medium Dave stepped onto the landing.

'Someone else is in the tower,' he said. 'They've got Catseye. I don't know how. I've got Peachy watching the stairs and I ain't sure where Chickenwire is.'

Teatime looked back to Sideney, who started prodding at the fourth lock again in a feverish attempt not to die.

'Why are you telling me? I thought I was paying you big strong men a lot of money to deal with this sort of thing.'

Medium Dave's lips framed some words, but when he spoke he said, 'All right, but what are we up against here? Eh? Old Man Trouble or the bogeyman or what?'

Teatime sighed.

'Some of the Tooth Fairy's employees, I assume,' he said.

'Not if they're like the ones that were here,' said Medium Dave. 'They were just civilians. It looks like the ground opened and swallowed Catseye up.' He thought about this. 'I mean the ceiling,' he corrected himself. A horrible image had just passed across his under-used imagination.

Teatime walked across to the stairwell and looked down. Far below, the pile of teeth looked like a white circle.

'And the girl's gone,' said Medium Dave.

'Really? I thought I said she should be killed.'

Medium Dave hesitated. The boys had been brought up by Ma Lilywhite to be respectful to women as delicate and fragile creatures, and were soundly thrashed if disrespectful tendencies were perceived by Ma's incredibly sensitive radar. And it was truly incredibly sensitive. Ma could hear what you were doing three rooms away, a terrible thing for a growing lad.

That sort of thing leaves a mark. Ma Lilywhite certainly could. As for the others, they had no objections in practice to the disposal of anyone who got between them and large sums of money, but there was a general unspoken resentment at being told by Teatime to kill someone just because he had no further use for them. It wasn't that it was unprofessional. Only Assassins thought like that. It was just that there were things you did do, and things you didn't do. And this was one of the things you didn't do.

'We thought . . . well, you never know . . .'

'She wasn't necessary,' said Teatime. 'Few people are.'

Sideney thumbed hurriedly through his notebooks.

'Anyway, the place is a maze—' Medium Dave said.

'Sadly, this is so,' said Teatime. 'But I am sure they will be able to find us. It's probably too much to hope that they intend something heroic.'

Violet and the oh god hurried down the stairs.

'Do you know how to get back?' said Violet.

'Don't you?'

'I think there's a . . . a kind of soft place. If you walk at it knowing it's there you go *through*.'

'You know where it is?'

'No! I've never been here before! They had a bag on my head when we came! All I ever did was take the teeth from under the pillows!' Violet started to sob. 'You just get this list and about five minutes' training and they even dock you ten pence a week for the ladder and I know I made that mistake with little William Rubin but they should of *said*, you're *supposed* to take any teeth you—'

'Er . . . mistake?' said Bilious, trying to get her to hurry.

'Just because he slept with his head under the pillow but they give you the pliers *anyway* and no one told *me* that you shouldn't—'

She certainly *did* have a pleasant voice, Bilious told himself. It was just that in a funny way it grated, too. It was like listening to a talking flute.

'I think we'd just better get outside,' he said. 'In case they hear us,' he hinted.

'What sort of godding do you do?' said Violet.

'Er . . . oh, I . . . this and that . . . I . . . er . . .' Bilious tried to think through the pounding headache. And then he had one of those ideas, the kind that only sound good after a lot of alcohol. Someone else may have drunk the drinks, but he managed to snag the idea.

'I'm actually self-employed,' he said, as brightly as he could manage.

'How can you be a self-employed god?'

'Ah, well, you see, if any other god wants, perhaps, you know, a holiday or something, I cover for them. Yes. That's what I do.'

Unwisely, in the circumstances, he let his inventiveness impress him.

'Oh, yes. I'm very busy. Rushed off my feet. They're always employing me. You've no idea. They don't think twice about pushing off for a month as a big white bull or a swan or something and it's always, "Oh, Bilious, old chap, just take care of things while I'm away, will you? Answer the prayers and so on." I hardly get a minute to myself but of course you can't turn down work these days.'

Violet was round-eyed with fascination.

'And are you covering for anyone right now?' she asked.

'Um, yes . . . the God of Hangovers, actually . . .'

'A God of Hangovers? How awful!'

Bilious looked down at his stained and wretched toga.

'I suppose it is . . .' he mumbled.

'You're not very good at it.'

'You don't have to tell me.'

'You're more cut out to be one of the important gods,' said Violet, admiringly. 'I can just see you as Io or Fate or one of those.'

Bilious stared at her with his mouth open.

'I could tell at once you weren't right,' she went on. 'Not for some horrible little god. You could even be Offler with calves like yours.'

'Could I? I mean . . . oh, yes. Sometimes. Of course, I have to wear fangs—'

And then someone was holding a sword to his throat.

'What's this?' said Chickenwire. 'Lover's Lane?'

'You leave him alone, you!' shouted Violet. 'He's a god! You'll be really sorry!'

Bilious swallowed, but very gently. It was a sharp sword.

'A god, eh?' said Chickenwire. 'What of?'

Bilious tried to swallow again.

'Oh, bit o' this, bit o' that,' he mumbled.

'Cor,' said Chickenwire. 'Well, I'm impressed. I can see I'm going to have to be dead careful here, eh? Don't want you smiting me with thunderbolts, do I? Puts a crimp in the day, that sort of thing—'

Bilious didn't dare move his head. But out of the corner of his eye he was sure he could see shadows moving very fast across the walls.

'Dear me, out of thunderbolts, are we?' Chickenwire sneered. 'Well, y'know, I've never—'

There was a creak.

Chickenwire's face was a few inches from Bilious. The oh god saw his expression change.

The man's eyes rolled. His lips said '. . . nur . . .'

Bilious risked stepping back. Chickenwire's sword didn't move. He stood there, trembling slightly, like a man who wants to turn round to see what's behind him but doesn't dare to in case he does.

As far as Bilious was concerned, it had just been a creak.

He looked up at the thing on the landing above.

'Who put that there?' said Violet.

It was just a wardrobe. Dark oak, a bit of fancy woodwork glued on in an effort to disguise the undisguisable fact that it was just an upright box. It was a wardrobe.

'You didn't, you know, try to cast a thunderbolt and go on a few letters too many?' she went on.

'Huh?' said Bilious, looking from the stricken man to the wardrobe. It was so ordinary it was . . . odd.

'I mean, thunderbolts begin with T and wardrobes . . .'

Violet's lips moved silently. Part of Bilious thought: I'm attracted to a girl who actually has to shut down all other brain functions in order to think about the order of the letters of the alphabet. On the other hand, *she's* attracted to someone who's wearing a toga that looks as though a family of weasels have had a party in it, so maybe I'll stop this thought right here.

But the major part of his brain thought: why's this man making little bubbling noises? It's just a *wardrobe*, for my sake!

'No, no,' mumbled Chickenwire. 'I don't *wanna*!'

The sword clanged on the floor.

He took a step backwards up the stairs, but very slowly, as if he was doing it despite every effort his muscles could muster.

'Don't want to what?' said Violet.

Chickenwire spun round. Bilious had never seen that happen before. People turned round quickly, yes, but Chickenwire just revolved as if some giant hand had been placed on his head and twisted a hundred and eighty degrees.

'No. No. No,' Chickenwire whined. 'No.'

He tottered up the steps.

'You got to help me,' he whispered.

'What's the matter?' said Bilious. 'It's just a wardrobe, isn't it? It's for putting all your old clothes in so that there's no room for your *new* clothes.'

The doors of the wardrobe swung open.

Chickenwire managed to thrust out his arms

and grab the sides and, for a moment, he stood quite still.

Then he was pulled into the wardrobe in one sudden movement and the doors slammed shut.

The little brass key turned in the lock with a click.

'We ought to get him out,' said the oh god, running up the steps.

'Why?' Violet demanded. 'They are *not* very nice people! I know that one. When he brought me food he made . . . suggestive comments.'

'Yes, but . . .' Bilious hadn't ever seen a face like that, outside of a mirror. Chickenwire had looked very, very sick.

He turned the key and opened the doors.

'Oh dear . . .'

'I don't want to see! I don't want to see!' said Violet, looking over his shoulder.

Bilious reached down and picked up a pair of boots that stood neatly in the middle of the wardrobe's floor.

Then he put them back carefully and walked around the wardrobe. It was plywood. The words 'Dratley and Sons, Phedre Road, Ankh-Morpork' were stamped in one corner in faded ink.

'Is it magic?' said Violet nervously.

'I don't know if something magic has the maker's name on it,' said Bilious.

'There *are* magic wardrobes,' said Violet nervously. 'If you go into them, you come out in a magic land.'

Bilious looked at the boots again.

'Um . . . yes,' he said.

I THINK I MUST TELL YOU SOMETHING, said Death.

'Yes, I think you should,' said Ridcully. 'I've got little devils running round the place eating socks and pencils, earlier tonight we sobered up someone who thinks he's a God of Hangovers and half my wizards are trying to cheer up the Cheerful Fairy. *We* thought something must've happened to the Hogfather. We were right, right?'

'*Hex* was right, Archchancellor,' Ponder corrected him.

HEX? WHAT IS HEX?

'Er . . . Hex thinks – that is, *calculates* – that there's been a big change in the nature of belief today,' said Ponder. He felt, he did not know why, that Death was probably not in favour of unliving things that thought.

MR HEX WAS REMARKABLY ASTUTE. THE HOG-FATHER HAS BEEN . . . Death paused. THERE IS NO SENSIBLE HUMAN WORD. DEAD, IN A WAY, BUT NOT EXACTLY . . . A GOD CANNOT BE KILLED. NEVER COMPLETELY KILLED. HE HAS BEEN, SHALL WE SAY, SEVERELY REDUCED.

'Ye gods!' said Ridcully. 'Who'd want to kill off the old boy?'

HE HAS ENEMIES.

'What did he do? Miss a chimney?'

EVERY LIVING THING HAS ENEMIES.

'What, everything?'

YES. EVERYTHING. POWERFUL ENEMIES. BUT THEY HAVE GONE TOO FAR THIS TIME. NOW THEY ARE USING PEOPLE.

'Who are?'

THOSE WHO THINK THE UNIVERSE SHOULD BE A LOT OF ROCKS MOVING IN CURVES. HAVE YOU EVER HEARD OF THE AUDITORS?

'I suppose the Bursar may have done—'

NOT AUDITORS OF MONEY. AUDITORS OF REALITY. THEY THINK OF LIFE AS A STAIN ON THE UNIVERSE. A PESTILENCE. MESSY. GETTING IN THE WAY.

'In the way of what?'

THE EFFICIENT RUNNING OF THE UNIVERSE.

'I thought it *was* run for us . . . Well, for the Professor of Applied Anthropics, actually, but we're allowed to tag along,' said Ridcully. He scratched his chin. 'And I could certainly run a marvellous university here if only we didn't have to have these damn students underfoot all the time.'

QUITE SO.

'They want to get *rid* of us?'

THEY WANT YOU TO BE . . . LESS . . . DAMN, I'VE FORGOTTEN THE WORD. UNTRUTHFUL? THE HOG-FATHER IS A SYMBOL OF THIS . . . Death snapped his fingers, causing echoes to bounce off the walls, and added, WISTFUL LYING?

'Untruthful?' said Ridcully. '*Me?* I'm as honest as the day is long! Yes, what is it *this* time?'

Ponder had tugged at his robe and now he whispered something in his ear. Ridcully cleared his throat.

'I am reminded that this is in fact the shortest day of the year,' he said. 'However, this does *not* undermine the point that I just made, although I thank my colleague for his invaluable support and constant readiness to correct minor if not downright trivial errors. I am a remarkably truthful man, sir. Things said at University council meetings don't count.'

I MEAN HUMANITY IN GENERAL. ER . . . THE ACT OF TELLING THE UNIVERSE IT IS OTHER THAN IT IS?

'You've got me there,' said Ridcully. 'Anyway, why're *you* doing the job?'

SOMEONE MUST. IT IS VITALLY IMPORTANT. THEY MUST BE SEEN, AND BELIEVED. BEFORE DAWN, THERE MUST BE ENOUGH BELIEF IN THE HOG-FATHER.

'Why?' said Ridcully.

SO THAT THE SUN WILL COME UP.

The two wizards gawped at him.

I SELDOM JOKE, said Death.

At which point there was a scream of horror.

'That sounded like the Bursar,' said Ridcully. 'And he's been doing so well up to now.'

The reason for the Bursar's scream lay on the floor of his bedroom.

It was a man. He was dead. No one alive had that kind of expression.

Some of the other wizards had got there first. Ridcully pushed his way through the crowd.

'Ye gods,' he said. 'What a face! He looks as though he died of fright! What happened?'

'Well,' said the Dean, 'as far as I can tell, the Bursar opened his wardrobe and found the man inside.'

'Really? I wouldn't have said the poor old Bursar was all that frightening.'

'*No*, Archchancellor. The corpse fell out on him.'

The Bursar was standing in the corner, wearing his old familiar expression of good-humoured concussion.

'You all right, old fellow?' said Ridcully. 'What's eleven per cent of 1,276?'

'One hundred and forty point three six,' said the Bursar promptly.

'Ah, right as rain,' said Ridcully cheerfully.

'I don't see why,' said the Chair of Indefinite Studies. 'Just because he can do things with numbers doesn't mean everything else is fine.'

'Doesn't need to be,' said Ridcully. 'Numbers is what he has to do. The poor chap might be slightly yoyo, but I've been reading about it. He's one of these idiot servants.'

'Savants,' said the Dean patiently. 'The word is savants, Ridcully.'

'Whatever. Those chaps who can tell you what day of the week the first of Grune was a hundred years ago—'

'—Tuesday—' said the Bursar.

'—but can't tie their bootlaces,' said Ridcully. 'What was a corpse doing in his wardrobe? And no one is to say "Not a lot," or anythin' tasteless like that. Haven't had a corpse in a wardrobe since that business with Archchancellor Buckleby.'

'We all warned Buckleby that the lock was too stiff,' said the Dean.

'Just out of interest, why was the Bursar fiddling with his wardrobe at this time of night?' said Ridcully.

The wizards looked sheepish.

'We were . . . playing Sardines, Archchancellor,' said the Dean.

'What's that?'

'It's like Hide and Seek, but when you find someone you have to squeeze in with them,' said the Dean.

'I just want to be clear about this,' said Ridcully. 'My senior wizards have spent the evening playing Hide and Seek?'

'Oh, not the whole evening,' said the Chair of Indefinite Studies. 'We played Grandmother's Footsteps and I Spy for quite a while until the Senior Wrangler made a scene just because we wouldn't let him spell chandelier with an S.'

'Party games? *You* fellows?'

The Dean sidled closer.

'It's Miss Smith,' he mumbled. 'When we don't join in she bursts into tears.'

'Who's Miss Smith?'

'The Cheerful Fairy,' said the Lecturer in Recent Runes glumly. 'If you don't say yes to everything her lip wobbles like a plate of jelly. It's unbearable.'

'We just joined in to stop her weeping,' said the Dean. 'It's amazing how one woman can be so soggy.'

'If we're not cheerful she bursts into tears,' said the Chair of Indefinite Studies. 'The Senior Wrangler's doing some juggling for her at the moment.'

'But he can't juggle!'

'I think that's cheering her up a bit.'

'What you're tellin' me, then, is that my wizards are prancing around playin' children's games just to cheer up some dejected fairy?'

'Er . . . yes.'

'I thought you had to clap your hands and say you believed in 'em,' said Ridcully. 'Correct me if I'm wrong.'

'That's just for the little shiny ones,' said the Lecturer in Recent Runes. 'Not for the ones in saggy cardigans with half a dozen hankies stuffed up their sleeves.'

Ridcully looked at the corpse again.

'Anyone know who he is? Looks a bit of a ruffian to me. And where's his boots, may I ask?'

The Dean took a small glass cube from his pocket and ran it over the corpse.

'Quite a large thaumic reading, gentlemen,' he said. 'I think he got here by magic.'

He rummaged in the man's pockets and pulled out a handful of small white things.

'Ugh,' he said.

'Teeth?' said Ridcully. 'Who goes around with a pocket full of teeth?'

'A very bad fighter?' said the Chair of Indefinite Studies. 'I'll go and get Modo to take the poor fellow away, shall I?'

'If we can get a reading off the thaumameter, perhaps Hex—' Ridcully began.

'Now, Ridcully,' said the Dean, 'I really think there must be some problems that can be resolved without having to deal with that damn thinking mill.'

Death looked up at Hex.

A MACHINE FOR THINKING?

'Er . . . yes, sir,' said Ponder Stibbons. 'You see, when you said . . . well, you see, Hex believes everything . . . but, look, the sun really will come up, won't it? That's its *job*.'

LEAVE US.

Ponder backed away, and then scurried out of the room.

The ants flowed along their tubes. Cogwheels spun. The big wheel with the sheep skulls on it creaked around slowly. A mouse squeaked, somewhere in the works.

WELL? said Death.

After a while, the pen began to write.

+++ Big Red Lever Time +++ Query +++

NO. THEY SAY YOU ARE A THINKER. EXTEND LOGICALLY THE RESULT OF THE HUMAN RACE CEASING TO BELIEVE IN THE HOGFATHER. WILL THE SUN COME UP? ANSWER.

It took several minutes. The wheels spun. The

ants ran. The mouse squeaked. An eggtimer came down on a spring. It bounced aimlessly for a while, and then jerked back up again.

Hex wrote: +++ The Sun Will Not Come Up +++

CORRECT. HOW MAY THIS BE PREVENTED? ANSWER.

+++ Regular and Consistent Belief +++

GOOD. I HAVE A TASK FOR YOU, THINKING ENGINE.

+++ Yes. I Am Preparing An Area Of Write-Only Memory +++

WHAT IS THAT?

+++ You Would Say: To Know In Your Bones +++

GOOD. HERE IS YOUR INSTRUCTION. BELIEVE IN THE HOGFATHER.

+++ Yes +++

DO YOU BELIEVE? ANSWER.

+++ Yes +++

DO . . . YOU . . . BELIEVE? ANSWER.

+++ **YES** +++

There was a change in the ill-assembled heap of pipes and tubes that was Hex. The big wheel creaked into a new position. From the other side of the wall came the hum of busy bees.

GOOD.

Death turned to leave the room, but stopped when Hex began to write furiously. He went back and looked at the emerging paper.

+++ Dear Hogfather, For Hogswatch I Want—

OH, NO. *YOU* CAN'T WRITE LETT— Death paused,

and then said, YOU CAN, CAN'T YOU.

+++ Yes. I Am Entitled +++

Death waited until the pen had stopped, and picked up the paper.

BUT YOU ARE A MACHINE. THINGS HAVE NO DESIRES. A DOORKNOB WANTS NOTHING, EVEN THOUGH IT IS A COMPLEX MACHINE.

+++ All Things Strive +++

YOU HAVE A POINT, said Death. He thought of tiny red petals in the black depths, and read to the end of the list.

I DON'T KNOW WHAT MOST OF THESE THINGS ARE. I DON'T THINK THE SACK WILL, EITHER.

+++ I Regret This +++

BUT WE WILL DO THE BEST WE CAN, said Death. FRANKLY, I SHALL BE GLAD WHEN TONIGHT'S OVER. IT'S MUCH HARDER TO GIVE THAN TO RECEIVE. He rummaged in his sack. LET ME SEE . . . HOW OLD ARE YOU?

Susan crept up the stairs, one hand on the hilt of the sword.

Ponder Stibbons had been worried to find himself, as a wizard, awaiting the arrival of the Hogfather. It's amazing how people define roles for themselves and put handcuffs on their experience and are constantly surprised by the things a roulette universe spins at them. Here am I, they say, a mere wholesale fishmonger, at the controls of a giant airliner because as it turns out all the crew had the Coronation Chicken. Who'd have thought it? Here am I, a housewife who merely went out this morning to bank the proceeds of the Playgroup Association's Car Boot Sale, on the run with one million in stolen cash and a rather handsome man from the Battery Chickens' Liberation Organization. Amazing! Here am I, a perfectly ordinary hockey player, suddenly realizing I'm the Son of God with five hundred devoted followers in a nice little commune in Empowerment, Southern California. Who'd have thought it?

Here am I, thought Susan, a very practically minded governess who can add up faster upside down than most people can the right way up, climbing up a tooth-shaped tower belonging to the Tooth Fairy and armed with a sword belonging to Death . . .

Again! I wish one month, just one damn *month*, could go by without something like this happening to me.

She could hear voices above her. Someone said something about a lock.

She peered over the edge of the stairwell.

It looked as though people had been camping out up here. There were boxes and sleeping rolls strewn around. A couple of men were sitting on boxes watching a third man who was working on a door in one curved wall. One of the men was the biggest Susan had ever seen, one of those huge fat men who contrive to indicate that a lot of the fat under their shapeless clothes is muscle. The other—

'Hello,' said a cheerful voice by her ear. 'What's *your* name?'

She made herself turn her head slowly.

First she saw the grey, glinting eye. Then the yellow-white one with the tiny dot of a pupil came into view.

Around them was a friendly pink and white face topped by curly hair. It was actually quite pretty, in a boyish sort of way, except that those mismatched eyes staring out of it suggested that it had been stolen from someone else.

She started to move her hand but the boy was there first, dragging the sword scabbard out of her belt.

'Ah, ah!' he chided, turning and fending her off as she tried to grab it. 'Well, well, well. My word. White bone handle, rather tasteless skull and bone decoration . . . Death himself's second favourite weapon, am I right? Oh, my! This must be Hogswatch! And this must mean that you are Susan Sto-Helit. Nobility. I'd bow,' he added, dancing back, 'but I'm afraid you'd do something dreadful—'

There was a click, and a little gasp of excitement from the wizard working on the door.

'Yes! Yes! Left-handed using a wooden pick! That's *simple*!'

He saw that even Susan was looking at him, and coughed nervously.

'Er, I've got the fifth lock open, Mister Teatime! *Not* a problem! They're just based on Woddeley's

Occult Sequence! Any fool could do it if they knew that!'

'*I* know it,' said Teatime, without taking his eyes off Susan.

'Ah . . .'

It was not technically audible, but nevertheless Susan could almost hear the wizard's mind back-pedalling. Up ahead was the conclusion that Teatime had no time for people he didn't need.

'. . . with . . . inter . . . est . . . ing subtleties,' he said slowly. 'Yes. Very tricky. I'll, er, just have a look at number six . . .'

'How do you know who I am?' said Susan.

'Oh, *easy*,' said Teatime. '*Twurp's Peerage*. Family motto *Non temetis messor*. We have to read it, you know, in class. Hah, old Mericet calls it the Guide to the Turf. No one laughs except him, of course. Oh yes, I know about you. Quite a lot. Your father was well known. Went a long way very fast. As for your grandfather . . . honestly, that motto. Is that good taste? Of course, *you* don't need to fear him, do you? Or do you?'

Susan tried to fade. It didn't work. She could feel herself staying embarrassingly solid.

'I don't know what you're talking about,' she said. 'Who are you, anyway?'

'I beg your pardon. My name is Teatime, Jonathan Teatime. At your service.'

Susan lined up the syllables in her head.

'You mean . . . like around four o'clock in the afternoon?' she said.

375

'No. I did say Teh-ah-tim-eh,' said Teatime. 'I spoke very clearly. Please don't try to break my concentration by annoying me. I only get annoyed at important things. How are you getting on, Mr Sideney? If it's just according to Woddeley's sequence, number six should be copper and blue-green light. Unless, of course, there are any *subtleties* . . .'

'Er, doing it right now, Mister Teatime—'

'Do you think your grandfather will try to rescue you? Do you think he will? But now I have his sword, you see. I wonder—'

There was another click.

'Sixth lock, Mister Teatime!'

'Really.'

'Er . . . don't you want me to start on the seventh?'

'Oh, well, if you like. Pure white light will be the key,' said Teatime, still not looking away from Susan. 'But it may not be all important now. Thank you, anyway. You've been most helpful.'

'Er—'

'Yes, you may go.'

Susan noticed that Sideney didn't even bother to pick up his books and tools, but hurried down the stairs as if he expected to be called back and was trying to run faster than the sound.

'Is that all you're here for?' she said. 'A robbery?' He was dressed like an Assassin, after all, and there was always one way to annoy an Assassin. 'Like a thief?'

Teatime danced excitedly. 'A thief? Me? I'm

376

not a thief, madam. But if I were, I would be the kind that steals fire from the gods.'

'We've already got fire.'

'There must be an upgrade by now. No, *these* gentlemen are thieves. Common robbers. Decent types, although you wouldn't necessarily want to watch them eat, for example. That's Medium Dave and exhibit B is Banjo. He can talk.'

Medium Dave nodded at Susan. She saw the look in his eyes. Maybe there was something she could use . . .

She'd need something. Even her hair was a mess. She couldn't step behind time, she couldn't fade into the background, and now even her hair had let her down.

She was normal. Here, she was what she'd always wanted to be.

Bloody, bloody damn.

Sideney prayed as he ran down the stairs. He didn't believe in any gods, since most wizards seldom like to encourage them, but he prayed anyway the fervent prayers of an atheist who hopes to be wrong.

But no one called him back. And no one ran after him.

So, being of a serious turn of mind under his normal state of sub-critical fear, he slowed down in case he lost his footing.

It was then that he noticed that the steps underfoot weren't the smooth whiteness they had been everywhere else but were very large, pitted flagstones. And the light had changed, and then they weren't stairs any more and he staggered as he encountered flat ground where steps should have been.

His outstretched hand brushed against a crumbling brick.

And the ghosts of the past poured in, and he knew where he was. He was in the yard of Gammer Wimblestone's dame school. His mother wanted him to learn his letters and be a wizard, but she also thought that long curls on a five-year-old boy looked very smart.

This was the hunting ground of Ronnie Jenks.

Adult memory and understanding said that Ronnie was just an unintelligent bullet-headed seven-year-old bully with muscles where his brain should have been. The eye of childhood, rather more accurately, dreaded him as a force like a personalized earthquake with one nostril bunged up with bogies, both knees scabbed, both fists balled and all five brain cells concentrated in a kind of cerebral grunt.

Oh, gods. There was the tree Ronnie used to hide behind. It looked as big and menacing as he remembered it.

But . . . if somehow he'd ended up back there, gods knew how, well, he might be a bit on the skinny side but he was a damn sight bigger than Ronnie Jenks now. Gods, *yes*, he'd kick those evil little trousers all the—

And then, as a shadow blotted out the sun, he realized he was wearing curls.

Teatime looked thoughtfully at the door.

'I suppose I should open it,' he said, 'after coming all this way . . .'

'You're controlling children by their teeth,' said Susan.

'It does sound odd, doesn't it, when you put it like that,' said Teatime. 'But that's sympathetic magic for you. Is your grandfather going to try to rescue you, do you think? But no . . . I don't think he can. Not here, I think. I don't think that he can come here. So he sent you, did he?'

'Certainly not! He—' Susan stopped. Oh, he *had*, she told herself, feeling even more of a fool. He certainly had. He was learning about humans, all right. For a walking skeleton, he could be quite clever . . .

But . . . how clever was Teatime? Just a bit too excited at his cleverness to realize that if Death— She tried to stamp on the thought, just in case Teatime could read it in her eyes.

'I don't think he'll try,' she said. 'He's not as clever as you, Mister Teatime.'

'Teh-ah-tim-eh,' said Teatime, automatically. 'That's a shame.'

'Do you think you're going to get away with this?'

'Oh, dear. Do people really say that?' And

suddenly Teatime was much closer. 'I've *got* away with it. No more Hogfather. And that's only the start. We'll keep the teeth coming in, of course. The possibilities—'

There was a rumble like an avalanche, a long way off. The dormant Banjo had awakened, causing tremors on his lower slopes. His enormous hands, which had been resting on his knees, started to bunch.

'What's dis?' he said.

Teatime stopped and, for a moment, looked puzzled.

'What's this what?'

'You said no more Hogfather,' said Banjo. He stood up, like a mountain range rising gently in the squeeze between colliding continents. His hands still stayed in the vicinity of his knees.

Teatime stared at him and then glanced at Medium Dave.

'He does *know* what we've been doing, does he?' he said. 'You did *tell* him?'

Medium Dave shrugged.

'Dere's got to be a Hogfather,' said Banjo. 'Dere's always a Hogfather.'

Susan looked down. Grey blotches were speeding across the white marble. She was standing in a pool of grey. So was Banjo. And around Teatime the dots bounced and recoiled like wasps around a pot of jam.

Looking for something, she thought.

'You don't believe in the Hogfather, do you?' said Teatime. 'A big boy like you?'

'Yeah,' said Banjo. 'So what's dis "no more Hogfather"?'

Teatime pointed at Susan.

'*She* did it,' he said. 'She killed him.'

The sheer playground effrontery of it shocked Susan.

'No I didn't,' she said. 'He—'

'Did!'

'Didn't!'

'Did!'

Banjo's big bald head turned towards her.

'What's dis about the Hogfather?' he said.

'I don't think he's dead,' said Susan. 'But Teatime *has* made him very ill—'

'Who cares?' said Teatime, dancing away. 'When this is over, Banjo, you'll have as many presents as you want. Trust me!'

'Dere's got to be a Hogfather,' Banjo rumbled. 'Else dere's no Hogswatch.'

'It's just another solar festival,' said Teatime. 'It—'

Medium Dave stood up. He had his hand on his sword.

'We're going, Teatime,' he said. 'Me and Banjo are going. I don't like any of this. I don't mind robbing, I don't mind thieving, but *this* isn't *honest*. Banjo? You come with me right now!'

'What's dis about no more Hogfather?' said Banjo.

Teatime pointed to Susan.

'You grab her, Banjo. It's all her fault!'

Banjo lumbered a few steps in Susan's direction, and then stopped.

'Our mam said no hittin' girls,' he rumbled. 'No pullin' dere hair . . .'

Teatime rolled his one good eye. Around his feet the greyness seemed to be boiling in the stone, following his feet as they moved. And it was around Banjo, too.

Searching, Susan thought. It's looking for a way in.

'I think I know you, Teatime,' she said, as sweetly as she could for Banjo's sake. 'You're the mad kid they're all scared of, right?'

'Banjo?' snapped Teatime. 'I said grab her—'

'Our mam said—'

'The giggling excitable one even the bullies never touched because if they did he went insane and kicked and bit,' said Susan. 'The kid who didn't know the difference between chucking a stone at a cat and setting it on fire.'

To her delight he glared at her.

'Shut up,' he said.

'I *bet* no one wanted to *play* with you,' said Susan. 'Not the kid with no friends. Kids know about a mind like yours even if they don't know the right words for it—'

'I *said* shut up! *Get* her, Banjo!'

That was it. She could hear it in Teatime's voice. There was a touch of vibrato that hadn't been there before.

'The kind of little boy,' she said, watching his face, 'who looks up dolls' dresses . . .'

382

'I *didn't!*'

Banjo looked worried.

'Our mam said—'

'Oh, to blazes with your mam!' snapped Tea-time.

There was a whisper of steel as Medium Dave drew his sword.

'What'd you say about our mam?' he whispered.

Now he's having to concentrate on three people, Susan thought.

'I bet *no one* ever played with you,' she said. 'I bet there were things people had to hush up, eh?'

'Banjo! You do what I tell you!' Teatime screamed.

The monstrous man was beside her now. She could see his face twisted in an agony of inde-cision. His enormous fists clenched and unclenched and his lips moved as some kind of horrible debate raged in his head.

'Our . . . our mam . . . our mam said . . .'

The grey marks flowed across the floor and formed a pool of shadow which grew darker and higher with astonishing speed. It towered over the three men, and grew a shape.

'Have you been a bad boy, you little perisher?'

The huge woman towered over all three men. In one meaty hand it was holding a bundle of birch twigs as thick as a man's arm.

The thing growled.

Medium Dave looked up into the enormous face of Ma Lilywhite. Every pore was a pothole. Every brown tooth was a tombstone.

'You been letting him get into trouble, our Davey? You have, ain't you?'

He backed away. 'No, Mum . . . no, Mum . . .'

'You need a good hiding, Banjo? You been playing with girls again?'

Banjo sagged on to his knees, tears of misery rolling down his face.

'Sorry Mum sorry sorry Mum noooohhh Mum sorry Mum sorry sorry—'

Then the figure turned to Medium Dave again.

The sword dropped out of his hand. His face seemed to melt.

Medium Dave started to cry.

'No Mum no Mum no Mum nooooh Mum—'

He gave a gurgle and collapsed, clutching his chest. And vanished.

Teatime started to laugh.

Susan tapped him on the shoulder and, as he looked round, hit him as hard as she could across the face.

That was the plan, at least. His hand moved faster and caught her wrist. It was like striking an iron bar.

'Oh, *no*,' he said. 'I don't *think* so.'

Out of the corner of her eye Susan saw Banjo crawling across the floor to where his brother had been. Ma Lilywhite had vanished.

'This place gets into your head, doesn't it?' Teatime said. 'It pokes around to find out how to deal with you. Well, *I*'m in touch with my inner child.'

He reached out with his other hand and grabbed her hair, pulling her head down.

Susan screamed.

'And it's much more fun,' he whispered.

Susan felt his grip lessen. There was a wet thump like a piece of steak hitting a slab and Teatime went past her, on his back.

'No pullin' girls' hair,' rumbled Banjo. 'That's *bad.*'

Teatime bounced up like an acrobat and steadied himself on the railing of the stairwell.

Then he drew the sword.

The blade was invisible in the bright light of the tower.

'It's true what the stories say, then,' he said. 'So thin you can't see it. I'm going to have such *fun* with it.' He waved it at them. 'So light.'

'You wouldn't *dare* use it. My grandfather will come after you,' said Susan, walking towards him.

She saw one eye twitch.

'He comes after everyone. But I'll be ready for him,' said Teatime.

'He's very single-minded,' said Susan, closer now.

'Ah, a man after my own heart.'

'Could be, Mister *Tea*time.'

He brought the sword around. She didn't even have time to duck.

And she didn't even try to when he swung the sword back again.

'It doesn't work here,' she said, as he stared at

it in astonishment. 'The blade doesn't *exist* here. There's no *Death* here!'

She slapped him across the face.

'Hi!' she said brightly. 'I'm the inner baby-sitter!'

She didn't punch. She just thrust out an arm, palm first, catching him under the chin and lifting him backwards over the rail.

He somersaulted. She never knew how. He somehow managed to gain purchase on clear air.

His free arm grabbed at hers, her feet came off the ground, and she was over the rail. She caught it with her other hand – although later she wondered if the rail hadn't managed to catch her instead.

Teatime swung from her arm, staring upwards with a thoughtful expression. She saw him grip the sword hilt in his teeth and reach down to his belt—

The question 'Is this person mad enough to try to kill someone holding him?' was asked and answered very, very fast . . . She kicked down and hit him on the ear.

The cloth of her sleeve began to tear. Teatime tried to get another grip. She kicked again and the dress ripped. For an instant he held on to nothing and then, still wearing the expression of someone trying to solve a complex problem, he fell away, spinning, getting smaller . . .

He hit the pile of teeth, sending them splashing across the marble. He jerked for a moment . . .

And vanished.

A hand like a bunch of bananas pulled Susan back over the rail.

'You can get into trouble, hittin' girls,' said Banjo. 'No playin' with girls.'

There was a click behind them.

The doors had swung open. Cold white mist rolled out across the floor.

'Our mam—' said Banjo, trying to work things out. 'Our mam was here—'

'Yes,' said Susan.

'But it *weren't* our mam, 'cos they *buried* our mam—'

'Yes.'

'We watched 'em fill in the grave and everything.'

'Yes,' said Susan, and added to herself, *I bet you did*.

'And where's our Davey gone?'

'Er . . . somewhere else, Banjo.'

'Somewhere nice?' said the huge man hesitantly.

Susan grasped with relief the opportunity to tell the truth, or at least not definitely lie.

'It could be,' she said.

'Better'n here?'

'You never know. Some people would say the odds are in favour.'

Banjo turned his pink piggy eyes on her. For a moment a thirty-five-year-old man looked out through the pink clouds of a five-year-old face.

'That's good,' he said. 'He'll be able to see our mam again.'

This much conversation seemed to exhaust him. He sagged.

'I wanna go home,' he said.

She stared at his big, stained face, shrugged hopelessly, pulled a handkerchief out of her pocket and held it up to his mouth.

'Spit,' she commanded. He obeyed.

She dabbed the handkerchief over the worst parts and then tucked it into his hand.

'Have a good blow,' she suggested, and then carefully leaned out of range until the echoes of the blast had died away.

'You can keep the hanky. Please,' she added, meaning it whole-heartedly. 'Now tuck your shirt in.'

'Yes, miss.'

'Now, go downstairs and sweep all the teeth out of the circle. Can you do that?'

Banjo nodded.

'What can you do?' Susan prompted.

Banjo concentrated. 'Sweep all the teeth out of the circle, miss.'

'Good. Off you go.'

Susan watched him plod off, and then looked at the white doorway. She was *sure* the wizard had only got as far as the sixth lock.

The room beyond the door was entirely white, and the mist that swirled at knee level deadened even the sound of her footsteps.

All there was was a bed. It was a large four-poster, old and dusty.

She thought it was unoccupied and then she

saw the figure, lying among the mounds of pillows. It looked very much like a frail old lady in a mob cap.

The old woman turned her head and smiled at Susan.

'Hello, my dear.'

Susan couldn't remember a grandmother. Her father's mother had died when she was young, and the other side of the family . . . well, she'd never had a grandmother. But this was the sort she'd have wanted.

The kind, the nasty realistic side of her mind said, that hardly ever existed.

Susan thought she heard a child laugh. And another one. Somewhere almost out of hearing, children were at play. It was always a pleasant, lulling sound.

Always provided, of course, you couldn't hear the actual words.

'No,' said Susan.

'Sorry, dear?' said the old lady.

'You're not the Tooth Fairy.' Oh, no . . . there was even a damn patchwork quilt . . .

'Oh, I *am*, dear.'

'Oh, Grandma, what big teeth you have . . . Good grief, you've even got a shawl, oh dear.'

'I don't understand, lovey—'

'You forgot the rocking chair,' said Susan. 'I always thought there'd be a rocking chair . . .'

There was a pop behind her, and then a dying creak-creak. She didn't even turn round.

'If you've included a kitten playing with a ball

389

of wool it'll go very hard with you,' she said sternly, and picked up the candlestick by the bed. It seemed heavy enough.

'I don't think you're real,' she said levelly. 'There's not a little old woman in a shawl running this place. You're out of my head. That's how you defend yourself . . . You poke around in people's heads and find the things that work—'

She swung the candlestick. It passed through the figure in the bed.

'See?' she said. 'You're not even *real*.'

'Oh, I am real, dear,' said the old woman, as her outline changed. 'The candlestick wasn't.'

Susan looked down at the new shape.

'Nope,' she said. 'It's horrible, but it doesn't frighten me. No, nor does that.' It changed again, and again. 'No, nor does my father. Good grief, you're scraping the bottom of the barrel, aren't you? I *like* spiders. Snakes don't worry me. Dogs? No. Rats are fine, I like rats. Sorry, is *anyone* frightened of *that*?'

She grabbed at the thing and this time the shape stayed. It looked like a small, wizened monkey, but with big deep eyes under a brow overhanging like a balcony. Its hair was grey and lank. It struggled weakly in her grasp, and wheezed.

'I don't frighten easily,' said Susan, 'but you'd be amazed at how angry I can become.'

The creature hung limp.

'I . . . I . . .' it muttered.

She let it down again.

'You're a bogeyman, aren't you?' she said.

It collapsed in a heap when she took her hand away.

'. . . Not *a* . . . *The* . . .' it said.

'What do you mean, *the*?' said Susan.

'*The* bogeyman,' said the bogeyman. And she saw how rangy it was, how white and grey streaked its hair, how the skin was stretched over the bones . . .

'The *first* bogeyman?'

'I . . . there were . . . I do remember when the land was different. Ice. Many times of . . . ice. And the . . . what do you call them?' The creature wheezed. '. . . The lands, the big lands . . . all different . . .'

Susan sat down on the bed.

'You mean continents?'

'. . . all different.' The black sunken eyes glinted at her and suddenly the thing reared up, bony arms waving. 'I was the dark in the cave! I was the shadow in the trees! You've heard about . . . the primal scream? That was . . . at *me*! I was . . .' It folded up and started coughing. 'And then . . . that thing, you know, that thing . . . all light and bright . . . lightning you could carry, hot, little sunshine, and then there was no more dark, just shadows, and then you made axes, axes in the forest, and then . . . and then . . .'

Susan sat down on the bed. 'There's still plenty of bogeymen,' she said.

'Hiding under beds! Lurking in cupboards! But,' it fought for breath, 'if you had seen me . . .

in the old days . . . when they came down into the deep caves to draw their hunting pictures . . . I could roar in their heads . . . so that their stomachs dropped out of their bottoms . . .'

'All the old skills are dying out,' said Susan gravely.

'. . . Oh, others came later . . . They never knew that first fine terror. All they knew,' even whispering, the bogeyman managed to get a sneer in its voice, 'was dark corners. I had *been* the dark! I was the . . . first! And now I was no better than them . . . frightening maids, curdling cream . . . hiding in shadows at the stub of the year . . . and then one night, I thought . . . why?'

Susan nodded. Bogeymen weren't bright. The moment of existential uncertainty probably took a lot longer in heads where the brain cells bounced so very slowly from one side of the skull to the other. But . . . Granddad had thought like that. You hung around with humans long enough and you stopped being what they imagined you to be and wanted to become something of your own. Umbrellas and silver hairbrushes . . .

'You thought: what was the point of it all?' she said.

'. . . frightening children . . . lurking . . . and then I started to watch them. Didn't really used to be children back in the ice times . . . just big humans, little humans, not *children* . . . and . . . and there was a different world in their heads . . . In their heads, that's where the old days *were* now. The old days. When it was all young.'

'You came out from under the bed . . .'

'I watched over them . . . kept 'em safe . . .'

Susan tried not to shudder.

'And the teeth?'

'I . . . oh, you can't leave teeth around, *anyone* might get them, do terrible things. I liked them, I didn't want anyone to hurt them . . .' it bubbled. 'I never wanted to hurt them, I just used to watch, I kept the teeth all safe . . . and, and, and sometimes I just sit here listening to them . . .'

It mumbled on. Susan listened in embarrassed amazement, not knowing whether to take pity on the thing or, and this was a developing option, to tread on it.

'. . . and the teeth . . . they remember . . .'

It started to shake.

'The money?' Susan prompted. 'I don't see many rich bogeymen around.'

'. . . money everywhere . . . buried in holes . . . old treasure . . . back of sofas . . . it adds up . . . investments . . . money for the tooth, very important, part of the magic, makes it safe, makes it proper, otherwise it's *thieving* . . . and I labelled 'em all, and kept 'em safe, and . . . and then I was old, but I found people . . .' The Tooth Fairy sniggered, and for a moment Susan felt sorry for the men in the ancient caves. 'They don't ask questions, do they?' it bubbled. '. . . You give 'em money and they all do their jobs and they don't ask questions . . .'

'It's more than their job's worth,' said Susan.

'. . . and then *they* came . . . stealing . . .'

Susan gave in. Old gods do new jobs.

'You look terrible.'

'. . . thank you very much . . .'

'I mean ill.'

'. . . very old . . . all those men, too much effort . . .'

The bogeyman groaned.

'. . . you . . . don't die here,' it panted. 'Just get old, listening to the laughter . . .'

Susan nodded. It was in the air. She couldn't hear words, just a distant chatter, as if it was at the other end of a long corridor.

'. . . and this place . . . it grew up round me . . .'

'The trees,' said Susan. 'And the sky. Out of their heads . . .'

'. . . dying . . . the little children . . . you've got to . . .'

The figure faded.

Susan sat for a while, listening to the distant chatter.

Worlds of belief, she thought. Just like oysters. A little piece of shit gets in and then a pearl grows up around it.

She got up and went downstairs.

Banjo had found a broom and mop somewhere. The circle was empty and, with surprising initiative, the man was carefully washing the chalk away.

'Banjo?'

'Yes, miss.'

'You like it here?'

'There's trees, miss.'

That probably counts as a 'yes', Susan decided.

'The sky doesn't worry you?'

He looked at her in puzzlement.

'No, miss?'

'Can you count, Banjo?'

He looked smug.

'Yes, miss. On m'fingers, miss.'

'So you can count up to . . . ?' Susan prompted.

'Thirteen, miss,' said Banjo proudly.

She looked at his big hands.

'Good grief.'

Well, she thought, and why not? He's big and trustworthy and what other kind of life has he got?

'I think it would be a good idea if you did the Tooth Fairy's job, Banjo.'

'Will that be all right, miss? Won't the Tooth Fairy mind?'

'You . . . do it until she comes back.'

'All right, miss.'

'I'll . . . er . . . get people to keep an eye on you, until you get settled in. I think food comes in on the cart. You're not to let people cheat you.' She looked at his hands and then up and up the lower slopes until she saw the peak of Mount Banjo, and added, 'Not that I think they'll try, mind you.'

'Yes, miss. I will keep things tidy, miss. Er . . .'

The big pink face looked at her.

'Yes, Banjo?'

'Can I have a puppy, miss? I had a kitten once, miss, but our mam drownded it 'cos it was dirty.'

Susan's memory threw up a name.

'A puppy called Spot?'

'Yes, miss. Spot, miss.'

'I think it'll turn up quite soon, Banjo.'

He seemed to take this entirely on trust.

'Thank you, miss.'

'And now I've got to go.'

'Right, miss.'

She looked back up the tower. Death's land might be dark, but when you were there you never thought anything bad was going to happen to you. You were beyond the places where it could. But here—

When you were grown up you only feared, well, logical things. Poverty. Illness. Being found out. At least you weren't mad with terror because of something under the stairs. The world wasn't full of arbitrary light and shade. The wonderful world of childhood? Well, it wasn't a cut-down version of the adult one, that was certain. It was more like the adult one written in big heavy letters. Everything was . . . *more*. More *everything*.

She left Banjo to his sweeping and stepped out into the perpetually sunlit world.

Bilious and Violet hurried towards her. Bilious was waving a branch like a club.

'You don't need that,' said Susan. She wanted some sleep.

'We talked about it and we thought we ought to come back and help,' said Bilious.

'Ah. Democratic courage,' said Susan. 'Well, they're all gone. To wherever they go.'

Bilious lowered the branch thankfully.

'It wasn't that—' he began.

'Look, you two can make yourselves useful,' said Susan. 'There's a mess in there. Go and help Banjo.'

'Banjo?'

'He's . . . more or less running the place now.' Violet laughed.

'But he's—'

'He's in charge,' said Susan wearily.

'All right,' said Bilious. 'Anyway, I'm sure we can tell him what to do—'

'No! Too many people have told him what to do. He *knows* what to do. Just help him get started, all right? But . . .'

If the Hogfather comes back now, you'll vanish, won't you? She didn't know how to phrase the question.

'I'm, er, giving up my old job,' said Bilious. 'Er . . . I'm going to *go on* working as a holiday relief for the other gods.' He gave her a pleading look.

'Really?' Susan looked at Violet. Oh, well, maybe if she believes in him, at least . . . It might work. You never know.

'Good,' she said. 'Have fun. Now I'm going home. This is a hell of a way to spend Hogswatch.'

She found Binky waiting by the stream.

The Auditors fluttered anxiously. And, as always happens in their species when something goes radically wrong and needs fixing instantly, they settled down to try to work out who to blame.

One said, It was . . .

And then it stopped. The Auditors lived by consensus, which made picking scapegoats a little problematical. It brightened up. After all, if everyone was to blame, then it was no one's actual *fault*. That's what collective responsibility meant, after all. It was more like bad luck, or something.

Another said, Unfortunately, people might get the wrong idea. We may be asked questions.

One said, What about Death? He interfered, after all.

One said, Er . . . not exactly.

One said, Oh, come on. He got the girl involved.

One said, Er . . . no. She got herself involved.

One said, Yes, but he told her . . .

One said, No. He didn't. In fact he specifically did *not* tell—

It paused, and then said, Damn!

One said, On the other hand . . .

The robes turned towards it.

Yes?

One said, There's no actual *evidence*. Nothing written down. Some humans got excited and decided to attack the Tooth Fairy's country. This is unfortunate, but nothing to do with us. We are shocked, of course.

One said, There's still the Hogfather. Things are going to be noticed. Questions may be asked.

They hovered for a while, unspeaking.

Eventually one said, We may have to take . . .

It paused, loath even to *think* the word, but managed to continue . . . a risk.

Bed, thought Susan, as the mists rolled past her. And in the morning, decent human things like coffee and porridge. And *bed*. *Real* things—

Binky stopped. She stared at his ears for a moment, and then urged him forward. He whinnied, and didn't budge.

A skeletal hand had grabbed his bridle. Death materialized.

IT IS NOT OVER. MORE MUST BE DONE. THEY TORMENT HIM STILL.

Susan sagged. 'What is? Who are?'

MOVE FORWARD. I WILL STEER. Death climbed into the saddle and reached around her for the reins.

'Look, I went—' Susan began.

YES. I KNOW. THE CONTROL OF BELIEF, said Death, as the horse moved forward again. ONLY A VERY SIMPLE MIND COULD THINK OF THAT. MAGIC SO OLD IT'S HARDLY MAGIC. WHAT A SIMPLE WAY TO MAKE MILLIONS OF CHILDREN CEASE TO BELIEVE IN THE HOGFATHER.

'And what were *you* doing?' Susan demanded.

I TOO HAVE DONE WHAT I SET OUT TO DO. I HAVE KEPT A SPACE. A MILLION CARPETS WITH SOOTY BOOTMARKS, MILLIONS OF FILLED STOCKINGS, ALL THOSE ROOFS WITH RUNNER MARKS ON THEM . . . DISBELIEF WILL FIND IT HARD GOING IN THE FACE

OF THAT. ALBERT SAYS HE NEVER WANTS TO DRINK
ANOTHER SHERRY FOR *DAYS*. THE HOGFATHER WILL
HAVE SOMETHING TO COME BACK TO, AT LEAST.

'What have I got to do now?'

YOU MUST *BRING* THE HOGFATHER BACK.

'Oh, must I? For peace and goodwill and the
tinkling of fairy bells? Who *cares*. He's just some
fat old clown who makes people feel smug at
Hogswatch! I've been through all this for some
old man who prowls around kids' bedrooms?'

NO. SO THAT THE SUN WILL RISE.

'What has astronomy got to do with the Hogfather?'

OLD GODS DO NEW JOBS.

The Senior Wrangler wasn't attending the Feast.
He got one of the maids to bring a tray up to his
rooms, where he was Entertaining and doing all
those things a man does when he finds himself
unexpectedly tête-à-tête with the opposite sex,
like trying to shine his boots on his trousers and
clean his fingernails with his other fingernails.

'A little more wine, Gwendoline? It's hardly
alcoholic,' he said, leaning over her.

'I don't mind if I do, Mr Wrangler.'

'Oh, call me Horace, *please*. And perhaps a little
something for your chicken?'

'I'm afraid she seems to have wandered off
somewhere,' said the Cheerful Fairy. 'I'm afraid
I'm, I'm, I'm rather dull company . . .' She blew
her nose noisily.

'Oh, I certainly wouldn't say that,' said the Senior Wrangler. He wished he'd had time to tidy up his rooms a bit, or at least get some of the more embarrassing bits of laundry off the stuffed rhinoceros.

'Everyone's been *so* kind,' said the Cheerful Fairy, dabbing at her streaming eyes. 'Who was the skinny one that kept making the funny faces for me?'

'That was the Bursar. Why don't you—'

'*He* seemed very cheerful, anyway.'

'It's the dried frog pills, he eats them by the handful,' said the Senior Wrangler dismissively. 'I say, why don't—'

'Oh dear. I hope they're not addictive.'

'I'm sure he wouldn't keep on eating them if they were addictive,' said the Senior Wrangler. 'Now, why don't you have another glass of wine, and then . . . and then . . .' a happy thought struck him '. . . and then . . . and then perhaps I could show you Archchancellor Bowell's Remembrance? It's got a-a-a-a very interesting ceiling. My word, yes.'

'That would be very nice,' said the Cheerful Fairy. 'Would it cheer me up, do you think?'

'Oh, it would, it *would*,' said the Senior Wrangler. 'Definitely! Good! So I'll, er, I'll just go and . . . just go and . . . I'll . . . ' He pointed vaguely in the direction of his dressing room, while hopping from one foot to the other. 'I'll just go and, er . . . go . . . just . . .'

He fled into the dressing room and slammed

the door behind him. His wild eyes scanned the shelves and hangers.

'Clean robe,' he mumbled. 'Comb face, wash socks, fresh hair, where's that Insteadofshave lotion—'

From the other side of the door came the adorable sound of the Cheerful Fairy blowing her nose. From this side came the sound of the Senior Wrangler's muffled scream as, made careless by haste and a very poor sense of smell, he mistakenly splashed his face with the turpentine he used for treating his feet.

Somewhere overhead a very small plump child with a bow and arrow and ridiculously un-aerodynamic wings buzzed ineffectually against a shut window on which the frost was tracing the outline of a rather handsome Auriental lady. The other window already had an icy picture of a vase of sunflowers.

In the Great Hall one of the tables had already collapsed. It was one of the customs of the Feast that although there were many courses each wizard went at his own speed, a tradition instituted to prevent the slow ones holding every-one else up. And they could also have seconds if they wished, so that if a wizard was particularly attracted to soup he could go round and round for an hour before starting on the preliminary stages of the fish courses.

'How're you feeling now, old chap?' said the

Dean, who was sitting next to the Bursar. 'Back on the dried frog pills?'

'I, er, I, er, no, I'm not too bad,' said the Bursar. 'It was, of course, rather a, rather a shock when—'

'That's a shame, because here's your Hogswatch present,' said the Dean, passing over a small box. It rattled. 'You can open it now if you like.'

'Oh, well, how nice—'

'It's from me,' said the Dean.

'What a lovely—'

'I bought it with my own money, you know,' said the Dean, waving a turkey leg airily.

'The wrapping paper is a very nice—'

'More than a dollar, I might add.'

'My goodness—'

The Bursar pulled off the last of the wrapping paper.

'It's a box for keeping dried frog pills in. See? It's got "Dried Frog Pills" on it, see?'

The Bursar shook it. 'Oh, how nice,' he said weakly. 'It's got some pills in it already. How thoughtful. They *will* come in handy.'

'Yes,' said the Dean. 'I took them off your dressing table. After all, I was down a dollar as it was.'

The Bursar nodded gratefully and put the little box neatly beside his plate. They'd actually allowed him knives this evening. They'd actually allowed him to eat other things than those things that could only be scraped up with a wooden spoon.

He eyed the nearest roast pig with nervous

anticipation, and tucked his napkin firmly under his chin.

'Er, excuse me, Mr Stibbons,' he quavered. 'Would you be so good as to pass me the apple sauce tankard—'

There was a sound like coarse fabric ripping, somewhere in the air in front of the Bursar, and a crash as something landed on top of the roast pig. Roast potatoes and gravy filled the air. The apple that had been in the pig's mouth was violently expelled and hit the Bursar on the forehead.

He blinked, looked down, and found he was about to plunge his fork into a human head.

'Ahaha,' he murmured, as his eyes started to glaze.

The wizards heaved aside the overturned dishes and smashed crockery.

'He just fell out of the air!'

'Is he an Assassin? Not one of their student pranks, is it?'

'Why's he holding a sword without a sharp bit?'

'Is he dead?'

'I think so!'

'I didn't even *have* any of that salmon mousse! Will you look at it? His foot's in it! It's all over the place! Do you want yours?'

Ponder Stibbons fought his way through the throng. He knew his more senior fellows when they were feeling helpful. They were like a glass of water to a drowning man.

'Give him air!' he protested.

'How do we know if he needs any?' said the Dean.

Ponder put his ear to the fallen youth's chest.

'He's not breathing!'

'Breathing spell, breathing spell,' muttered the Chair of Indefinite Studies. 'Er . . . Spolt's Forthright Respirator, perhaps? I think I've got it written down somewhere—'

Ridcully reached through the wizards and pulled out the black-clad man by a leg. He held him upside down in his big hand and thumped him heavily on the back.

He met their astonished gaze. 'Used to do this on the farm,' he said. 'Works a treat on baby goats.'

'Oh, now, *really*,' said the Dean, 'I don't—'

The corpse made a noise somewhere between a choke and a cough.

'Make some space, you fellows!' the Archchancellor bellowed, clearing an area of table with one sweep of his spare arm.

'Hey, I hadn't had any of that Prawn Escoffé!' said the Lecturer in Recent Runes.

'I didn't even know we *had* any,' said the Chair of Indefinite Studies. 'Someone, and I name no names, Dean, shoved it behind the soft-shelled crabs so they could keep it for themselves. I call that cheap.'

Teatime opened his eyes. It said a lot for his constitution that it survived a very close-up view of Ridcully's nose, which filled the immediate universe like a big pink planet.

'Excuse me, excuse me,' said Ponder, leaning over with his notebook open, 'but this is vitally important for the advancement of natural philosophy. Did you see any bright lights? Was there a shining tunnel? Did any deceased relatives attempt to speak to you? What word most describes the—'

Ridcully pulled him away.

'What's all this, Mr Stibbons?'

'I really should talk to him, sir. He's had a near-death experience!'

'We all have. It's called "living",' said the Archchancellor shortly. 'Pour the poor lad a glass of spirits and put that damn pencil away.'

'Uh . . . This must be Unseen University?' said Teatime. 'And you are all wizards?'

'Now, just you lie still,' said Ridcully. But Teatime had already risen on his elbows.

'There was a sword,' he muttered.

'Oh, it's fallen on the floor,' said the Dean, reaching down. 'But it looks as though it's— Did I do that?'

The wizards looked at the large curved slice of table falling away. Something had cut through everything – wood, cloth, plates, cutlery, food. The Dean swore that a candle flame that had been in the path of the unseen blade was only half a flame for a moment, until the wick realized that this was no way to behave.

The Dean raised his hand. The other wizards scattered.

'Looks like a thin blue line in the air,' he said, wonderingly.

'Excuse me, sir,' said Teatime, taking it from him. 'I really must be off.'

He ran from the hall.

'He won't get far,' said the Lecturer in Recent Runes. 'The main doors are locked in accordance with Archchancellor Spode's Rules.'

'Won't get far while holding a sword that appears to be able to cut through anything,' said Ridcully, to the sound of falling wood.

'I wonder what all that was about?' said the Chair of Indefinite Studies, and then turned his attention to the remains of the Feast. 'Anyway, at least this joint's been nicely carved . . .'

'Bu-bu-bu—'

They all turned. The Bursar was holding his hand in front of him. The cut surface of a fork gleamed at the wizards.

'Nice to know his new present will come in handy,' said the Dean. 'It's the thought that counts.'

Under the table the Blue Hen of Happiness relieved itself on the Bursar's foot.

THERE ARE . . . ENEMIES, said Death, as Binky galloped through icy mountains.

'They're all dead—'

OTHER ENEMIES. YOU MAY AS WELL KNOW THIS. DOWN IN THE DEEPEST KINGDOMS OF THE SEA, WHERE THERE IS NO LIGHT, THERE LIVES A TYPE

OF CREATURE WITH NO BRAIN AND NO EYES AND NO MOUTH. IT DOES NOTHING BUT LIVE AND PUT FORTH PETALS OF PERFECT CRIMSON WHERE NONE ARE THERE TO SEE. IT IS NOTHING EXCEPT A TINY *YES* IN THE NIGHT. AND YET . . . AND YET . . . IT HAS ENEMIES THAT BEAR ON IT A VICIOUS, UNBENDING MALICE, WHO WISH NOT ONLY FOR ITS TINY LIFE TO BE OVER BUT ALSO THAT IT HAD NEVER EXISTED. ARE YOU WITH ME SO FAR?

'Well, yes, but—'

GOOD. NOW, *IMAGINE WHAT THEY THINK OF HUMANITY.*

Susan was shocked. She had never heard her grandfather speak in anything other than calm tones. Now there was a cutting edge in his words.

'What are they?' she said.

WE MUST HURRY. THERE IS NOT MUCH TIME.

'I thought you always had time. I mean . . . whatever it is you want to stop, you can go back in time and—'

AND MEDDLE?

'You've done it before . . .'

THIS TIME IT IS OTHERS WHO ARE DOING IT. AND *THEY* HAVE NO RIGHT.

'What others?'

THEY HAVE NO NAME. CALL THEM THE AUDITORS. THEY RUN THE UNIVERSE. THEY SEE TO IT THAT GRAVITY WORKS AND THE ATOMS SPIN, OR WHATEVER IT IS ATOMS DO. AND THEY HATE LIFE.

'Why?'

IT IS . . . IRREGULAR. IT WAS NEVER SUPPOSED TO HAPPEN. THEY LIKE STONES, MOVING IN

CURVES. AND THEY HATE HUMANS MOST OF ALL. Death sighed. IN MANY WAYS, THEY LACK A SENSE OF HUMOUR.

'Why the Hog—'

IT IS THE THINGS YOU BELIEVE WHICH MAKE YOU HUMAN. GOOD THINGS AND BAD THINGS, IT'S ALL THE SAME.

The mists parted. Sharp peaks were around them, lit by the glow off the snow.

'These look like the mountains where the Castle of Bones was,' she said.

THEY ARE, said Death. IN A SENSE. HE HAS GONE BACK TO A PLACE HE KNOWS. AN EARLY PLACE . . .

Binky cantered low over the snow.

'And what are we looking for?' said Susan.

YOU WILL KNOW WHEN YOU SEE IT.

'Snow? Trees? I mean, could I have a clue? What are we here for?'

I TOLD YOU. TO ENSURE THAT THE SUN COMES UP.

'Of *course* the sun will come up!'

NO.

'There's no magic that'll stop the sun coming up!'

I WISH I WAS AS CLEVER AS YOU.

Susan stared down out of sheer annoyance, and saw something below.

Small dark shapes moved across the whiteness, running as if they were in pursuit of something.

'There's . . . some sort of chase . . .' she conceded. 'I can see some sort of animals but I can't see what they're after—'

Then she saw movement in the snow, a blurred, dark shape dodging and skidding and never clear. Binky dropped until his hooves grazed the tops of the pine trees, which bent in his wake. A rumble followed him across the forest, dragging broken branches and a smoke of snow behind it.

Now they were lower she could see the hunters clearly. They were large dogs. Their quarry was indistinct, dodging among snowdrifts, keeping to the cover of snow-laden bushes—

A drift exploded. Something big and long and blue-black rose through the flying snow like a sounding whale.

'It's a pig!'

A BOAR. THEY DRIVE IT TOWARDS THE CLIFF. THEY'RE DESPERATE NOW.

She could hear the panting of the creature. The dogs made no sound at all.

Blood streamed onto the snow from the wounds they had already managed to inflict.

'This . . . boar,' said Susan. '. . . It's . . .'

YES.

'They want to *kill* the Hogf—'

NOT KILL. HE KNOWS HOW TO DIE. OH, YES . . . IN THIS SHAPE, HE KNOWS HOW TO DIE. HE'S HAD A LOT OF EXPERIENCE. NO, THEY WANT TO TAKE AWAY HIS REAL LIFE, TAKE AWAY HIS SOUL, TAKE AWAY EVERYTHING. THEY MUST NOT BE ALLOWED TO BRING HIM DOWN.

'Well, stop them!'

YOU MUST. THIS IS A HUMAN THING.

The dogs moved oddly. They weren't running but flowing, crossing the snow faster than the mere movement of their legs would suggest.

'They don't look like real dogs . . .'

NO.

'What *can* I do?'

Death nodded his head towards the boar. Binky was keeping level with it now, barely a few feet away.

Realization dawned.

'I can't *ride* that!' said Susan.

WHY NOT? YOU HAVE HAD AN *EDUCATION*.

'Enough to know that pigs don't let people ride them!'

MERE ACCUMULATION OF OBSERVATIONAL EVIDENCE IS NOT PROOF.

Susan glanced ahead. The snowfield had a cut-off look.

YOU MUST, said her grandfather's voice in her head. WHEN HE REACHES THE EDGE THERE HE WILL STAND AT BAY. HE MUST NOT. UNDERSTAND? THESE ARE NOT REAL DOGS. IF THEY CATCH HIM HE WON'T JUST DIE, HE WILL . . . NEVER BE . . .

Susan leapt. For a moment she floated through the air, dress streaming behind her, arms outstretched . . .

Landing on the animal's back was like hitting a very, very firm chair. It stumbled for a moment and then righted itself.

Susan's arms clung to its neck and her face was buried in its sharp bristles. She could feel the heat under her. It was like riding a furnace.

And it stank of sweat, and blood, and pig. A lot of pig.

There was a lack of landscape in front of her.

The boar ploughed into the snow on the edge of the drop, almost flinging her off, and turned to face the hounds.

There were a lot of them. Susan was familiar with dogs. They'd had them at home like other houses had rugs. And these weren't that big floppy sort.

She rammed her heels in and grabbed a pig's ear in each hand. It was like holding a pair of hairy shovels.

'Turn left!' she screamed, and hauled.

She put everything into the command. It promised tears before bedtime if disobeyed.

To her amazement the boar grunted, pranced on the lip of the precipice and scrambled away, the hounds floundering as they turned to follow.

This was a plateau. From here it seemed to be all edge, with no way down except the very simple and terminal one.

The dogs were flying at the boar's heels again.

Susan looked around in the grey, lightless air. There had to be somewhere, some way . . .

There was.

It was a shoulder of rock, a giant knife-edge connecting this plain to the hills beyond. It was sharp and narrow, a thin line of snow with chilly depths on either side.

It was better than nothing. It was nothing with snow on it.

The boar reached the edge and hesitated. Susan put her head down and dug her heels in again.

Snout down, legs moving like pistons, the beast plunged out onto the ridge. Snow sprayed up as its trotters sought for purchase. It made up for lack of grace by sheer manic effort, legs moving like a tap dancer climbing a moving staircase that was heading down.

'That's right, that's right, that's—'

A trotter slipped. For a moment the boar seemed to stand on two, the others scrabbling at icy rock. Susan flung herself the other way, clinging to the neck, and felt the dragging abyss under her feet.

There was nothing there.

She told herself, *He'll catch me if I fall, he'll catch me if I fall, he'll catch me if I fall* . . .

Powdered ice made her eyes sting. A flailing trotter almost slammed against her head.

An older voice said, *No, he won't. If I fall now I don't deserve to be caught.*

The creature's eye was inches away. And then she knew . . .

. . . Out of the depths of eyes of all but the most unusual of animals comes an echo. Out of the dark eye in front of her, someone looked back . . .

A foot caught the rock and she concentrated her whole being on it, kicking herself upward in one last effort. Pig and woman rocked for a moment and then a trotter caught a footing and the boar plunged forward along the ridge.

Susan risked a look behind.

The dogs still moved oddly. There was a slight jerkiness about their movements, as if they flowed from position to position rather than moved by ordinary muscles.

Not dogs, she thought. Dog shapes.

There was another shock underfoot. Snow flew up. The world tilted. She felt the shape of the boar change when its muscles bunched and sent it soaring as a slab of ice and rock came away and began the long slide into darkness.

Susan was thrown off when the creature landed, and tumbled into deep snow. She flailed around madly, expecting at any minute to begin sliding.

Instead her hand found a snow-encrusted branch. A few feet away the boar lay on its side, steaming and panting.

She pulled herself upright. The spur here had widened out into a hill, with a few frosted trees on it.

The dogs had reached the gap and were milling round, struggling to prevent themselves slipping.

They could easily clear the distance, she could see. Even the boar had managed it with her on its back. She put both hands around the branch and heaved; it came away with a crack, like a broken icicle, and she waved it like a club.

'Come on,' she said. 'Jump! Just you try it! Come *on*!'

One did. The branch caught it as it landed, and then Susan spun and brought the branch around on the upswing, lifted the dazed animal off its feet and out over the edge.

For a moment the shape wavered and then, howling, it dropped out of sight.

She danced a few steps of rage and triumph.

'Yes! Yes! Who wants some? Anyone else?'

The other dogs looked her in the eye, decided that no one did, and that there wasn't. Finally, after one or two nervous attempts, they managed to turn, still sliding, and tried to make it back to the plateau.

A figure barred their way.

It hadn't been there a moment ago but it looked permanent now. It seemed to have been made of snow, three balls of snow piled on one another. It had black dots for eyes. A semi-circle of more dots formed the semblance of a mouth. There was a carrot for the nose.

And, for the arms, two twigs.

At this distance, anyway.

One of them was holding a curved stick.

A raven wearing a damp piece of red paper landed on one arm.

'Bob bob bob?' it suggested. 'Merry Solstice? Tweetie tweet? What are you waiting for? Hogswatch?'

The dogs backed away.

The snow broke off the snowman in chunks, revealing a gaunt figure in a flapping black robe.

Death spat out the carrot.

HO. HO. HO.

The grey bodies smeared and rippled as the hounds sought desperately to change their shape.

YOU COULDN'T RESIST IT? IN THE END? A MISTAKE, I FANCY.

He touched the scythe. There was a click as the blade flashed into life.

IT GETS UNDER YOUR SKIN, LIFE, said Death, stepping forward. SPEAKING METAPHORICALLY, OF COURSE. IT'S A HABIT THAT'S HARD TO GIVE UP. ONE PUFF OF BREATH IS NEVER ENOUGH. YOU'LL FIND YOU WANT TO TAKE ANOTHER.

A dog started to slip on the snow and scrabbled desperately to save itself from the long, cold drop.

AND, YOU SEE, THE MORE YOU STRUGGLE FOR EVERY MOMENT, THE MORE ALIVE YOU STAY . . . WHICH IS WHERE I COME IN, AS A MATTER OF FACT.

The leading dog managed, for a moment, to become a grey cowled figure before being dragged back into shape.

FEAR, TOO, IS AN ANCHOR, said Death. ALL THOSE SENSES, WIDE OPEN TO EVERY FRAGMENT OF THE WORLD. THAT BEATING HEART. THAT RUSH OF BLOOD. CAN YOU NOT FEEL IT, DRAGGING YOU BACK?

Once again the Auditor managed to retain a shape for a few seconds, and managed to say: you cannot do this, there are rules!

YES. THERE ARE RULES. BUT YOU BROKE THEM. HOW DARE YOU? *HOW DARE YOU?*

The scythe blade was a thin blue outline in the grey light.

Death raised a thin finger to where his lips might have been, and suddenly looked thoughtful.

AND NOW THERE REMAINS ONLY ONE FINAL QUESTION, he said.

He raised his hands, and seemed to grow. Light flared in his eye sockets. When he spoke next, avalanches fell in the mountains.

HAVE YOU BEEN NAUGHTY . . . OR NICE?

HO. HO. HO.

Susan heard the wails die away.

The boar lay in white snow that was now red with blood. She knelt down and tried to lift its head.

It was dead. One eye stared at nothing. The tongue lolled.

Sobs welled up inside her. The tiny part of Susan that watched, the inner baby-sitter, said it was just exhaustion and excitement and the backwash of adrenalin. She couldn't be crying over a dead pig.

The rest of her drummed on its flank with both fists.

'No, you can't! We *saved* you! Dying isn't how it's supposed to go!'

A breeze blew up.

Something stirred in the landscape, something under the snow. The branches on the ancient trees shook gently, dislodging little needles of ice.

The sun rose.

The light streamed over Susan like a silent gale. It was dazzling. She crouched back, raising her forearm to cover her eyes. The great red ball turned frost to fire along the winter branches.

Gold light slammed into the mountain peaks,

making every one a blinding, silent volcano. It rolled onward, gushing into the valleys and thundering up the slopes, unstoppable . . .

There was a groan.

A man lay in the snow where the boar had been.

He was naked except for an animal skin loincloth. His hair was long and had been woven into a thick plait down his back, so matted with blood and grease that it looked like felt. And he was bleeding everywhere the hounds had caught him.

Susan watched for a moment, and then, thinking with something other than her head, methodically tore some strips from her petticoat to bandage the more unpleasant wounds.

Capability, said the small part of her mind. A rational head in emergencies.

Rational something, anyway.

It's probably some kind of character flaw.

The man was tattooed. Blue whorls and spirals haunted his skin, under the blood.

He opened his eyes and stared at the sky.

'Can you get up?'

His gaze flicked to her. He tried moving and then fell back.

Eventually she managed to pull the man up into a sitting position. He swayed as she put one of his arms across her shoulders and then heaved him to his feet. She did her best to ignore the stink, which had an almost physical force.

Downhill seemed the best option. Even if his brain wasn't working yet, his feet seemed to get the idea.

They lurched down through the freezing woods, the snow glowing orange in the risen sun. Cold blue gloom lurked in hollows like little cups of winter.

Beside her, the tattooed man made a gurgling sound. He slipped out of her grasp and landed on his knees in the snow, clutching at his throat and choking. His breath sounded like a saw.

'What *now*? What's the matter? What's the matter?'

He rolled his eyes at her and pawed at his throat again.

'Something stuck?' She slapped him as hard as she could on the back, but now he was on his hands and knees, fighting for breath.

She put her hands under his shoulders and pulled him upright, and put her arms around his waist. Oh, gods, how was it supposed to go, she'd gone to *classes* about it, now, didn't you have to bunch up one fist and then put the other hand around it and then pull *up* and *in* like *this*—

The man coughed and something bounced off a tree and landed in the snow.

She knelt down to have a look.

It was a small black bean.

A bird trilled, high on a branch. She looked up. A wren bobbed at her and fluttered to another twig.

When she looked back, the man was different. He had clothes now, heavy furs, with a fur hood and fur boots. He was supporting himself on a stone-tipped spear, and looked a lot stronger.

Something hurried through the wood, barely visible except by its shadow. For a moment she glimpsed a white hare before it sprang away on a new path.

She looked back. Now the furs had gone and the man looked older, although he had the same eyes. He was wearing thick white robes, and looked very much like a priest.

When a bird called again she didn't look away. And she realized that she'd been mistaken in thinking that the man changed like the turning of pages. All the images were there at once, and many others too. What you saw depended on how you looked.

Yes. It's a good job I'm cool and totally used to this sort of thing, she thought. Otherwise I'd be rather worried . . .

Now they were at the edge of the forest.

A little way off, four huge boars stood and steamed, in front of a sledge that looked as if it had been put together out of crudely trimmed trees. There were faces in the blackened wood, possibly carved by stone, possibly carved by rain and wind.

The Hogfather climbed aboard and sat down. He'd put on weight in the last few yards and now it was almost impossible to see anything other than the huge, red-robed man, ice crystals settling here and there on the cloth. Only in the occasional sparkle of frost was there a hint of hair or tusk.

He shifted on the seat and then reached down

to extricate a false beard, which he held up questioningly.

SORRY, said a voice behind Susan. THAT WAS MINE.

The Hogfather nodded at Death, as one craftsman to another, and then at Susan. She wasn't sure if she was being thanked – it was more a gesture of recognition, of acknowledgement that something that needed doing had indeed been done. But it wasn't thanks.

Then he shook the reins and clicked his teeth and the sledge slid away.

They watched it go.

'I remember hearing,' said Susan distantly, 'that the idea of the Hogfather wearing a red and white outfit was invented quite recently.'

NO. IT WAS REMEMBERED.

Now the Hogfather was a red dot on the other side of the valley.

'Well, that about wraps it up for *this* dress,' said Susan. 'I'd just like to ask, just out of academic interest . . . you were sure I was going to survive, were you?'

I WAS QUITE CONFIDENT.

'Oh, *good*.'

I WILL GIVE YOU A LIFT BACK, said Death, after a while.

'Thank you. Now . . . tell me . . .'

WHAT WOULD HAVE HAPPENED IF YOU HADN'T SAVED HIM?

'Yes! The sun would have risen just the same, yes?'

NO.

'Oh, come *on*. You can't expect me to believe *that*. It's an astronomical *fact*.'

THE SUN WOULD NOT HAVE RISEN.

She turned on him.

'It's been a long night, Grandfather! I'm tired and I need a bath! I don't need silliness!'

THE SUN WOULD NOT HAVE RISEN.

'Really? Then what would have happened, pray?'

A MERE BALL OF FLAMING GAS WOULD HAVE ILLUMINATED THE WORLD.

They walked in silence for a moment.

'Ah,' said Susan dully. 'Trickery with words. I would have thought you'd have been more literal-minded than that.'

I AM NOTHING IF NOT LITERAL-MINDED. TRICKERY WITH WORDS IS WHERE *HUMANS* LIVE.

'All right,' said Susan. 'I'm not stupid. You're saying humans need . . . *fantasies* to make life bearable.'

REALLY? AS IF IT WAS SOME KIND OF PINK PILL? NO. HUMANS NEED FANTASY TO BE HUMAN. TO BE THE PLACE WHERE THE FALLING ANGEL MEETS THE RISING APE.

'Tooth fairies? Hogfathers? Little—'

YES. AS PRACTICE. YOU HAVE TO START OUT LEARNING TO BELIEVE THE *LITTLE* LIES.

'So we can believe the big ones?'

YES. JUSTICE. MERCY. DUTY. THAT SORT OF THING.

'They're not the same at all!'

YOU THINK SO? THEN TAKE THE UNIVERSE AND

GRIND IT DOWN TO THE FINEST POWDER AND SIEVE IT THROUGH THE FINEST SIEVE AND THEN *SHOW* ME ONE ATOM OF JUSTICE, ONE MOLECULE OF MERCY. AND YET— Death waved a hand. AND YET YOU ACT AS IF THERE IS SOME IDEAL ORDER IN THE WORLD, AS IF THERE IS SOME . . . SOME *RIGHTNESS* IN THE UNIVERSE BY WHICH IT MAY BE JUDGED.

'Yes, but people have *got* to believe that, or what's the *point*—'

MY POINT EXACTLY.

She tried to assemble her thoughts.

THERE IS A PLACE WHERE TWO GALAXIES HAVE BEEN COLLIDING FOR A MILLION YEARS, said Death, apropos of nothing. DON'T TRY TO TELL *ME* THAT'S RIGHT.

'Yes, but people don't think about that,' said Susan. Somewhere there was a bed . . .

CORRECT. STARS EXPLODE, WORLDS COLLIDE, THERE'S HARDLY ANYWHERE IN THE UNIVERSE WHERE HUMANS CAN LIVE WITHOUT BEING FROZEN OR FRIED, AND YET YOU BELIEVE THAT A . . . A BED IS A NORMAL THING. IT IS THE MOST AMAZING TALENT.

'Talent?'

OH, YES. A VERY SPECIAL KIND OF STUPIDITY. YOU THINK THE WHOLE UNIVERSE IS INSIDE YOUR HEADS.

'You make us sound mad,' said Susan. A nice warm bed . . .

NO. YOU NEED TO BELIEVE IN THINGS THAT AREN'T TRUE. HOW ELSE CAN THEY *BECOME*? said Death, helping her up on to Binky.

'These mountains,' said Susan, as the horse rose. 'Are they *real* mountains, or some sort of shadows?'

YES.

Susan knew that was all she was going to get.

'Er . . . I lost the sword. It's somewhere in the Tooth Fairy's country.'

Death shrugged. I CAN MAKE ANOTHER.

'Can you?'

OH, YES. IT WILL GIVE ME SOMETHING TO DO. DON'T WORRY ABOUT IT.

The Senior Wrangler hummed cheerfully to himself as he ran a comb through his beard for the second time and liberally sprinkled it with what would turn out to be a preparation of weasel extract for demon removal rather than, as he had assumed, a pleasant masculine scent.* Then he stepped out into his study.

'Sorry for the delay, but—' he began.

There was no one there. Only, very far off, the sound of someone blowing their nose mingling with the *glingleglingleglingle* of fading magic.

The light was already gilding the top of the Tower of Art when Binky trotted to a standstill on the air beside the nursery balcony. Susan

---

*It was, in fact, a pleasant masculine scent. But only to female weasels.

climbed down onto the fresh snow and stood uncertainly for a moment. When someone has gone out of their way to drop you home it's only courteous to ask them in. On the other hand . . .

WOULD YOU LIKE TO VISIT FOR HOGSWATCH DINNER? said Death. He sounded hopeful. ALBERT IS FRYING A PUDDING.

'*Frying* a pudding?'

ALBERT UNDERSTANDS FRYING. AND I BELIEVE HE'S MAKING JAM. HE CERTAINLY KEPT TALKING ABOUT IT.

'I . . . er . . . they're really expecting me here,' said Susan. 'The Gaiters do a lot of entertaining. His business friends. Probably the whole day will be . . . I'll more or less have to look after the children . . .'

SOMEONE SHOULD.

'Er . . . would you like a drink before you go?' said Susan, giving in.

A CUP OF COCOA WOULD BE APPROPRIATE IN THE CIRCUMSTANCES.

'Right. There's biscuits in the tin on the mantel-piece.'

Susan headed with relief into the tiny kitchen.

Death sat down in the creaking wicker chair, buried his feet in the rug and looked around with interest. He heard the clatter of cups, and then a sound like indrawn breath, and then silence.

Death helped himself to a biscuit from the tin. There were two full stockings hanging from the mantelpiece. He prodded them with professional satisfaction, and then sat down again and observed the nursery wallpaper. It seemed to be pictures of rabbits in waistcoats, among other fauna. He was not surprised. Death occasionally turned up in person even for rabbits, simply to see that the whole process was working properly. He'd never seen one wearing a waistcoat. He wouldn't have expected waistcoats. At least, he wouldn't have expected waistcoats if he hadn't had some experience of the way humans portrayed the universe. As it was, it was only a blessing they hadn't been given gold watches and top hats as well.

Humans liked dancing pigs, too. And lambs in hats. As far as Death was aware, the sole reason for any human association with pigs and lambs was as a prelude to chops and sausages. Quite why they should dress up for children's wallpaper as well was a mystery. Hello, little folk, this is what you're going to eat . . . He felt that if only he could find the key to it, he'd know a lot more about human beings.

His gaze travelled to the door. Susan's governess coat and hat were hanging on it. The coat was grey, and so was the hat. Grey and round and dull. Death didn't know many things about the human psyche, but he did know protective coloration when he saw it.

Dullness. Only humans could have invented it. What imaginations they had.

The door opened.

To his horror, Death saw a small child of unidentifiable sex come out of the bedroom, amble sleepily across the floor and unhook the stockings from the mantelpiece. It was halfway back before it noticed him and then it simply stopped and regarded him thoughtfully.

He knew that young children could see him because they hadn't yet developed that convenient and selective blindness that comes with the intimation of personal mortality. He felt a little embarrassed.

'Susan's gotta poker, you know,' it said, as if anxious to be helpful.

WELL, WELL. INDEED. MY GOODNESS ME.

'I fort – *thought* all of you knew that now. Larst – *last* week she picked a bogey up by its nose.'

Death tried to imagine this. He felt sure he'd heard the sentence wrong, but it didn't sound a whole lot better however he rearranged the words.

'I'll give Gawain his stocking and then I'll come an' watch,' said the child. It padded out.

ER . . . SUSAN? Death said, calling in reinforcements.

Susan backed out of the kitchen, a black kettle in her hand.

There was a figure behind her. In the half-light the sword gleamed blue along its blade. Its glitter reflected off one glass eye.

'Well, *well*,' said Teatime, quietly, glancing at Death. 'Now this *is* unexpected. A family affair?'

The sword hummed back and forth.

'I wonder,' said Teatime, 'is it *possible* to kill Death? This must be a very special sword and it certainly works *here* . . .' He raised a hand to his mouth for a moment and gave a little chuckle. 'And of course it might well not be regarded as murder. Possibly it is a civic act. It would be, as they say, The Big One. Stand up, sir. You may have some personal knowledge about your vulnerability but I'm pretty certain that Susan here would quite *definitely* die, so I'd rather you didn't try any last-minute stuff.'

I *AM* LAST-MINUTE STUFF, said Death, standing up.

Teatime circled around carefully, the sword's tip making little curves in the air.

From the next room came the sound of someone trying to blow a whistle quietly.

Susan glanced at her grandfather.

'I don't remember them asking for anything that made a noise,' she said.

OH, THERE HAS TO BE SOMETHING IN THE STOCKING THAT MAKES A NOISE, said Death. OTHERWISE WHAT IS 4.30 A.M. *FOR*?

'There are children?' said Teatime. 'Oh yes, of course. Call them.'

'Certainly not!'

'It will be instructive,' said Teatime. 'Educational. And when your adversary is Death, you cannot help but be the good guy.'

He pointed the sword at Susan.

'I *said* call them.'

Susan glanced hopefully at her grandfather. He nodded. For a moment she thought she saw the glow in one eye socket flicker off and on, Death's equivalent of a wink. *He's got a plan. He can stop time. He can do anything. He's got a plan.*

'Gawain? Twyla?'

The muffled noises stopped in the next room. There was a padding of feet and two solemn faces appeared round the door.

'Ah, come in, come *in*, curly-haired tots,' said Teatime genially.

Gawain gave him a steely stare.

His next mistake, thought Susan. If he'd called them little bastards he'd have them bang on his side. But they know when you're sending them up.

'I've caught this bogeyman,' said Teatime. 'What shall we do with him, eh?'

The two faces turned to Death. Twyla put her thumb in her mouth.

'It's only a skeleton,' said Gawain critically.

Susan opened her mouth, and the sword swung towards her. She shut it again.

'Yes, a nasty, creepy, horrible skeleton,' said Teatime. 'Scary, eh?'

There was a very faint 'pop' as Twyla took her thumb out of her mouth.

'He's eating a bittit,' she said.

'Biscuit,' Susan corrected automatically. She started to swing the kettle in an absent-minded way.

'A creepy bony man in a black robe!' said Teatime, aware that things weren't going in quite the right direction.

He spun round to face Susan. 'You're fidgeting with that kettle,' he said. 'So I expect you're thinking of doing something creative. Put it down, please. Slowly.'

Susan knelt down gently and put the kettle on the hearth.

'Huh, that's not very creepy, it's just bones,' said Gawain dismissively. 'And anyway Willie the groom down at the stables has promised me a real horse skull. And anyway I'm going to make a hat out of it like General Tacticus had when he wanted to frighten people. And anyway it's just standing there. It's not even making woo-woo noises. And anyway *you're* creepy. Your eye's weird.'

'Really? Then let's see how creepy I can be,' said Teatime. Blue fire crackled along the sword as he raised it.

Susan closed her hand over the poker.

Teatime saw her start to turn. He stepped behind Death, sword raised . . .

Susan threw the poker overarm. It made a ripping noise as it shot through the air, and trailed sparks.

It hit Death's robe and vanished.

He blinked.

Teatime smiled at Susan.

He turned and peered dreamily at the sword in his hand.

It fell out of his fingers.

Death turned and caught it by the handle as it tumbled, and turned its fall into an upward curve.

Teatime looked down at the poker in his chest as he folded up.

'Oh, no,' he said. 'It couldn't have gone

through you. There are so many ribs and things!'

There was another 'pop' as Twyla extracted her thumb and said, 'It only kills monsters.'

'Stop time *now*,' commanded Susan.

Death snapped his fingers. The room took on the greyish purple of stationary time. The clock paused its ticking.

'You *winked* at me! I thought you had a *plan*!'

INDEED. OH, YES. I PLANNED TO SEE WHAT YOU WOULD DO.

'Just *that*?'

YOU ARE VERY RESOURCEFUL. AND OF COURSE YOU HAVE HAD AN EDUCATION.

'*What?*'

I DID ADD THE SPARKLY STARS AND THE NOISE, THOUGH. I THOUGHT THEY WOULD BE APPRO-PRIATE.

'And if I *hadn't* done anything?'

I DARESAY I WOULD HAVE THOUGHT OF SOME-THING. AT THE LAST MINUTE.

'That *was* the last minute!'

THERE IS ALWAYS TIME FOR ANOTHER LAST MINUTE.

'The children had to watch that!'

EDUCATIONAL. THE WORLD WILL TEACH THEM ABOUT MONSTERS SOON ENOUGH. LET THEM RE-MEMBER THERE'S ALWAYS THE POKER.

'But they saw he's human—'

I THINK THEY HAD A VERY GOOD IDEA OF WHAT HE WAS.

Death prodded the fallen Teatime with his foot.

STOP PLAYING DEAD, MISTER TEH-AH-TIM-EH.

The ghost of the Assassin sprang up like a jack-in-the-box, all slightly crazed smiles.

'You got it right!'

OF COURSE.

Teatime began to fade.

I'LL TAKE THE BODY, said Death. THAT WILL PREVENT INCONVENIENT QUESTIONS.

'What did he do it all for?' said Susan. 'I mean, why? Money? Power?'

SOME PEOPLE WILL DO ANYTHING FOR THE SHEER FASCINATION OF DOING IT, said Death. OR FOR FAME. OR BECAUSE THEY SHOULDN'T.

Death picked up the corpse and slung it over his shoulder. There was a sound of something bouncing on the hearth. He turned, and hesitated.

ER . . . YOU DID *KNOW* THE POKER WOULD GO THROUGH ME?

Susan realized she was shaking.

'Of course. In this room it's pretty powerful.'

YOU WERE NEVER IN ANY DOUBT?

Susan hesitated, and then smiled.

'I was quite confident,' she said.

AH. Her grandfather stared at her for a moment and she thought she detected just the tiniest flicker of uncertainty. OF COURSE. OF COURSE. TELL ME, ARE YOU LIKELY TO TAKE UP TEACHING ON A LARGER SCALE?

'I hadn't planned to.'

Death turned towards the balcony, and then seemed to remember something else. He fumbled inside his robe.

I HAVE MADE THIS FOR YOU.

432

She reached out and took a square of damp cardboard. Water dripped off the bottom. Somewhere in the middle, a few brown feathers seemed to have been glued on.

'Thank you. Er . . . what is it?'

ALBERT SAID THERE OUGHT TO BE SNOW ON IT, BUT IT APPEARS TO HAVE MELTED, said Death. IT IS, OF COURSE, A HOGSWATCH CARD.

'Oh . . .'

THERE SHOULD HAVE BEEN A ROBIN ON IT AS WELL, BUT I HAD CONSIDERABLE DIFFICULTY IN GETTING IT TO STAY ON.

'Ah . . .'

IT WAS NOT AT ALL CO-OPERATIVE.

'Really . . . ?'

IT DID NOT SEEM TO GET INTO THE HOGSWATCH SPIRIT AT ALL.

'Oh. Er. Good. Granddad?'

YES?

'Why? I mean, why did you do all this?'

He stood quite still for a moment, as if he was trying out sentences in his mind.

I THINK IT'S SOMETHING TO DO WITH HARVESTS, he said at last. YES. THAT'S RIGHT. AND BECAUSE HUMANS ARE SO INTERESTING THAT THEY HAVE EVEN INVENTED DULLNESS. QUITE ASTONISHING.

'Oh.'

WELL THEN . . . HAPPY HOGSWATCH.

'Yes. Happy Hogswatch.'

Death paused again, at the window.

AND GOOD NIGHT, CHILDREN . . . EVERYWHERE.

*   *   *

The raven fluttered down onto a log covered in snow. Its prosthetic red breast had been torn and fluttered uselessly behind it.

'Not so much as a lift home,' it muttered. 'Look at this, willya? Snow and frozen wastes, everywhere. I couldn't fly another damn inch. I could starve to death here, you know? Hah! People're going on about recycling the whole time, but you just try a bit of practical ecology and they just . . . don't . . . want . . . to . . . know. Hah! I bet a *robin*'d have a lift home. Oh *yes*.'

SQUEAK, said the Death of Rats sympathetically, and sniffed.

The raven watched the small hooded figure scrabble at the snow.

'So I'll just freeze to death here, shall I?' it said gloomily. 'A pathetic bundle of feathers with my little feet curled up with the cold. It's not even as if I'm gonna make anyone a good meal, and let me tell you it's a disgrace to die thin in my spec—'

It became aware that under the snow was a rather grubbier whiteness. Further scraping by the rat exposed something that could very possibly have been an ear.

The raven stared. 'It's a *sheep*!' it said.

The Death of Rats nodded.

'A *whole* sheep!'*

SQUEAK.

---

*Which had died in its sleep. Of natural causes. At a great age. After a long and happy life, insofar as a sheep can be happy. And would probably be quite pleased to know that it could help somebody as it passed away . . .

'Oh, wow!' said the raven, hopping forward with its eyes spinning. 'Hey, it's barely cool!'

The Death of Rats patted it happily on a wing.

SQUEAK-EEK. EEK-SQUEAK . . .

'Why, thanks. And the same to you . . .'

Far, far away and a long, long time ago, a shop door opened. The little toymaker bustled in from the workshop in the rear, and then stopped, with amazing foresight, dead.

YOU HAVE A BIG WOODEN ROCKING HORSE IN THE WINDOW, said the new customer.

'Ah, yes, yes, yes.' The shopkeeper fiddled nervously with his square-rimmed spectacles. He hadn't heard the bell, and this was worrying him. 'But I'm afraid that's just for show, that is a special order for Lord—'

NO. I WILL BUY IT.

'No, because, you see—'

THERE ARE OTHER TOYS?

'Yes, indeed, but—'

THEN I WILL TAKE THE HORSE. HOW MUCH WOULD THIS LORDSHIP HAVE PAID YOU?

'Er, we'd agreed twelve dollars but—'

I WILL GIVE YOU FIFTY, said the customer.

The little shopkeeper stopped in mid-remonstrate and started up in mid-greed. There *were* other toys, he told himself quickly. And this customer, he thought with considerable prescience, looked like someone who did not take no for an answer and seldom even bothered to ask the question. Lord Selachii would be angry, but Lord Selachii wasn't here. The stranger, on the other hand, was here. Incredibly here.

'Er . . . well, in the circumstances . . . er . . . shall I wrap it up for you?'

NO. I WILL TAKE IT AS IT IS. THANK YOU. I WILL LEAVE VIA THE BACK WAY, IF IT'S ALL THE SAME TO YOU.

'Er . . . how did you get *in*?' said the shopkeeper, pulling the horse out of the window.

THROUGH THE WALL. SO MUCH MORE CONVENIENT THAN CHIMNEYS, DON'T YOU THINK?

The apparition dropped a small clinking bag on the counter and lifted the horse easily. The shopkeeper wasn't in a position to hold on to anything. Even yesterday's dinner was threatening to leave him.

The figure looked at the other shelves.

YOU MAKE GOOD TOYS.

'Er . . . thank you.'

INCIDENTALLY, said the customer, as he left, THERE IS A SMALL BOY OUT THERE WITH HIS NOSE FROZEN TO THE WINDOW. SOME WARM WATER SHOULD DO THE TRICK.

Death walked out to where Binky was waiting in the snow and tied the toy horse behind the saddle.

ALBERT WILL BE VERY PLEASED. I CAN'T WAIT TO SEE HIS FACE. HO. HO. HO.

*　　*　　*

As the light of Hogswatch slid down the towers of Unseen University, the Librarian slipped into the Great Hall with some sheet music clenched firmly in his feet.

As the light of Hogswatch lit the towers of Unseen University, the Archchancellor sat down with a sigh in his study and pulled off his boots.

It had been a damn long night, no doubt about it. Lots of strange things. First time he'd ever seen the Senior Wrangler burst into tears, for one thing.

Ridcully glanced at the door to the new bathroom. Well, he'd sorted out the teething troubles, and a nice warm shower would be very refreshing. And then he could go along to the organ recital all nice and clean.

He removed his hat, and someone fell out of it with a tinkling sound. A small gnome rolled across the floor.

'Oh, another one. I thought we'd got rid of you fellows,' said Ridcully. 'And what are you?'

The gnome looked at him nervously.

'Er . . . you know whenever there was another magical appearance you heard the sound of, er, bells?' it said. Its expression suggested it was owning up to something it just knew was going to get it a smack.

'Yes?'

*The gnome held up some rather small handbells and waved them nervously. They went **glingleglingleglingle**, in a very sad way.*

'Good, eh? That was me. I'm the Glingleglingleglingle Fairy.'

'Get out.'

'I also do sparkly fairy dust effects that go twing too, if you like . . .'

'Go away!'

'How about "The Bells of St Ungulant's"?' said the gnome desperately. 'Very seasonal. Very nice. Why not join in? It goes: "The bells [clong] of St [clang] . . ." '

Ridcully scored a direct hit with the rubber duck, and the gnome escaped through the bath overflow. Cursing and spontaneous handbell ringing echoed away down the pipes.

In perfect peace at last, the Archchancellor pulled off his robe.

The organ's storage tanks were wheezing at the rivets by the time the Librarian had finished pumping. Satisfied, he knuckled his way up to the seat and paused to survey, with great satisfaction, the keyboards in front of him.

Bloody Stupid Johnson's approach to music was similar to his approach in every field that was caressed by his genius in the same way that a potato field is touched by a late frost. Make it loud, he said. Make it wide. Make it all-embracing. And thus the Great Organ of Unseen University was the only one in the world where you could play an entire symphony scored for thunderstorm and squashed toad noises.

Warm water cascaded off Mustrum Ridcully's pointy bathing cap.

Mr Johnson had, surely not on purpose, designed a perfect bathroom – at least, perfect for singing in. Echoes and resonating pipeways smoothed out all those little imperfections and gave even the weediest singer a rolling, dark brown voice.

And so Ridcully sang.

'—as I walked out one dadadadada for to something or other and to take the dadada, I did espy a fair pretty may-ay-den I think it was, and I—'

The organ pipes hummed with pent-up energy. The Librarian cracked his knuckles. This took some time. Then he pulled the pressure release valve.

The hum became an urgent thrumming.

Very carefully, he let in the clutch.

Ridcully stopped singing as the tones of the organ came through the wall.

Bathtime music, eh? he thought. Just the job.

It was a shame it was muffled by all the bathroom fixtures, though.

It was at this point he espied a small lever marked 'Musical pipes'.

Ridcully, never being a man to wonder what any kind of switch did when it was so much easier and quicker to find out by pulling it, did so. But instead of the music he was expecting he was rewarded simply with several large panels sliding silently aside, revealing row upon row of brass nozzles.

The Librarian was lost now, dreaming on the

wings of music. His hands and feet danced over the keyboards, picking their way towards the crescendo which ended the first movement of Bubbla's Catastrophe Suite.

One foot kicked the 'Afterburner' lever and the other spun the valve of the nitrous oxide cylinder.

Ridcully tapped the nozzles.

Nothing happened. He looked at the controls again, and realized that he'd never pulled the little brass lever marked 'Organ Interlock'.

He did so. This did not cause a torrent of pleasant bathtime accompaniment, however. There was merely a thud and a distant gurgling, which grew in volume.

He gave up, and went back to soaping his chest.

'—running of the deer, the playing of . . . huh? What—'

Later that day he had the bathroom nailed up again and a notice placed on the door, on which was written:

'Not to be used in any circumstances. This is IMPORTANT.'

However, when Modo nailed the door up he didn't hammer the nails in all the way but left just a bit sticking up so that his pliers would grip later on, when he was told to remove them. He never presumed and he never complained, he just had a good working knowledge of the wizardly mind.

They never did find the soap.

*   *   *

Ponder and his fellow students watched Hex carefully.

'It can't just, you know, *stop*,' said Adrian 'Mad Drongo' Turnipseed.

'The ants are just standing still,' said Ponder. He sighed. 'All right, put the wretched thing back.'

Adrian carefully replaced the small fluffy teddy bear above Hex's keyboard. Things immediately began to whirr. The ants started to trot again. The mouse squeaked.

They'd tried this three times.

Ponder looked again at the single sentence Hex had written.

+++ Mine! Waaaah! +++

'I don't actually think,' he said, gloomily, 'that I want to tell the Archchancellor that this machine stops working if we take its fluffy teddy bear away. I just don't think I want to live in that kind of world.'

'Er,' said Mad Drongo, 'you could always, you know, sort of say it needs to work with the FTB enabled . . . ?'

'You think that's better?' said Ponder, reluctantly. It wasn't as if it was even a very realistic interpretation of a bear.

'You mean, better than "fluffy teddy bear"?'

Ponder nodded. 'It's better,' he said.

Of all the presents *he* got from the Hogfather, Gawain told Susan, the best of all was the marble.

And she'd said, what marble?

And he'd said, the glass marble I found in the fireplace. It wins all the games. It seems to move in a different way.

The beggars walked their erratic and occasionally backward walk along the city streets, while fresh morning snow began to fall.

Occasionally one of them belched happily. They all wore paper hats, except for Foul Ole Ron, who'd eaten his.

A tin can was passed from hand to hand. It contained a mixture of fine wines and spirits and something in a can that Arnold Sideways had stolen from behind a paint factory in Phedre Road.

'The goose was good,' said the Duck Man, picking his teeth.

'I'm surprised you et it, what with that duck on your head,' said Coffin Henry, picking his nose.

'What duck?' said the Duck Man.

'What were that greasy stuff?' said Arnold Sideways.

'That, my dear fellow, was *pâté de foie gras*. All the way from Genua, I'll wager. And very good, too.'

'Dun'arf make you fart, don't it?'

'Ah, the world of haute cuisine,' said the Duck Man happily.

They reached, by fits and starts, the back door

of their favourite restaurant. The Duck Man looked at it dreamily, eyes filmy with recollection.

'I used to dine here almost every night,' he said.

'Why'd you stop?' said Coffin Henry.

'I . . . I don't really know,' said the Duck Man. 'It's . . . rather a blur, I'm afraid. Back in the days when I . . . think I was someone else. But still,' he said, patting Arnold's head, 'as they say, "Better a meal of old boots where friendship is, than a stalled ox and hatred therewith." Forward, please, Ron.'

They positioned Foul Ole Ron in front of the back door and then knocked on it. When a waiter opened it Foul Ole Ron grinned at him, exposing what remained of his teeth and his famous halitosis, which was still all there.

'Millennium hand and shrimp!' he said, touching his forelock.

' "Compliments of the season",' the Duck Man translated.

The man went to shut the door but Arnold Sideways was ready for him and had wedged his boot in the crack.*

'We thought you might like us to come round at lunchtime and sing a merry Hogswatch glee for your customers,' said the Duck Man. Beside

---

*Arnold had no legs but, since there were many occasions when a boot was handy on the streets, Coffin Henry had affixed one to the end of a pole for him. He was deadly with it, and any muggers hard-pressed enough to try to rob the beggars often found themselves kicked on the top of the head by a man three feet high.

him, Coffin Henry began one of his volcanic bouts of coughing, which even *sounded* green. 'No charge, of course.'

'It being Hogswatch,' said Arnold.

The beggars, despite being too disreputable even to belong to the Beggars' Guild, lived quite well by their own low standards. This was generally by careful application of the Certainty Principle. People would give them all sorts of things if they were certain to go away.

A few minutes later they wandered off again, pushing a happy Arnold who was surrounded by hastily wrapped packages.

'People can be so kind,' said the Duck Man.

'Millennium hand and shrimp.'

Arnold started to investigate the charitable donations as they manoeuvred his trolley through the slush and drifts.

'Tastes . . . sort of familiar,' he said.

'Familiar like what?'

'Like mud and old boots.'

'Garn! That's *posh* grub, that is.'

'Yeah, yeah . . . ' Arnold chewed for a while. 'You don't think we've become posh all of a sudden?'

'Dunno. You posh, Ron?'

'Buggrit.'

'Yep. Sounds posh to me.'

The snow began to settle gently on the River Ankh.

'Still . . . Happy New Year, Arnold.'

'Happy New Year, Duck Man. And your duck.'

'What duck?'

'Happy New Year, Henry.'

'Happy New Year, Ron.'

'Buggrem!'

'And god bless us, every one,' said Arnold Sideways.

The curtain of snow hid them from view.

'Which god?'

'Dunno. What've you got?'

'Duck Man?'

'Yes, Henry?'

'You know that stalled ox you mentioned?'

'Yes, Henry?'

'How come it'd stalled? Run out of grass, or something?'

'Ah . . . it was more a figure of speech, Henry.'

'Not an ox?'

'Not *exactly*. What I *meant* was—'

And then there was only the snow.

After a while, it began to melt in the sun.

THE END

THUD!
by Terry Pratchett

Koom Valley? That was where the trolls ambushed the dwarfs, or the dwarfs ambushed the trolls. It was far away. It was a long time ago.

But if he doesn't solve the murder of just one dwarf, Commander Sam Vimes of Ankh-Morpork City Watch is going to see it fought again, right outside his office.

With his beloved Watch crumbling around him and war-drums sounding, he must unravel every clue, outwit every assassin and brave any darkness to find the solution. And darkness is *following* him.

Oh . . . and at six o'clock every day, without fail, with no excuses, he must go home to read *Where's My Cow?*, with all the right farmyard noises, to his little boy.

There are some things you *have* to do.

Thud! is the thirtieth novel in the now legendary *Discworld* series.

'Anything in a Pratchett story is capable of being transformed into something else – from a joke to a profound observation, from a fact of our social world to pure and lively fantasy'
A. S. Byatt, *The Times*

'*Thud!* has a serious theme: racial intolerance. That Pratchett can explore this while still making us laugh is a tribute to the integrity of his created world . . . Extremely funny but it's also very nar the knuckleduster'
Scotland on Sunday

0552152676
9780552152679

CORGI BOOKS

TERRY PRATCHETT'S FAMOUS *DISCWORLD*® SERIES NOW AVAILABLE ON TAPE AND CD!

The now legendary *Discworld*® series are available in Corgi audio.
And for the first time some *Discworld*® titles are also available on CD.

'Pure fantastic delight'
Time Out

Each title comes abridged on two tapes or three CDs lasting approximately three hours.

0552 14017	1	THE COLOUR OF MAGIC	£10.99 incl VAT
0552 15222	6	THE COLOUR OF MAGIC CD	£14.99 incl VAT
0552 14018	X	THE LIGHT FANTASTIC	£9.99 incl VAT
0552 15223	4	THE LIGHT FANTASTIC CD	£14.99 incl VAT
0552 14016	3	EQUAL RITES	£9.99 incl VAT
0552 15224	2	EQUAL RITES CD	£14.99 incl VAT
0552 14015	5	MORT	£9.99 incl VAT
0552 15225	0	MORT CD	£14.99 incl VAT
0552 14011	2	SOURCERY	£9.99 incl VAT
0552 15226	9	SOURCERY CD	£14.99 incl VAT
0552 14014	7	WYRD SISTERS	£9.99 invl VAT
0552 15227	7	WYRD SISTERS CD	£14.99 incl VAT
0552 14013	9	PYRAMIDS	£9.99 incl VAT
0552 15298	6	PYRAMIDS CD	£14.99 incl VAT
0552 14012	0	GUARDS! GUARDS!	£9.99 incl VAT
0552 15299	4	GUARDS! GUARDS! CD	£14.99 incl VAT
0552 14572	6	ERIC	£9.99 incl VAT
0552 14010	4	MOVING PICTURES	£9.99 incl VAT
0552 15300	1	MOVING PICTURES CD	£14.99 incl VAT
0552 14009	0	REAPER MAN	£10.99 incl VAT
0552 15301	X	REAPER MAN CD	£14.99 incl VAT
0552 14415	0	WITCHES ABROAD	£9.99 incl VAT
0552 15302	8	WITCHES ABROAD CD	£14.99 incl VAT
0552 14416	9	SMALL GODS	£9.99 incl VAT
0552 15303	6	SMALL GODS CD	£14.99 incl VAT
0552 14417	7	LORDS AND LADIES	£9.99 incl VAT
0552 15318	4	LORDS AND LADIES CD	£14.99 incl VAT
0552 14423	1	MEN AT ARMS	£9.99 incl VAT
0552 15317	6	MEN AT ARMS CD	£14.99 incl VAT
0552 14424	X	SOUL MUSIC	£9.99 incl VAT
0552 15320	6	SOUL MUSIC CD	£14.99 incl VAT
0552 14425	8	INTERESTING TIMES	£9.99 incl VAT
0552 15322	2	INTERESTING TIMES CD	£14.99 incl VAT
0552 14426	6	MASKERADE	£9.99 incl VAT
0552 15324	9	MASKERADE CD	£14.99 incl VAT
0552 14573	4	FEET OF CLAY	£9.99 incl VAT
0552 15326	5	FEET OF CLAY CD	£14.99 incl VAT
0552 14574	2	HOGFATHER	£9.99 incl VAT
0552 14684	6	JINGO	£10.99 incl VAT
0552 14650	1	THE LAST CONTINENT	£9.99 incl VAT
0552 14653	6	CARPE JUGULUM	£9.99 incl VAT
0552 14720	6	THE FIFTH ELEPHANT	£10.99 incl VAT
0552 14793	1	THE TRUTH	£9.99 incl VAT
0552 60188	3	THIEF OF TIME	£10.99 incl VAT
0552 14898	9	NIGHT WATCH	£10.99 incl VAT
0552 15074	6	NIGHT WATCH CD	£14.99 incl VAT
0552 15161	0	MONSTROUS REGIMENT	£9.99 incl VAT
0552 14940	3	MONSTROUS REGIMENT CD	£14.99 incl VAT
0552 14942	X	GOING POSTAL	£9.99 incl VAT
0552 15228	5	GOING POSTL CD	£14.99 incl VAT
0552 15362	1	THUD!	£10.99 incl VAT
0552 15363	X	THUD!	£14.99 incl VAT

All Transworld titles are available by post from:
Bookpost, PO Box 29, Douglas, Isle of Man IM99 1BQ
Credit cards accepted. Please telephone +44(0)1624 836000, fax +44(0)1624 837033,
Internet http://www.bookpost.co.uk or
e-mail: bookshop@enterprise.net for details.
Free postage and packing in the UK.
Overseas customers allow £2 per book (paperbacks) and £3 per book (hardbacks).

A LIST OF OTHER TERRY PRATCHETT TITLES
AVAILABLE FROM CORGI BOOKS

THE PRICES SHOWN BELOW WERE CORRECT AT THE TIME OF GOING TO PRESS.
HOWEVER TRANSWORLD PUBLISHERS RESERVE THE RIGHT TO SHOW NEW
RETAIL PRICES ON COVERS WHICH MAY DIFFER FROM THOSE PREVIOUSLY
ADVERTIZED IN THE TEXT OR ELSEWHERE.

All Transworld titles are available by post from:
Bookpost, PO Box 29, Douglas, Isle of Man IM99 1BQ
Credit cards accepted. Please telephone +44(0)1624 836000, fax +44(0)1624 837033,
Internet http://www.bookpost.co.uk or
e-mail: bookshop@enterprise.net for details.
Free postage and packing in the UK.
Overseas customers allow £2 per book (paperbacks) and £3 per book (hardbacks).